Praise for the novels of Heather Graham

"An incredible storyteller."
—*Los Angeles Daily News*

"Graham wields a deftly sexy and convincing pen."
—*Publishers Weekly*

"If you like mixing a bit of the creepy with a dash of sinister and spine-chilling reading with your romance, be sure to read Heather Graham's latest...Graham does a great job of blending just a bit of paranormal with real, human evil."
—*Miami Herald* on *Unhallowed Ground*

"Eerie and atmospheric, this is not late-night reading for the squeamish or sensitive."
—*RT Book Reviews* on *Unhallowed Ground*

"The paranormal elements are integral to the unrelentingly suspenseful plot, the characters are likable, the romance convincing, and, in the wake of Hurricane Katrina, Graham's atmospheric depiction of a lost city is especially poignant."
—*Booklist* on *Ghost Walk*

"Graham's rich, balanced thriller sizzles with equal parts suspense, romance and the paranormal—all of it nail-biting."
—*Publishers Weekly* on *The Vision*

"Heather Graham will keep you in suspense until the very end."
—*Literary Times*

"Mystery, sex, paranormal events. What's not to love?"
—*Kirkus* on *The Death Dealer*

Also by HEATHER GRAHAM

NIGHT OF THE WOLVES
HOME IN TIME FOR CHRISTMAS
UNHALLOWED GROUND
DUST TO DUST
NIGHTWALKER
DEADLY GIFT
DEADLY HARVEST
DEADLY NIGHT
THE DEATH DEALER
THE LAST NOEL
THE SÉANCE
BLOOD RED
THE DEAD ROOM
KISS OF DARKNESS
THE VISION
THE ISLAND
GHOST WALK
KILLING KELLY
THE PRESENCE
DEAD ON THE DANCE FLOOR
PICTURE ME DEAD
HAUNTED
HURRICANE BAY
A SEASON OF MIRACLES
NIGHT OF THE BLACKBIRD
NEVER SLEEP WITH STRANGERS
EYES OF FIRE
SLOW BURN
NIGHT HEAT

The Bone Island Trilogy

GHOST SHADOW
GHOST NIGHT
GHOST MOON (September 2010)

HEATHER GRAHAM

ghost NIGHT

Recycling programs for this product may not exist in your area.

ISBN-13: 978-0-7783-2815-5

GHOST NIGHT

For questions and comments about the quality of this book please contact us at Customer_eCare@Harlequin.ca.

www.MIRABooks.com

Printed in U.S.A.

For Scott Perry, Josh Perry,
Frasier Nivens, Sheila Clover-English,
Victoria Fraasa, Brian O'Lyaryz
and the great and fun folks
with whom I've been on some strange
and entertaining filming expeditions.

Key West History Time Line

1513—Ponce de Leon is thought to be the first European to discover Florida for Spain. His sailors, watching as they pass the southern islands (the Keys), decide that the mangrove roots look like tortured souls and call them "Los Martires," or the Martyrs.

Circa 1600—Key West begins to appear on European maps and charts. The first explorers came upon the bones of deceased native tribes, and thus the island was called the Island of Bones, or Cayo Hueso.

The Golden Age of Piracy begins as New World ships carry vast treasures through dangerous waters.

1763—The Treaty of Paris gives Florida and Key West to the British and Cuba to the Spanish. The Spanish and Native Americans are forced to leave the Keys and move to Havana. The Spanish, however, claim that the Keys are not part of mainland Florida and are really North Havana. The English say the Keys are a part of Florida. In reality, the dispute is merely a war of words. Hardy souls of many nationalities fish, cut timber, hunt turtles—and avoid pirates—with little restraint from any government.

1783—The Treaty of Paris ends the American Revolution and returns Florida to Spain.

1815—Spain deeds the island of Key West to a loyal Spaniard, Juan Pablo Salas of St. Augustine, Florida.

1819–1922—Florida is ceded to the United States. Salas sells the island to John Simonton for $2,000. Simonton divides the island into four parts, three going to businessmen Whitehead, Fleming and Greene. Cayo Hueso becomes more generally known as Key West.

1822—Simonton convinces the U.S. Navy to come to Key West—the deepwater harbor, which had kept pirates, wreckers and others busy while the land was scarcely developed, would be an incredible asset to the United States. Lieutenant Matthew C. Perry arrives to assess the situation. Perry reports favorably on the strategic military importance but warns the government that the area is filled with unsavory characters—such as pirates.

1823—Captain David Porter is appointed commodore of the West Indies Anti-Pirate Squadron. He takes over ruthlessly, basically putting Key West under martial law. People do not like him. However, starting in 1823, he does begin to put a halt to piracy in the area.

The United States of America is in full control of Key West, which is part of the U.S. Territory of Florida, and colonizing begins in earnest by Americans, though, as always, those Americans come from many places.

Circa 1828—Wrecking becomes an important service in Key West, and much of the island becomes involved in the activity. It's such big business that over the next twenty years, the island becomes one of the richest per capita areas in the United States. In the minds of some, a new kind of piracy has replaced the old. Although wrecking and salvage are licensed and legal, many a ship is lured to its doom by less than scrupulous businessmen.

1845—Florida becomes a state. Construction begins on a fort to protect Key West.

1846—Construction of Fort Jefferson begins in the Dry Tortugas.

1850—The fort on the island of Key West is named after President Zachary Taylor.

New lighthouses bring about the end of the golden age of wrecking.

1861—January 10, Florida secedes from the Union. Fort Zachary Taylor is staunchly held in Union hands and helps defeat the Confederate Navy and control the movement of blockade-runners during the war. Key West remains a divided city throughout the Great Conflict. Construction begins on the East and West Martello Towers, which will serve as supply depots. The salt ponds of Key West supply both sides.

1865—The War of Northern Aggression comes to an end with the surrender of Lee at Appomattox Courthouse. Salvage of blockade runners comes to an end.

Dr. Samuel Mudd, deemed guilty of conspiracy for setting John Wilkes Booth's broken leg after Lincoln's assassination, is incarcerated at Fort Jefferson, the Dry Tortugas.

As salt and salvage industries come to an end, cigar making becomes a major business. The Keys are filled with Cuban cigar makers following Cuba's war of independence, but the cigar makers eventually move to Ybor City. Sponging is also big business for a period, but the sponge divers head for waters near Tampa as disease riddles Key West's beds and the remote location make industry difficult.

1890—The building that will become known as "the little White House" is built for use as an officer's quarters at the naval station. President Truman will spend at least 175 days here, and it will be visited by Eisenhower, Kennedy and many other dignitaries.

1898—The USS *Maine* explodes in Havana Harbor, precipitating the Spanish-American War. Her loss is heavily felt in Key West, as she had been sent from Key West to Havana.

Circa 1900—Robert Eugene Otto is born. At the age of four, he receives the doll he will call Robert, and a legend is born, as well.

1912—Henry Flagler brings the Overseas Railroad to Key West, connecting the islands to the mainland for the first time.

1917—On April 6, the United States enters World War I. Key West maintains a military presence.

1919—Treaty of Versailles ends World War I.

1920s—Prohibition gives Key West a new industry—bootlegging.

1927—Pan American Airways is founded in Key West to fly visitors back and forth to Havana.

Carl Tanzler, Count von Cosel, arrives in Key West and takes a job at the Marine Hospital as a radiologist.

1928—Ernest Hemingway comes to Key West. It's rumored that while waiting for a roadster from the factory, he writes *A Farewell to Arms.*

1931—Hemingway and his wife, Pauline, are gifted with the house on Whitehead Street. Polydactyl cats descend from his pet, Snowball.

Death of Elena Milagro de Hoyos.

1933—Tanzler removes Elena's body from the cemetery.

1935—The Labor Day Hurricane wipes out the Overseas Railroad and kills hundreds of people. The railroad will not be rebuilt. The Great Depression comes to Key West, as well, and the island, once the richest in the country, struggles with severe unemployment.

1938—An Overseas Highway is completed, U.S. 1, connecting Key West and the Keys to the mainland.

1940—Hemingway and Pauline divorce; Key West loses her great writer, except as a visitor.

Tanzler is found living with Elena's corpse. Her second viewing at the Dean-Lopez Funeral Home draws thousands of visitors.

1941—December 7, "a date that will live in infamy," occurs, and the U.S. enters World War II.

Tennessee Williams first comes to Key West.

1945—World War II ends with the Armistice of August 14 (Europe) and the Surrender of Japan, September 2.

Key West struggles to regain a livable economy.

1947—It is believed that Tennessee Williams wrote his first draft of *A Streetcar Named Desire* while staying at La Concha Hotel on Duval Street.

1962—The Cuban Missile Crisis occurs. President John F. Kennedy warns the United States that Cuba is only ninety miles away.

1979—The first Fantasy Fest is celebrated.

1980—The Mariel Boatlift brings tens of thousands of Cuban refugees to Key West.

1982—The Conch Republic is born. In an effort to control illegal immigration and drugs, the United States sets up a blockade in Florida City, at the northern end of U.S. 1. Traffic is at a stop for seventeen miles, and the mayor of Key West retaliates on April 23, seceding from the U.S. Key West Mayor Dennis Wardlow declares war, surrenders and demands foreign aid. As the U.S. has never responded, under international law, the Conch Republic still exists. Its foreign policy is stated as, "The Mitigation of World Tension through the Exercise of Humor." Even though the U.S. never officially recognizes the action, it has the desired effect; the paralyzing blockade is lifted.

1985—Jimmy Buffet opens his first Margaritaville restaurant in Key West.

Fort Zachary Taylor becomes a Florida State Park (and a wonderful place for reenactments, picnics and beach bumming).

Treasure Hunter Mel Fisher at long last finds the *Atocha*.

1999—First Pirates in Paradise is celebrated.

2000–Present—Key West remains a unique paradise itself, garish, loud, charming, filled with history, water sports, family activities and down-and-dirty bars. "The Gibraltar of the East," she offers diving, shipwrecks and the spirit of adventure that makes her a fabulous destination, for a day, or forever.

Prologue

South Bimini
September

The sound of the bloodcurdling scream was as startling as the roar of thunder on a cloudless day.

Vanessa Loren immediately felt chilled to the bone, a sense of foreboding and fear as deep-seated as any natural instinct seeming to settle into her, blood, body and soul.

So jarring! It brought casual conversation to a halt, brought those seated to their feet, brought fear to all eyes. It was the sound of the scream, the very heartfelt terror within it, which had been lacking during the day's work.

The ocean breeze had been beautiful throughout the afternoon and evening; it seemed almost as if the hand of God was reaching down to gently wave off the last dead heat of the day, leaving a balmy temperature behind as the sun sank in the western horizon with an astonishing palette of crimson, magenta, mauve and gold.

The film crew had set up camp on the edge of the sparse pine forest, just yards away from the lulling sound of the ocean. The Bahamian guides who had brought them and worked with them had been courteous, fun and knowledgeable, and there was little not to like about the project, especially as night fell and the last of the blazing, then pastel, shades faded into the sea, and it and the horizon seemed to stretch as one, the sky meeting the ocean in a blur.

A bonfire burned with various shades from brilliant to pale in the darkness, and the crew gathered around as it grew dark. South Bimini was sparsely inhabited, offering a small but popular fisherman's restaurant and little more, unlike the more tourist-friendly North Bimini, where numerous shops, bars and restaurants lined what was known as The King's Highway in Alice Town.

They had taken it a step further than South Bimini, choosing to film on one of the several little uninhabited islands jutting out to the southwest. One with a name that had greatly appealed to Jay.

Haunt Island.

A long time ago, there had been a pirate massacre here. Over the years, truth and legend had merged, and it was this very story that Vanessa had used in her script for the low-budget horror film they were shooting.

So infamous years ago, Haunt Island was currently just a place where boaters came now and then. An island filled with scrub and pines, a single dock and an abundance of beach. Out here, tourism wasn't plentiful—the terrain remained wild and natural, beloved by naturalists and campers.

There had been more people in their group, but now they were down to ten. There were Georgia Dare and Travis Glenn, the two actors playing the characters who remained alive in the script; Jay Allen, director; Barry Melkie, sound; Zoe Cally, props, costumes and makeup; Carlos Roca, lighting; Bill Hinton, and Jake Magnoli, the two young production assistants/lighting/sound/gophers/wherever needed guys; their Bahamian escort and guide, Lew Sanderson; and Vanessa herself, writer and backup with the cameras and underwater footage.

It was all but a wrap. The historical legend filled with real horror that was sure to be a box-office hit on a shoestring budget had been all but completed, and they'd been winding down, crawling out of their tents to enjoy the champagne, laughing and lazing against the backdrop of the sunset and the breeze.

And then the sound of the scream, so much more chilling and horrible than any sound Georgia Dare had managed to emit throughout the filming.

Until that moment, Vanessa Loren had enjoyed the project. It was simple enough—a low-budget horror flick that actually had a plot. She had written the script. In addition, she and Jay were financially committed to the project, which made them both willing to work in any capacity. She was ready to do instant rewrites as needed because of the actors and the environment, and she could film underwater shots and even pitch in as second camera for many of the land shots.

Jay, the director, was planning on making a bundle; he was counting on the success of such films as *The Blair Witch Project* and *Paranormal State.* Vanessa and Jay had known each other forever, and had both gone to film school at NYU. He'd contacted her while she was working back in Miami after she'd gotten her master's degree at the University of Miami. He'd talked the good talk on getting together and finding a few investors to finance a really good low-budget flick.

Luckily, she had just been nicely paid for work she had done writing and filming an advertisement for dive gear. It had been one of the few projects she had worked on that hadn't been rewritten by a dozen people before coming to fruition—and it had been a sixty-second spot.

Jay agreed with her that if they were going to do the project, an independent endeavor, it had to be done really well. However, they were also looking for commercial success. So the script was well written but also included the usual assortment of teen-slasher-flick characters—the jock who counted his conquests with scratches on his football helmet, the stoner guitar boy, the struggling hero, the popular slut coming on to the hero and the good-girl bookworm. So far, two characters had been killed in the water, two had disappeared from the boat—and two had to fight the evil, reborn pirates on land and sea and somehow survive until help could come to the patch of sand where they'd been grounded in the Atlantic.

The scream.

Vanessa had been sitting by the fire, sipping a glass of champagne and chatting with Jay, Lew and Carlos. They'd broken it open just a few minutes earlier, taking a minute to relax before they all gathered to cook dinner over the fire and the camp stoves they'd brought and finish off the rest of the champagne.

At the scream, she, like the others, stopped what she was doing. They looked at one another in the eerie light produced by the flames in the darkness, then bolted up and started running toward the sound.

Vanessa was in the lead when Georgia came tearing down the beach toward them. Vanessa caught the young woman, trying to hold her, trying to find out what had happened. "Georgia! Stop, stop!" Georgia Dare, a stunning twenty-one-year old blonde, stared at her with eyes as wide as saucers. "Georgia, it's me, Vanessa. What's wrong?"

"Nessa…Nessa…oh my God, oh, no, no…!"

Georgia started to scream again, trying to shake Vanessa's hold.

"Georgia!"

By then, everyone had come, bursting out of their camp tents, forgetting whatever task they had been involved in.

The others gathered behind her while Jay came forward. "Georgia, damn it, what the hell kind of a prank is this?" he demanded. Once, Georgia had tried to pretend that a stunt knife was real and that she'd been stabbed by a woman from the Retirees by the Sea trailer park back in the Keys.

"The bones, the bodies…they are alive, they don't like us, they're going to kill us…they're angry…we'll all die!" Georgia blurted.

"Damn it, I've had it," Jay said with disgust, turning away. Most of the others did the same.

Vanessa didn't. Georgia was shaking violently. *And that scream! The sound of that scream still seemed to be chilling her blood.*

"They're going to kill us all. Kill us all," Georgia said. Her eyes fell directly on Vanessa's then, and she was suddenly as strong as a sumo wrestler, breaking free from Vanessa's hold and gripping her shoulders instead. "They're real! They're going to kill us, don't you understand, we have to get out of here! They're coming out of the sand. I saw them…the arms, the hands, the skulls… I saw them, coming out of the sand."

"Georgia, Georgia, please, stop it. Hey, come on, we're filming a horror movie, remember?" Vanessa asked gently. "The guys probably set up some of the props to scare you," She frowned suddenly. "What were you doing alone, way down on the beach?"

"Travis and I…Travis and I… Travis is gone."

Travis Glenn was the male lead, an exceptionally beautiful if not terribly bright young man.

"Okay, where is Travis?"

"Gone. Gone. The pirate took him."

"The pirate?"

Georgia shook her head. "Maybe he wasn't a pirate. I didn't see him very clearly. But he was evil—he was like an evil shadow, skulking in the darkness. Travis was yelling, and he went after the shadow. He was mad. He thought you all were playing tricks. And then this monster came out of the sand, but he wasn't right, he seemed to jerk around, like his bones were put back together wrong. And he took Travis and I started screaming and ran."

Jay came back, hands on his lean hips, chest glistening in the darkness. "Slap her! Nessa, don't look so damned concerned. She's jerking us around and it isn't funny. Damn you, Georgia. Look, I realize this isn't anything major-budget, but the crew has worked hard and everyone is tired—and you're acting like a complete bitch! It's just not the time for practical jokes. Slap her, knock her out of it, Vanessa!"

Vanessa glared at him and shook her head. Georgia wasn't that good an actress. She had disagreed with casting the young woman, but she had looked phenomenal on film.

"Let's go down to the beach and see what scared her," Vanessa suggested. She looked back at Lew, a big, broad-shouldered Bahamian man who had been one of their guides. "Do you think there's anything down at the beach, Lew?"

"Sand," he told her.

"Let's go see."

Georgia jerked away from her, shaking her head vehemently. "No, no, no! I am not going back there. I am not going back!"

Carlos Roca, their lighting engineer, came toward them. He'd been close to both actors, and Georgia liked him. Vanessa did, too. He was a nice guy—even-tempered and capable. He took Georgia's hands. "Hey, hey. I'll stay here with you, and we'll sit by the fire with the others while Lew, Jay and Vanessa go check it all out. How's that?"

Georgia looked up at him. Huge tears formed in her eyes and she nodded. "Travis is dead," she told him. "Travis is dead."

Jay looked at Zoe, who worked with the props, makeup and buckets of stage blood they'd been using. He glared sternly at her, then turned to Bill and Jake, the young production assistants, earning credit from the U of Miami. "Hey, you guys didn't rig anything, did you—any practical jokes?"

Zoe looked at him with incredulous disdain. "No. No, we did not."

Jay looked from face to face and was obviously satisfied with the chorus of denials.

"All right, we'll check it out," Jay said.

"Yes, yes. Come on, let's do this," Lew said with his pleasant and easy Bahamian accent. "We'll find Travis and see what's going on. Miss Georgia, you're going to be just fine, honey."

But Georgia shook her head. "Travis is dead," she repeated.

"I'll light some torches from the fire," Lew offered.

"I don't believe we're doing this," Jay said, tired and irritated as they started down the beach. "I made a mistake in casting, that's for sure. We're filming a legend, a horror flick, for God's sake. She's letting it all get to her. This is crazy."

Lew chuckled softly. "Ah, yes, well, that's the way it is with American slasher flicks, eh? Two young people drink and wander off into the woods or the pines to make love, and then the monster comes upon them. They are mistaken. This is Bimini. There are no monsters."

Vanessa stopped. They had come to the edge of the beach. A pine forest came almost flush with the water after a rise in the landscape.

"Nothing," Jay said. "There's nothing out here at all."

Vanessa raised her torch to look around. She froze suddenly. There was nothing there now, but just feet from her, the sand looked as if it had been raked, and it was damp as well, as if someone had dumped buckets of water twenty feet inland from the shore.

"Look," she said.

"Someone was playing a joke on her—on her and Travis, maybe," Jay said. He swore. "We've got one more day of filming to tie up loose ends, and I guess it's natural that someone just feels the need to play practical jokes."

"But where is Travis?" Vanessa asked.

Lew was hunkered down by the disturbed sand. "Interesting," he said.

"What?" Jay asked.

"It does look like something burst outward from the sand—more than it looks as if someone were digging in it," Lew said. "As if it erupted, and was then smoothed over."

"We work with great props and special-effects people," Jay said dryly. "Let's get back. I'm tired as hell. Someone has to have some kind of sleeping pill Georgia can take."

"I'm not sure she should be taking a pill—" Vanessa began.

"I am," Jay interrupted her. "I need to sleep tonight!"

"I'll take Georgia in with me," Vanessa volunteered. She surprised herself. She hadn't disliked Georgia; she just found the woman to be a little…vapid. But that night, she felt sorry for her. Georgia had dropped out of high school, certain that an actress didn't need an education. She'd spent several years working as a model at car and boat shows, and Jay had discovered her because she'd gotten a local spot on television promoting a used-car dealer. Vanessa had to admit that Georgia might not be the most talented actress she knew, but she had been professional and easy to work with. She was pretty sure that Georgia had never gotten a lot of support from her parents or anyone else.

She also knew that she had been lucky. She had been raised by parents who had cared more about their children than anything else in life. Her mother and father had been avid historians, readers, writers and divers, and they had done everything in their power to put their two children through college. She loved history and she loved diving. Her actual forte was in script writing, but in Hollywood, that was a difficult route, with scripts being rewritten so many times that you seldom recognized your own work at the end, and you seldom received credit for a project, either. It had been necessary, in her mind, to learn cameras as well, and with her background, underwater work was a natural. She was driven and she was passionate about her work, so she'd jumped at the chance to work on this movie when Jay called her.

Jay loved horror movies, and they had loved each other forever. Not as boyfriend and girlfriend—they had known each other since grade school in the small town of Micanopy, Florida. He had a chance with this movie, and she wanted him to have his chance. She wanted this chance for herself, too.

She had said from the beginning that she was in only if she got her own tent.

But tonight she'd bring Georgia in with her and be a mother hen.

Carlos had been settling the young woman down; the two were sitting by the fire with large plastic cups—Vanessa was pretty sure they contained something a lot harder than champagne. As Vanessa, Jay and Lew returned, Georgia jumped to her feet, staring at them. "See? See? I told you!"

Jay took Georgia by the shoulders and tried to be calm and reassuring. "Georgia, all I can think is that Travis is playing some kind of a trick on you, sweetie."

"No, no! You have to go look for Travis!" Georgia said.

"I guess we should," Vanessa said quietly.

Jay stared at her with aggravation. "Look for him? Oh, please! You know damned well that Travis is the one who played this ridiculous joke, or he's in on it! And there's nothing there, Georgia. No hands, no skulls, no monsters. Georgia, you've got to get some sleep. I need some sleep."

"No, no, I saw it!" Georgia said, shaking her head in fear. She glared furiously at Jay. "I have to get out of here. I won't stay here!" she insisted.

"You've got to be joking!" Jay declared irritably. "Georgia, you were touting used cars, for God's sake! This could make you the new scream queen!"

Georgia was obviously terrified beyond caring. "I don't care! I don't care if I spend the rest of my life as a waitress. I have to get off this island—now. Now!"

"It's dark!" Jay reminded her.

"Hey, hey, it's all right, we're fifty miles from Miami, and we've got a good speedboat. I can take her in and be back to help with any follow-up or backup shots that we need tomorrow," Carlos offered.

"What if we need *the actress?*" Jay demanded. "I haven't looked through the sequences we shot today."

Carlos looked at Vanessa. "If Nessa doesn't mind,

she's the same height and build and has long blond hair. She can fill in."

"Yes, yes, Vanessa can fill in! You can be my stunt double!" Georgia said enthusiastically.

"For joy, for joy," Vanessa murmured. But she was still disturbed by the young woman's absolute terror. Georgia was ambitious. Was she really so terrified that she would walk away from what could be a big break for her?

She realized that everyone was staring at her.

"Sure. Whatever is needed," she said dryly to Jay. Of course she would do it. They both had a lot of hard work—not to mention their finances—tied up with this.

"I'll be back in the morning," Carlos promised. "Look, seriously, it's what? Seven-thirty, eight o'clock now? I can make Miami in a few hours. I'll get a night's sleep and head back by five or six tomorrow morning."

It was agreed. In another hour, Carlos and Georgia were off.

Vanessa found herself sitting by the fire with the others, sipping champagne once again, though it had lost its taste.

"I still think we should look for Travis," she said.

Zoe let out an irritated "tsking" sound. "That jerk! He's out there somewhere, laughing at everyone, and not caring that he's put a real bug in the production."

"And messing with the props. When he walks up laughing and swaggering in the morning, I think we should give him a good right hook," Barry said.

Silence fell.

"Hey, we could sit here and tell ghost stories!" Bill suggested.

They all glared at him. Apparently, no one was in the mood.

For a while, they did reflect upon the many disappearances and oddities that had occurred in the Bermuda Triangle, but even that didn't last long.

It was only nine-thirty when Vanessa opted for bed. She lay awake, watching the patterns of the low-burning fire playing upon the canvas roof of her tent. She thought about the ridiculousness of filming the movie—the hours of getting the characters into makeup and how, to save money, they had all taken on so many different tasks. Jay and Carlos had played the vengeful pirates, coming out of the sea, and she had supplied some of the sound effects and acted as the kidnapped and murdered Dona Isabella.

Her script was honestly good, based on history and legend. Once, the Florida Keys and the Bahamas had been areas of lawlessness, ruled by pirates. An infamous pirate captain, Mad Miller, and his mistress, Kitty Cutlass, had gone on a wild reign of terror, taking ship after ship, or so legend said. Then all had gone wrong. They had taken a ship bearing the beautiful and rich Dona Isabella. They had sunk her ship, killed most of the crew and, presumably, planned on ransoming Dona Isabella. She had been sailing from Key West to Spain, back to her wealthy husband, when she had been taken. But nothing had happened as planned. Legend said that Kitty Cutlass killed Dona Isabella in a fit of rage, and on Haunt Island, Mad Miller went *really* mad and massacred the remaining crew and many of his own men.

Finally, his pirate ship had sunk off Haunt Island, caught in the vengeful winds of a massive storm. Vanessa had based her script on the legend, doing what research she could, with contemporary teenagers finding themselves victims of bitter ghosts risen from the sand and the sea. As a screenplay, the story provided amazing fodder for the imagination. Filming had actually been fun. There had been some amusing accidents along the way, but none that had caused any harm. Bill had fallen into one of the buckets of blood, and Jake had come bolting up out of the water once, terrified of a nurse shark. She liked the people she was working with, and so, for the most part, it had been enjoyable. A crash shoot—all of it done within three weeks. And Jay was right—it could hit big at the box office.

She still felt disturbed and uneasy, although she wasn't alone. The tents were no more than a few feet apart. Jay, who had been bunking with Carlos, was next to her. Bill and Jake were on her left side. Lew, as secure a figure as anyone might ever want to meet, was just beyond Zoe.

But she was still afraid. It was as if Georgia's gut-wrenching scream had awakened something inside her that knew something was coming, something that she dreaded.

At eleven o'clock, she was still staring at the canvas. She didn't have anything really strong to help her sleep, but she decided on an over-the-counter aid. In another half an hour, she was asleep.

It might have been the pill. She slept, but she tossed and turned and awakened throughout the night. And she dreamed that Georgia was standing in front of her, giant tears dripping down her cheeks. "I told you, I told you there were monsters!"

Georgia's image disappeared.

She dreamed of giant shadow figures rising over her tent and of seaweed monsters rising out of the ocean, growing and growing and devouring ships, boats and people, and reaching up to the sky to snatch planes right from the atmosphere.

She awoke feeling better, laughing at herself for the absurdity of her dreams.

She didn't believe in seaweed monsters—sea snakes, yes, sharks and other demons of the real world, but seaweed monsters, no.

When she had nightmares, they were usually more logic-based—being chased in the darkness by a human killer, finding out she was in a dark house alone with a knife-wielding madman.

It had been Georgia. Georgia and that terrifying scream.

She blinked, stretched and rose. Taking off the long T-shirt nightgown she'd worn, she put on a bathing suit, ready to hit the beach. There were showers in the heads on both boats the crew had been using, the *Seven Seas* and the *Jalapeño.* Of course, one boat wouldn't be back until Carlos returned. It was a bright and beautiful morning, and she felt that a good dousing in the surf would be refreshing.

She stepped out of her tent. The morning sun was shining, but the air retained a note of the night's pleasant coolness. The sea stretched out before her, azure as it could only be in the Bahamas. Jay and Zoe were already up, and one of them had put the coffeepot to brew on the camp stove.

"Morning!" Jay called.

"Morning!" she returned. "How long till coffee?"

"Hey! As fast as it brews!" Jay told her.

Zoe giggled. "What? Did you think this film had a budget for a cook?"

Vanessa walked on out to the water. It was delightful; warm, but not too warm. So clear she could easily see the bottom, even when she had gone out about twenty-five feet from shore and the depth was around ten feet. The current of the Gulf Stream was sweeping the water around to the north; she decided to fight it and swim south, then let it bring her on back offshore from the campsite.

She swam a hard crawl, relaxed with a backstroke, worked on her butterfly and went back to doing the crawl, and then decided that she had gone far enough. She had angled herself in toward shore, so she paused a minute, standing, smoothing back her hair.

It was then that she looked toward the shore.

She would have screamed, but the sound froze in her throat.

She stood paralyzed, suddenly freezing as if she were a cube of ice in the balmy water.

The bones…the bodies…

Georgia's terrified words of the night before seemed to echo and bounce in her mind.

Then she did scream, loud and long. And she found sense and logic, amazingly, and started shouting for the others to come.

The bones…the bodies…

They were there. There was no sign of the boat, but Georgia Dare and Travis Glenn were there—in the sand. Their heads, eyes glaring open, were posed next to one another, staring toward the sea. Inches away from each, arms stretched out of the sand as well—just as props had done in the filming. It was as if they desperately reached out for help as the earth sucked them down, leaving only those pathetic heads, features frozen in silent screams.

Jay had reached the scene. He was shaking and staring, in shock and denial. He shouted. "Travis, what is this, damn it! Georgia—no! No, no, no! Where is Carlos? What kind of a stunt is this?" Jerking like a mechanical figure, Jay went to touch the actor's head, as if he could wake him up or snap him out of whatever game he was playing.

The head rolled through the sand. The body wasn't attached.

Jay himself began to scream.

Frozen still, shaking from a sudden cold that threatened never to leave her, Vanessa remained just offshore. She didn't move until Lew had gotten the authorities, until a kindly Bahamian official came and wrapped a towel around her shoulders, and led her away.

1

2 years later
Key West

Before him, frond coral waved in a slow and majestic dance, and a small ray emerged from the sand by the reef, weaving in a swift escape, aware that a large presence, possibly predatory, was near.

Sean O'Hara shot back up to the surface, pleased with his quick inspection of Pirate Cut, a shallow reef where divers and snorkelers alike came to enjoy the simple beauty of nature. It was throughout history a place where many a ship had met her doom, crushed by the merciless winds of a storm. Now only scattered remnants of that history remained; salvage divers of old had done their work along with the sea, salt and the constant shift of sands and tides and weather that remained just as turbulent through the centuries.

It was still, he decided, a great place to film.

He hadn't opted for scuba gear that day—it had been just a quick trip, thirty minutes out and thirty back in, early morning, just to report to his partner, David

Beckett, so they could talk about their ever-changing script and their plans for their documentary film.

Because Sean was an expert diver, he seldom went diving alone. Good friends—some of the best and most experienced divers in the world—had died needlessly by diving alone. But a free dive on a calm day hadn't seemed much of a risk, and he was pleased that he had taken off early in the morning. Most of the dive boats headed out by nine, but few of them came to Pirate Cut as a first dive, and it wouldn't get busy until later in the day.

And out in the boat, he wasn't exactly *alone.*

Bartholomew was with him.

Climbing up the dive ladder at the rear of his boat, *Conch Fritter,* he tossed his flippers up and hauled himself on board. His cell phone sat on his towel, and the message light was blinking. Caller ID showed him that he'd been called from O'Hara's, his uncle's bar.

"I thought about answering it, but refrained."

Sean turned at the sound of the voice. Bartholomew was seated at the helm of the dive boat, feet in buckle shoes up on the wheel, a *National Geographic* magazine in his hands.

Bartholomew was getting damned good at holding things.

"Thank you for refraining. And tell me again, why the hell are you with me? You hate the water," Sean said, irritated. He pushed buttons on his phone to receive his messages, staring at Bartholomew.

"Love boats, though," Bartholomew said.

Sean groaned inwardly. It was amazing—once he hadn't believed in Bartholomew. Actually, he'd thought the ghost might have been one of his sister Katie's imaginary friends. He realized he either had to accept that she was crazy or that there was a ghost. At that time, Sean couldn't see or hear Bartholomew.

But that had been a while ago now. While solving the Effigy Murders—as the press wound up calling them—he'd ended up with his head in a bandage and stitches in his scalp.

It was the day the damned stitches had come out that he'd first seen the ghost—as clearly as if he had physical substance—sitting in a chair next to the hospital bed.

Sean listened to his messages. The first, from David Beckett, asking him what time he wanted to go out. Sean grinned. David was in love—and sleeping late. Sean was glad, since it seemed that his old friend was in love with his sister, Katie, and she was in love with him. They'd both seen some tough times, and Sean was happy for them.

The next message was from his uncle just asking him to call back.

He did so. Still, he didn't learn much. His uncle just wanted him to come to the bar. Sean told him it would take him about forty-five minutes, and Jamie said that was fine, just to come.

"So what's up?" Bartholomew asked.

"Going to the bar, that's all," Sean said. He was curious. Jamie wasn't usually secretive.

"Can you keep a hand on the helm? Bring her straight in?" Sean asked Bartholomew as he brought up the anchor. Securing it, he added, "Jeez, am I crazy asking you that?"

Bartholomew looked at him with tremendous indignation.

"Really! That was absolutely—churlish of you! If there's one thing I know, it's a lazy man's boat like this!"

Sean grinned. "I'll be in the head in the shower for about fifteen minutes. That's all you need to manage."

"It'll be great if we pass the Coast Guard or a tour boat!" Bartholomew cried.

Sean ignored him. He just wanted to rinse off the sea salt—his uncle had him curious.

He showered, dried and dressed in the head and cabin well within his fifteen minutes. In another twenty, he was tying up at the pier.

Duval Street was quiet.

As he walked from the docks to O'Hara's, Sean mused with a certain wry humor that Key West was, beyond a doubt, a place for night owls. He was accustomed enough to working at night—or even partying at night—but he was actually more fond of the morning hours.

"What do you think Jamie wants?"

Sean heard the question again—for what seemed like the tenth time now—and groaned inwardly without turning to look at the speaker. *Imagine, once he had* wanted *to see the damned ghost!*

Oh, he could see Bartholomew way too clearly now, though when he had first come home to Key West—hearing that David Beckett was in town and worried for his sister's safety—he had come with his longtime fear for Katie's mind. She had always seemed to sense or see things. But that had been Katie, not him.

Bartholomew had apparently wanted to be known, though at first he proved his presence by moving things around.

Then Sean had seen him in that damned chair in the hospital room. Now he could see the long-dead privateer as easily as he could see any flesh-and-blood, living person who walked into his life.

He cursed the fact.

He had never believed in ghosts. He'd never wanted to believe. In fact, he'd warned Katie not to ever talk about the fact that she had "strange encounters" or had been "gifted" or "cursed" from a young age. The majority of the world would think that she should be institutionalized.

He wasn't pleased that he saw Bartholomew. Now he had the fear that he would one day wind up institutionalized himself.

And he was far from pleased that the dapper centuries-old entity had now decided to affix himself to Sean.

"I will not answer you. I will never answer you in public," Sean said.

Bartholomew laughed. "You just answered me. Then again, we're hardly in public, you know. I think the whole island is still asleep. Besides, you're a filmmaker. An 'artiste!' People will happily believe that you are eccentric, and it's your brilliance causing you to speak to yourself."

"Right. Don't you feel that you should go and haunt my sister?" Sean asked.

"I believe she's busy."

"I'm busy," Sean said.

"Look, I'm apparently hanging around for something," Bartholomew said. "Others have gone on, and I haven't. You seem to be someone I must help."

"I don't need help."

"You will, I'm sure of it," Bartholomew said.

Sean kept walking.

"So what do you think he wanted?" Bartholomew persisted.

"I don't know," Sean said flatly. "But he wanted something, and that's why I'm going to see him." He cast a glance Bartholomew's way. The privateer—hanged long ago for a deed he hadn't committed—was really quite a sight. His frock coat and stockings, buckle shoes, vest and tricornered hat all fit his tall, lean physique quite well. In his lifetime, Sean thought dryly, he had probably made a few hearts flutter. Sadly, he had died because of the death of the love of his life, and an act of piracy blamed upon him. However, after haunting the island since then, he had recently found a new love, the "lady in white," legendary in Key West. When they filmed their documentary, Sean meant to make sure that he covered Bartholomew's case and those of his old and new loves.

He'd heard once that ghosts remained on earth for a reason. They wanted to avenge their unjust deaths, they needed to help an ancestor or they were searching for truth. There were supposedly ghosts who were caught in time, reenacting the last moments of their lives. But that was considered "residual haunting," while Bartholomew's determination to remain on earth in a spectral form was known as "active" or "intelligent" haunting.

Bartholomew had been around for a reason—he had

been unjustly killed. But Sean couldn't figure out why he remained now. His past had been aligned with David Beckett and his family, and Sean had to admit that Bartholomew had been helpful in solving the Effigy Murders, all connected to the Becketts.

Maybe he had stayed because of the injustice done to him and because he still felt that he owed something to the Becketts. All Sean knew was that he had been Katie's ghost—if there was such a thing—and now he seemed to be with him all the time.

Sean liked Bartholomew. He had a great deal of wit and he knew his history. He was loyal and might well have contributed to saving their lives.

But it was unnerving from the get-go to realize that you were seeing a ghost. It was worse realizing that the ghost was no longer determined to stick to Katie like glue, but had moved on to him. He was a good conversationalist—and thus the problem. Sean was far too tempted to talk to him, reply in public and definitely appear stark, raving mad upon occasion.

Ghosts were all over the place, Bartholomew had informed him. Most people felt a whisper in the breeze, sometimes a little pang of sorrow, and if the ghost was "intelligent" and "active," it might enjoy a bit of fun now and then, creating a breeze, causing a bang in the dark of night, and so on. Katie had real vision for the souls lurking this side of the veil. So far, thank God, he'd seen only Bartholomew, and maybe a mist of others in the shadows now and then.

Sean had been damned happy before he'd "seen" a ghost at all.

Pirate Cut, he noted mentally. A good place to begin

shooting. They hadn't known in Bartholomew's day that the reefs needed to be protected. They had brought their ships to the deep-water plunge just off the reef many times. Bartholomew knew for a fact that the legend about the area was true—ships of many nations had foundered here in storms, been cut up on the reefs and left to the destruction of time and the elements. But there was treasure scattered here, treasure and history, even if it had been picked over in the many years since.

It would also make for beautiful underwater footage. The colors were brilliant; the light was excellent. And it was near the area where Bartholomew had allegedly chased and gunned down a ship and murdered those aboard. Falsely accused, in the days after David Porter's Pirate Squadron had been established, he had been hanged quickly, and it had been only after his unjust death that his innocence had been proven.

It was a good story for a documentary. Especially considering the events of the recent past, when a madman had decided that it was his ancestor who had been wronged and that the Becketts were to pay.

The whole story needed to be told, and it would.

And perhaps, if he managed to get Bartholomew's story out there, with any luck Bartholomew might "see the light" and move on to the better world he believed he would find.

It was true that Bartholomew was not a bad guy and that, if he were flesh and blood, he'd be great to hang out with. But with Katie engaged to David Beckett now and basically living at the Beckett house, it seemed that Bartholomew was really all his.

And no way out of it—it was awkward. Disconcerting.

And he was starting to look as if he walked around talking to himself. So much for an intelligent and manly image, Sean thought dryly.

"Bartholomew, please, stop talking to me. You're well aware that I look crazy as all hell when people see me talking to you, right?" Sean demanded.

"I keep telling you, you're an artist. And a true conch," Bartholomew said. "Born and bred on the island. Tall, with that great red hair, good and bronzed—hey, fellow, a man's man as they say," Bartholomew told him, waving a ringed hand in the air. "Trust me—you're masculine, virile, beloved and—an artist. You're allowed to be crazy. And, good God, man—this is Key West!"

"Right. Then the tourists will have me arrested," Sean said.

They'd reached O'Hara's, toward the southern end of Duval. Sean cast Bartholomew a warning glare. Bartholomew shrugged and followed Sean in.

Sean walked straight up to the bar. Jamie O'Hara himself was working his taps that day.

"Hey, what's up?" Sean asked, setting his hands on the bar and looking at Jamie, who was busy drying a beer glass.

It was early in the day—by Key West bar standards. Just after eleven. Jamie, when he was in town, usually opened the place around eleven-thirty, and whoever of his old friends, locals, or even tourists who wandered in for lunch early were served by Jamie himself. He cooked, bussed and made his drinks, poured his own Guinnesses—seven minutes to properly fill a Guinness glass—and he did so because he liked being a pub owner and he was the kind of employer who liked people, his employees and his establishment. He could handle the place in the early hour—unless there was a festival in town. Which, quite often, there was. Starting at the end of this week, he'd have double shifts going on—Pirates in Paradise was coming to town.

At this moment, though, O'Hara's was quiet. Just Jamie, behind the bar.

Jamie was the perfect Irish barkeep—though he had been born in Key West. He, like Sean's dad, had spent a great deal of time in the "old country" visiting their mother's family—O'Casey folk—and he and Sean's dad had both gone to college in Dublin. Jamie could put on a great brogue when he chose, but he could also slip into a laid-back Keys Southern drawl. Sean had always thought he should have been an actor. Jamie said that owning a pub was nearly the same thing. He had a rich head full of gray hair, a weather-worn but distinguished face, bright blue eyes and a fine-trimmed beard and mustache, both in that steel-gray that seemed to make him appear to be some kind of clan chieftain, or an old *ard-ri,* high king, of Ireland. He was well over six feet, with broad shoulders and a seaman's muscles.

Jamie indicated the last booth in the bar area of the pub, which was now cast in shadow.

He realized that someone was sitting in the booth.

He couldn't help but grin at his uncle. "You're harboring a spy? A double agent? Someone from the CIA working the Keys connection?"

Sean knew that bad things—very bad things—could happen, even in Key West, Florida, "island paradise" though it might be. He'd seen them. But someone hiding in the shadows seemed a bit out of the ordinary.

Jamie shrugged and spoke softly. "Who knows why she's sitting in the dark? She's a nice kid. Came in here, I guess, 'cause the world seems to consider it neutral ground or something. She heard about you and David and the documentary you two are going to film together."

Sean frowned. "We've had ads in the papers for crews for the boats and the filming. David and I have been setting up for interviews at his place."

"What do you want from me, son, eh? She came in here, knowing I was related to the O'Hara looking to film about Key West and her mysteries. I said yes, and she asked if there was any way she could speak to you alone."

"She's applying for a job? Then she should go about it just like all the others and ask for an interview," Sean said, annoyed. He couldn't really see the woman in the corner, but he thought she seemed young. Maybe she was trying to secure a position by coming through the back door, flirting, drawing on his uncle's sympathies.

"I don't think that it's work she's looking for, but I don't know. She's pretty tense. She wanted to know about the recent business down here—you know, all the nasty stuff with the murders—and she was mainly wanting to know, so it seemed, how you all coped with the bad things going on. Like, frankly, were you a pack of cowards, was it really all solved by the police, did I think that you were capable people—and did you really know the area."

"Oh, great. She sounds like someone I really want to hire!" Sean said.

Jamie laughed. "She's not that bad—she was dead

honest in the questions she asked me. She didn't use the word *coward,* that was mine. There's something I like about her, Sean. Talk to her. She seems tense and nervous—and somehow, the real deal." His uncle leaned closer to him. "There's some mystery about this girl, and yet something real. Talk to her. Oh, and by the way, she is really something. She's got every diving certificate, advanced, teacher, you name it. She's gotten awards for her writing, and oh—hmm. She happens to have amazing blond hair, giant blue eyes and a shape to die for, nephew. Check it out. Go ahead. What's the matter, boy, scared?"

Sean looked at his uncle in surprise and laughed. Scared? No. He was at least intrigued. Couldn't hurt to talk to the woman. He and David were anxious to get started on their project because it was important to both of them—and it was also what they were best known for in their separate careers. But they were discussing just what bits and pieces and stories they would use for their documentary. Bartholomew's situation was a must, Robert the Doll was a must, and the bizarre, true and fairly recent history of Elena and Count von Cosel was also a must. It wouldn't be Key West if they didn't touch on Hemingway and the writing connection. And there had to be pirates, wreckers, sponge divers and cigar makers, and how the Conch Republic became the Conch Republic. But as to exactly what they were using and what they were concentrating on, they were still open. They hadn't made any hard-and-fast decisions yet, but since David was home and planning a wedding with Sean's sister, they had decided that, at long last, they should work together. Friends in school who hadn't seen each other in a decade, they had both gone the same route—film. Once the tension and terror of a murderer at work in Key West had died down, David had decided he was going to stay home awhile. That had a lot to do with the fact that he was in love with Sean's sister, Katie O'Hara. But David was a conch, too—born and bred in Key West from nearly two generations of conchs. David belonged here.

Sean had stayed away from home a lot, too. But now he was excited about the idea of working with David—and working on a history about Key West and the surrounding area, bringing to light what truth they could discover that lay behind many of the legends. One thing had never been more true—fact was far stranger than fiction. But as he knew from living here, fact could become distorted. Tourists often asked which form of a story told by a tour guide was the true one. He and David meant to explore many of the legends regarding Key West—and, through historical documents, letters and newspapers of each era, get to the heart of the truth. Fascinating work. He loved his home. Key West was the tail end of Florida, an oddity in time and place. An island accessible only by boat for much of its history. Southern in the Civil War by state, Union by military presence.

Bartholomew suddenly let out a soft, low whistle, almost making Sean jump. He gritted his teeth and refused to look at the ghost.

"Pretty, pretty thing!" Bartholomew said. "I'd have been over there by now, not wondering if there was some secret agenda behind it all!"

Somehow, Sean refrained from replying. He even kept smiling and staring straight at his uncle.

"Are you going to stare at the shadows? Or are you at least going to let the girl have her say?" Jamie demanded. "I'll bring coffee," he added.

"I know where the coffee is, thanks, Uncle," Sean said. He came behind the bar to pour himself a cup, trying to get a better look at the woman at the booth.

She was waiting for him. There was no looking at her surreptitiously—she was staring back at him. She was still in the shadows, but his uncle seemed to be right about one thing—she was stunning. She had the kind of cheekbones that were pure, classic beauty—at eighty, she'd still be attractive with that bone structure. Her hair was golden and pale and simply long, with slightly rakish and overgrown bangs. He didn't think she spent a lot of money in a boutique salon; the shades of color had come from the sun and the overgrown, rakish look was probably because she didn't spend much time getting it cut.

She was dressed more like a native than a tourist—light cotton dress with a little sweater over her shoulders. Down here, the days were often hot, tempered only by the ocean and gulf breezes that were usually present. But inside, it could be like the new ice age had come—because of the heat, businesses were often freezing. Jamie kept his swinging doors to the outside open sometimes—it was a Key thing. Trying to be somewhat conservative in the waste of energy, the air blasted in the back, not near the front.

Coffee in hand, he walked back to the booth at last. "Hi. I'm Sean O'Hara. We're doing interviews tomorrow and the next day at the old Beckett house, because, I'm assuming you know, it's a joint project between David Beckett and myself." He offered her his hand.

She accepted it. Her grip was firm. Her palms were slightly callused, but they were nice, tanned. Her fingers were long and she had neat nails, clipped at a reasonable length rather than grown out long.

Her eyes were steady on his.

"I'm Vanessa Loren," she said. "I have real experience and sound credentials, but that's not exactly why I'm here, or why I wanted to meet with you here."

He shrugged, taking a seat opposite her in the booth.

"All right."

She suddenly lifted both hands and let them fall. "I've actually practiced this many times, but I'm not sure where to begin."

"You've—practiced?" Sean asked. "Practiced an interview for a job?"

She nodded. "I've practiced trying to explain. This is really important to me."

"All right. Start anywhere," Sean said.

She lowered her head, breathing in deeply. Then she looked at him again. "Unless you've been under a rock, you must have heard about the Haunt Island murders."

He blinked and tried to remember. He'd been filming in the Black Sea two years ago, but he had heard about the bizarre murders. Members of a film crew had been gruesomely slain on an island just southwest of South Bimini. Though uninhabited, the island belonged to the Bahamas.

He hadn't moved into the booth and hadn't left room

for Bartholomew. However, the ghost had followed him to the booth, and leaned against the wall just across from them.

"Yes, I heard something about the murders," he said carefully.

"I was with the film crew," she said. "One of my best childhood friends was the director, and I was the script-writer. We both put money into the venture, and we were doing double duty. When I say low budget, I mean low budget. But we had it together—we knew what we were doing, and we worked incredibly hard. The film wasn't going to win an Oscar, but we had hopes of having it picked up by a national distributor."

"Don't know much about that," Bartholomew said sorrowfully, as if he were part of the conversation.

"You were making a film, and people were brutally killed," Sean said, ignoring Bartholomew. He didn't want to feel sympathy for her. Sadly, there were a number of unsolved mysteries that had little chance of being solved. He vaguely remembered some of the newspaper articles his sister had e-mailed him at the time—a lot of people were chalking the tragedy up to the mystery of the Bermuda Triangle. "What are you trying to tell me, or ask me?"

She took a deep breath. "It's really all the same area—the same area you're doing a documentary on. Do you know how many boaters go from the Intracoastal, South Florida, say Fort Lauderdale and Miami, out to Bimini and then on to Key West?" she asked. "Or vice versa. We're all connected here."

"I know that," he said, feeling oddly irritated. "We always intended to do a documentary on the area."

"This is a story that shouldn't just be included, it should be the main focus," she said somberly.

"Why?"

"Because it's an unsolved mystery. And there's a killer or killers out there."

"Sadly, there are many killers on the loose at any given time. I'm not sure what we can do for you. David and I are not law enforcement," Sean said. "And if we were, Haunt Island is still the Bahamas."

"It doesn't sound as if law enforcement has had much luck yet," Bartholomew interjected.

"I was there when it happened," she said quietly. "The truth must be discovered."

"But we're just doing a documentary," Sean protested.

"You're doing a documentary on history—and oddities and mysteries. You'll never find a better mystery," she said flatly. "I admit, the script was written for what would basically be a teenage-slasher-type flick," she said. "But it was based on history. Key West and Bahamian history."

He shook his head. "All right, I'm still getting lost here. You were filming a movie based on history, but it was a slasher film? Low budget? A historical slasher film? You're talking big money there."

She shook her head. "Not with the people we had working with us. The new digital age has helped a hell of a lot. And we had easy access to costumes—we bought most of them here, some from the shop on Front Street, and some at Pirates in Paradise. We refitted one of our boats, and with a little digital finesse, we had a pirate ship, which could become pirate ships. We knew what we were doing—I'm talking about people with real degrees in film and real experience—and more. It was our project."

"I'm listening. Tell me more."

"You're from here and you're working on history," she said. "You must have heard of the *Santa Geneva*—and Mad Miller and his consort, Kitty Cutlass, and the murder of Dona Isabella."

He nodded slowly. He knew the legend. All Key West kids knew the stories about pirates in the area. They made great tales at campfires. "A piece of pirate lore," he said.

"Yes, and if you're following pirate lore, you should be following that story. It was past the Golden Age of Piracy. It was after David Porter came here to clear out the pirates. There were still Spaniards living here, naturally. Dona Isabella was a wealthy woman, with homes in Madrid and Key West. She was married to Diego, a very wealthy Spanish merchant. She was kidnapped off a Spanish ship, the *Santa Geneva*. They say she was never ransomed because Mad Miller, the pirate, fell in love with her—and because of that, she wound up dead. Some say that Mad Miller murdered her in a frenzy, because she loathed him. Some say that Kitty Cutlass, furious over her lover's adoration for another woman, was the one to kill her. At any rate, she supposedly wound up dead in the company of the pirates. It's thought that she survived until the pirates reached Haunt Island, where they might have drawn in for ship repairs. Some of Mad Miller's men then massacred the remaining crew members of the *Santa Geneva*, and members of their own crew who were in revolt over what had happened. Thus the name, obviously, Haunt Island, and the legend."

"I still don't see—" Sean began.

"Dona Isabella lived in Key West. Her ship, a Spanish ship, left from Key West. The pirates raided her in American waters. Off of *Key West.* Mad Miller came from Key West. Let's see—Kitty Cutlass began as a prostitute in a shack on Duval. Mr. O'Hara, this is an amazing story that has everything to do with the documentary you want to film. You're a fool if you haven't already thought of using the legend—and the truth of what happened to the members of our film crew," she said.

All right—that was aggravating. But there was something desperate in her voice that kept him from entirely losing his temper.

"Okay, Miss Loren. You have a good story. What, exactly, is it that you want? I've told you, we're not any form of law enforcement. I can't go over to the Bahamas and just solve your mystery for you."

She inhaled again, staring at him. She let out a long breath of air. She seemed to physically square her shoulders, as if seeking strength and resolve.

"I know that, and..." She paused, wincing. "Look, I'm sorry. I'm just passionate about my feelings on this. First, I need you to hire me. I'm good—really good. I swear. You can check all my references," she said.

"I would definitely do so, no matter what," he said.

"I'd bet good money that she has excellent references," Bartholomew said.

Sean locked his jaw, determined not to turn, or respond to the ghost in any way.

"No one is hired unless David and I agree," he said to Vanessa.

"That is certainly understandable," she said. Again, she paused. "I know all about David Beckett, as well. I know that he was once accused of murder, and I know how desperate he was to find the truth. And the truth was discovered. I can't believe that he wouldn't understand how I feel, or be sympathetic to my cause."

Sean felt tension steal through his body. The Effigy Murders had been bad, very bad. He still felt they were all recovering from the terrible things that had happened. He still had scars beneath his hairline.

David would be sympathetic, he knew.

"Go on," he said quietly.

"Then—I think you need to make me your assistant. I'm excellent at managing a schedule, and I can write a scene, narrative, interview questions, anything you need, at the drop of a hat. I know you do a lot of your own scheduling and writing. That's why I say *assistant.* I went to film school. When needed, I can handle any kind of a camera. I'm fit so I can tote and carry. The filmmaker in you must see what there is here—a legend that remains a mystery, historical and contemporary. You can look for the *Santa Geneva,* you can really follow the path of those who came before you. And if you leave out piracy, and the stamping out of the pirates, and the supposed massacre on Haunt Island, you're doing a disservice to everyone."

He leaned back. "If this is such a great documentary, why don't you do it yourself?" he demanded.

She leaned back, biting her lower lip. "Well, for

one, I don't have the kind of money you need for a documentary. And..."

"And?"

She leaned forward. "Look, I'll work cheap. I'll work harder than anyone you ever imagined."

He leaned back, shaking his head. "I'd like to help you, I'd really like to help you. But it seems as if you're chasing something, and I'm not—I'm not what you're looking for. If these murders haven't been solved, you need a private investigator. You need—"

"Have you ever tried to look for a private investigator who specializes in water, legends and boats?" she asked irritably.

He hesitated for a moment. "Look, from what I understand, every agency possible was involved in that case. If there are no clues, there are no clues."

"No one wanted to follow through on the legend—or the history," she said, exasperated.

He felt his fingers tense around his coffee cup and he stared at her. "You're trying to tell me that pirates returned to massacre your friends?" he asked.

Something about the tightening in her lips and the way that she stared at him caused him to feel as if he should be ashamed—as if he had spoken out of turn.

But he hadn't. And he couldn't explain to her that he knew what ghosts were capable of doing, and what they weren't. As a matter of fact, he knew a few of them....

"That's not what I'm suggesting at all," she said.

"Then?"

"I—don't know, exactly," she said, looking away. "Here's the thing. We've had this movie stowed since it happened. But...people know about it. I'm afraid we'll get an offer from a major distributor. My partner would gladly sell. I don't want to sell—not unless I can get some justice for those who were involved. I don't want to make money on sensationalism, on something…something unsolved. I've gotten Jay to agree that I can try one more time to discover the truth."

"I—"

"Please. Please just tell me that you'll consider doing it?" she asked.

He stared at her, not knowing what to say.

No. A flat-out no would be a great answer. He and David hadn't set anything in stone as yet, but…no. This one had to be a no. They both had their individual exemplary careers, they knew what they were doing. They could write themselves.

"I'm sorry. I just don't think my partner will agree," Sean said.

"Will you ask David Beckett?" she queried stubbornly.

He smiled. "Will you quit asking if I talk to him and he says no?"

She smiled. "You're— Look, I know I'm asking a lot without much to offer. But I am really good at what I do, and if you give me a few weeks, I promise, I'll help to make anything you want to do come out as brilliantly as possible. I'll be slave labor, I swear."

"I don't want slave labor."

"I'll be the best damned assistant you've ever had," she swore.

"Take her up on it!" Bartholomew said. "Hell, my boy! Take her up on it just for the pleasure of having her upon your wretched little boat."

"I'll talk to David," he said.

"You really will. And…and if he's hesitant, if there's any chance, will you let me try to persuade him, as well?" she asked.

He forced an even smile. *No, just say no!*

He asked himself if he would be so torn, so tempted, if the person asking him wasn't this young woman, not just beautiful, but…strong. So confident in her ability that she would swear she could make his work the best ever.

Ability.

The way she looked.

The sound of her voice.

The mystery involved. Yes, he knew the damned legend. And hell yes, he was curious.

"Look," he began.

But she wasn't looking at him. She was looking at the door. She let out a little cry of surprise and gladness.

Sean swung around. His sister had just come in the door.

He looked at Vanessa Loren.

Ah, hell.

Hell.

The young woman knew Katie. He should have figured.

He stared back at her, irritated, and suddenly certain that it was all over.

"You know my sister," he said.

She glanced at him while rising. "Yes, I know Katie. I've been on a few dive boats with her, and of course, I bring friends in here for Katie-okie when I'm down…."

She started to head out to see Katie. He set his fingers around her wrist, drawing her back.

She didn't jerk away, but then his hold was pretty firm. Those huge, cornflower-blue eyes of hers lit on him.

He smiled coldly. "You know my uncle, too, don't you? And my uncle knew just who you were and what you wanted."

"I've met Jamie before, yes," she admitted. "Katie can explain it all to David, if you don't want to, but I know that she'll convince him that I'm right. I came to you first, because Katie told me that David had said all the major decisions were going to be yours, so if you just agree—"

He stood, releasing her wrist.

"I don't like being played," he said flatly. "Good day, Miss Loren."

She didn't call after him.

Bartholomew did.

"Sean! Oh, come on, Sean. I can help you with this, I was around when it all happened," the dapper buccaneer cried to him. "Sean, oh, do come on! If I were flesh and blood, I'd be on this like a mosquito at a topless bar! Sean!"

Sean passed Katie near the doorway. "Hey, sis," he said, kissed her cheek, and kept on going.

They'd all just survived near death. They had dealt with total insanity.

He would have to be insane himself to get into something like this again.

"Mr. O'Hara!"

She had followed him out. The lithe and dignified

Miss Loren had come rushing out, and now she stood on the sidewalk, staring after him.

Despite himself, he paused.

She walked to him, her chin high. "I never meant to play anyone," she said. "I'm just desperate for help. You don't understand," she said.

"I think I do," he told her.

"No, no, you don't. I have reason to believe that someone must find out what happened, not just for those who were killed, but…"

"But what?"

"Other things have happened. Bad things. Not involved with filming, but with other boaters who disappeared near Haunt Island."

"The sea can be huge and merciless, Miss Loren. And sadly, throughout history, many a boat and ship have disappeared without a trace."

"There's more to it. I know there's more to it, and I'm afraid."

"Afraid of what?"

"I'm afraid that if the truth isn't discovered, more people will die. That there will be blood and death… a massacre again, and maybe this time, here, in Key West."

2

Vanessa walked back into O'Hara's, trying to feel as if she hadn't just been crushed in a major defeat.

Katie was sitting at the bar, talking to her uncle. She watched Vanessa as she came up and took the stool next to her. Vanessa had known Katie forever, or so it seemed. They'd met when Katie's school had brought a group of Key West students up to dive the springs and Vanessa's school had been hosting the week of camp. She wasn't sure if she'd liked her at first, being ten and wary of kids who came from cool places like Key West. But she'd been paired with Katie, who had an exceptional voice, for the talent show, and Vanessa had been her harmony and backup act, and they'd won the grand prize—two new regulators for their scuba equipment. That had begun the friendship. Of course, they'd been kids living almost four hundred miles away from one another even if it was the same state, but they'd kept up as much as possible, visiting one another at their respective colleges and meeting whenever they could.

By the time they had been able to get together in Key West, or anywhere in the Keys, Sean had been gone most of the time, so it really wasn't that strange that she'd never had a chance to meet him before.

It seemed odd that the O'Haras could so clearly resemble one another and yet look so different. When she'd asked Jamie O'Hara what Sean looked like, he told her that Katie was Sean in a dress. That wasn't true at all. Sean was very tall, three or four inches over six feet, with a linebacker's shoulders. Katie was slim and willowy. While Katie had auburn hair, Sean's was lighter, though with the same streaks of red. Katie's eyes were a hazel green while Sean's were more of a golden color. He had almost classic features, just like Katie, but he looked like a man who had braved the wind many a time, and his jaw leaned toward the square side.

Maybe that had just been because he'd been talking to her—and she sensed that she'd irritated him.

"Maybe I should have mentioned first that I knew you both," Vanessa said dryly to Katie.

Katie smiled and swirled a stirrer in her coffee cup. "Ha-ha. Perhaps he's feeling as if we're ganging up on him! Oh, well, Sean is just being—Sean. He'll get over it. Really, I think the lure of the mystery will get to him, once he thinks it all out. I think." She looked at Vanessa with concern. "But…are you sure you should be doing this? Maybe you should just leave it all alone."

"You know I can't do that—you know you couldn't do that! Hey, I've talked to people around here. *You* plunged headfirst into finding out what had happened in David's past, a pretty dangerous occupation, so I heard," Vanessa said.

"Yes, but I didn't realize at the beginning that there

were going to be more bodies," Katie murmured. "And David was determined."

"All right, then, let me put it this way—could *you* just forget about it? Katie, I saw that poor girl the night she disappeared—and wound up dead. She was terrified. There was something on that beach. Other people go over there still, despite what happened."

Katie frowned. "But nothing has happened since, right?"

"Not on Haunt Island," Vanessa said.

"What happened otherwise?" Katie asked.

"In two years' time? I don't know everything, but I'm suspicious every time I hear about any bad things happening. I know about one boat that disappeared in that area. A charter boat on its way to Bimini about a year ago. Disappeared, as in vanished."

"Things don't really disappear in the Bermuda Triangle," Katie said. "It was just that for years, we didn't know what had happened. But they found the planes that went down years ago, after World War II. They finally found them. No one knows why they went down, but they certainly have educated theories. So a charter boat didn't really *disappear*—it's out there somewhere."

"Well, one of Jay's boats disappeared," Vanessa said flatly. "It disappeared—and Travis and Georgia were found dead on the beach."

Katie looked at her sympathetically. "The Bahamian authorities, Florida State authorities, and even the FBI got in on the investigation, Vanessa. There's a problem with the ocean—when things go down, they may go down miles. There are storms, there are currents. There were no clues on the island." She cleared her throat. "They, um, never found the rest of the bodies, right?"

Vanessa shook her head. "I'd say they actively investigated for months...maybe even a year. The torsos, hips and legs were never found. God, I can't even believe I'm saying that!"

"But there was a suspect, right? Carlos...someone?"

"Carlos Roca," Vanessa told her. "But he was a good guy. A friend."

"Okay, so, no matter how you might think that he was a good guy, and even if he was a friend, you have to admit, Vanessa, it does appear as if Carlos had already killed Travis, and that when he said he'd take Georgia back to Miami, he was lying. What he did was kill her, get the boat down the beach, find where he'd stashed Travis's body, and stage the heads and arms. Then he stole the boat and dumped the rest of the bodies into the ocean. Oh, Vanessa, I know you don't want to believe that. But there's no other explanation."

"Carlos would have popped up somewhere. And the boat would have been found."

Katie let out a long sigh. "Nessa, the boat could have gotten into trouble—and it might have sunk. And Carlos might have gone down with it. God knows where he might have tried to go from Haunt Island. But that boat's out there somewhere. I don't know about the bodies anymore—fish are ravenous little creatures, really—and not so little, often. Time, salt water..."

"Isn't David's cousin, Liam, a detective now? Could he know something?" Vanessa asked.

"Yes, I talked to him after you called me. He was

never in on that investigation. He'd heard about it, of course, but he didn't have anything to do with it."

Jamie O'Hara strode down the bar to where the two of them were sitting. "Don't you be worrying, Miss Loren. If I know my nephew, and I think I do, he'll come around."

Katie arched a brow at Jamie. "Uncle Jamie, don't go getting her hopes up, hmm?"

Jamie winked at Vanessa.

"You think he'll come around, too, don't you, Katie?"

Katie frowned. Then she sighed. "Yes, I started on David this morning, so…well, we'll see. But, Vanessa, I don't want you to be so—obsessed. I know my brother and David, and I know that they're fascinated by mysteries like this, but…you have to understand," she added quietly. "David came home determined to discover the truth behind a ten-year-old murder case because *he* had been accused of murder."

"Yes, I know," Vanessa said. She'd read all about the insanity that had first driven David Beckett out of Key West, and then home. Naturally. She had been friends with Katie O'Hara for years. She had read every word in the papers when the case had been solved, and that had brought her back here. Key West had two of its own native conchs—David Beckett and Sean O'Hara—about to embark on a film project that would bring to light many of the mysteries that surrounded the area throughout the decades and even centuries. David Beckett had a military background, and Sean O'Hara had filmed in many dangerous places, had received a great deal of defensive training and certainly knew how to take care of himself. Beckett also had a cousin who was a detective with the Key West police. They were the right people to at least explore the waters, and the story, and make her feel at the very least as if she were doing all that she could to find out just what had happened to Georgia, Travis—and Carlos Roca.

"Oh, I mean, David's a great person!" Katie said, quickly defending the love of her life. "You have to understand, it's not that he wouldn't care, or that he wouldn't be horrified—but he's not FBI, a cop or any other kind of law enforcement." She brightened suddenly. "Hey, I'll set up a meeting with Liam. I mean, if Liam gets into it, maybe he could help us out."

"That would be great—thanks, Katie. I'd like to meet him and hear what he thinks, because I'm sure he had to have heard about it, at least when it was all taking place."

"Well," Jamie said, "well and good. Now you can't sit here in the bar, moping about all day. Go enjoy the fall. Beautiful days we've got going here now. Days that are the kind that bring people south. Get—get out of bar, go and do something."

"Hey, I know that my friend Marty—big-time into pirates—is getting ready for his booth and show for the Pirates in Paradise performances this year. Let's go give him a hand—he loves to talk pirates. I bet he knows all about that pirate you were using for your horror movie, Mad Miller. And I can almost guarantee you he knows about Kitty Cutlass and Dona Isabella, too."

"Katie," Vanessa said, "I did tons of research. And I love the history—love it!—but we're talking about people murdered just two years ago."

"But you were filming history, right?"

Vanessa grimaced. "Well, history—fractured beyond belief—that we were using for a slasher flick."

"So I'll call Liam. We'll have dinner. We'll have him over to the house."

"David will be there, right? I mean—you are living with David at the Beckett house, right?" Vanessa asked her.

"David will be on your side," Katie said. "I'll call while we head over to Marty's."

"How do you know that you'll convince David to be on my side?" Vanessa asked.

Katie laughed. "I can be very persuasive. No, all kidding aside, they should agree to follow your mystery. It's good film. They'll be delving into piracy, the founding of the area—and something that's contemporary and horrible. People like justice and a satisfactory ending. No one can bring the dead back to life, but there is something to be said for closure. We don't feel that we failed those who died if we can figure out a riddle and bring a killer to justice."

"I may have you do all the talking," Vanessa told her.

"It will work out," Katie said.

Vanessa wasn't at all sure that she believed Katie, but she had to keep trying. She had exhausted other possibilities. She had plagued many law-enforcement agencies, and people had been kind and they had said the right things. But the case, though open, was not being actively investigated. Her only recourse was filmmakers—and those with a preplanned budget and a plan. *And* a wealth of knowledge about the history of the area.

"Great," Vanessa said. She smiled at the elder O'Hara behind the bar. "Thank you, Jamie. Katie, let's go play with the pirates."

Clear air turbulence in the Bermuda Triangle.

That was one of the main causes listed on a number of the flights—major commercial flights and smaller, private craft—that had plunged a thousand feet or more or had trouble in the last few decades.

There were other losses, however. A number of disappearances in the area known as the Bermuda Triangle. It wasn't officially an area at all, and had only become so in latter history—the U.S. Board of Geographical Names didn't recognize it as a place with a name at all. Superstition ruled a lot of what people believed about the area, and it had a doppelgänger on the other side of the world called "the Devil's Sea" by Japanese and Filipino people.

The most widely accepted scientific explanation for the strange events in the area had to do with magnetism. In the Bermuda Triangle, magnets might point "true north" in contrast to "magnetic north," which had to do with circumnavigating the earth. The compass variations could be as great as twenty degrees, which would definitely cause havoc when attempting to reach a destination.

Sean leaned back in his computer chair, studying the screen.

The next theory had to do with gas—gas from the sea itself. Subterranean beds shifting due to underwater landslides could cause a vast leakage of methane gas. An Englishman from Leeds University had proposed the theory as late as the 1990s that the weight of the gas in the water could cause a ship to sink like a rock and also that the gas in the air could cause instantaneous combustion of a fuel-filled jet in seconds flat. Boom.

The first odd occurrence went all the way back to Christopher Columbus, who, along with several of his men, reported mass compass malfunctions, a massive bolt of fire that suddenly fell from the sky into the sea and then strange lights on the horizon—all in the area of the Bermuda Triangle.

Switching from site to site on the Internet, Sean had to admit that he found what he was reading fascinating.

But from magnets and gas, the theories went off into other realms, ones he was certain he couldn't buy himself.

Aliens. Apparently, the belief that aliens were responsible for the disappearances was more widespread than he'd wanted to know. Some people believed that extraterrestrials had brought down a massive ship hundreds of years ago. That ship was down below the ocean floor. Sometimes the aliens were angry and destructive. Sometimes, to perform their evil deeds in their evil laboratories, they would send out their own vessels to snag ships or planes and bring them down below the surface.

Some people believed that they made trips to earth only now and then to snatch planes from the sky and ships from the sea.

Another theory had to do with the lost city of Atlantis. The psychic Edgar Cayce, who passed away in 1945, had claimed that he—and many other people—were reincarnated residents of the doomed Atlantis. He said that the city had not been in the Old World at all but near Bimini, in the Bahamas. The people had been highly advanced and used fire crystals for their power—fire crystals that had gotten out of hand and exploded, thus causing the sinking of Atlantis. There were still fire crystals deeply embedded in the ocean, and their power surged sometimes, causing ships, people, planes and debris to disappear. He prophesied that Atlantis would rise again in 1968 or '69.

In 1968, the Bimini Road or Bimini Wall was discovered—a rock formation of rounded stones beneath the sea near North Bimini that definitely bore the appearance of an ancient great highway. Some geologists argued that it was a natural highway; others were convinced that it might have been a manmade structure dating back three to four thousand years.

Sean had seen the Bimini Wall, and it was fascinating, but he wasn't a structural scholar, so he couldn't determine if the wall had been there forever, lurking beneath sand and the elements, or if it had been manmade.

He didn't believe that Cayce had once been a citizen of the fabled Atlantis.

Another man had put forth a crystal theory—Ray Brown. While diving in the area in 1970, he had gotten cut off from his friends. He'd found an underwater cave. The cave had been extraordinary. He'd seen a pyramid formation against a beautiful aquamarine light. Obviously, some higher intelligence had been at work in the cave, creating the light, the formation and the smooth workmanship within the cave.

He'd found a crystal sphere in the pyramid, and taken

it. When he'd left the cave, he'd heard a voice telling him to get out and never to return.

Sean sat back, shaking his head, puzzled. If he'd ever found such a cave, he'd have partners and film crew down in the water before he ever came out of it.

Ray Brown didn't do that.

He didn't tell the world about his remarkable experience.

He brought his crystal to a psychics fair in Phoenix in 1975.

If his cave had ever been discovered or the secret of the crystal divulged, Sean didn't know about it, nor, going from site to site to site on the Internet, could he find any mention of it—the cave, that was. There was mention only of the crystal.

Behind him, Bartholomew sniffed.

"God! Would you not read over my shoulder?" Sean asked.

Bartholomew ignored the question.

"They are referring to the Gulf Stream. They are referring to an area that, even in my day, was one of the most heavily traveled sea passages in the world. The current is always five to six knots, storms rise up constantly out of nowhere, and statistically, it would be almost impossible for things not to happen in the area. Ah, but absurd things do happen. So is there a Bermuda Triangle? Or is it just the natural state of the world?" he queried.

"I believe that you're right about the fact that the sea can be dangerous, the Gulf Stream can be treacherous and human beings can make errors. There was a case just a few years ago where seven fishermen were out.

The captain had sailed the waters more than thirty years. They left on a clear day, and a rogue wave overturned the boat. They weren't five nautical miles from shore, but after the wave hit, the boat overturned. Two died and five were found alive. If the five hadn't been recovered, it would have been another case for the Bermuda Triangle, because no trace of the fishing boat was ever discovered and they were in relatively shallow waters, close to shore, when it happened. I don't believe in crystals or aliens. Who knows? Maybe a city was sunk thousands of years ago—I've been places where they know that one day the volcanoes beneath the surface will blow—and old islands will go down and new ones will be formed. Hawaii will sink—hell, one day, Florida will sink. That's the planet. But as far as people being *murdered* by the Bermuda Triangle, crystals, aliens, or even a subspecies of humanity with gills—I don't believe it for an instant."

Bartholomew laughed. "That from a man carrying on a conversation with a ghost!"

Sean glared at him.

"Hey!" Bartholomew protested. "I'm just pointing out that there is more in the world than what most people are willing to see or accept. But frankly, I'm with you. I don't believe in aliens—not from other planets. Oh, there may be life out there, but I have a feeling that life might be fungi or sponges. And no one sees the future—except for God. I've been around a very long time. I've been able to observe quite a bit. Like the fact that you're thinking about all of this because you've spent the day on the computer."

"Is there no one else you can go haunt?" Sean asked him. "Where is your beautiful lady in white?"

Bartholomew waved a hand in the air. "I'll see her later."

A ghost, yes. He was talking to a ghost. Not his fault—he blamed that on Katie! So he was talking to a ghost, and calling others absurd!

"Ghosts are different," Bartholomew said, as if reading his mind. "We *were,* we lived and breathed. Energy doesn't die—and we are the result. Most human beings have a religious or spiritual belief, and if you believe in what you don't see, as in God, then it's not such a stretch to believe that souls exist. And we all know that even among the living, some people can communicate and some can't. But I do agree with you. The perpetrator of the evil deeds surrounding the film crew was not the Bermuda Triangle, the power of a crystal or a little green man popping out of the ocean. There's a live person, homicidal, organized and possibly psychotic," he finished.

Sean stared at him, hiding a smile.

"I have spent some time in the police station, obviously," Bartholomew said. "Actually, it's quite something. People are always saying 'I'd just love to be a fly on the wall.' Well, that is one thing about departing one's earthly form. I am able to be a fly on the wall."

"Ah, so you're an expert now on all things law enforcement," Sean teased.

"No, I'm gifted at listening to other people—and you may never know when you need the services of an excellent eavesdropper."

"Point noted, thank you. Isn't it time for high tea, or something like that?" Sean asked.

"I'm off to find my dear beauty in white," Bartholomew said. "Be nice to me, Sean O'Hara—I believe I'm still here to watch out for you, so you just may find that you need me!"

Bartholomew walked to the door, and disappeared through it.

Sean turned back to the computer and keyed in the name *Vanessa Loren.*

"Fascinating!" Marty said to Vanessa. She and Katie had joined him at his house on Fleming Street. It was what they called a "shotgun" house, built with a long hall or breezeway, so that if the front and back doors were both open, you could fire a shotgun and the bullet would run right through the house. Basically, the plan was to keep the air going through the house at all times, since it had been built long before air-conditioning became a customary feature in homes in the hot, subtropical climes of the Keys.

Marty seemed like a very nice guy. Vanessa had actually seen him before, stopping in at O'Hara's for Katie's business, Katie-oke. O'Hara's was always pleasant and laid-back, and a lot of locals planning acts for different festivals, private parties or any such ventures spent time there. The bar had the kind of comfortable feel that worked for locals and tourists alike. Vanessa hadn't met Marty formally before, but she'd seen him do a good job with a pirate bellow in a rollicky sea shanty.

His house was decorated to fit the man. There were a number of ship's bells, ships in bottles, old figureheads, anchors and other paraphernalia from the past set up around the house; he was a collector of books, music, logs, parchments, deeds, old money and more. The place was eclectic and comfortable. Vanessa thought that he must have a small fortune in the place as far as the value of some of the antiques would go, but it was still comfortable and casual.

"Fascinating!" Marty repeated, then he looked sheepish and rueful. "Oh, that's terrible, that's really terrible of me to say. I'm so, so sorry about your friends, of course. And I suppose it all did terrible things to the futures of those who survived. But that it all happened when you were working on a movie about Mad Miller and Kitty Cutlass… I've always been intrigued by the tales of people that have come down to us. History. People make it so dry. This date and that date. It's not dates schoolchildren should be remembering—it's the people. History should be like a reality show—or *Oprah.* No, *Jerry Springer.* People love the weaknesses, the cruelty and sometimes even the honor of others!"

"Maybe an enterprising person will get it together that way one day, Marty," Katie said.

"Aha!" Marty told her happily. "That's exactly what I'm doing at the fort this year. An interview with a few of our notorious pirates and their consorts. You have to come. Better yet, you could be consorts, harlots, barmaids—"

"I have to work, Marty," Katie reminded him.

"I'm hoping to be working," Vanessa said.

Marty sighed, disappointed, and studied Vanessa. "Have you not worked for the last two years—since the incident on Bimini?"

"No, no, I've been working, Marty. I'm doing all right. You know the commercial for the new underwater camera that any two-year old can use? I wrote it."

Marty shuddered. "All those two-year-olds!"

"It was fun, actually. We shot in a lovely private pool, and the kids were really adorable," Vanessa assured him.

Marty still looked at her worriedly. "You okay down here? Where are you staying?"

"She's got a perfectly good room at my house or with David and me—she won't take either," Katie said.

"I'm just down Duval, perfect location, a little room for rent above one of the shops," Vanessa told him. "And I'm quite happy."

"But what if you're not safe?" Marty asked.

"I'm right on Duval, in the midst of the tourist horde. There's someone up just about all hours of the night, and the cops are out in droves. I'm safe. Look, I've been bugging police and anyone else you can think of for two years—whatever happened, happened. It's sliding by, and that's why I'm so concerned. This killer might lie dormant for a long time, then swoop down on another group of unsuspecting boaters."

Marty stood. "Well. Just in case you didn't come across this in your research, I have something to show you."

He walked over to the large buffet where a ship's dining bell held the central position. Reaching behind it, he pulled out a framed picture. He turned to her with pleasure in his eyes. "Dona Isabella!" he told her.

Vanessa walked over to study the picture. It was a pen-and-ink drawing of a woman in an elegant gown circa the early eighteen hundreds. Her hair was loose, curling around her shoulders. The artist had captured the beauty of the woman, and something more—something that was partly flirtatious and might also be cunning. She could see that the sketch had been titled "The Mystery of a Woman."

"How do you know that this is Dona Isabella?" Vanessa asked.

Marty smiled, proud of his acquisition. He opened the frame, showing the old parchment on which the portrait had been sketched, and the signature of the artist. Len Adams had sketched the picture, and he had written, "Dona Isabella at Tea with a Friend, 1834."

"I've had it authenticated, of course," Marty said. "Len Adams is known down here—his pieces are coveted. He died very young of tuberculosis, so he doesn't have an extensive body of work. He came here because he was dying in the north. He died anyway. But he sketched many wonderful portraits."

Vanessa was fascinated by the picture, and suddenly felt guilty about her slasher-film script. Of course, in the movie, Dona Isabella had been the victim of Kitty Cutlass, quickly in the film, and quickly out. It had been Kitty Cutlass who'd returned from her watery grave to join with the ghost of Mad Miller to wreak murder, mayhem and havoc upon the unsuspecting teens sailing to Bimini and on Haunt Island.

"Oh, girl, you're one after my own heart!" Marty said, appreciating the way she looked at the picture. "I'll copy it for you—won't be the original, but you'll have the beauty anytime you choose. Poor thing! So lovely, such a coquette and so tragically young to be a victim."

He looked at Vanessa. "Boy, that would be something, wouldn't it? What if your people were killed because the ghosts of Mad Miller and Kitty Cutlass are out there, cruising between Key West and Bimini, right into the Triangle, alive through some wild magnetic source?"

Vanessa stared at him.

He gave her a tap on the shoulder. "Joshing with you, girl. But if you want more pirate history, you come on back here anytime, all right? And if you need anything at all, you come to see me. I'm like a Key West structure, an institution, always here, and I wouldn't be anywhere else in the world."

She thanked him, and she and Katie said goodbye.

"Do you think that the murders might have had something to do with the story you were filming?" Katie asked as they walked. "No, wait. We'll wait until we all get together, and then we'll talk about it. I don't want to make you repeat it all over and over."

They stopped in front of the Beckett house and Vanessa looked up at the grand facade. "So you're living in the Beckett house!" Vanessa teased.

Katie shrugged. "Life is pretty bizarre, just like death."

"So it seems," Vanessa agreed.

Katie opened the front door with a key and they stepped into the hallway. She paused. "I guess they're already here," she said. They walked through the large parlor, through the kitchen and to the back porch, handsomely furnished with white wicker and plush jungle-colored cushions. There were three men there already—not just the two tall, dark-haired men Vanessa assumed to be Liam and David Beckett, but Sean O'Hara, as well.

They all stood as Vanessa and Katie came into the room.

She envied Katie, who walked comfortably up to David Beckett and slipped an arm around him. There was something nicely sure and confident in the motion, and more so in David's smile of response. They were happy.

David and Liam shook hands with Vanessa and were pleasant and cordial. Sean, of course, she had already met.

He waited quietly.

Then the awkward silence fell at last.

"Why doesn't everyone sit, and I'll get some drinks and snacks," Katie suggested.

Great! Vanessa glared at her, feeling as if she had suddenly been thrown to the wolves.

But she was the one who wanted help!

She sat stiffly, folding her hands around her knees as she looked at the three. "Perhaps this is way out of bounds. But I don't know where else to go from here."

"Start at the beginning," David suggested. "Sean has told us what you want us to do—but start back at the beginning, the film shoot you did, everything that happened that night and everything that happened after."

Vanessa decided to start out looking straight ahead, and then she decided to speak as naturally as possible and not avoid anyone's eyes. "I've loved Key West since I was a child, since my father first brought me down here. When my friend Jay Allen came to me saying that he wanted to make a film, the first thing that came to my mind was the story of Mad Miller, his mistress, Kitty Cutlass, and the murder of poor Dona Isabella. Everything went fine, and we were down to a skeleton crew—Georgia and Travis, the last characters who remained alive, Jay and myself, of course, two young production assistants, Bill Hinton and Jake Magnoli, and Barry Melkie, our soundman. Zoe was everything as far as props, costume and makeup, with the help of Bill and Jake. Oh, and of course, Carlos Roca. Lew, our Bahamian guide, was there, too. That night, we had just about wrapped, and I was by the fire… Jay was there, I'm not sure who else at first, but everyone was just winding down. Suddenly, Georgia came screaming down the beach—she'd seen heads sticking out of the sand, arms. She described a scene that was the exact one in which we found her and Travis the following morning."

"You found Georgia and Travis?" David asked.

She nodded gravely.

"You found the bodies?" Sean asked.

"I did," Vanessa said. "Lew and Jay came quickly down to the beach, then the others…and then the Bahamian authorities."

"Let me see if I've got this straight, though," Sean said. "Georgia and Travis were found dead. Georgia had been running down the beach. Where was Travis?"

"No one knew," Vanessa said.

"Then why didn't you look for him?" Sean asked.

"Frankly, we thought he was part of a huge prank being pulled on Georgia. Jay was aggravated with him. We did go down the beach—Lew, Jay and I—and there was nothing there. Except—"

"Except?" Liam asked.

"The sand where we later found the two had been churned up. It looked as if maybe there had been something stuck in the sand."

"And that didn't bother you?" Sean asked.

"We were filming a horror movie. We thought that someone was playing an elaborate prank, and, as I said, that Travis was involved in the prank. I'm afraid that a lot of pranks are carried out on film sets," Vanessa said evenly. She took a deep breath. "Anyway, Georgia was in terror—she wasn't going to stay on the island. She was having an absolute fit, so Carlos said that he could take her into Miami and head back first thing in the morning. We all thought it was best. But Georgia and Travis were found on the beach, and Carlos and the boat disappeared."

"I'm not sure there's much of a mystery there," Sean said. "Apparently, Carlos stole the boat after he killed the two."

"I don't believe it, not for a minute," Vanessa said. "The police, the Coast Guard, the FBI—every known agency looked for the boat and Carlos, but it was as if they had vanished. What you don't understand is that Carlos Roca wasn't capable of doing something so horrible. He was one of the most gentle people I've ever met."

"I wasn't in on the investigation, but I do remember it," Liam said. "And I'm sorry to tell you this, but most of those law-enforcement agencies believe that Carlos Roca did murder the two young people and steal the boat."

"I don't care what they believe!" Vanessa said.

She was surprised when Sean said, "Of course,

there's another scenario. Someone else hijacked the boat, someone who might have already taken Travis. That person either killed Carlos first to take control of Georgia or had Carlos knocked out somewhere. Then did the grisly deed on the island and dumped Carlos in the Atlantic."

David leaned forward. "Okay, here's the curious part—where was Travis? Had he been killed and his body hidden? And was it possible for someone to have killed him, hidden his body and managed to go after Carlos and Georgia in the boat, get back to the island without being seen, find the one body, stage the gruesome death scene, and then get rid of Carlos? And how, with the alarm that must have gone out, could they have gotten away with the boat? Everyone in the Bahamas, South Florida and all of the Caribbean would have been on the alert."

"Well, stealing the boat, gassing it up, changing it—that seems the easiest part of it," Sean said.

"I agree with you—where Travis was when the whole thing started would be a nice piece of the riddle."

"Dead," Vanessa said softly.

"Probably dead, but where? And how was he killed, and then not found until later?" Sean mused.

"These are the questions everyone has asked time and time again, and they haven't found the answers. But they aren't people who know the legends, know the area—"

"Snacks and beer!" Katie announced cheerfully from the hallway.

She set nachos with steaming cheese and other ingredients on the coffee table and passed around the tray she carried with ice-cold beer bottles.

Vanessa accepted a beer with a gaze that said both "Thanks" and "How could you have left me alone in here?"

Katie smiled. "I know you all," Katie said, sitting, "and there isn't a better mystery out there!"

"I have a lot of work to do now," Liam said. "And it's a bad time, a very bad time, at the station."

"Nothing has been decided," Sean said.

"We've all agreed to talk about it. We've talked about focusing on a number of mysteries and legends, but we haven't decided what our focus is going to be," David said. "It's Sean's decision. I am gung-ho on the idea of pooling our resources and working locally, but Sean's been doing the budget, mapping and research, so it's his decision."

"Yes, but if you're thinking about the story, I ought to be on the trip," Liam said. He looked at Vanessa. "It hasn't occurred to you to be afraid? The killer or killers were never caught. They might still be out there," he said.

"Afraid?" she asked softly. "I still have nightmares. I see Georgia alive and screaming, and I see the heads and the arms sticking out of the sand. I remember being terrified of the dark for nearly a year. And then I got very angry, and I finally figured out that I'd probably have nightmares for the rest of my life if I didn't do something to discover the truth. I think the killer is a coward—he worked in the dark, at night. I think there has to be a way to stand against him. That starts with finding him—and when he's found, I don't care if they give him life or the death penalty, just so long as he can never do anything so horrible to anyone else, ever again."

She stood up. They were going to agree, or they weren't.

"I'll let you all talk," she said. "Katie knows where to find me. Thank you for your time."

Afraid? Yes, she'd been so afraid....

Her only fear now was that they would say no.

The *Happy-Me* sat off the coast of Bimini in shallow water. Jenny and Mark Houghton and their friends Gabby and Dale Johnson had planned on camping on the beach, but they had gotten lazy. They hadn't tied up at the dock because they'd kept the boat in the shallow water, and talked so late that the sun had gone down.

Both retired, the couples motored the short distance to Haunt Island several times a year.

Gabby and Dale had gone to bed, Mark was still topside and Jenny was humming as she put away the last of the dishes. They'd dined on spaghetti and meatballs, heated up in the microwave.

She was startled to hear her husband call her name. "Jenny!"

She nearly dropped the dish in her hand, it had been so quiet. She set it on the counter and hurried up the ladder to the deck. For a moment, it struck her that they might as well be alone in the world. Entirely alone. There were a few stars in a black-velvet sky, and it seemed that there was no horizon, the sea melded with the sky. The lights of the *Happy-Me* were colorful and brave against the night—and pitiful, as well.

"Hand me the grapple pole there, quickly, Jenny," Mark said, leaning over the hull and staring into the water.

"What?"

She was concerned. Mark had been given a clean bill of health after having suffered a heart attack on his seventieth birthday, but he thought himself a young man still, at times. And he was acting like a crazy one now.

"That one," he said, spinning around. There was a grappling hook on a long pole set in its place in metal brackets against the wall of the cabin.

"But, Mark—"

"Please, Jenny, please—there's someone in the water!"

She heard it then: a gasped and garbled plea for help.

While Mark continued to stare into the water, Jenny reached for the hook, almost ripping it from the wall to bring to Mark.

He stuck it out into the water, calling out, "Here, here, take this, we'll get you aboard!

"Ah!" he murmured. Jenny saw that someone had the pole and that Mark was managing to pull the person closer to the boat.

"The flashlight, get a flashlight!" Mark said.

Jenny turned to do so. As she did, she heard another gasping sound, and within it a little cry of terror.

She spun around.

The sound was coming from Mark.

Because someone…*something*…was rising from the sea.

It couldn't be. It was a bony pirate, half-eaten, so it appeared, in rags. Bones and rags, and it was laughing....

"No!" Jenny gasped herself.

The *thing* reached out and grabbed Mark around the neck. It lifted him and tossed him overboard. Jenny started to scream in protest, horrified for Mark, her companion, friend, lover, husband for all of her life.

And then...

In terror herself. For her own life.

Because now the *thing* pulled a sword. A fat sword. Maybe it wasn't a sword. Maybe it was a machete. Maybe it was...

Her last conscious thought was, *What the hell does it matter what it is?*

It swung in the night.

She never managed to scream. Her windpipe was severed before she could do so. She dropped to the deck, her head dangling from the remnants of her neck.

"Quickly," said the one to the other, joining him on board. "Quickly. The other two, before they wake up!"

The deck was drenched as they walked across it and down the ladder to the cabin below.

Gabby and Dale never woke up.

For a while, the *Happy-Me* rolled in the gentle waves of the night, beneath the velvet darkness of the sky.

Then it sank to a shallow grave.

3

Vanessa had the dreams again that night.

They had started the night on the island when Georgia had talked about the monsters, left the island with Carlos—and wound up murdered with her head on the sand.

For the first weeks after the incident, they'd come frequently. They would start with her being Isabella, rising from the sea in her period gown, covered with seaweed.

Vanessa had agreed to play the small role of Isabella, and the day when they had filmed her in the costume had turned out to be fun—after she'd calmed down from being aggravated. There she had been in that gown, floating—a corpse that had come to the surface, about to open its long-dead eyes—and they were supposed to have been filming from beneath her. But in the middle of the shoot, they'd gotten distracted by a school of barracuda, and she'd looked up at last to see that the boat was far away and there was no sign of the others. She was a good swimmer, but the seas were beginning to rise and the gown was heavy. She lay there cursing them, then called out, hoping someone on the boat would hear her.

The boat had come around at last with Jay and the others on board. They'd been thrilled with their footage of the barracuda—which usually left people alone, unless they had something on them that sparkled and attracted the attention of the predators. Incredulous, she'd asked if they'd gotten the shots of her, floating in the water. Oh, yes, they'd done so. Then, seeing her face, Jay had been entirely contrite, and everyone had tripped over themselves trying to appease her for the afternoon.

But in her dreams, she didn't see Isabella as herself. She saw her dead, murdered, empty sockets where her eyes should be, yet seeming to see, face skeletal and pocked with the ravages of the sea, bits of bone and skull peeking through decomposing flesh. The woman stared at her as if she were the enemy, and all around her, huge black shadows seemed to form, and they were made of seaweed and *evil.*

Then she was alone on the beach at Haunt Island, and they were coming after her, and she didn't run because there was nowhere to go to escape the darkness and evil, she simply stood there, staring at them, as they seemed to grow larger and larger and come closer and closer, and she could smell the rot of flesh and a stagnant sea and she could almost feel the salt spray of the ocean.

Right before they embraced her, she awoke with a start.

For a moment she was disoriented in the darkness of her room. Then she heard a whistle from below her window, the wheels of a late-night taxi going somewhere and the laughter of the few drunken revelers still on the street, and her eyes adjusted to the darkness. She was in her little studio room atop the bathing suit and T-shirt shop on Duval Street. A glance at the faceplate of her phone told her that it was just about 2:00 a.m.

She stared at the ceiling for a while, angry with herself. She wasn't afraid of ghosts or sea monsters. Someone real and alive had happened upon the island. A real person had killed her friends—and she just couldn't believe it was Carlos. Carlos was probably dead. She hated the fact that everyone *assumed* that he'd been the killer, when he probably died trying to protect Georgia from whatever sick maniac had come upon them. It was chilling to think that the killer had to have been on the island with them when Georgia had first screamed, when they had all thought that Travis was fine somewhere, laughing at the cruel joke he had played on Georgia. They should have looked harder for Travis that night.

And yet, who would have really suspected anything? They were a large enough group. They'd been enjoying the shoot, and even the pristine isolation of Haunt Island.

She probably lay there for hours, and then drifted off.

Vanessa's phone rang at 8:00 a.m. She knew, because the jarring sound caused her to bolt up, and she saw the time immediately. She fumbled to retrieve it from the stand next to the bed and answered breathlessly.

"Yes?"

"Vanessa?"

She felt as if her heart stood still for a moment. The voice sounded like that of Sean O'Hara.

"Yes?"

"Are you awake? Sorry if I woke you."

He wasn't one bit sorry, she thought.

"I was awake," she said. So she was lying. She wasn't sure what she had said or done exactly that had seemed to raise a barrier of hostility within him—other than that she did want him to take his project and turn it to her purpose.

"Ready to let me see your stuff?" he asked.

"Pardon?"

"Diving, filming," he said. Was there a touch of mockery in his tone? Was he amused that she might have thought that he meant something else?

"Of course. Anytime. Does this mean that—"

"It means I want to see if you're as good as your credentials," he said flatly.

"Of course. Where do you want me, when, and with what equipment?"

"I have equipment. You probably want your own regulator and mask."

"Of course. What about cameras?"

"Mine are excellent quality."

"So are mine."

"Let's see if you know my equipment, and my methods," he said. "And if I hire you, it's going to be as my assistant, remember? Hauling, toting. But…it won't hurt to see what you can do with a camera. You never know when you may need some backup."

"All right."

"Meet me at the dock in half an hour. My dive boat is the *Conch Fritter.* I'll be setting her up."

"I'll be there," she promised.

For a moment she couldn't afford to waste, she just sat there, staring at her phone. He hadn't agreed.

But he hadn't said no.

And in the water, she could prove herself.

She blinked, then shot out of bed. She had thirty minutes to shower, find a suit and run down the seven or so blocks to the boat docks.

And there had to be a cup of coffee somewhere along the way.

Vanessa Loren was all business when she arrived at the dock precisely on time. She was wearing a huge tank-type T-shirt over a bathing suit and carried a dive bag in one hand, a large paper cup of coffee in the other. Her hair was swept back in a band at her nape and she was wearing large dark sunglasses.

"Hand over the bag," he said politely.

"I can manage," she told him.

She could. Without needing a handhold of any kind for balance, she made the short leap from the dock to the deck with amazing dexterity, never in danger of losing so much as a drop of coffee—not that the company didn't serve its coffee with A-one lids.

He shrugged as she landed. "Suit yourself. Want to grab that line aft?"

"Sure."

Bartholomew leaned casually against the rail, arms crossed over his chest. "She's got quite the physical prowess, and yet she's light and sleek as a cat. I say, hire her on! Trust me, the women of my day were seldom adept at working on any ship. Ah, this is but a boat. There you go."

Sean wanted to tell Bartholomew that there had been a number of famous and infamous women working upon pirate ships, but since Bartholomew was indignant at the term *pirate,* he'd deny it. And he knew that Bartholomew was going to goad him all afternoon.

He refrained from replying.

He went to the fore to release the front line and she scurried to release the one aft. He didn't speak to her as he guided the *Conch Fritter* out of the harbor.

Bartholomew, however, kept up a running conversation.

"Ah, what a lovely day. Truly lovely day! Calm seas, a beautiful sky and just the tiniest kiss of autumn in the air. I do remember this reef—we forced a few Spaniards into her sharp tentacles, we did. Glorious sailing! Oh, and by the way—you do know that this is the area where Mad Miller supposedly attacked the *Santa Geneva* and kidnapped Dona Isabella. Alas, the ship upon which she sailed sank to the bottom of the sea with the nasty, evil creatures upon the pirate ship, Mad Miller's flagship, slicing up many a man as he begged for mercy, cast into the water, drowning!"

Slicing them might have been a mercy, if they were drowning, Sean thought, but he kept silent.

As he cleared the channel, Vanessa came and took the companion seat by the helm.

"Ah, but she looks lovely there!" Bartholomew commented.

She did. She was relaxed, enjoying the wind that whipped around them as they sped through the water. The *Conch Fritter* wasn't new, but she was a thirty-eight-foot Sea Ray custom Sundancer, and Sean loved her. She did twenty knots with amazing comfort—she wasn't going to outrun a real powerboat by any means, but she could move. The cockpit was air-conditioned and equipped with two flat-screen TVs, and there were three small sleeping cabins, the captain's cabin at the fore and two lining the port and starboard sides. There was a small galley and main cabin as well, and the helm sat midway through the sleek design with a fiberglass companion seat that offered plenty of storage. He'd had her outfitted with a helm opening and an aft boarding ladder with a broad platform, and portside and starboard safe holds for dive tanks.

"Yes, yes, you love your boat," Bartholomew said, rolling his eyes. "And she is a thing of beauty! But then again, can anything rival the gold of that young woman's hair, the sea and sky that combine in her eyes?" he asked with an exaggerated sigh.

Sean thought, *I will not look at you, you scurvy spectral bastard.*

"Where are we going?" Vanessa asked above the hum of the motor.

"Pirate Cut—it's a close, easy dive," Sean said.

"We don't even need tanks," she commented.

"Ah, she knows the reef!" Bartholomew said. "Frankly, it seems that everything this young woman has said to you is true."

"If you want to stay down and film we need tanks and equipment," Sean said pleasantly to Vanessa.

She flushed and looked away, but it was obvious that she knew the reef, and probably knew it fairly well.

She did. She knew exactly where they were going, and how long it was going to take to get there. When they were still five minutes away, she stood and dug into her bag. She worked with a dive skin, not a suit, but a skin, light and not providing warmth. He actually liked a skin himself—a skin protected a diver against the tentacles of small and unseen jellyfish.

But he hadn't brought one.

By the time he'd stopped the motor and dropped anchor, she had on her skin and dive booties. Dive booties could be good, too, he had to admit. He'd brought neither his skin nor booties, but he didn't always wear them. She'd attached her regulator to a buoyancy-control vest and tank—the one next to the tank he'd prepared for himself. She wasted no time.

"What are we using?" she asked him.

He opened his storage container. He loved his equipment; he could spend hours perusing new camera equipment on the Internet.

He had many makes and models of video and still cameras, lighting systems and sound recorders, though often sound was added after shooting. He chose a Sony that day, with a Stingray Plus housing.

"Want help with your BCV and tank?" he asked.

"Nope, thank you."

He'd worked on dive boats growing up; tanks were heavy, it was easy to go off balance with them. Most people didn't mind help rising with them.

He let her go on her own.

She buckled into the vest and rose carefully, her mask on her head, her regulator ready. She proceeded carefully to the edge, slipped her regulator in her mouth and entered in a smooth backward flip. She had managed the weight on her slim body without any difficulty. All right, so she was trying to be one of the guys, not a hindrance, not someone on a crew who couldn't manage basic tasks.

She surfaced, and he handed her the camera equipment. She removed her regulator and asked him, "What am I filming?"

"Something artistic," he told her. "And I'm right behind you."

She nodded, but she wasn't waiting around at the surface. She could handle the camera housing fine while releasing air from her BCV. She sank below the surface.

"What a woman!" Bartholomew said. "Why, if I were only flesh and blood..."

"But you're not," Sean told him.

He hurried into his own gear and followed in her wake.

Pirate's Cut was a beautiful place to dive. The water was clear, and visibility was amazing. Staghorn coral rose and wafted in the movement of the water, while torch and pineapple coral in dazzling shades grew around it. Tiny fish darted here, there and everywhere, while a large grouper, at least three hundred pounds, decided to swim at her side.

It did make for beautiful filming. She shot the coral with the tiny fish and panned slowly around to the giant grouper.

There was a drop-off near the shallow area of the reef, and she followed it down; she knew that the ocean went to no more than a hundred feet at the drop-off. She eased down about another twenty feet, aware that Sean was near her then, watching her. He came to her, motioning for the camera. She frowned behind her mask but handed it to him. He indicated her side, and she saw that the giant grouper was still following her, like a pet dog. She shrugged and swam slowly alongside the fish while Sean took footage. She reached out and stroked the side of the fish. He circled her—hoping for a handout, she was certain. Divers must have recently come to the reef with food to encourage the creature to come near. It was amazing that he hadn't wound up on a dinner plate himself.

He lingered a little while longer, and then swam off.

Sean returned the camera to her. She decided to go to the bones of the old sunken ship that was assumed to be the *Santa Geneva.* She'd been a wooden-hulled ship and had broken up, however it was that she'd gone down. She was really nothing but wooden bones now, since the sea had caused the disintegration of most of the hull. Vanessa still loved the wreck. It was possible to imagine the size of the ship, where the masts had been, the hold, the cabins, the quarters.

She looked through the camera as she neared a section of the remains.

She almost choked, and started in the water.

Through the lens, she saw a figurehead.

Impossible. The figurehead was long gone.

She looked again, and for a moment, she could have sworn that she was seeing a woman's face—and the sleek lines of a beautifully crafted figurehead.

She blinked, and it was gone.

She moved the camera away for a moment and lowered herself down to the ruins. She shook the image of the figurehead and filmed the length of the ruins, taking in the fish, the barnacles growing on those sad bare bones that remained.

Something crusted rose from the bed of sand on the floor of the ocean that held the wreck. It was just a dot on the sand, but through the lens, it seemed to be something. Vanessa moved down and reached out, gently swishing sand from the object. She wasn't sure what it was, it was so encrusted, but it was odd, so she picked it up.

Sean was behind her. He eased himself down on his knees and she showed him what she had discovered. He took the camera from her and pointed upward. He was ready to surface.

They had moved a good hundred feet from the boat and stopped at thirty-three feet to pressurize. Sean reached the dive platform and ladder before she did. He set the camera down on the platform and threw his flippers on board as she grasped hold of the platform. The sea rocked around them, but Sean ably drew himself up and turned to reach for her. She hesitated only briefly and then accepted his hand, throwing her flippers up as well and climbing up the ladder.

They came through the little custom hatch to the deck of the Sea Ray and he spun her around without asking, unlatching her tank.

"I'll get yours," she said.

He didn't protest but accepted her help and stowed the tanks. He came back to her and asked for the object she had picked up from the ocean floor.

He turned it around and around in his hand. "I have friends to take this to," he murmured.

Vanessa felt a sudden, eerie sweep of air around her. She spun around, looking for…

Something.

But there was nothing around her.

Still, she was suddenly cold. She could remember the figurehead she had seen through the camera lens with a frightening clarity—since it hadn't really been there. And now…

This. This chilling sensation that…

They weren't alone.

Sean looked at her suddenly. "What's wrong?" he asked her.

She shook her head. "Nothing. A goose walked over my grave, I guess. What do you think it is?"

"A coin…or a pendant. I think you've found a real relic," he told her.

"Really?"

"Well, we could find out it's a 1950s Timex or something…I don't know enough to take a chance trying to get the ocean crust off it, but as I said, I have friends who do this professionally. We'll bring it to them. I'm driving in. Want water, beer, soda? They're in the cooler, over there, portside. Help yourself."

He pulled down the dive flag and drew in the anchor—it was automatic, all he had to do was push a button. The Sea Ray was definitely nice.

He went to the helm, starting the motor, taking the wheel. She still had the crazy feeling that they weren't alone, that the air was charged.

She grabbed a couple of bottles of water out of the cooler and hurried back to the companion seat.

"So—did I pass inspection?" she called to Sean,

more to start a conversation than because she was really ready for an answer.

He didn't reply; he was looking straight ahead with a small smile on his face. The wind had ruffled his hair, he was in board shorts and nothing else, and his chest was gleaming bronze and powerfully muscled. She was startled to feel a stirring of admiration or something worse, even—attraction.

It was the smile, she thought.

He reached for sunglasses, and leaned casually against the captain's seat rather than sitting.

She eased back in the companion chair, tired from the night before. She closed her eyes and allowed herself just to feel.

The figurehead had seemed so real…

Her eyes flew open. She almost bolted out of the chair.

The figurehead! The figurehead with its beautiful face…

The same face she had in her own possession, her copy of the artist's rendering of Dona Isabella.

4

Vanessa Loren knew how to work and how to move. She seemed familiar with every aspect of equipment and the importance of rinsing off their dive gear and his camera rigging as soon as they got back to the dock. When they were done, she slipped her oversize T-shirt back on and looked at him expectantly.

"Tell her she's hired," Bartholomew said. He was stretched out on his back on the aft seat, hands crossed behind his head, hat over his eyes, as if he still needed to shade them from the sun. One leg dangled over the other in lazy comfort. "Tell her that she's hired, and you're doing the story. You know you're going to do it. She's a scriptwriter, she knows cameras, she knows boats, and she sure seems to have a great work ethic. Not to mention great legs as long as a yardarm and… well, nothing wrong with the rest of her, either."

Sean ignored Bartholomew. He smiled at Vanessa. "You know we'll do a background check," he told her.

"Go for it," she said, looking off into the distance. She seemed distracted.

He nodded. "Oh, the object you found—I'm going to take it to friends who have a small shop on

Simonton—they usually work privately, but they have a little storefront. It's called Sunken Treasures. You're more than welcome to take it yourself, if you prefer. You discovered the piece."

"I trust you to take it—I'm not after treasure," she told him. Her hair was still damp; her eyes seemed the most brilliant blue he had ever seen, filled with honesty. There was something as she stood there, her answer to him filled with trust and disinterest, that seemed to catch at his throat. Or his heart.

Or, admittedly, other parts of his anatomy. Even wet, she was stunning. And yet beauty itself never created such an appeal. Maybe it was her energy or vitality. Or the way she seemed filled with warmth and vibrant, sleek movement—even when she stood still. He wanted to step closer to her, as intrigued by the woman as the mystery she brought.

He stepped back.

"All right, but you'll know where it is," he told her.

She smiled. The smile seemed a little distant. She looked around him and seemed confused, then shrugged, as if returning to the subject. "Thanks. I'll, uh, talk to you later, then?" she asked.

"Yes. I'll talk to you later," he assured her.

"Thank you."

She was sincere.

And yet it was odd. She still seemed distracted as she walked away. Sean watched her go, puzzled.

"She senses me—that's what's going on," Bartholomew said, rising and adjusting his hat. "She's got the sense—it's not developed, but she's got something. I know—trust me. I spent a few of my early years in this rather awkward state playing tricks on people. There are those who will never sense a thing, and there are those who always get a feeling...but don't really know what it is. She's gifted, I'd say."

"Wonderful. She's tracking a murderer—seriously, that's what she wants to do—and you're doing your best to make her jump at every whisper of breeze," Sean said.

"Excuse me! I don't really have much to do with it. Well, maybe I do. I mean, ghosts can make an effort, as you know...but I wasn't doing anything."

"That's not exactly true—since you talked a blue streak all day. Now I have to think over some things."

Bartholomew shrugged. "But you know you're going to work with her."

"It's not just my decision. David has to decide on this, as well."

"David's going to do whatever you want to do."

"The point is, really, there's nothing new that we're going to discover. Say Carlos Roca did it—he's long gone. Say someone else did it—that someone has managed to change the boat so that no one would ever recognize her, and they're probably living in Brazil by now," Sean said.

"You know better than anyone that it's never too late to seek the truth," Bartholomew said.

"Bartholomew, you're like an old fishwife. Quit nagging. The story is intriguing. I have to see how I'm going to fit it in with the rest of the history we want to put out there—touching on enough, creating a story line—"

"You were creating a documentary about legends and mysteries in this area. Fits right in," Bartholomew said.

"Hey, look—isn't that the lady in white?" Sean asked, pointing toward the center of Mallory Square. There was no one there, but Bartholomew looked. He glared at Sean. "She has a name, you know. Lucinda, Miss Lucinda Wellington—Lucy."

"Well, it's just damned adorable to see you so smitten, my friend," Sean said.

Bartholomew shook his head. "You won't distract me. Lucy and I have a lovely relationship. We walk every afternoon through the cemetery, strolling and reading the headstones. And sometimes we stroll down Duval and observe the tourists. Ah, I can smell the rum, so it seems, at times. But, Sean O'Hara, God knows why, it seems I'm here still to help you, and my beautiful lady in white, dear Lucy, seems glad enough to be with me."

"Great. Just great. Well, why don't you go see if she's in the cemetery now. I'm going to take a shower and then bring whatever that encrusted piece is that Vanessa found over to Jaden and Ted."

He left the ghost on deck and went down to the *Conch Fritter*'s head. Twenty minutes later, he headed to his friends' shop, curiously flipping the thing—trinket or treasure—in his hand.

Back in her room, Vanessa showered for a long time, luxuriating in the heat of the water, trying not to think. She emerged, and, convincing herself that she was overtired and suffering from the nightmares again, she went to the dresser and stared at the copy of the likeness of Dona Isabella that Marty had given her the day before.

She'd never heard that any ship had sailed with a figurehead carved as a replica of Dona Isabella.

Of course. There was no figurehead. She was exhausted, and she'd spent the morning trying to prove that she was more efficient than the Energizer bunny.

She dressed quickly and looked at the time. One o'clock. She realized that she was starving and still really exhausted. Okay, she was pretty sure that she'd pulled the morning off quite well—she'd been efficient, she'd gotten good footage, the giant grouper had certainly allowed Sean to get some good footage of her with the fish, and she'd discovered something at the bottom of the ocean, where the ship had wrecked and broken up nearly two hundred years ago.

She could take a nap.

Food and a nap.

And maybe a drink to help her relax. She was just a few feet away from the Key West Smallest Bar. Food, something good and stiff and a long nap.

She had imagined the figurehead in the water. But, really, if she thought about it, if she was going to imagine images, maybe in her mind the poor martyred Dona Isabella was trying to help her, she wanted the history known, she wanted the world to know what horrible villains Mad Miller and Kitty Cutlass had been.

Sleep.

And she would quit seeing things.

And with any luck, she wouldn't dream.

Sunken Treasures was located on Simonton. The proprietors, Jaden Valiente and Ted Taggart, were friends of Sean's from school. They'd lived and worked together for years without choosing to marry, but they seemed happy, had no children, kept five cats in the small store, and appeared pleased with every aspect of their lives. They never fought, which was nice, since Sean was good friends with both of them. He'd traveled so much working that he hadn't been home much since high school, but when he was in Key West, with the two of them, it was as if he had never left.

"Hey!" Jaden said, looking up from her workstation as he entered. Ted was across the room at an identical station. They were both equipped with bright, twist-neck lamps, bottles with all kinds of solutions and brushes with varying degrees of bristles. The shop was decorated with old broadsides and sailing paraphernalia from every century and decade. It was eclectic and had one showcase—where they displayed the reproduction pieces that they made, much more affordable than the real items that could be purchased many places in the city.

Jaden looked at him through magnifying glasses that made her eyes appear huge. They were warm brown eyes, and she had curly brown hair past her shoulders that gave her the look of a new age hippie. Ted had the same look—he was wearing a Grateful Dead T-shirt and he also had curly brown hair that he wore long, a curly brown beard and mustache and an easygoing smile.

"Nice to see you in our neck of the woods. We usually have to go to karaoke down at O'Hara's and warble out an old Cream number to get to see you, Sean," Ted said, grinning.

"Speak for yourself. I do not warble, I sing delightfully off-key," Jaden said. "What's up?"

"A young woman diving with me this morning made a discovery," Sean said.

"Oh? What?" Jaden asked, coming around from her workstation.

Sean produced the piece. "Right now, God knows, it could be anything, but…this kind of growth and debris upon it, whatever it is, it looks as if it has been out there awhile."

Jaden took it from him, studying it. Ted came around, as well. "Looks old," he said.

"Is it a coin?" Sean asked.

"Looks more like a medallion…a brooch? Where was it found?" Jaden asked.

"Pirate Cut," Sean told her.

"That's where the *Santa Geneva* went down under pirate attack," Ted said. "Other ships, too. The water is so deep and then the shallow reef juts up—caught lots of ships over time."

"We were diving over the bone structure—what's left—of the *Santa Geneva*," Sean said.

"Cool!" Jaden looked at Ted with a pleased smile. "This really could be something."

"I'd have thought that, over the years, almost everything of any value had already been brought up," Sean said.

"For shame, Sean O'Hara!" Jaden said. "The sea is ever a cruel mistress, and you never know what's been found and what hasn't—especially over time. I'll get on it right away," Jaden promised. "And carefully!"

"I knew you would," Sean told her.

"It would be spectacular if this were a documented piece of jewelry!" Jaden said enthusiastically.

"Did you get any of it on film?" Ted asked him.

"Yes, some of the discovery."

"'Cause you're going to work with David Beckett and do a really cool documentary, right?" Ted asked. "Wow—and you start off by finding a treasure from the *Santa Geneva*. Lord, do I love that story!"

"Romantic in an icky kind of tragic way," Jaden agreed.

"Gorgeous Dona Isabella captured, her ship sunk in Pirate's Cut!"

"Apparently when Mad Miller attacked the ship, he swept Dona Isabella from it first. And of course, he was supposed to be asking her husband for a ransom," Jaden said. "But he fell in love with her."

"And infuriated Kitty Cutlass!" Ted said dramatically.

"The ship was blown to smithereens, most of the crew killed in the water, but some of them taken prisoner as well for slave labor," Jaden said.

Looking at them, Sean shook his head and smiled. "You two should take it on the road. You're very dramatic."

"Well, who knows what really happened?" Jaden asked with a shrug. "All that is fact is that Mad Miller did attack the ship and he did kidnap Dona Isabella. And Kitty Cutlass was madly in love with Mad Miller. I mean, supposedly, Mad Miller was in love with Kitty Cutlass, so why kidnap Dona Isabella unless it was for ransom, and she had a rich husband, and whether they were living apart or not, he would have paid the ransom, just for the sake of his pride. But, no—Dona Isabella is murdered, some say *by* Kitty Cutlass, and the crew of the *Santa Geneva* who were taken prisoner rather than murdered or left to drown at the site were then massacred on Haunt Island. Oh! And those other murders took place on Haunt Island just about two years ago—now, there's a story for you, Sean.

"Hey, who were you with?" Jaden asked him curiously. "Who is the 'young woman'?"

"Her name is Vanessa Loren. And, yes—I see you're starting to frown. If you were following the newspapers when members of the film crew were killed on Haunt Island, you heard the name. She was one of the survivors."

"Whoa—wow!" Ted said. "Man—perfect. Why, you have an excellent story going there. Hey—what is she like? How did she wind up here?"

"My God, I can't even imagine how horrible that must have been—not that we haven't had our share of our own absurdities around here lately," Jaden said. "Whoa, whoa, whoa! Did she come to see you on purpose?"

"Yes," Sean said.

"Can't wait to meet her!" Ted told Jaden.

"Now, wait—" Sean said, frowning.

"Oh, come on. We're not going to say anything to her. We won't embarrass you!" Jaden protested.

"It's not that—I just can't imagine she really likes being quizzed constantly on what happened. It must have been pretty—horrifying."

"Ah, but you two have something in common. You were almost killed by a madman," Ted pointed out.

"But Sean's madman was caught—and no one knows

what happened to the other," Jaden said. "Oh, it is a mystery! I'd love to know what happened on that island. Most people, of course, think it was that fellow who was supposed to take the actress home.... Rodriquez... Rod..."

"Roca. Carlos Roca," Sean said.

"What does she think?" Ted asked.

"I'm dying to see what she looks like!" Jaden said.

"Just be nice when you meet her," Sean said. *He was defending her. Well, these were his friends, but they were professing some intrusive curiosity.*

"And you might have found a relic. Like Ted said, wow, cool!" Jaden said happily.

"You know what some people think?" Ted asked, nodding sagely.

"What?"

"It's the Bermuda Triangle," Ted said, as if it were fact.

"Ted, ships get lost, planes go down, and many so-called victims of the so-called Bermuda Triangle have been found. Ships have sunk."

"Aha! But throughout the years, they've found ghost ships out there, too. Ships with absolutely nothing wrong with them—but no one aboard. Hey, come on! You can order DVDs from the educational channels on the Bermuda Triangle," Ted argued.

"The Bermuda Triangle did not decapitate two people and leave their heads and arms in the sand," Sean said.

"Ugh. Scary!" Jaden said.

"Who says that there isn't some form of really vicious creature making its home in the Triangle?" Ted asked.

"They're finding new species of fish constantly—things like the megamouth shark that was supposed to be extinct. They *know* that giant squid exist, but they know almost nothing about the habits of the creatures," he said triumphantly.

"A giant squid didn't do it either, Ted," Sean said.

"Ah! But what happened to the boat? If there's an explanation, go ahead—you find it!"

"A half-dozen law enforcement agencies, including the Coast Guard, couldn't find it—I'm not so sure I'm going to," Sean said.

"And what about the killer? If it's a man, he's out there somewhere. Or, like I said, he's a victim of the Triangle. The Bermuda Triangle harbors some form of evil, and that evil got into the man, and then the man killed the actor and actress."

"You sure it wasn't aliens?" Sean asked dryly.

"Evil aliens living in the Triangle!" Ted agreed.

"I don't think that Sean's accepting any of your theories, my love," Jaden said. "Sean, before he starts to argue UFOs, I suggest you get out of here. I'm going to get right on this piece—I'm really excited, it just might be something unique and historic. I'll call you later, okay?"

"Be good to that young woman," Ted advised. "Poor thing!"

"Yes, be kind," Jaden admonished.

They were staring at him like a pair of proud parents on prom night. "I'll do my best," Sean said. He offered a grimace, waved and left the shop.

Key West was a small island. Pretty soon, everyone would be talking. And like Ted, most people liked to believe there was *something* about the Bermuda Triangle. Or aliens.

As he headed out, his phone rang. It was Liam Beckett. "I've checked out everything possible on your Miss Loren."

"She's not exactly *my* Miss Loren," Sean protested.

"Well, she came to you," Liam said. "Anyway, she appears to be everything that she claims on paper. She went to college, and she's worked on prestigious projects since. Apparently, she invested about fifty thousand dollars into filming the movie and her partner, Jay Allen, did the same. But it doesn't seem that she's in any financial trouble—in fact she was recently very well paid for a project. I have a list of her work, some of which can be pulled up on YouTube."

"I don't know why I had you do extensive work on her background," Sean said. "I didn't think that you'd find anything."

"She's the real deal, so it seems."

"Thanks."

"So?"

"So?"

"So, if you're doing this—I want in on it. I have to apply quickly for the time. Hey, you two are going to need me. Yeah, yeah, you're tough guys, but I'm a cop, and three of us who completely trust each other are better than two. You need me," Liam repeated.

"You were always invited, whatever the end choices. I just didn't think that you could get off with everything that has gone on lately."

"Oh, no. I'm there," Liam said. "I'll see you later."

"You will?"

Liam laughed. "Katie-oke at O'Hara's. David sips a beer and munches on conch fritters every night she works, as if he's still afraid to let her out of his sight."

Yes, I understand that feeling. So why am I even considering doing this?

Because he knew, too, what it was like not to know the truth, to mistrust your best friends and wonder as the years rolled by.

"You are going to be following the route of the film crew, aren't you?" Liam asked.

He wanted to protest again that he wasn't working alone, that the business venture was between him and David Beckett.

But David had already handed the decision over to him.

"Yes," he said simply. "I'll see you later tonight."

He headed over to the Beckett house; that afternoon, they were interviewing for positions for the shoot.

One, he knew, was already taken. Two. Liam was in, as well. And if they were all going, well, then, he could guarantee that his sister would be with them, as well.

There would be two boats, as always planned.

It occurred to him that the film crew who met the tragic and traumatic fate had also started out from Key West with two boats. Wasn't that the point? He mocked himself.

They were re-creating history. Seeking the truth.

And they were probably fools.

But, he determined, they'd be fools who came on the journey aware and alert—and well armed.

The Smallest Bar in Key West was very small. Vanessa had gotten to know several of the bartenders, and they were nice—even when she just wanted to order a soda or a bottle of water. She was certain that they knew who she was—her picture had been in the papers and on the news.

The afternoon had gone well. The warm shower, food and the Irish car bomb the bartender had suggested had done a number on her and she'd slept like the dead for almost four hours. Once she awoke and thought about the night, she didn't want to be alone and she didn't want to sit by the phone waiting to see if Sean was going to call her.

She decided to head south on Duval for O'Hara's. Katie should have been setting up the karaoke by then. Not that she had to set up much—it was her uncle's bar, and nothing was going to happen to any of her equipment there.

As she walked down the street, she knew that many of the shopkeepers and servers at outside restaurants watched her as she went by. Just another reminder that people would not quickly forget her face, or the story that was associated with it.

Such gruesome murders did not occur without a great deal of sensationalism.

She wondered sometimes if whoever had killed Travis and Georgia—she didn't believe for a minute that it had been Carlos Roca—had relished the attention that the killings had brought. The police had questioned both her and Jay about their enemies. To the best of her knowledge, she didn't have any. Nor did Jay. They had led simple lives, gone to college, gone out into the world, worked really hard and survived. That had come from a lot of twenty-hour days at film school, but they had paid off. She knew she was lucky, too; she knew the water, thanks to her father.

Ah, her father! As far as her parents knew, right now she was just in the Keys with Katie. She knew they wouldn't be happy if they knew what she was doing—trying to retrace the steps she had previously taken and find out if there was an answer anywhere. Maybe, if she had convinced Sean, they would find nothing. But she would have the satisfaction of knowing that she had tried everything that was in her power to find out the truth.

When she reached O'Hara's, she found that Katie and David were seated at the bar. Katie was ready to go when the time rolled around, and she was snacking on conch fritters with David and sipping a soda. The two were in deep conversation when she arrived. She wondered what they were talking about—they shut up the moment they saw her.

David Beckett stood politely, offering her the stool next to Katie. She tried to tell him to sit, but he wouldn't, so she thanked him and sat down. "I hear we're on," Katie said happily.

"We are?" Vanessa asked.

"Sean called and asked if I was sure it was a direction I willing to go in—and I must say I'm intrigued. We've had Liam studying what information he can from various sources, and it is one of the most disturbing mysteries of recent time," David told her.

Katie looked at Vanessa with triumph. She had an "I told you so" look in her eyes.

"We started interviewing for researchers and our film crew today," David said.

"And how did that go?"

David grinned. "Sean said that not one of the people we saw had your credentials. But some seemed okay. We actually have a number of friends who are top-notch, but most of them are already committed to projects—it's tough, even for the best people, so when something is up, you commit fast. And I admit, we didn't set this up ahead very far, which might have helped in that area."

"I'm still sure you can find the people you need," Vanessa said.

"Oh, yeah. But it would have been easier to hit the folks we know—and whose work and work ethic we know," David said.

"Everyone has to start somewhere," Vanessa said.

"That's true, and now I have to go to work," Katie said. "I'm counting on both of you if it's a dead crowd," she added.

Vanessa smiled and shook her head. "A group number!" Katie said.

There were about twenty people in the bar when Katie started up, singing a number with a friend of hers, Clarinda, who was also one of the night servers at O'Hara's. The two sang a country number that was beautiful and sexy. By the time they finished, other people were walking in the door.

"I don't think that she's going to have any problem with this crowd not getting up," Vanessa told David.

"Probably not. We're off the hook. Oh, and she's trying to get Clarinda to get up enough confidence to take it over when she's not here," David said.

"Oh?"

David smiled. "You don't think we'll all be going on this excursion without Katie, do you?"

Vanessa smiled. "So it's a done deal?" she asked.

"It seems to be so," David told her. "I heard about your dive today—and that you might have discovered a relic of some kind."

"Hopefully. And hopefully, it is a real relic, and not a watch lost recently that encrusted quickly," Vanessa said.

"I don't think so," David said, "Sean has a good eye for things like that. The sea can play games, that's for certain, but anyone who has grown up diving down here has found something lost from a boat from some period of time—he'd probably know if it was just a twenty-year-old barnacle crustation."

"I found it awfully easily."

"The current is always moving and the sand is always shifting," David reminded her.

She faced the doorway where, in ones, twos and threes, others were now coming into the bar. She saw Marty and he waved to her as he headed up to Katie and her computer area to request a song.

"Ah, good, Marty is here. We'll be getting a good sea shanty," David said.

She smiled at him and noted the door again.

She stiffened where she sat at the stool, dead straight.

She didn't believe it, didn't believe that she was seeing the man who was walking in.

A man obviously looking for someone.

Her.

5

Sean arrived at his uncle's bar around nine-thirty. Katie-oke was in full swing.

He saw David at one of the high-top tables in the rear of the karaoke area and came to sit by him at one of the free bar stools. There was one left; Bartholomew sat in it as if he and Sean had come in together like any friends out for a drink together.

David acknowledged Bartholomew's presence with a nod. He could hear Bartholomew at times and see his faint outline at certain times, too. Sean didn't think that David had any kind of a sixth sense, but Bartholomew had become so entwined in the events that had nearly cost all of them their lives that David did have a sense of him. It was often a relief for Sean to be with his sister and David, who knew about Bartholomew's presence. That way, when the pirate goaded him, he could reply without appearing to be talking to an imaginary friend.

"Liam here yet?" he asked.

"Not yet. But I talked to him after you did. Seems he's in on this one way or the other," David said.

"Which is great—having a skilled cop with us cannot be bad," Sean said.

"You really think that we might have trouble?" David asked.

"Two people were murdered, maybe three, when they were making the film. I think that the only rational explanation is that Carlos Roca was the killer, and that he's out there somewhere. But will he come after our crew? Probably not. He got away with murder—and a good boat. I don't think he'd come back. Is there the possibility of something going wrong, such as idiot drug smugglers, human traffickers? Sure, always. We both know that. So it's good to have a cop along. We can watch each other's backs. Yeah, I like that," Sean said.

"The pickings seemed slim today at the interviews," David said.

Sean shrugged. They had talked to a couple of "possible people." He wished he could have Frazier, from Key Largo, but he was working on a *National Geographic* project. There were other friends he'd known for years and years. Of course, they could delay the project. But now, he didn't want to.

"We'll be all right," David said. "You know Katie is coming. And she can help with lights, sound...cameras. She says she hung around you enough when you first got into it, and we've been out doing some fooling around filming on the reefs since we decided to do this."

"Two and two," Bartholomew said. "Always close enough to be in easy vision, that's the way to do it."

David gazed in his direction. "And which boat will you be on?"

"Whichever appears to be more comfortable. Or, perhaps, more in danger," he said.

"You'll leave Lucinda, Lucy—your lady in white—for that kind of time?" Sean asked Bartholomew. He realized, oddly enough, that as much as he didn't want to be "haunted," he did think it was a good thing that Bartholomew was ready for the trip.

"Can't leave you folks alone. And who knows, maybe Lucy will be up for the voyage. Though she does hate the water. And boats," Bartholomew admitted.

"A long time to be away," Sean noted, mumbling so that only David could hear him.

Bartholomew slowly lifted an aristocratic brow. "Time is irrelevant, my dear boy. You must remember, Lucy and I have both been drifting these streets for many, many a year now. We'll be fine with a few weeks apart—as they say, absence makes the heart grow fonder." He frowned. "Alas, you should be worrying about a living vision of grace and beauty!" Bartholomew said gravely, looking toward the booths in the bar area.

"What?" Sean turned to stare.

Vanessa Loren was seated in one of the booths, oblivious to his presence—and all else, including the slightly inebriated college student attempting a rap number on stage. She was facing a man; Sean could see shoulders and a head of dark hair. She was speaking passionately, and seemed to be upset.

"Who is it?" Sean asked David, frowning. "I didn't know Vanessa was in here."

"I don't know who it is, and you didn't ask about her. We were talking. She saw that fellow in the doorway and excused herself, telling me it was an old friend she was surprised to see."

"Really?" Sean said.

So who was the guy?

Yeah, right, and what was it to him?

That morning she had attracted him. In fact, he realized, he was more than attracted, and he didn't want to be. He wanted everything professional, every single decision he made. But she had slipped into him, mind, soul and substance, since he had first seen her sitting here in O'Hara's, and he wondered if that was why he had wanted to fight anything she had to say to him—it was far safer, it was far more *professional* not to be attracted to an employee, especially when employment started out with such a story.

All right, face it, he didn't want her bothered by anyone. All right, in all honesty, he wasn't sure what he wanted, but he didn't want her there with anyone else.

He had no right to feel that way—he still barely knew her. A day of diving did not a long-term friend make, nor did standing near her, realizing just what a chemical mystique she possessed, give him the right to go interrupting her conversations with other men.

He stood. He suddenly felt as if he were a jealous boyfriend, irked that his girlfriend was flirting with someone else. Ridiculous feeling—but she had pursued him, determined on her course of action. And people *had* been murdered. He'd agreed to what she wanted—he did have a right to find out why she appeared to be so disturbed.

If she was happy speaking with an old friend, fine.

But if she wasn't, well, she had appealed to him for help in one way already.

Even as he approached the booth, he didn't think that this was anyone with whom Vanessa had an intimate relationship. They were on opposite sides of the booth. Her hands went from the table to the air as she spoke but never touched his. When he was speaking, she sat leaning back, arms crossed over her chest, and she seemed annoyed.

He reached the end of the booth. The man was talking, but he fell silent when Sean arrived and started to get up. He was about Vanessa's age, tall, well built and well bronzed, as if he spent a lot of time in the sun.

Sean set a hand on his shoulder. "Sit, sit, sorry, I didn't mean to interrupt a conversation. I just came by to say hello to Vanessa."

"Hello, Sean," Vanessa said, her voice tight.

"Sean—Sean O'Hara?" the man asked.

"Yes. And…you are?"

The young man stood quickly, offering his hand. "Jay. Jay Allen."

Jay Allen.

Producer, director and the man who had lost a small fortune because of the murders on Haunt Island.

"Please, sit down, please, please, join us," Jay said.

Vanessa didn't seem to want to have anyone—more specifically him—join them. Her jaw was set at a rigid angle and she stared at Jay as if her eyes were vivid blue daggers.

He was definitely going to join them.

Vanessa didn't move; she didn't look away from Jay

and she appeared rigidly angry. Sean slid in beside Jay as he scooted to the inside edge of the booth.

"Frankly, I'm here to apply for work—with you," Jay said.

Sean thought that Vanessa kicked Jay under the table.

"Oh?" Sean asked.

Jay nodded. "I heard that Vanessa was down here and that there were filmmakers about to embark on a historical documentary. I was working—filming tourists while they played with dolphins—in the Bahamas."

"I see," Sean said.

"I'm— Honestly, I know everything—or at least something about everything—from shooting, lighting, sound, editing, you name it. Seriously, ask Vanessa. Oh, and I have a boat. It's got some equipment. I can work anything on any vessel you've got, my diving certificate is a master's and I wash dishes," he said. "I've directed, but don't worry—it's not an obsession. I can take direction, as well."

Jay seemed earnest. It was just too bizarre—him being here, right after he had agreed to film in the direction Vanessa had petitioned.

Or maybe it wasn't bizarre at all. Vanessa was here. Maybe she'd been elected to be the one to get under his skin and get it all going.

He stared at Vanessa. Obviously, she knew what he was thinking. Or she had known exactly what his thoughts might naturally be once Jay had shown up.

"I didn't know Jay was coming in," she said flatly.

"Sure," he said.

"Hey, look, I just arrived with a tremendous amount

of hope," Jay said. "I went down like a lead balloon in all that, you have to realize."

"Two—possibly three—people are dead," Vanessa said sharply.

"Oh, of course! I mean, that's the most important part of all this, the really tragic part," Jay said. "And they deserve justice. And if Carlos is innocent and out there somewhere...alive, well, we owe the truth to him, too, right? And if he did murder poor Travis and Georgia, and he didn't get swallowed up by the Bermuda Triangle, he deserves to go to prison. Or be executed. The whole thing *screams* for answers, don't you agree?"

"Answers, yes," Sean agreed. "Whether there's a prayer in hell that a set of filmmakers could get the answers, I don't know."

"I'm good, I swear, ask Vanessa," Jay said.

"Vanessa?" Sean asked politely.

"He's good. He knows boats and he can dive," she said, still not facing Sean. Her cheeks seemed flushed.

"I'll take it all under consideration," Sean said. "And, of course, discuss it with my partner."

He started to rise.

"Please. Please consider me," Jay said. He sounded humble. Sincere.

And desperate.

"I can't tell you what it means to me. Honestly—yes, yes, other than the dead—this didn't affect anyone as badly as me. I can't tell you... I still spend my life wondering," Jay said.

Sean shook his head. "There's not even a real suggestion that we can find any answers," he said.

"Please," Jay repeated.

"I'll discuss it with the others," Sean said. He left then, aware that Vanessa's eyes were following him as he walked across the room.

He hadn't realized that Bartholomew had been behind him until he felt the pressure when the ghost bumped into him.

"Such a skeptic!" Bartholomew said.

"Sorry, I don't like it."

"Don't like what?" Bartholomew demanded.

"I decide to go her way—and suddenly her old friend is here, asking for a job."

"She didn't know he was going to come here," Bartholomew said.

"Are you sure?"

"She seems honest. I don't think she knew."

"Either that, or she was just hoping to use David and me as saps."

"Ouch. There's a chip on your shoulder, my friend. Wait—better call it a boulder."

"I intend to be careful," Sean said.

"So—what is there to be so careful about? I'd say that it's natural. If you'd been involved in something like that and you heard that someone was doing anything that touched upon the mystery, wouldn't you jump it on it like a starving tick on an Irish wolfhound?"

"A starving tick on an Irish wolfhound?" Sean repeated.

"I make my point—and if you tell me no, I'll call you a liar of the worst kind."

"All right, yes, I'd be after anything that could get me close again," Sean admitted. He paused. His sister was singing an old Beatles number, giving all due honor to the Fab Four. He paused, clapping, and watching David clap, watching the pleasure on his face. The world seemed so strange. David Beckett was seriously in love with Katie. It was nice. It was the kind of thing you had to admire—and envy.

He gave himself a mental shake. He'd had his share of relationships, most of which had ended decently, and he was long past the stage where he understood anyone who tried to hook up with a stranger in a bar purely for the purpose of sex. But somehow, looking at his sister and David, he felt a strange sense of emptiness he'd never known. He'd liked his life; come and go as you please, come and go anywhere in the world. Appreciate family and old friends, and look for new adventures. But now…

He took his stool back at the high-top table with David.

"So?" David asked.

"That is Jay Allen—the director of the movie that went so astray," Sean explained.

"Ah, the plot thickens," David said.

"He thinks it's strange that Jay just appeared," Bartholomew said, rolling his eyes. He jumped up suddenly.

"What? What is it?" Sean asked sharply.

"Lucinda lingers just outside. You'll excuse me…?" Bartholomew asked.

"Why doesn't Mistress Lucinda just come in?" Sean asked. "Damn, Bartholomew, the way you jumped up…I thought something had happened. Invite the lovely and ethereal Miss Lucy in."

He shuddered. "Good God, she'd never!" he said.

"Wait—are you insulting my uncle's establishment?" Sean teased.

"No, you're forgetting that such an establishment as O'Hara's didn't really exist in my lady's day. Quite frankly, there was a house of disrepute on this very corner back then, and it was certainly no place where Lucinda would come. That's why she wanders so much. Of course, she knows that it's not a house of prostitution now, but still…memories will linger."

With a touch to his hat, he was gone. Sean watched him. Out on Duval, a rather staggered trail of tourists was wandering by. Oblivious to them, Bartholomew met his Lucy, his lady in white, in the street. He took both her hands in his own and looked down into her eyes, laughing at something she said. The tourists continued to move on by…smiling, chatting to one another, unaware of the tenderness that went on beneath their noses. One young woman paused and looked in their direction, and then smiled. The young man at her side paused as well, asking her what she saw, what made her smile, so it appeared. She shrugged and replied, stood on her toes and briefly kissed his lips, and then kept moving.

Sean saw Liam beyond the door. Like the young woman, he paused, as if sensing something there. But he didn't see the ghostly duo. He shrugged and came on in. He took the seat Bartholomew had vacated.

Liam knew about Bartholomew. One night, they had tried to explain. Liam tried to believe them; he just couldn't. He didn't see Bartholomew, or hear his voice. He didn't show his skepticism, but Sean knew it was there. Liam seemed to think they were victims of a shared hysterical hallucination, but he didn't voice his thoughts or his doubts.

"How's the hiring going?" Liam asked them both. Clarinda came by then, asking them what they'd like. Sean ordered a Guinness, wondering if the dark mellow tones would lighten his mood. Liam opted for one as well, musing that it sounded good when Sean ordered it.

"We met some folks who are possibilities. I'd take one Frazier Nivens over the six people we saw today, but he's working," Sean said.

"You're doing all right though, really," Liam argued. "You've got me and Katie—and Vanessa. David and you, and you'll be fine with a few more people. I'm not great, but I'm a solid backup guy on the boat and I can hold an extension and boom arm when you're recording on deck—good muscles for that. I did it enough for both of you when we were kids and recording backyard bands and some of our great oceanic discoveries like old work boots. And I can haul anything you need in the water."

"Hey, Liam, we're thrilled with you going. Hate the idea of you taking time off now, though," David said. "It's such a bad time."

"You know you are always wanted," Sean assured him. "And I've just had another applicant."

"Someone in the bar?" Liam asked.

Sean indicated Vanessa Loren's booth. "Jay Allen—Vanessa's friend, and the director of the ill-fated film shoot."

"Ah," Liam said. "And what are you thinking?"

"I don't know," Sean said. "I'm irritated in a way—it's

kind of like Vanessa was sent in as a vanguard, and now he's here."

"Send in beauty, and then bring the beast?" Liam asked dryly.

"She pretends to be—or is—unaware that he planned on coming," Sean said.

"And it may be the truth," David told him.

"I don't like the idea of being used," Sean said.

"Liam, want to be in charge of another background check?" David asked his cousin.

Liam grinned. "Way ahead of you guys. I checked out everyone on that film crew. I even did cursory checks into the one or two day jobbers they took on in different locations, and the other four cast members. Jay Allen appears to be clean as a whistle. Got through school with excellent marks—and perfect attendance, for whatever that is worth. He's never been arrested, pays his bills on time and works out of Palm Beach most of the time now—that's where he has his office. He directed segments of a historical series set up in Virginia, chronicling the men in the Civil War. And he won an award for editing. He's got good reports from every employer. They say that he is imaginative, dedicated and responsible."

"And no corpses turned up anywhere else he worked, right?" Sean asked.

"No. The movie project collapsing caused him to fall into a steady decline, though, I'm afraid. He lost his personal savings, obviously—just like Vanessa," Liam said.

"But she's doing all right?" Sean asked.

"Yes—maybe because she wasn't the director of the

project. Who knows why certain people wind up suffering and others don't?" Liam said.

"Okay, say we take on Jay Allen. It might not be a bad thing," David said. "If we've agreed we're following this trail, why not?"

"Give me a timetable, and I'll get it all legit through the Bahamian authorities," Liam said.

"I'll set up a schedule tomorrow," Sean said. "We'll take Jay Allen on with us, mainly because I'd like to interview him when we get to Haunt Island but also because I'd like to have a lot of footage edited on a daily basis, seeing how we're moving on. It will be great if it's not something we have to do ourselves, since it's so time-consuming. I'd like to start with Marty, dressed up in his pirate best, telling the tale of the *Santa Geneva,* Mad Miller, Kitty Cutlass and poor Dona Isabella. That will explain Vanessa's script—and the quest we're heading out on, to find the truth. Marty is a great character. He can also tell some of the pirate lore and history in general without becoming dry—or downright boring."

"It sounds like a plan to me. Set it up," David said.

Sean saw Vanessa and Jay stand; they headed together over to the table where Liam, David and Sean were sitting together. "David, Liam, this is Jay Allen. He and Sean just met. He's applying for work on the project."

Her voice was clear, but there was no emotion in it. She was angry and covering it up.

Jay offered his hand. The introduction was acknowledged.

"I'm heading on out for the evening. I hope you'll

consider me for your crew. I truly can never explain just how much this project means to me," Jay said.

"We may find nothing. We may just rehash the same old, same old," David said.

"I'd like to be aboard, just for my own peace of mind, retrace every step—and see if there wasn't something of importance that we never gave to the police," Jay said.

His words sounded reasonable, and they would certainly appeal to David.

"Well, like I said, I'm out of here," Jay said. "I'm at Paradise Inn, and—" he paused to write a number on a cocktail napkin "—this is my cell number."

"Plan on meeting us here tomorrow at one o'clock," Sean said. "We're going to do an interview with a friend who's an expert in pirate lore and Key West history. I'm going to have you edit the footage and we'll see what we get."

Jay brightened and grabbed Sean's hand, pumping it. "Great. Great. You won't regret it, I swear. I can stand in as well, in almost any capacity. Whatever you need. Thank you. Thank you." He looked around the table, animated, humble and grateful. "Thank you, thank you all." He turned to Vanessa. "Nessa, want a walk back to your place?" he asked her.

She shook her head. "You're south, I'm north. I'm fine. But thanks. I'm going to hang around a few more minutes," she told him.

"Nothing is too far south or north around here, you know," Jay said.

"I'm fine, really. Thanks."

Jay nodded to her, and nodded toward the table again. He backed away. "My equipment or—"

"Ours, thanks," Sean said.

Jay nearly knocked into a table as he left, still looking at them all the while, as if they would change their minds if he didn't. Finally, he was out the door.

David had already risen to drag a chair over to their table for Vanessa.

When she sat, David said, "Well, this is interesting."

She shook her head. "I had no idea he knew anything about this, or that he was anywhere nearby at the moment."

"Right," Sean murmured.

"So," Liam said quickly, "you two are old friends?"

She nodded. "Micanopy is not a big place," she said. "We went through twelve years of school together—I've known him since I was four or five. He is a good filmmaker, and he's serious when he says that he'll do anything, anything at all. That's why our initial project had seemed so exciting. It was mainly our money, and we were willing to do what it took to get the movie made. And it is true, he's excellent at editing. He has the instinct for it, which, in my mind, at least, is one of the hardest parts of any production. Slow, hard, tedious—and amazingly important to a final project. Honestly, I admit, I was angry that he suddenly showed up and wanted me to…introduce him to you all, but…he is good."

She sounded so damned honest. Sean didn't know why he still felt a strange twist inside. He wanted to trust her. Maybe he wanted to trust her too much.

She hadn't left, Sean knew, because she had felt the

need to talk to the three of them. Was she protesting too much?

"Would you like a drink?" David asked her.

She shook her head. "Thanks, no. I'm going to head out, too. I just wanted to…I wanted to talk to you for a few minutes, try to explain."

"It's fine. We'll see what he's worth on the project tomorrow," David said.

"Do you want me to come, too?" Vanessa asked.

"No, that's not necessary," Sean said quickly. "You proved your ability today." He stood. "I'll walk you back," he told her.

She smiled. "That's not necessary. I've walked Duval alone a…a zillion times. I'll be fine."

"I wasn't going to because it was necessary. I was going to walk you down because I wanted to," Sean said.

"All right, then, sure. I'll just say good-night to Katie."

She walked to the stand. A man of about sixty was onstage. He was doing a damned good Sinatra imitation with his version of "Fly Me to the Moon."

She kissed Katie on the cheek; Katie looked up and waved to Sean. She was smiling. He walked to the computer area himself and kissed his sister on the top of the head. "Tomorrow, kiddo," he told her. "Ready?" he asked Vanessa.

She nodded.

They walked through the high-top tables in the karaoke area and said good-night to David and Liam. "Can you grab the tab?" Sean asked David.

"Got it. I'm not too worried—I know the owner," David said.

Sean waved a hand and walked Vanessa out.

The south end of Duval was quiet as they walked along. Down by the inn where Vanessa was staying, there would still be activity at Sloppy Joe's, Captain Tony's, Rick's, Irish Kevin's and maybe a few more. It would probably be a mild crowd though. On Friday and Saturday nights, it was a wild crowd. When any of the festivals was going on, anything went.

"I really didn't know anything about Jay looking to join on," Vanessa said.

"Yes. That's what you've said. Several times."

"But you don't believe me," she said flatly, turning her blue eyes on him. The woman really looked like a damned angel. Her hair was like a halo, blond, and bleached lighter by the sun. Not really an angel. She wasn't delicate, he had learned that by watching her in action. She was really just about perfect. Too perfect. He felt jealous, though he barely knew her. He wanted to strangle Jay Allen because he seemed to be so close to her. He wanted to know if—in the years of their *friendship*—they had ever been intimate. Information he had no right to. He barely knew her.

He wanted her. She was gorgeous, she was sensual, she was lithe, athletic. He was imagining far too much about her.

That meant he had to stay the hell away.

"Look, it's not that I don't believe you, it just seems all too opportune," he said. "But my partner agrees that it's interesting, and we'll see how Jay does tomorrow."

"I should be there," she said.

He shook his head. "Let's see how he stands on his own, okay?"

"All right."

They were coming closer to the northern end of Duval, where revelers were still out. Too many people for a real conversation. All seemed to be having fun—a few were inebriated.

"Watch out," he murmured. A group, nicely dressed and not composed of teenagers, seemed to be having a bit of a problem navigating the streets. He thought a tall stout man was about to run into Vanessa. He took her hand and pulled her out of the way.

She laughed. "Thanks."

"Here we are," he said.

She nodded. "The stairway is up the back, through the garden gate." She rummaged in a pocket for her key.

"I'll walk you around," he said.

"All right, thanks."

They passed through a little walkway. It led to the back. There was nice foliage along the way, but the inn was basic, just some rooms over a storefront. No charming tables and chairs outside, no pool, nothing but access to the rooms.

Sean knew that it was filled with spring-breakers and bachelor and bachelorette parties.

"I'm surprised you chose this place," he told her. "It gets awfully loud."

"I wanted the loud," she said.

"Oh?"

"And the activity—cops around most of the time, lots of people at all hours."

"Are you afraid?" he asked her, frowning and setting his hands on her shoulders.

"No, I'm not really afraid. But I like people and noise."

He nodded. "All right. But you do know my sister well, so it seems. She owns the house we grew up in, though I'm living there now and Katie has moved in with David. Both places are huge. You're on the project now. You're welcome to come stay at either."

"Thank you." It seemed there was a slight tremor in her voice. "I thought I should stand on my own until we get going with this."

"Your choice," he told her.

"Thank you." She looked at him for a long moment. He found that he really was in love with her eyes. Other assets as well, but her eyes…

The moment grew awkward. He pulled his hands away and shoved them in his pockets. "All right. I'll talk to you tomorrow, then."

"Actually…" she began, and then hesitated.

"Actually, what?" he queried.

"Well, I am your assistant, and a writer. I have a list of interview questions. I wrote them up, assuming you'd be interviewing an expert on the pirate era, and with Pirates in Paradise gearing up, it seemed to make sense. And Marty is amazing. I mean, it's your project, you have your own questions, and once Marty gets going, but…"

"I'll take your questions," he told her.

"I'll be right back," she told him. She turned the key,

entered the hallway and ran up the stairs. She returned within a minute flat, an envelope in her hands.

He grinned. "You are on the ball," he told her.

"I swear, we're good at what we do. I'm good at what I do. Honestly."

"I believe you." He cleared his throat. "I'm still waiting to hear back from Jaden and Ted."

"Of course. Um, well, see you then."

The door was still ajar. He opened it for her, and she entered the hallway. He watched as she ran up the stairs. The door closed behind her, and Sean pushed it so that it would close firmly and lock. He turned away and headed for his own place.

He barely knew her.

If he'd admitted it to himself, that didn't matter. He wanted her to be everything that she seemed. He wanted to know more about her. Everything.

Two people had died. Maybe a third.

And the mystery was intriguing. The only way to really understand it, to try to figure out what *could* have happened, was to follow the same trail.

They would do so.

Two boats.

He'd make sure that Vanessa was on his.

And that Jay Allen wasn't.

That night, it was the heads.

Vanessa was sound asleep, and the world was pleasant and dark, and then the darkness began to lift. She was walking along the shore, and it was beautiful, pristine white sand, the ocean in all its glorious shades of aqua and blue, light and deep. She heard the sound of the waves and felt the sand and the pleasant wash of the waves over her toes.

And then she reached them. Georgia's head, with her arms in front of her, stuck out of the sand, and Travis's head, his arms in front, as well.

"Vanessa, see! I told you I wasn't lying!" Georgia said angrily.

"And I don't play bad practical jokes on people," Travis said. "Why didn't you all look for me, why did you just assume I was being an ass?" Travis demanded.

"Oh!" Georgia said. Her arms moved in the sand with the exclamation, and she pointed down the shore. "They were having champagne. They were celebrating. And they all got mad at me! Then Carlos…"

"Then Carlos what?" Vanessa cried out.

"Carlos…Carlos…" Georgia said. "I don't know. Come help me. Oh, wait. I can't get out of here. I have no legs. I have no torso. Why didn't you believe me, Vanessa, why didn't you believe me?"

"Be careful. They'll get you, too," Travis warned. He blew a lock of his hair out of his eyes. "They'll get you, too."

"And you can be with us, just heads, talking heads, sitting in the sand," Georgia said.

"We have arms," Travis reminded her.

"Yes, we have arms," Georgia agreed, and they both waved their hands in the air.

"Be careful, Vanessa, be careful, you need the truth, or you can join us…heads and arms and hands, hands and heads…here, in the sand."

"In fact," Travis said, "you need to come closer and closer…."

* * *

She awoke with a start. She was shaking, clammy with sweat. She inhaled on a deep breath and wondered if the nightmares would ever stop.

It was day. She glanced at the cheap alarm on the bedside table. Almost 9:00 a.m. She would get up, walk down to the Internet café, read some e-mails and drink lots of coffee. A shower would be wonderful, so wonderful now.

She ran her hands over the bed as she pushed herself from it. She frowned as her hands went over something gritty.

Sand.

She jumped out of the bed. There were a million explanations for it. She'd spent the day diving. There was dirt and sand everywhere.

The pile on her bed was pristine and white.

With a shout of irritation, she whisked it off the bed and to the floor, and hurried into the bathroom.

There were tons of explanations....

Yeah, right. The explanation, ridiculous and horrible, that came to her mind was simple and sad. Georgia and Travis were haunting her. They blamed her for not doing more. They...

They needed the truth, justice, closure.

Somehow, she had to give it them.

Before she became nothing more than a head and arms in the sand herself.

6

One o'clock rolled around and Sean, Jay and David went to film at Marty's place. Marty told them that they didn't need to pay him for an interview on his love of pirates and the sea, but they insisted and he shrugged it off. He seemed pleased enough to meet Jay, and he was more than helpful as they set up for the shoot in his eclectic house. When they were set, Sean did the questioning, admitting to himself that the questions Vanessa had written were excellently phrased and led Marty quickly in the right direction.

David filmed, Jay was recruited for lighting, and Marty was assured that it didn't matter if he made mistakes or wanted to go back, it was fine. The footage would be edited.

It went well. Marty was a natural showman, and if any man looked like an old pirate, it was Marty. He talked about the early days of Key West—the very early days, when the Calusa Indians were around, through the Spanish period, the English period, the Spanish period, and then the days when Florida—and Key West—became a territory of the United States. He knew his piracy and could trace it through the sixteen, seventeen and eighteen hundreds—and he could even tell hair-raising tales of modern-day piracy.

Sean led him to talking about the attack on the *Santa Geneva,* Mad Miller and Kitty Cutlass.

"Ah, well, there's a story!" Marty said, his eyes blazing. "Mad Miller was born and bred on the island, just like his paramour, Kitty Cutlass. Kitty was a saloon girl, right on Duval Street, and let me tell you, they were rough places back then, shacks, they were. Some say she was a sweet girl gone bad, and some say she was born pure evil. Mad Miller was working a rich man's merchant vessel when he turned it around and made her a pirate ship. He managed to take a gunboat down and steal her cannons, then reworked the merchant ship into a fine pirate vessel with twenty guns. Now, it's said that the early days were good days—Mad Miller would blast a merchant ship or any enemy ship to smithereens, but he'd always pick up the survivors, and he never kidnapped a soul for ransom, just left them all beached somewhere. Ah, but then the battle of the sexes began! There's always a woman, right? In any story. Except in this story, there were two. Key West had barely become an American territory, Admiral David Porter had just begun his campaign with his Mosquito Squadron to clear out the pirates, when Mad Miller and his crew came upon the *Santa Geneva.* Relations with Spain were doing fine—God knew, enough Spaniards were still living here. Now Dona Isabella was a great beauty of her day. Black eyes, black hair, fair skin, white bosom and wasp waist, and she lived a fine life of society right around the Southern tip of Duval—the house is long gone now, though a fine residence still stands where it once was. She was married to Don Diego de Hidalgo, a man highly respected in his native Spain, where he chose to reside most of the time. Dona Isabella had just left Key West to return to Spain—her husband wanted her back with him—when Mad Miller and his crew lit out after her ship, said to carry great riches upon it. But it seemed that Mad Miller suddenly changed his ways—he took a number of the surviving crew captive, but it's said that his men slashed to death those in the water who were begging to be saved. From the point of the attack—near Pirate Cut and the Pirate Cut reef—Mad Miller sailed off to his safe harbor at Haunt Island, a nearly desolate islet off South Bimini. There it's said that Mad Miller and his crew massacred the survivors—even the beautiful Dona Isabella. Of course, much of what we suspect is theory, since no one knows what really happened. But there were rumors among other men of unsavory repute that Mad Miller had gone insane with desire for Dona Isabella and that Kitty Cutlass, in a jealous rage, had murdered her. Mad Miller then left Haunt Island, ready to attack more ships, but it wasn't to be. He met his demise not at the end of a hangman's noose but in the midst of the fury of the Atlantic. A hurricane came through, and Mad Miller's ship was sunk with all aboard, and all his treasure. This is known because another ship caught in the weather made it back. The hazardous conditions prevented any type of rescue operation, and frankly, since the ship that reported her foundering was a part of the Mosquito Squadron, it's likely that the men watched her go down with laughter on their lips—when they weren't fighting to stay afloat themselves!"

Marty stopped speaking and looked at Sean and then David and then Sean again.

"Wonderful. You were great, Marty."

"Yeah? Really?" Marty asked.

"Wonderful!" Jay said. He looked really pleased. "Marty, you're so damned good, it's going to be easy for me to appear to be the world's most talented editor. When I'm done, you'll see what I can do. You're going to love the final footage."

"I know it's going to be good," David said.

"One more thing, Marty. Will you do one of your sea shanties for us?"

"A privilege, boys, a privilege!" Marty said. He went for his old guitar in the corner. "Should have a squeeze box, really, but this will do."

"Give us a chance to move the lights and the camera around a bit," Sean said. Marty nodded happily and practiced strumming his string and tuning the instrument.

"Ready," Sean said. "And we can film several takes, so you're under no pressure."

Marty grinned, strummed and sang.

"Oh, the sea, she is my lady,
E'er my lady true,
For the lady t'was my lady
Back upon the shore"

Mary strummed the last chord, set the guitar down and grinned.

"Cut," Sean said. "Perfect!"

"Great," David agreed.

"Should we do another, for safety's sake?" Marty asked anxiously.

David glanced and Sean and shrugged with a grin.

"Sure, we've got the time, the people, and you—you're an amazing intro, Marty," Sean said.

Marty was pleased. He blushed. He picked up his guitar again, explained that it was an old sea shanty his father had taught him, one that had come down from old pirating days.

The next take was even better. Marty was just warming up.

They spent a while longer there, letting Marty go over a few facts and figures from history and the area, and then they wrapped it up.

While they packed the equipment, Jay asked, "Can I get started immediately on the footage, show you just what you'll be getting?"

Sean hesitated, wondering what his problem was with Jay. Of course, he knew. Allen was close with Vanessa Loren. He was being unreasonable.

"Yes."

"I'll go back now—"

"Go to my place. I've got the equipment set up that you need," Sean said.

Jay nodded with pleasure. "You won't be disappointed."

"If that comes out well enough, you'll be wanting to take some shots at the setup for Pirates in Paradise, down by Fort Zachary Taylor," Marty said. "Costumes, knives, swords, reproductions of all kinds. Pirate food and grog. Hey, everybody wants to be a pirate. Everybody wants to be Johnny Depp in *Pirates of the Caribbean,* huh?"

They all agreed that Johnny Depp had done wonders for piracy, and then left the house at last. David went on to find Katie, and Sean took Jay Allen to his house, to the back, where he had his computer set up with all the software Jay might need.

And where he found Bartholomew, reading the screen—and pushing the keys.

"What the hell?" Jay murmured.

Sean reached over and pushed the escape key and then keyed in for his film system.

"You might have just said 'move,'" Bartholomew said. "Or, more politely, 'Bartholomew, old fellow, I need the computer now. Would you mind?'"

Sean didn't respond.

"You're good to go," he told Jay.

"You'll see, you'll see—and you'll want me more than you ever expected," Jay promised, sitting down to get started.

"Go for it," Sean told him.

"You're not going to watch over my shoulder, are you?" Jay asked.

Leave this guy alone in his house?

"Don't worry—I'll be here, looking over his shoulder!" Bartholomew assured him.

Sean lowered his head to hide a smile. It was perfect. He could leave and yet know every single thing that went on in his house while Jay was there.

"Actually, no. I need to see a few friends," Sean assured him.

"Okay, I'll lock up," Jay told him. "When I'm done. I'll leave it in a 'Marty' file for you to find when you get back."

"Great," Sean agreed. "All right, then. I'll call you if I don't see you."

He walked to the door. Bartholomew had taken another chair, at the table, his feet plunked upon it. He was watching Jay Allen with narrowed eyes.

When he headed for the door, Jay called him back. "You really don't know how much I appreciate this opportunity."

Sean nodded, and left.

With the door closed, he smiled. Bartholomew could be a true pest, an annoyance, taunting him when a response would make Sean appear to be totally insane.

But the old pirate/privateer was actually a damned good guy.

Oddly enough, a damned good friend.

Vanessa didn't want to stay in her room at the inn, and she had been sincerely un-invited to be involved in the day's shoot with Marty. She had decided to go explore down by the grounds at Fort Zachary Taylor, wearing a bathing suit beneath a cover-up dress, and force herself to stay calm and away from anyone with the name Beckett or O'Hara.

The main events of Pirates in Paradise weren't taking place yet, but Vanessa learned from the first "pirate" she encountered that the booths would be starting to open the next day with eager, friendly vendors—all in pirate attire, of course—and that the first parties would take place that night. She was invited to come—he'd get her in free. She thanked him, said that she wasn't sure and explored a lot of the merchandise.

At one booth, she found a beautiful display of

reproduction jewelry. As she looked through the pieces she was impressed. The booth carried pen-and-ink drawings of various ships, lists of their manifests, the pirate "code of honor" and many more bills of lading and other pieces of the past, all historic copies.

She started when she looked up after studying one case to see that the picture above it was of Dona Isabella. Or at least it was a likeness similar to that which Marty had given her.

The girl attending the booth, a pretty young thing who looked to be no more than a teenager, came before her smiling. She was in a corset, skirt and big billowing blouse, with a tricorn hat perched atop her head.

"She startles everyone," the girl said. "Dona Isabella, I mean. What a gorgeous creature—to die so sadly. Do you know the story?"

"Yes, actually, I do," Vanessa told her.

"She's supposed to haunt a lot of places, you know. Pirate Cut for one—a few divers swear that they've seen her! And, let's see—she haunts the south end of Duval Street, where she supposedly lived. And Haunt Island, of course. I mean, what would Haunt Island be without a few haunts?"

Vanessa smiled. She didn't want to talk about Haunt Island.

"What's this?" she asked, pointing to the piece in the display case that had drawn her attention. It was a jeweled pendant, a mermaid studded with various precious stones.

"Oh, this is a reproduction of one of Dona Isabella's necklaces. Beautiful, isn't it?" She giggled. "There was description of it in the ship's manifest. There were always three manifests, you know. One for the ship's owner, one on the ship and one left with the dockmaster's office from the original embarkation point of a ship's journey. This pendant was in the manifest—well, not *this* pendant, it's a reproduction, of course—and, as you can see, Dona Isabella is wearing it in this picture, which is another copy, of an oil painting that hangs in a museum in Spain."

"It's gorgeous. Truly, absolutely gorgeous," Vanessa said.

"And more reasonable than you would think. Okay, truthfully? It's done in ten carat—if I'd had my say, it would be fourteen carat at the very least. Eighteen for such a piece would be closer to the original. And the jewels—that really looks like a ruby, but it's a garnet. And that's not a sapphire, it's blue topaz, and the yellow stones are citrine."

"How much?" Vanessa asked.

The girl smiled and told her. The piece was more than affordable. Vanessa bought it.

She looked at an exhibition that was going to be on food, and she glanced through the costume racks, remembering when the world had been bright, when she had done so with high excitement, thinking that she and Jay were about to produce their first full movie. That was then, this was now. She walked around and saw some excellent outfits—should Sean and David want them for anything—then moved on to the beach.

It was a decent day, even though they were into fall. The air temperature was still rising to eighty-five, and the water at the shore was only about ten degrees cooler.

She'd grown up in the chilly freshwater springs of north Florida, so it was a lovely temperature to her.

She lay on the sand, slipped on her sunglasses and watched the waves.

She tried not to think about the fact that she was ready to kill Jay. She could remember the look in Sean O'Hara's eyes when he had met Jay, when Jay had said that he was applying for work. She looked like the agent sent in to scope it out.

What was, was.

Except that she needed the truth more than Jay.

She needed to silence the nightmares.

To keep from thinking too much, she headed into the water. She swam awhile, working her muscles, then ambled back toward the shore, watching a father play with his children—a boy of about ten and a little girl, around five—and as she walked, not paying attention, she crashed into someone. A hard body. She stepped back awkwardly and quickly apologized. Hands shot out to steady her.

It was Sean.

"Hey," she said.

"Hey, yourself. You're hard to find," he told her.

"Well, I would have been easier, if I'd known you were looking for me."

He smiled. "I called."

"Oh—my phone is with my towel and bag, on the shore."

"Ah."

"So—you were looking for me. How'd the filming go?" She realized she was shivering. It was getting later than she realized; the sun was beginning to sink, and while the temperature was still far from cold, being wet made her shiver.

He arched a brow to her. "Not that badly, trust me, no need to shake."

She laughed. "Sorry, I'm suddenly freezing."

"Then let's get out and get you a towel."

"It's a good plan," she said.

She hurried ahead of him and found her towel. He had worn cutoff chinos into the water, and just the edges were wet. He reached for the polo shirt he had thrown on the sand near her things and skinned it over his head. She towel dried quickly and slid on her dress, and still she was shaking.

"Ah, you know what you need?" he asked, taking her discarded towel and wrapping it around her shoulders and rubbing them.

"Dry clothing?" she suggested.

"A hot toddy—and Irish whiskey. I know where they make the best."

"Would that be a place south on Duval known as O'Hara's? I hear that it's a real hangout for actual locals—conch-type people—and that the tourists crash in sometimes, wanting to hang with the locals," she said with a smile.

"That's the place," he agreed.

He was pleasant and easy, charming, in fact. She wondered how she would have felt about him if they'd met on different footing. If she'd just come in with Katie somewhere and it had been, oh, Vanessa, you've met my brother, Sean, right? No, after all these years, imagine. Well, anyway, then, Sean, this is Vanessa, Vanessa, Sean.

She had chosen their meeting. Katie had offered to introduce him. She hadn't wanted friendship to be a part of it. Maybe she had made a mistake. What did it matter? She was getting what she had set out for—another chance to discover what had happened. At the very least, a chance to feel that she had done everything in her power.

"So, seriously, how did it go?" she asked.

"Brilliantly. Better. I don't know if I would have thought of having an intro with Marty if I hadn't wanted to see what Jay could do. And Marty was wonderful. He's a natural before the camera, and he absolutely loves his history, so it was all great. Jay is editing now."

"He brought all his equipment?"

"No, he's at my house."

She was silently impressed—with Jay. She was surprised that Sean would trust a stranger with his work system, and she said so.

"You left him—at your house—alone."

"Yes."

"You're a trusting soul."

"Hardly."

"But?"

She started to sink in the sand while taking a step. He took her hand. The feel was a jolt. A nice one. She liked the scent of him, too. Ocean and…him. Clean and fresh.

She didn't want to feel so attracted.

She didn't want to break free from his hand.

She walked casually, thanking him.

"I looked around at costumes today. This is really one of the best places to purchase. A lot of the retailers have researched the period thoroughly. They have great poet's shirts, vests, jackets, hats, corsets, blouses, skirts—you name it. Oh! I bought a piece today. A replica of one worn by Dona Isabella," she said.

He nodded and continued walking.

The vendors had covered up their wares; some were still around, chatting, eating sandwiches and keeping a firm eye on their goods, while others were off, trusting in hired security.

"I drove down here. Let's get to my car," Sean said.

They hurried along, Sean still holding her hand. He unlocked the car and opened the passenger-side door for her.

It was a car she might have expected for him, and she liked it. A Jeep. New enough, but not brand-new, a car that could go just about anywhere. It fit Sean very well, down-to-earth, utilitarian, and somehow, though anyone could buy the car, it seemed rugged and sensual and masculine.

She really had to stop her mind from wandering in that direction.

It was difficult. A St. Nicholas medallion hung from the rearview mirror, and she wasn't surprised to see that he honored the patron saint of the sea. An O'Hara's sticker was on the front windshield, low, on the passenger side. The rear of the Jeep was filled with a stack of neatly piled clothing, as if he had just been to the laundry, though she wasn't sure why he would go out since she was certain that the house—which had actually been bought by Katie—had a washer and dryer.

He saw her looking at the stack of clothing. He winced. "I suck at it so I take it to the Laundromat to get it done for me. I've had too many white and beige things wind up an ultrafeminine shade of pink."

Vanessa laughed. Good God, she found even that endearing.

"Let me see your piece," he told her.

She dug in her tote and took out the box that carried the mermaid pendant.

He took it and stared at it, and then at her.

"What?" she demanded. Something about the way he looked at her made her shiver.

"I just saw this same piece," he told her.

"Oh? Did you go by the vendors?" she asked. Her voice seemed faint.

And hopeful.

He shook his head slowly. She thought she knew his answer before he spoke, and she was oddly afraid without knowing why.

"This is the piece you found at the shipwreck site the other day. Where the *Santa Geneva* went down. It's—it's the exact piece," he said at last.

They were at O'Hara's, where they had run into Katie and David. Sean had gotten Vanessa the promised Irish coffee. It was delicious. At O'Hara's, there were equal parts Irish whiskey and Drambuie in with the coffee, along with a generous dollop of real whipped cream. The night was pleasantly cool with a southwesterly breeze, making the hot drink perfect.

She was still in her bathing suit, and the damp and the salt and the sand were irritating, and she was certain that her hair looked like windblown spiderwebs. If they were all about to take part in filming on boats and at sea, she supposed, they should all get accustomed to one another in wet and scraggly mode.

"Well, if it's the original, eighteen or twenty-four karat, with rubies and sapphires, it's worth a mint," David said.

"I imagine," Sean agreed.

"What will you do with it?" Katie asked.

"Do with it?" Vanessa said blankly. "Well, I don't actually see it as mine. I was on a trial run for the film when I happened upon it. I don't know—it should be in a museum, I guess. It's confusing, though. It should really belong to Sean and David, I think. Isn't that the way it works when you're working for someone? Like Mel Fisher had all kinds of divers, but the finds were his—right?"

Sean laughed. "After he fought the state for a decade," he said. "But he won. Nowadays, in territorial waters, it's twenty-five percent to the state. The rest is yours. Jaden was beside herself with excitement when she called me. She says that it's stunning. I haven't had a chance to get over and see it in person yet. All I have is the picture she sent to my phone. She and Ted had a party tonight, so she locked it up tight. We'll go and see it in person in the morning."

"Wonderful," Vanessa said. She wasn't sure it was wonderful at all. She wished that she hadn't found it. She could only imagine the terror of the woman who had worn it. By legend, Dona Isabella hadn't died on the ship—she had been murdered with the others on Haunt Island, probably by Kitty Cutlass. In the movie script, she'd written in a spectacular scene of the beauty floating in the water. It was unlikely that had been the case—Dona Isabella's bones were somewhere beneath the sands of Haunt Island.

Kitty Cutlass had most probably perished in the storm.

"Yes, that sounds fine," Vanessa said.

"Oh my God!" Katie said. "You don't sound excited. Vanessa, that's a real historical find. It's amazing. I've been on those reefs all my life. I found an old boot and a high school ring from Miami High, class of '75. Hey, this is...treasure!"

Vanessa smiled and nodded. "I've got to get to work," Katie said. She rolled her eyes.

"I'm going to go to Sean's and see what Jay has done with the footage we took this morning," David said. "Katie...do you mind? I'll be back before you close."

Katie laughed and touched David's face tenderly. "I worked here long before you came back, my love. But, hey, I do appreciate walking home together, so thanks."

She went off to introduce her show; a blonde girl was waiting impatiently to sing.

"So let's head down to my house," Sean said.

"Well, I'm off to shower and change," Vanessa said, slipping from her stool. She paused. "Thank you, Sean, the Irish coffee was delicious."

"Glad you enjoyed it," Sean said, standing, as well. "Don't you want to see the footage? I put some together from the dive, as well."

"Sure, but..." She grimaced, indicating what she was wearing. "I really need to shower and change."

"That's easy enough. We'll walk by your place, and I'll wait for you."

"No, no, that's all right. It will take me a few minutes."

"Not a problem," David assured her.

"Sure—we haven't looked in the T-shirt shop windows for a while," Sean said, but he was smiling. "Actually, Irish Kevin's has a great band. We can hang out and listen, and when you're ready, head to my place."

"You're forgetting something," she told him.

"What?"

"Your car."

"It's fine here. I'll get it in the morning. There won't be anyplace to park on lower Duval. I've left it before—it will be fine."

Duval was crazy at night, with many people dressed up. Open containers were legal in Key West, and many a pirate and his dame walked about with their grog in a leather-bound drinking vessel of some kind or another. Some looked great and truly played the part.

"Hey, we wouldn't be hard put to find extras, if we were filming a smashing pirate scene," Sean said dryly.

"It's happened every year for about a decade," Vanessa said. "No surprise there."

"One of the parties is happening," David said. "I think it's down on Mallory Square, but I'm not sure. It won't be in full swing for a while."

"And hopefully, we'll be out of here by then," Sean said, grinning.

"Hey, I think it's great. They do reenactments and all kinds of cool historical stuff. Kids can come to it, and face it, Key West isn't always kid-friendly," Vanessa said.

"Excuse me—I was a kid here, and I came out just fine," Sean said.

"I grew up here, too. So we stayed off Duval growing up," David said. "We had the water. Boats, the sea, diving. What more could you ask?"

They reached Vanessa's place. When Vanessa ran up to shower and change, Sean and David walked across the street to Irish Kevin's. She would find them there when she was ready.

She showered and shampooed, and though she was in a hurry, she discovered that she was determined to be thorough. She shaved her legs, dried her hair with the blow-dryer and despite herself, opted for makeup. She chose a knit dress that was both casual and slinky, and though appalled at her choice, she went for heeled sandals.

Dressing up as if out on the hunt, she mocked herself.

It wasn't her—it wasn't the way she lived.

And yet, that night, it was.

Impatient at last, she gave her hair a last brush and hurried out. As she crossed the street, whistles followed her from the tiny bar next door. She blushed and was glad.

The two men were hanging at the entrance to Irish Kevin's—the music could be heard clearly from there. The band *was* good, playing something from Three Dog Night that she hadn't heard in years and years but sounded absolutely great.

"Shall we?" Sean said, seeing her.

David whistled. "What a transformation."

She laughed. "Thank you."

Sean cleared his throat. "Yes, you look great. But transformation? David, are you implying that she doesn't look great wet, in sand, with ratty hair?"

"Not in the least. And I'd have never said *ratty* hair," David protested.

"Hmm. You're right. I do apologize!" Sean said.

She grinned. "Thank you both, I'm pretty sure. Should we go and see if Jay is still at your house?"

They agreed. She walked between the two of them as they traveled the short distance from Duval to the O'Hara house.

Vanessa remembered it well. She had stayed here with Katie many a time.

It hadn't changed much, though Katie had added a few little touches that made it her own. There were new seascapes on the walls, light, new upholstery on the furniture that still seemed to fit the Victorian period of the house, and there was a new entertainment center with a flat-screen TV in the parlor. Walking into the house was comfortable. She'd spent good times there.

"You know my house?" Sean asked her.

"I spent a lot of nights here," she said.

"Pity. And I never knew," Sean murmured.

"Hey! You're back!" Jay called from the rear of the house, once an open porch, then a screened porch, now a glassed-in family room.

They headed toward the sound of Jay's voice.

The rear of the house *had* changed. It was all Sean O'Hara's now, with several screens set up, a large computer, camera equipment here and there, microphones, booms and more. Jay was in a twirling office chair at the computer.

"Nessa, old gal, you've made it with the boys! I'm so glad. This is great stuff, great!" Jay said enthusiastically.

"He's shy, never toots his own horn," Vanessa said dryly.

"Let's see it," Sean said.

Jay hit a key that sent the film to the largest of the screens in the room. They moved around to perch on chairs to watch. As she took a seat on the divan by the back of the house, Vanessa felt a chill sweep through her and something almost like a gentle touch on her arm. She looked around, certain one of the men was near her. But Sean was perched on a stool and David had taken the wicker wingback chair to her far right. Neither was anywhere near her.

And Jay was at the computer chair still, arms crossed over his chest.

Vanessa had to admit that the footage was fantastic. Marty was an amazing subject and storyteller, and Jay had the editing just right. It ran approximately three minutes, with an extra twenty seconds of the old pirate historian playing his sea shanty. In all, it was fabulous footage.

"Well?" Jay demanded.

"You're good," Sean said.

"Yes, very good," David agreed.

"Am I hired? Please?" Jay begged.

Sean was still staring at the screen, though it was dark. "Yes," he said. "You're hired."

Jay let out a yelp of joy. He sprang from the chair and came to Vanessa, pulling her from her seat, swirling her around the room. "Thank God, thank God!"

She didn't share his elation. She felt her cheeks redden, and she nodded.

Sean rose, ignoring the two of them. "This is what we got the other day," he told David. He hit a few keys. Sean narrated what had been shot, and she knew that, beyond a doubt, she would watch the documentary even if she had nothing to do with it. His voice was a captivating tenor with the right inflection at every moment. There was footage she hadn't even realized he had taken as she set her mask and slipped off the side of the boat. Her shots of the reef with the brilliant fish flashed by as he explained the wrecks and the delicacy of the reefs, along with the dangers they had, and still did, create. There was footage of her with the grouper as he talked about the wonder of the reef today—and then went into the sinking of the *Santa Geneva* as she was beset by pirates. He talked about the legend, about the film crew, and how they had chosen, in presenting unsolved mysteries, to focus on the legend of the *Santa Geneva,* Mad Miller, Kitty Cutlass and the sad plight of Dona Isabella. That legend had given rise to many others."

"Wow. You did that just shooting with the two of you?" Jay said. "Hey, what am I talking about? I was doing a motion picture with a small crew that did extra duty as stunt doubles!"

"You're a walking wonder, Jay," Vanessa said, teasing him, and yet, she realized, her tone was dry. She was still angry with him. He shouldn't have just shown up. He should have called her.

But then again, she had barged in. No, she had set up an appointment. Jay had used her.

"I am a walking wonder, Nessa," Jay said, grinning.

But then he sighed. "I just wish I knew what had happened."

"All right," Sean said. "Tomorrow, we'll get together and go through everything you did from the time you came to Key West to start filming. Since this was planned as a documentary, there's an outline and a list of shoots, but no actual script. Things will change now, some, but I don't want to make the changes until you've given me your story from start to finish."

Jay nodded gravely. "All right."

"We might make another dive where the *Santa Geneva* went down, too," he said.

"Hey, you're the boss. Bosses," Jay said, looking from Sean to David.

"What now?" Vanessa asked.

Sean smiled. "Dinner. No one has had any."

"Oh, man, great idea. I'm starving," Jay said.

David rose and said, "How about Turtle Kraals? Tourists are out, but it's a guaranteed relaxed atmosphere and it's on the water."

"Sounds good to me," Sean agreed.

They walked the back streets down to Turtle Kraals and the docks. The air was pleasantly cool and the walking was beautiful. She was next to Sean, who was somewhat quiet, while Jay walked next to David, talking enough for everyone.

"Beginning to end," he said. "You know what I remember, clearer than anything? Just how annoyed I was with Georgia. If I'd only known…if we'd only looked for Travis. But we weren't expecting anything. I'd been on Haunt Island dozens of times. Boaters come and go. And of course we did everything by the book, notifying the Bahamian authorities, even hiring Bahamian tour guides just to keep everything legit. And that on our budget. I still can't figure it, I just can't figure it. I didn't see any other boats during the day. I know that most of the authorities believe that Carlos Roca killed Travis earlier in the day, and killed Georgia when he pretended he was going to take her home. Why? I can't begin to fathom. And why stage the bodies in the way that he did? None of it makes any sense. You'd think there had been a ghost," he said with disgust.

Then, oddly, he jumped and spun around.

"What the hell was that?" Jay demanded.

"We're in front of you," Vanessa reminded him.

"Must have been the wind," Sean said, still walking and not looking back.

"That was one hell of a wind," Jay said.

"Oh, we get those now and again down here," David said.

They walked on and arrived at the restaurant. Sean knew the right people. He smiled and chatted with the hostess, and they wound up with a perfect table, one that overlooked the water of the historic seaport. It was a pleasant place, named for something not so pleasant, really. It was where turtles had once been stored until it was time for them to be sent to whatever restaurant or manufacturer or distributor of turtle soup and turtle steak was ready for them. Nowadays, turtles were protected, and the wildest events here that included the reptiles were the turtle races held on certain days of the week.

They ordered, and Vanessa excused herself, saying she wanted to look at the moon over the water. She walked out and realized someone was behind her. She turned to see that Sean had followed her. "Beautiful night," he said. "Perfect weather. Calm seas and a full moon."

"Yes, perfect," she agreed.

There was a silence between them for a moment. It wasn't awkward, and yet Vanessa knew he was about to say something. And he did.

"You know, there's something underneath everything here. On the surface, what happened was a horrible, gruesome tragedy, a heinous crime. The kind that couldn't be repeated. But now we're about to go the same route. Have you ever wondered if the person—or persons—responsible might find out what you're doing, be afraid that you know something and come after you?"

She inhaled deeply. "I did my best to convince you to make your film following our route. But it might have been the wrong thing. If you're afraid in any way—"

He shook his head impatiently, interrupting her. "I'm not afraid. We've been on a dangerous route before. I'll have myself, David, Liam and maybe a few other people I know well and trust with my life. I'm worried about you. All right, I don't think you ought to be in that room on Duval Street. Yes, it's Duval, yes, there are cops around. If you don't want to stay at my house—or Katie's house—go and stay with Katie and David at David's house."

"It just…it would be awkward, either way," she murmured.

"I can ask Jay to stay, as well," he said.

She spun around to look at him. "Hey, I can honestly be the perfect gentleman," he told her.

"Must you always be?" she asked him.

He arched a brow and smiled. She looked quickly away, wondering what she had been thinking to speak so rashly. She stared at the water. "Good God, I'll be on a boat again with Jay. I love him, he's a good friend, but he drives me crazy when the contact is constant!"

As she stared into the water, images seemed to form within it. As she looked, it rippled.

Fish. Fish were always moving about.

But it wasn't a school of fish moving. Something seemed to be rising, coming to the surface. She wanted to grab Sean's hand and find out if he saw it, too, but she seemed to be frozen in place. She knew what it was.

The image of the figurehead. The figurehead that bore the facial features of Dona Isabella.

She turned away from the water. "All right," she said. "Thank you. I'll stay at your house. I appreciate the offer. I'll move in tonight, after dinner, if that's all right with you."

He seemed startled by her sudden change of mind. He looked at the water.

And saw nothing.

"Perfect," he said softly. "Shall we go in? Food is probably about ready."

She nodded, looking up at him with her wide, beautiful eyes. They caught the opalescence of the water and sky and seemed especially hypnotic. He cleared his throat. "I'm going to give Liam a call and see what your other friends are up to now," he told her.

"What? What friends?"

"Your crew from your movie shoot."

Her brows shot up. "You're going to hire us all on?" she asked.

"Well, we're following the trail that you and Jay and your crew followed for the movie. I thought we should use everyone who was involved in the film shoot."

She blinked and nodded.

"Is there something wrong?"

She shook her head. "No, I think it's brilliant. But it's not as if we were all the best of friends. We worked well together but I had never met Bill Hinton or Jake Magnoli until the shoot. I've known Barry and Zoe through different projects during the years, but... I'm sure, though, that Jay would have information on how to reach them."

"Don't worry about it. Liam will find them."

"Okay," she said.

"Great. We'll get on it."

She still stared at him, wondering why she felt quite so paralyzed that night.

"Are you all right?" he asked her. "Seriously? Do you not want the others—"

"Oh, no! Of course I do," she said.

He smiled.

She gave herself a shake. Something didn't seem to be boding well for her, but she didn't understand her feelings of dread. She tried to shake them off.

"Food!" she said. "I think I need food."

He slipped an arm around her shoulders and led her in.

And the feel of him was good.

7

The scream awakened Sean like a bolt out of the blue.

He had been sleeping soundly, glad to have Vanessa under his roof. He didn't know why he was suddenly worried about her sleeping in what should have been a fairly safe haven, but maybe it had been recent events here that had gotten him so worried. And maybe he was looking for something closer. Ass. Any fool in his right mind would want more. She reeked of beauty and sensuality.

Just having her in the house was some kind of a strange primitive pleasure.

But the scream ripped him from any thoughts except the possibility of danger, and he tore out of his own room and down the hall to where she slept in Katie's room.

"Vanessa!" He turned the light on, seeking whatever threat she faced.

But there was nothing there. She was up on her knees, staring into the sudden light, blinking furiously. She was more than decently clad in a massive cotton T-shirt, and he didn't hesitate to rush to her, slide onto the bed and take her shoulders, shaking her slightly, bringing her focus to him.

"Vanessa, what? What happened?"

She didn't reply for a minute. Then her eyes focused on his and a flood of color filled her cheeks.

"Oh, God! I am so sorry. I never thought that I…that I screamed aloud," she said.

She was shaking. He pulled her toward him, leaning her against him where he sat on the bed. "It's all right. What? A nightmare?"

"It used to always be the same. Now it's changing. First, I just saw the heads in the sand. Then they began talking to me. Asking me how and why I let it happen. Travis wants to know why we didn't even look for him. Georgia wants to know why we didn't believe her when she screamed about monsters…and now…"

"Now?"

"Now, on top of Travis and Georgia, I keep dreaming about Dona Isabella. It makes me think that I am losing it and I certainly had no right coming here and getting you and David involved. Except that, of course, I don't think these nightmares will ever stop if…if there can't be an answer somewhere out there."

"Hey!" He found himself smoothing back her hair. "It's all right. I understand. And David and I aren't coming into this blindly. We know what happened. We consider ourselves worthy of the task, honestly. We're good at what we do, and we know how to defend ourselves. Liam is a cop, and he's coming. We'll stack the decks with the right people, Vanessa."

She looked up at him. "How? You were saying that

you weren't getting exactly what you wanted, so many of your friends were already involved in projects."

"It will happen. I'm going to try to recruit old Marty, and maybe even Jamie. It will be fine. Tomorrow, we'll do some more shooting on the reef with the four of us working and see how it falls out."

"Lew will come to the beach again. He was there, and he saw," she said.

"Lew…?"

"Our Bahamian guide," she said.

"Of course," he said. "David has already sent ahead to the Bahamian government, getting film permits and letting them know our location plans. We'll soon need a list of the crew, though I believe he's submitted certain names already…. Listen, about your screaming…"

"Yes?"

"Never be afraid if you scream in the night here. We've had our share of fear and dread, and there's nothing to be ashamed of when it regards fear," he said.

He wanted to melt into her being suddenly. Those eyes. Huge and blue and staring so trustingly into his.

Great. When holding her made every sexual instinct in him scream away in silent agony.

Yes, come to my house, it will be perfectly safe! he mocked himself.

She smiled.

"Do you want me to stay here? Until you fall asleep?" he asked her.

"Oh, I really couldn't ask you to do that," she said, offering a small laugh. "And I'm sorry. It is embarrassing. I am competent! And you'll never believe that if I keep screaming in the middle of the night."

"Apples and oranges," he assured her.

She smiled again. "Stay," she said.

"Your wish, my command," he told her. "Well, for tonight, anyway."

That brought a true smile to her lips. She crawled up to one side of the bed. "Really awkward, huh? I was about to plump the pillow, asking you to come up. But that would be rather…oh, God, the whole situation is very…"

He laughed. "Premature. That's all. Quite frankly, every time I see you, I'm more under some kind of a spell. I'm fascinated with your knowledge and talents. And there's the simple fact that you love the water as much as I do. Then again, it could be how beautiful you are. God knows, you're probably vibrant and vital when you sleep. Stop me if there's someone in your life and I'm going on ridiculously," he said.

"There's no one in my life. Dating is really out of the question when you're the wrong kind of screamer," she said dryly.

He laughed and moved up to the pillow. He drew her head down on his chest. "Sleep, my dear, in comfort, I hope. You're safe from the evils of the world—and me—for the night."

"I think you might be too good to be true," she whispered.

"Oh, nothing is that good, and certainly not me," he assured her gruffly.

He smoothed her hair. It felt like silk.

He felt her breathing against him. Felt her warmth, her form, close to his.

A sense of longing filled him. Not just the burning need for sex she could create.

Longing. For something more.

Tonight, he would be content.

Thank God, she didn't scream again. Waking, Vanessa opened her eyes and realized that she was sprawled atop Sean. For a moment, she didn't dare move, and then she did so. He was awake, watching her. She flushed and winced.

"I'm so sorry. Did you sleep all right?" she asked him.

"Beautifully," he assured her.

"Thank you for staying with me."

"My pleasure."

"Sure."

"Well, it could have been greater pleasure," he teased.

She grew serious. "I didn't ask last night, what about you?" she asked him. "Is there any involvement in your life?"

He shook his head. "I haven't been home that long. Before, I moved too much. The Black Sea, the Great Barrier Reef. Loch Ness. The Great Lakes. The Bahamas."

"You've really been everywhere," she noted.

"Everywhere—and nowhere," he murmured. He rolled over and rose. "I'll put coffee on. Are you a breakfast person? I'm a decent cook—that's what happens when you live on boats half the time. You get desperate and learn how to cook."

"But no laundry, eh?" she teased.

"Hey, I packed enough for what I needed. Laundry was done onshore. Eating is a necessity on a daily basis. So, you a breakfast person?"

"Sure, only I help cook," she said.

He nodded. "Actually, there's already coffee on. Programmed it last night. I'm going to jump in the shower. Help yourself whenever you're ready."

"Thanks."

He left the room. Vanessa walked into her own bathroom and met her reflection in the mirror. She was still flushed. She washed her face, brushed her teeth and thought about the shower.

Then she thought about the night.

She thought about his words, and about the way he had behaved.

She winced, hesitated, caught her breath.

He was everything she wanted, as well. Yes, he was gorgeous, tall, bronzed, well muscled, with his striking, rugged and intriguing face. Classical features. Golden eyes. But it wasn't just the tempting pull of his equally sculpted build.

It was the sea. The things he loved. The way he behaved. Even his bark when he was angry. Even the way he looked at her when he was wary, skeptical. It was in his movement, in his words.

She didn't step into her own shower. She walked down the hall, knowing which room was his from days gone by. She listened and heard the sound of the water flowing in his shower.

"Sean?" She tentatively pushed open the door to his room and walked through it. The bathroom door was ajar and the water was flowing.

She stepped closer. “Sean?”

The shower curtain jerked open and he looked out, alert and anxious.

“What’s wrong?”

“Nothing, nothing!” she declared quickly. So much for being a femme fatale with a casual and sensual style.

“I—oh, God, I’m not at all good at this. I thought that maybe…we could shower together. I mean the way that you were speaking last night, it didn’t seem quite out of the question,” she said.

His shoulders eased. A broad smile slowly creased his features and he looked down for a moment, and then back to her.

“The shower will work better if you come in naked,” he told her.

She laughed, breathless and more than a little nervous. She slipped from her panties, drew the huge T-shirt over her head and walked over to join him. Unabashedly, he looked her up and down.

“Well, since bathing suits leave little to the imagination, I can’t say that I haven’t noticed the infinitely fine attributes you possess. But reality is far superior to anything I imagined.”

“Where on earth did you get your language skills?” she demanded.

He pulled her under the spray beneath him. The water was warm and delightful. His body was pure fire and magnificent against hers.

“You don’t like my language skills?” he asked.

“No, no, they’re fine! Lovely, really,” she assured him.

"Maybe I should stop speaking," he said. He did so, pressing his lips down upon hers. The touch was electric, and his kiss was perfect, gentle, tasting at first, his mouth molding to hers. And then, as their bodies crushed closer together, it deepened to something forceful and coercive, volcanic in the rush it created within her. Or maybe it was the molten-steel feel of his body, the rise of his erection against her lower abdomen. All she knew was that what she had started so tentatively was now urgent. While the warm water coursed around them, she felt a buildup of arousal within her that seemed insane and yet so wonderful she wanted to experience it forever.

Their hands moved upon one another. They found the soap, used it, lost it, crashed into one another finding it again. Suds covered them, making their flesh slick and sleek, and then the water rinsed off the suds, and they were together again, just holding each other for a moment beneath the spray. She laid her head against his neck and felt the throb of his pulse. She felt his hand slide down her hip, between her thighs. He lifted her, with the water still sending out spray and steam; he held her high, then brought her down, guiding her down on him. She wound her arms around his neck and her legs around his waist, and he balanced against the fiberglass of the shower as he eased completely into her, his eyes on hers. Then he began to move.

She didn't know if it was him, if it was the simple fact that they were there, just as they began, with the pounding sound, water and steam, but nothing had ever seemed more erotic to her, and the way that he moved was an arousal unlike any other. She clung to him, arched and writhed to his lift and fall, and gave herself over to the pure carnal rawness of the experience. Far too soon she realized that she was burning and frantic and climaxing. She felt a final great thrust from him, shuddered, and eased slowly down on him, but he held her against the fiberglass until the sound of the water was just that again and the spray and the mist kept them warm, even as they cooled.

His lips found hers again, wet, hard, wonderful. He kissed her deeply, her wet hair entangled in his fingers.

He groped for the faucet at last, stopping the spray. Still nearly on top of her, his lips just inches away, he said, "Try and get me out of bed at night, hmm?"

"I think that you're quite lovely in bed, actually," she said.

"I hope you'll think I'm even lovelier now."

She nodded.

"Towels," he said.

"Pardon?"

"I'll get towels."

"Oh, yes, that would be lovely, too."

He stepped from the shower and produced two towels, large towels, with sailing motifs. She wrapped hers around herself and stepped out into the bedroom. His private quarters were neat. He had books stacked on his bureau, most of them sea charts, or books on great sailing ships, some on diving, and one or two fiction. His furniture was solid mahogany without Victorian carving, more in an old west Mission style. It was a personal place, too, though. Not just bare. There were pictures of dive trips and sailing and foreign shores. On the dresser, too, sat a family photo: Katie and Sean, their mother and father. It was a wonderful room. Probably because she had just decided sex with Sean was wonderful, everything in the world about him was wonderful, as well.

"How's the room?" he asked. "Am I passing muster?"

She laughed. "The room, let me see. Solid, manly furniture. Good photos. Good reading material. Sparse and neat—belongs to a man, most obviously, accustomed to tight spaces on a boat. It's really unbelievable that he still messes up his laundry, but hey, in the list of could-be faults, that is quite a small one."

"What about the bed?" he inquired.

"Oh, definitely macho. Studly, even. A lovely bed. Something I'd actually love to try out tonight."

"Why wait for tonight?" he asked her.

Why wait?

Words coming from his lips were as arousing as the most provocative touch....

And it would be rather senseless at this point to argue the feeling...

She turned into his arms. Towels were lost. What was lost from the steam and spray of the shower was found in slow discovery, touch after touch, complete intimacy. There was the wonder of finding every little scar and wound upon his body, learning where it had come from—a dive into shallow water when he had been a kid; a cut from a catfish, oh, so dumb and he knew it; the only fight he'd gotten into in junior high, and, of course, she should have seen the other guy. There was so much laughter, so much sensuality as she kissed each little wound, as he returned the questionnaire, as they lay entwined until the touches and kisses became breathless and ever more predetermined and purposely provocative, hot and wet and aimed at erogenous zones. They melded together again, holding still for that perfect moment as he thrust deeply into her, then letting basic instinct come into play, the renewed desperation for fulfillment. The sheets became entangled and damp, and still they lay locked together, ever moving, writhing, arching, until the sweet moment of climax burst upon them, and they fell into one another's arms, damp, depleted, sated and smiling breathlessly. Vanessa listened to the thunder of his heart as it slowed and felt her own, and they seemed to meld, as well.

She rolled away from him and jumped to her feet, heading for the door.

"Hey!" he called.

"We have to start the day," she replied.

"So we do—but we could lie here a moment quietly, couldn't we?" he asked.

She caught the door frame and looked back at him. "Maybe you could," she said softly, and ran out, heading for the shower in Katie's room.

When the water came down on her this time, it came with the memory of joining him, and she burned beneath the water, both amazed and glad for what she had done, and yet horrified. She wasn't sure what had possessed her, but she was certain she had never done anything that had felt more perfect and right as it had progressed. It was new, it was magnificent, and all that she wanted to do was be with him, hear his voice and the laughter, and discover again and again how easy it was to lie with him, what an absolute wonder it was to get to know him.

It was crazy. She had just seduced the man who was more or less her employer, a good friend's brother and someone with whom she was about to embark on a strange mission. Not good.

Oh, yes, good, very good, but...

He was showered again and dressed for the boat when she came down. Coffee had brewed and there was a cup waiting for her by where he sat at the counter, perusing the newspaper. He signaled to it as he saw her. "I just talked to David. He's gotten hold of Jay, and we're going to do some more footage at Pirate Cut. Are you a vegetarian?"

"What? Um, no."

"Good. Bacon is in the microwave and I'm about to put the eggs on. We have about half an hour, then we meet them down at the docks."

"Okay, sounds good," Vanessa said.

He stood and walked around to the oven, tested his fry pan and poured the egg mixture into it, then added chopped onions, peppers, mushrooms and tomato.

"So, you are a cook," she said.

He turned to her. "And you might pop that bread in the toaster, if you like."

"Aye, aye, captain."

"Ah, such a reply is necessary only on a boat!" he teased.

Vanessa popped the toast into the toaster. As she did so, she had the strange sensation that something cold passed behind her.

And Sean was looking in that direction, frowning.

"Is there a draft in the house?" she asked.

He shrugged. "A ghost—so I've been told."

Vanessa smiled. "Really?"

"It's actually a very old place, you know. But I think there was a structure here before, long, long ago, when the pirates were at their heyday. Real butter? Or the fake spray stuff?"

"What?"

"Which do you prefer?"

"Real butter."

"In the refrigerator. I heard it's not really that bad for you unless you consume the whole stick."

"All things in moderation, so they say."

He added cheese to the omelets while she got the butter and spread it on the toast. There was orange juice in the refrigerator, and she poured a glass for each of them. He directed her to the microwave as he flipped the omelet, slid it onto a plate and separated it to slide half onto a second plate. They set it all on the counter and took their seats again.

"Do you have a copy of your original script with you?" he asked her. "The script you wrote for the movie."

"Sure. It's still in my computer," she told him.

"Can you give me a rundown?"

"We started from Key West, with three couples meeting up to take a trip out to Haunt Island. The usual college-age crew—Jay was hoping to reel in the seventeen- to twenty-one-year-old crowd. There was the good girl, the one you liked, the nerd…you know, the usual slasher cast. We had permits, of course, and filmed them getting together at the dock. They went diving at Pirate Cut, and they made fun of the story of Dona Isabella, and drew up silly pictures of Mad Miller and Kitty Cutlass. Then they did this ridiculous thing, like a game of Bloody Mary, but they called up Mad Miller. The first death occurs when one of the kids sees a woman floating in the water and goes to help her, but when he turns her over, her face is skeletal and eaten away. When he shrieks and tries to get away, the sea ghost of Mad Miller drags him down, cutting him up in the water. We're talking true teen-slasher flick," she said, grimacing apologetically.

"I understand someone trying to break in—and make a living," Sean said. "Many a director has cut his teeth on a slasher flick, and some have made very respectable livings on that alone." He seemed thoughtful as he munched on his toast. "Go on."

"Well, the rest on board are terrified, of course, and they try to perform a ritual that will let the poor murdered Dona Isabella rest—and send Mad Miller and Kitty Cutlass to hell. One by one they end up dead as the boat limps toward the closest land—Haunt Island. Of course, the heroine, Georgia Dare, is something of a scholar and she discovers that Haunt Island was where everyone was massacred. In the script, Mad Miller and Kitty Cutlass come after them, but Georgia and her boyfriend—Travis, of course—find a way to raise the massacred dead, and they come to life and destroy Mad Miller and Kitty Cutlass, and then sink back into the sand. Simple, basic—some history, some ridiculous witchery, even if I did write it myself—good, gory teen fare."

"What schedule did you follow filming?" he asked.

"I have that in my notebook, too. Oddly enough, most of the scenes were in order, and that was because we were so cost-conscious that we didn't want to pay actors when we didn't need them," Vanessa explained. "Obviously, we filmed the scenes at Pirate Cut first, and then we filmed at a few of the reefs up by Key Largo, and then made our way over to South Bimini and finally Haunt Island. When Carlos and Georgia left on the night she was killed, they were supposedly heading straight for Miami."

"And you don't believe that Carlos Roca was a brilliant psychopath, pretending to be a great guy and savoring all the possibilities when Georgia went nuts and wanted to go home?" Sean asked.

"No. If he were that good an actor, he would have been in front of the camera, would have been there for years, and garnered a few Oscars," Vanessa said with certainty. "But here's the thing, of course—he's gone. He can't defend himself. I don't know what I really even think that we can get out of this, but Carlos is another reason I'd so desperately love to find the truth. He might be a victim, too, and stand accused for this in the memory of his family and loved ones. It isn't right."

"We may do this and wind up with nothing more than an interesting documentary that merely gives rise to more questions," Sean warned.

"It's more than anyone else is doing right now," she said.

"True. But, objectively, I can't blame the Coast Guard, the Bahamian police, the FBI or any other law-enforcement agency. They've hit a brick wall. It's impossible to drain the ocean—by today's technology, at any rate. I'm sure that all over the Southeastern United States and at Caribbean ports, people are still on the lookout for the boat."

"Right—and how hard do you think they're looking now? People forget, and they move on. Other crimes happen. It's sad, but true," Vanessa said. "And by the way, you do make an excellent omelet."

He grinned. "Yep, I do dishes well, too. It's only the laundry thing that escaped me. But how about you clean up for me, I'll get David on the phone, gather some supplies and meet you down at the dock. We'll get your buddy Jay out there as well today, and I'll interview both of you while we're on the *Conch Fritter.*"

"I'm great at dishes," she assured him.

He set his in the sink. He carefully kept his distance from her. He wanted the day to be productive. At this moment, touching her would be counterproductive.

It was a beautiful day. Calm seas, bright sun, cool air.

Jay was called upon to act as cameraman, though David and Sean set up the shot. They spoke about beginning their documentary. They were both excellent speakers, and it was a really good and casual segment, explaining that they were going to follow the legend and speaking about the events that had occurred on the recent film shoot. They talked about the fact that Vanessa was Katie's friend and had come to them, and how they were they hoping to shed some light on the mystery.

Sean then repositioned himself and the camera so that he in turn could interview Jay about the film. Sean explained to David where he would want sea charts and other visual aids edited in, and they all seemed to be getting along quite well.

Katie had come on board with David, so there were five of them out. When they were ready to go into the water, Katie determined that she was just going to lie in the sun—she was tired. It was a busy time at O'Hara's, and she was trying to make sure that Clarinda would be ready to take over for her when they set out through the Bermuda Triangle for the Bahamas.

On film again, Sean explained that they were looking for good footage of the "bones," or the wreck field of the *Santa Geneva.* Over the years, with storms and currents, wreckage could move for miles. The initial sinking or breakup of a ship could begin the process, and time could keep it going into eternity. The site was fairly shallow, and it was popular with divers; you would think it had been picked clean by salvage divers in the eighteenth century, and yet still more relics had been found in the present, including the mermaid pendant Vanessa had discovered.

Jay paired up with David, and Vanessa naturally paired up with Sean.

It was cool in the water, but Vanessa's skin was still enough for her. Sean and the other men also opted for skins.

Vanessa was thrilled that the sea was clear that day and the visibility was amazing. She hovered with Sean just below the surface, trying to capture the enormity of the spread of the wreck over the years, and the size and shape of the ship itself. Overlays could be edited in that would describe the *Santa Geneva* when she was afloat—and how she had been blasted by the pirate ship and came to sink and break up, forced onto the reef now known as Pirate Cut.

The ship had sunk north to south, and it was actually from a position of about five feet below the surface that Vanessa discovered she was getting the best long shot of the bones of the ship. It was amazing to see the shape and tragically disjointed outline of what had once been a regal and majestic sailing ship. She moved slowly and smoothly over the bones of the wreckage, keeping a straight sweep of the site, and then panning in slowly to show what divers saw as they got closer. If it wasn't known that a great ship had gone down, a diver might have explored the wreckage for a long time without knowing what it was when he got too close.

She adjusted the zoom, and it was then that she saw something from the periphery of her eyes.

The figurehead.

A chilling sensation burned through her as cold and hot as dry ice.

She drew the camera away and looked down at the site. The *Santa Geneva* seemed settled, at peace, in her sunken graveyard.

How many had died in this area? The pirates had given the ship a vicious cannon salvo; they had boarded to kill and maim with cutlasses and pistols, and kidnapped Dona Isabella for the ransom she would bring. Those who had fought, who had perished in the water, were here somewhere, now long gone, flesh eaten, bones bleached and disarticulated, food for the creatures of the sea. Ghosts and memories were all that remained.

Vanessa looked through the lens again.

And there she was, hazy at first, seeming to look up from jagged coral and sand, the myriad of fish in their amazing colors—and the remains of the deck of the *Santa Geneva* far below.

Vanessa wanted to scream but knew she'd choke, spitting out her regulator. She wanted to give a swift kick with her flippers, burst up the few feet to the surface, leave the water and never come near the reef again.

But it went against everything she had been fighting to do!

Maybe she had let it all play on her mind too much; the nightmares were always tearing into her life, and she wasn't crazy at all, she was simply finding ways to seek and find anything that she could.

The image of the figurehead was probably some other minor clue that went into the fantastic computer of the human brain and manifested in an eerie manner.

She had to believe that, and she had to follow the figurehead, because, so far, it had led her to a mermaid pendant, and it might lead her to...

She couldn't let it scare her. She had to believe in a logical explanation.

She kicked, and her body surged into the depths rather than surfacing.

She was about fifty yards west of where she had found the locket. She eased more air out of her BCV to settle on the bottom. It seemed that she was near the body, or actual remaining structure of the wreck. Jagged and beautiful coral rose to her right—the drop-off pitched to a hundred feet and then two hundred feet to her left.

She began to move the sand, not knowing what she was looking for. There wasn't a spark of light—the reflection of the sun on an object—or anything to suggest that she would make a find.

She felt Sean come down near her, concerned—she had made a swift descent, but they were still no more than fifty feet down.

He tapped her shoulder.

She looked at him and smiled, and returned to her task of shifting sand.

Her heart skipped a beat and thundered. After several minutes, she touched something. Something hard.

She turned. She could see Sean's eyes behind his mask. He was staring at her with great concern. She caught his hand and brought it down to the sand.

He felt what she felt. He still frowned, but he seemed incredulous, as well.

He began working in the sand. She carefully set the shoulder strap of the camera around her and began to dig, as well.

Whatever they had discovered, it was large. A fair amount of work brought them to realize that they had found the top of something. It was about five feet by three, and appeared to go deeply into the sand. With what they had—their hands—they weren't going to be able to dig it out.

Sean motioned to her that they needed to surface. She nodded.

He went up first on the dive ladder; she knew that he did so should she need help with the weight of her tank. She was good, though, and seldom needed help, but she allowed him to steady her as she climbed up. Katie came aft where they stood, helping each other remove their tanks and vests.

"I was about to come after you," she said sternly. "David and Jay have been up—they're in the cabin. David was convinced you knew your air consumption.... I guess you did."

"We found something," Vanessa told Katie breathlessly.

"What?" Katie asked.

"Ah—something?" Sean said, smiling.

"As in? A cannon? An anchor? A big fish?" Katie asked, exasperated.

"I don't know," Sean said. He went over to the ice chest for water, brought out two and tossed one to Vanessa. "We have to go back down. I have two blowers. I don't know if it will be enough, but it will definitely help. Whatever it is, it's buried deep. I honestly think it's a treasure chest. To the best of my knowledge, gold and jewels have been brought up many times, but treasure chests…I think only one or two have ever come up. This is buried. It's like it sank into the sand, and because of that, it's preserved. It's the right size, and it seems that it was wood, covered in leather. I believe the leather is disintegrating, but the chest is very solid. Lead-lined maybe. I've got to tell David." He paused, turned, took Vanessa's cheeks between his hands and kissed her quickly on the lips.

Katie stared with surprise.

Sean, oblivious, headed for the cabin.

Katie stared at Vanessa. "I guess you two are getting along all right."

Vanessa nodded. She felt something at her back and

swung around, but no one was there. Katie, watching her, looked guilty suddenly.

"Is everything all right?" Katie asked.

"Yes, of course. This boat just gets…strange drafts, I guess," she said.

Katie gasped suddenly. "A treasure chest! Do you think he's right?"

Vanessa shook her head. "I don't know. It's something—it's hard."

"How did you find it?"

"Digging in the sand."

"How did you know where to dig in the sand?" Katie asked.

"I don't know. Something just led me there."

"Wow. Like…something led you to the mermaid pendant?"

Vanessa shrugged, wishing that Katie wasn't looking at her so probingly. "I don't know—I really don't."

Katie nodded, frowning. The three men appeared, coming from the cabin. "New tanks, all of us, and two blowers…if it's heavy, we're probably going to need some kind of winch and tackle," David said.

"I think we should go for it now," Sean said. "This could be the find of the century. All right, the *Atocha* was probably the find of the century. But…no. We go for it now. We can set up a winch. We're talking fifty feet down. I have enough rope to set up a winch. Katie may not be able to handle it alone.… Four of us will go down and set it—and someone will come back."

"We'll take the blower first?" David asked.

Sean grinned. "Yeah—we'll make sure we do have something," he said. "But we do. I know we do. The pendant Vanessa found was real—it belonged to Dona Isabella. Jaden said it's a beautiful piece. I don't know exactly what we've got—or what Vanessa has. Rule of thumb is twenty-five percent to the state, but every find is subject to maritime law, and we are in Florida waters. Let's go down—" He paused. "Vanessa? You good for a second dive?"

"Of course."

Sean secured his portable blowers and checked that they were clean and ready for use, murmuring that it had been a long time since he'd had them out.

Within minutes, they were diving in, one by one, David and Sean carrying the handheld blowers, which looked like vacuum cleaners. Sean had a keen sense of direction and led the way, never glancing at his compass. When they reached the object, David and Jay ran their hands over it.

Sean motioned Jay and Vanessa out of the way and he and David went to work on opposite sides of the object. Little by little, they began to create wedges.

Sand flew in a fury.

Then both turned the blowers off and waited.

Sand settled.

And there it was. It still needed a great deal of digging to come free, but it was evident that they had indeed made a discovery.

It was a chest. A pirate's chest.

A treasure chest.

8

David wound up working with Katie on deck. Vanessa helped, but Jay and Sean seemed to have a system for rigging the rope around the chest, and she hovered within easy call if they beckoned for her assistance. Eventually, the sand was dug out enough; rope was gotten around the chest, and Sean tugged on the rope, letting David know it was time to work the winch.

They guided the chest as it began a slow and careful ascent to the surface.

When they breached the water, there were several hectic moments as they moved as quickly as they could to board the boat, shed their gear and guide the heavy chest aboard, as well.

When they were finished, they all collapsed on the deck. Jay began to laugh; it was contagious. Then there were high fives all around, and David went down and broke out the beer.

"Not to ruin this party, but we still don't know what we have," Katie pointed out.

"True," Sean said. He ruffled his sister's hair. "It's treasure. Come on, be a ray of sunshine, huh?"

"I'm not so sure I like treasure," Katie said, frowning. "Well, it's Vanessa's treasure."

Vanessa shook her head. "It's a group treasure, whatever it is!" she said.

"You found it," Katie reminded her.

Sean had gone to the chest. The old, encrusted lock that held it closed was firmly in place. It seemed to be sealed as tightly as if the long-ago owners had welded it shut.

"We can break the lock, but I don't think that's going to help. The damned thing is heavy as hell—and it looks like they might have welded it or something. They wanted it to be sealed, watertight," he said.

"We can take it to Jaden and Ted. They'll know the best thing to do," David said.

"They'll know, yes," Katie said. "And we should be getting back in. We're going to lose the sun any minute. And I have to go to work."

Sean smiled. "Are you afraid of the dark, Katie? You never were. Work! You work all the time. You can be a little late. This is a treasure chest."

"Yes. I know it's a chest. I'm so excited. But we're not going to open it here," Katie said.

Vanessa realized that she, too, wanted to be back onshore. There was something about the trunk that suddenly made her feel uncomfortable. It was wet, dark with age, still covered in sand, but the lock, encrusted, seemed somehow ominous. She felt ridiculously superstitious. Someone had locked the trunk carefully. They had sealed it.

For a reason.

What the hell was in it?

Yes, it did look like it belonged in a Robert Louis Stevenson novel. Or in Mel Fisher's museum. It was dome-topped and handsome, even in its current state. Maybe it was just the way Katie was acting.

Vanessa wished that she had never found it.

The strangest thing was that she wasn't certain she felt the same way as Katie. Katie seemed scared. Vanessa wasn't certain that she was scared. Yes, yes, she was scared. The chest was…

An instrument…of something else?

Ridiculous. None of them even knew what was in it.

"We'll head in right now," Sean assured his sister. He seemed puzzled by her reaction and paused to give her a hug. "It may be treasure," he said.

"And it may not," she told him. She waved a hand in the air. "Maybe it's documents. A captain's log, something like that."

"To me, that would be a greater treasure," Sean said.

"Pieces of paper?" Jay queried glumly.

Sean laughed. "Come on, you must know the value of that kind of paper."

"Yeah. Historic!" Jay said. "I say it's going to be pieces of eight! Gold and silver ingots. We know the *Santa Geneva* sank there. And she had come from Columbia to Cuba—and to Key West to bring Dona Isabella and others back to Spain. There had to have been great treasures on the ship!"

"I say that it's going to be gold and silver because the damned thing is heavy as hell," Sean said.

Katie moved back by Vanessa. She waved a hand in

the air. "Boys, boys! Bring this boat back in—or I'll take the helm!"

Sean grinned at her and started the engines.

Vanessa glanced at her. "He doesn't want you driving his boat?"

"Oh, he'd let me, but I hit the dock once. It was rather an expensive error," Katie said. She tried to grin. The grin failed.

Sean, David and Jay remained excited. Sean was at the helm, but David and Jay hovered with him. They gestured as they spoke, all enthusiastic.

Vanessa jumped off the boat quickly to help with the ties when they arrived at the dock. By then, she didn't even want to be on the boat with the chest. It was ridiculous, but she felt uneasy. It was so stupid! She didn't usually let herself behave so ridiculously. Even when they had found the bodies of Travis and Georgia…or what had remained of them, she hadn't been uneasy. She had been horrified, and then angry. They had been so young. They had been so cruelly robbed of their lives. And someone was getting away with it.

She was tired. Certainly, that was it.

As if reading her mind, Sean looked over at her. "You all right?"

She nodded. "Hey—I'm going to run back to the inn and get the rest of my things."

"I'll meet you there."

"Are you two coming by tonight?" Katie asked. "I'm going to change for work."

"I'll be home soon," David promised, pausing to kiss her, smiling and smoothing her hair back.

"Boys, boys—take your time. Vanessa and I will be

fine," Katie assured him. She looked at Vanessa. "We can walk part of the way together."

"Perfect," Vanessa said.

She was on the dock; Sean was on the boat. He smiled at her. "I won't be all that long, really. I'll come to the inn and get you. We definitely need a big drink at ye olde family bar tonight!"

She was glad to see him so enthusiastic.

Jay was staring at her, too. He gave her a thumbs-up, glad because she was proving that the two of them were worth something.

"What do you think our problem is?" Vanessa asked Katie as they started toward Front Street.

"I don't know—weird, isn't it? I was as excited as anyone when we started—then it came aboard. Creepy. Hey, we are probably idiots. If that thing is filled with treasure, even after the state gets hold of it, we'll be in nice shape."

"Katie, all of us are working. None of us is desperate for a treasure. Okay, maybe Jay. He went through a serious funk after…after everything with the movie went so badly. He didn't work a lot. I think he's been working lately, but…not doing what he wants. Underwater weddings, scuba trips…just enough to keep going. He thought we would have been in the big bucks once the movie went to a distributor. But then it was all so horrible…"

"Well, we'll leave it to the boys," Katie said, rolling her eyes. "And Jaden and Ted have worked with some of the most amazing finds. Treasure after treasure. They'll get it unsealed without compromising anything. Now, that is amazing! Sealed and preserved. We need to be happy."

"Sure," Vanessa said. She wrinkled her face in perplexity and stopped to stare at Katie. "It's absurd. I was excited. Now I'm not. What made the difference?"

"I don't know…I don't know. Maybe we should go back tomorrow to see Marty—he'll be getting his shows going and all by now. We'll get him to talk about Dona Isabella. Maybe that will help us somehow."

"I did a lot of research—I was nuts about the legend. It was so tragic. I'm not sure what else Marty can tell us," Vanessa said.

"Can't hurt, right?" Katie said.

"Can't hurt," Vanessa agreed.

She was surprised when Katie wrapped her arms around herself, shivering. "Sorry—goose bumps. I'm glad Sean is coming back for you."

"I'd be fine," Vanessa said. She was glad, too.

"Come into Katie-oke. That'll make you feel normal!" Katie assured her.

Vanessa nodded. She and Katie hugged quickly, then went their separate ways.

She was glad to head down Duval. The tourists and bright lights helped her shake her feelings of unease.

She was surprised when she hesitated as she neared her inn and decided she'd like a break instead of going right inside.

She walked onto the patio restaurant next to the shop and decided that she'd like one drink. There was a small empty table and she sat at it. Despite the fact that it was busy, a waitress came her way fairly quickly, and she opted for a whiskey with cola.

Her drink came and she sipped it, watching the activity. Yes, Pirates in Paradise was happening. A trio, dressed as pirates, was playing back at the small bandstand.

She smiled, closed her eyes for a moment and sipped her drink. She opened her eyes, feeling more relaxed and focused on taking in her environment.

The next table was filled with would-be pirates. It was fun to see the different ensembles. Women were fond of the corsets—which could be bought on Front Street or on the grounds of Fort Taylor. The skirts were in a multitude of colors and lengths. Despite the fact that Key West pirates most often appeared to be very authentic, a few women were in short, sexy costumes from well-known short, sexy costume manufacturers.

Some wore them better than others.

Everyone seemed to have a good time, though.

As she casually surveyed a group at a nearby table, a woman turned toward her.

She was a wench.

A well-done wench.

She was a pretty woman with strawberry-blond hair that was wild and curled down her back. She wore no hat of any kind. Her blouse, beneath her corset, was billowing and a shade of off-white that looked to be unbleached cotton. Her skirt was long, but with ties that could hike it up so that it wouldn't constantly sweep the ground.

She looked a bit tired, a bit worn.

And she looked right at Vanessa.

Vanessa smiled in return.

The woman's mouth moved as she spoke. She was

saying something to Vanessa. The beat to "Joy to the World" was pounding in the distance, and there was a great deal of conversation and laughter all around them.

And yet Vanessa thought that she heard her.

"It's not what it seems. Help me, I'll help you."

She was a stranger; it couldn't be what she was saying. Frowning, Vanessa rose, ready to walk over to the woman and introduce herself, prove that she was saying something else.

She stood. A heavyset man in a giant frock coat walked between the tables.

Vanessa knew that he didn't see her; politely, she gave way.

But as she headed for the other table, she stopped. The chair where the strawberry blonde had been sitting was empty.

Vanessa looked around; she had to be somewhere nearby.

She would just ask the people where their friend had gone. The chair she had vacated was quickly filled by the man in the giant frock coat. She approached the group, who looked at her with friendly smiles.

"Hello?" said one of the women, her smile open and generous.

"Hi, all. You look great," Vanessa told them.

"Thank you," the man in the giant frock coat said. He stood. "Care to join us? This is great for us—we're having the time of our lives. Jessy—that's my wife over there—teaches high school history, so for history buffs, this is just cool."

"Can we get you a drink?" another woman asked politely. "I'm Gena, Jessy's sister."

Introductions went around.

"No, thank you so much on the drink. Actually, I was looking for your friend. She was trying to tell me something, and I couldn't hear her," Vanessa explained.

"Our friend?" Jessy asked. "We're all here. Oh, I mean, we're meeting all kinds of new friends—this is like grown-up costume-party fun right along with a fabulous learning experience! Like minds and all that. But…our whole group is here."

"There was a woman…sitting here," Vanessa said. "A strawberry blonde."

They all stared at her.

"Oh!" Gena said suddenly. "I think I might know who you mean, but I'm afraid she isn't our friend."

"Who are you talking about?" her sister asked.

"Oh, she was around… I don't know who she is," Gena explained. "But she sure looked great! Kind of like a prostitute of old. I saw her, but she wasn't one of our friends."

"She was sitting right here," Vanessa said.

They all looked at her blankly, probably regretting that they had asked her over.

At least Gena had seen the woman, too.

She smiled and rose. "Ah, well, I must have been mistaken. Thank you—and have a wonderful time!"

They assured her that they would.

Vanessa turned around, returned quickly to her own table and set money on her check. She picked up her drink, drained it and left. She really needed to wash off the salt. She wanted to shower.

She wanted Sean to come back for her. She wanted to be with him.

"There's something wrong with it," Bartholomew said flatly, crossing his arms over his chest. "Can't you tell? Both Katie and Vanessa reacted to it—and you should trust Katie's very acute sixth sense!"

"Well, genius, you were around when it all happened. You tell me what's wrong with the trunk!" Sean said. He was aggravated. What was the matter with all of them? It was the find of a lifetime. He wanted to be excited about it. In fact, he realized, he'd been so damned excited, they hadn't filmed any of it, except when Vanessa had first found the damned thing.

"I was around at the time, yes. I didn't run in the same circles as Dona Isabella. I knew that she was a beauty—I saw her in the streets. She was surrounded by servants. She had a grand house. Her husband never came from Spain, and she controlled all his properties here. Now, I did meet Mad Miller, and in my mind, he wasn't so mad. And Kitty Cutlass…well, if she went crazy and killed a bunch of people, it was only because she was madly in love with Mad Miller. But this trunk… you found it away from the ship?"

"Not far from the debris field. It wasn't on coral—or in the remains of the ship. But I don't know what you think that means. Debris travels. It can spread out for miles—you know that." Sean paused and looked toward the dock. David and Jay were there; they had called Jaden and Ted, and the couple was coming with their truck to bring the chest back to their place of business. They would study and analyze it and figure out how to open it with the most integrity toward the chest itself and whatever just might be inside. Ted also knew a great deal more about reporting finds to the state and the legal filing that needed to be done.

"I don't like it, I don't like it, I don't like it," Bartholomew said.

"What's not to like about the possibility of a cache of historical coins?" Sean asked.

Bartholomew shook his head. "You don't need to make a fortune. You're a lucky man. You do what you love for a living, and you make a good living at it."

"That from a pirate," Sean moaned.

"Privateer," Bartholomew said irritably.

"You're right—I don't need a hoard of riches. It's not that, Bartholomew. I believe in learning about the past—I believe in museums. I believe in finding out the truth about what happened, and every little clue gives us something more on that end. What's bothering you? What do you feel?"

"I'm a ghost. I don't feel. Well, not really," Bartholomew said.

"You're certainly ready at all times to give an opinion."

"Actually, I do have a…oh, all right, I have a feeling. But I don't really understand it. Is it Pandora's box?" Bartholomew asked softly. "I don't think so. But it is something…that may change things. Does that make any sense?"

"It may change the way we look at the past," Sean suggested.

Bartholomew shrugged. "I think your friend onshore is already counting his riches," he said.

Jay stood with David, still gesturing, excited.

As Sean watched, he saw Ted and Jaden arrive with their truck. A fair group of tourists and locals had formed in the parking lot beyond the restaurant and the docks, all looking anxiously to see what was going on.

"They're here!" Jay called, spinning around to make sure that Sean had heard him.

Sean nodded. David and Jay returned to the boat, hopping onto the deck. Now that it was out of the water, the chest was manageable, just awkward, especially with three of them. But Ted came hurrying from the passenger side of the truck, leaving Jaden to maneuver it as close to the end of the dock as she could.

"Cool! Cool, oh my God! Cool!" Ted announced, jumping on the deck of the *Conch Fritter.* "Every man to an edge. We'll get her to our place. I can't wait, I can't wait. I want to keep it in a mist until we see how it will do out of the water. This is amazing. Cool, cool, cool!"

They hunkered down, the four of them. Between them, the weight didn't seem that bad. Sean estimated that whatever was actually inside the chest weighed between a hundred and a hundred and twenty pounds.

They moved easily enough with it—moving quickly. They got it onto a tarp Ted had stretched out over the bed of the truck.

"Sean, your find, you go with Ted," David said. "I'll hose down and secure the *Conch Fritter.* Then I'll head straight over."

"Sure. I'll help David," Jay said without enthusiasm.

David laughed. "No, go with Sean. Never mind—stay with me. We'll both get there faster."

"Yeah, let's do it!" Jay said.

Before Sean could crawl into the cab, Jay was racing back to the *Conch Fritter.*

Sean slid in next to Jaden, leaning forward between the driver and passenger seats. She gave him a kiss on the cheek and grinned. "You are on a roll!"

"Vanessa is on a roll. I have no idea how she found it," he said.

Ted climbed in and slammed the door. "Drive, woman, drive!" he said.

In a matter of minutes they were back at the shop. They didn't have to worry about weight or statistics; Ted and Jaden had carts and ramps, and they quickly had it down, still on a tarp, in one of their temperature-controlled rooms where the air was heavy with moisture.

Jaden and Ted looked over the trunk and discussed the best way to attack it. Obviously, they didn't have a key, and if they did, the lock was probably too degraded to open with it. They did, however, have a friend who was a locksmith.

He was called.

They were going to have to wait.

If they were going to have to wait, Sean wanted to bring Vanessa back.

"All right, I'm going to call David," he told Ted. "I'll run and grab a quick shower, stop by for Vanessa, and we'll all meet back here in an hour. How's that?"

"An hour?" Ted said. He loved the old, treasure and a mystery.

"Ted, we have to wait for the locksmith," Jaden reminded him.

"We could just need a little oil," Ted said hopefully. "You know what works wonders? Olive oil, not that I was really thinking about olive oil on this. WD-40."

"We'll do it right. Run on, Sean. I'll chill some champagne!" Jaden said happily.

Vanessa told herself that she wasn't afraid of her own room. She was. She didn't want to be alone anymore. She just wanted to go back to Sean's. She'd get the rest of her things later.

She showered fast, scrubbed her face, towel dried her body and her hair, dressed in an A-line knit dress and sandals and ran back down the stairs. The sun was setting, and it would be dark soon. She was glad she was on Duval Street—and that pirates and wenches and drunken frat boys were plying the sidewalk.

She headed into the little bar again but ordered a soda. She could still feel the warmth of the whiskey and didn't want to appear to be as inebriated as the frat boys. It was while she was there, idly sitting on one of the four stools in the place and watching the crowd, that she nearly choked and fell off.

She wasn't seeing any kind of an apparition.

No one dressed in pirate attire.

To her amazement, Zoe Cally and Barry Melkie, props, costumes, makeup and sound on their ill-fated film, stood in front of the Irish bar, drinking beer, deep in conversation.

She jumped up and ran across the street. "Hey!"

Zoe turned to look at her. She was a pretty girl, small and delicate, with large brown eyes and light hair. She smiled, and the smile was bright and welcoming.

"Vanessa!" Zoe cried with pleasure.

"Hey, you!" Barry said. He picked her up to give her a huge bear hug. He was a big man, about six foot three and well muscled, in his midthirties.

Barry set her down, grinning as broadly as Zoe. "This is unbelievable! How cool. We were just talking about you and Jay, and thinking that we should call you."

Zoe laughed. "We were talking because we read an advertisement. There are these guys planning a documentary on weird stuff in Key West and environs," Zoe said.

"I know, I know!" Vanessa said. She started to speak again, but Zoe interrupted her enthusiastically.

"Imagine our surprise when *they* called us!" Zoe said.

"Hey, let me buy you a beer, Vanessa," Barry said. "We'll explain."

Vanessa explained how she and Jay were already working with Sean and David. "Sean just called you and my Lord, you got here quickly!" she said.

Zoe giggled. "We were close. We got here last night."

"And guess what? I mean, I think this was all really supposed to happen. I have already called the kids," Barry said proudly.

"The kids?" Vanessa said.

"The kids—our kids, our grad students. You know,

both those bozos managed to graduate and get work, can you imagine?" Barry asked.

Vanessa felt her heart sinking. "You mean Bill Hinton and Jake Magnoli?"

"Well, of course, what other kids did we work with?" Zoe asked, confused.

"Vanessa, come on, let me buy you a beer," Barry said.

"I—I can't right now. I'm waiting for Sean," Vanessa explained.

"And Jay?" Zoe asked, grinning.

"And Jay," she said.

Zoe smiled. "I am so glad. I'm so glad we were already heading here. This is going to be so important, so cathartic, for all of us. We were there! We saw Travis and Georgia. Vanessa, you of all people must understand how we feel!"

"Of course," Vanessa agreed softly.

"This is an amazing opportunity. We've all been ripped apart by nightmares. We've all been like zombies since it happened," Barry said.

"And you're happy, right?" Zoe asked. "You want to work with us again? We were all giving our hearts to that project of Jay's!"

"Of course I'd want to work with you again. I came at Sean O'Hara full blast, but then Jay showed up, and I had no idea Jay was coming, but it *looked* as if I had planned a way to wheedle everyone in," Vanessa said. "I'm thrilled now that they're fascinated by the whole project and want all of us to be crew—and to be interviewed."

"Oh, so cool. So great," Zoe said.

"Do they know that you're here yet?" Vanessa asked.

"Don't think so," Barry said.

"We wanted to do some catching up and all. We've been on separate projects," Zoe said. "We've all been on separate projects, I guess."

"Yeah. Why don't you do some catching up with us?" Barry asked Vanessa.

"I can't right now. But Sean will be glad to hear that you're here in Key West and that you're gung-ho with their plan. Look, there's a bar called O'Hara's down on the other end of Duval. Show up down there around ten o'clock and I'll introduce you."

"All right, sounds great," Zoe said.

"Okay, later," Vanessa said.

Zoe slipped her arm through Barry's and they headed off, waving. Vanessa wandered back across the street to the patio restaurant.

She felt acutely uncomfortable, and she wasn't sure why. After all, Sean had said just last night that he'd ask Liam to get hold of the others.

She ordered another drink.

There were the key words. *Just last night.*

And they were already here.

Well, it made sense, really. She had desperately wanted to reach Sean and David when she had heard about their project and that they were hiring crew. So…

To her surprise, she had to call out to Sean to stop him from heading around her building to the stairs to the upper stories. He had showered and changed into jeans and a short-sleeved cotton shirt, so he had evidently been home.

"Hey!" he said, surprised to see her waiting for him at the bar.

"Did you open the trunk?" she asked anxiously.

"Not yet. Jaden and Ted wanted to call a locksmith, so I decided the group should get together for the grand opening. David and I are partners and Katie is his...well, those two will wind up married, and she's my sister. You discovered the chest. And Jay—well, as I said, *you* discovered the chest, and you brought Jay in."

"I didn't bring Jay in," Vanessa protested. She winced inwardly. She was aggravated. Sean kept speaking casually, but it was apparent that he *believed* that she had brought Jay in on the project. Jay was her friend, but she *hadn't* brought him in on the project. "I didn't mean that in a bad way," she said. "I've known him forever. He is a good friend. But I didn't bring him in."

"Well, it would hardly seem fair to exclude one person who was on the *Conch Fritter* today, would it?" Sean asked her.

Vanessa smiled. The more she was with him, the more she *liked* him. Which was good, of course. The sexual attraction was so strong, but really liking some-one was...important.

Did he really like *her? Would he do so if he knew that she saw strange things in the water? He knew about the nightmares, of course.*

But she had been through an enormous trauma. Any psychiatrist would say so.

"So let's head on over to the shop!" he said.

"All right," she said, but she pulled back a minute,

her hand on his arm. "Wait. Zoe Cally and Barry are here."

His eyebrows shot up with surprise. "Wow. I just asked Liam to try to reach them last night."

"They were coming here to ask you for work," she explained.

"So where are they now?" he asked. His eyes were narrowed, and he was staring at her strangely. Maybe he was just staring at her, and she felt guilty. She shouldn't feel guilty. She hadn't done anything.

"I told them to come to O'Hara's tonight," she said.

"All right. That was definitely fast. Let's go see about the trunk."

He slipped an arm around her shoulders. He frowned, and she turned, certain there was someone behind her.

But there was no one.

As they walked, the sun sank completely, and the majestic colors that had filled the western sky faded away. A misty gray followed the sunset, twilight, with darkness coming quickly.

She had never been afraid of the dark.

She was glad of Sean's arm around her shoulders.

And for how long would that be? she wondered. *He didn't seem to be the type of man who would want a woman long who was afraid of the dark, afraid of her own shadow, afraid of being alone in broad daylight.*

She was uncertain about her feelings regarding the trunk. She knew that Sean was excited, and she wanted to feel the same way. The odd thing was that she was now feeling more confused than ever. At first, she had felt that the object was…

Evil.

Now, she wasn't sure.

Object. Inorganic. Not good or evil!

They came around the corner and headed to the front door of the shop. Sean knocked, since it was closed for actual business, and Jaden came around to let them in. She didn't seem disturbed at all, but excited.

"They haven't opened the chest!" she said. "Ricky—he's our locksmith—he got the old lock open without destroying it. David and Ted are breaking the seal. Oh, lordy, lordy, this is exciting! I've never, never seen anything like it! Oh, and Ted called a maritime lawyer he knows, so the claim is being filed. It's amazing! Just the chest is amazing!"

Vanessa smiled. "Wonderful."

"Let's get in," Sean said. He looked at Vanessa. "Hey, I don't know your dousing secret, but it's unbelievable. The trunk, and its contents, are yours."

She shook her head. "Hey, I'm one of the crew. I'm grateful that we're doing this. I remain in your debt."

He touched her face. "No debt," he said softly. "No one forced my hand—I chose to set off in your direction, and I think it's going to be a great decision."

She nodded.

"Let's go!" Jaden urged.

They walked on through to the workroom. Ricky was working extremely carefully with crowbars, small hammers and chisels.

Katie was standing back with Jay. Her arms were crossed over her chest. She tried to offer a cheerful smile as they arrived.

"Oh, while they're finishing up, Vanessa, you haven't even seen the piece you found the other day!" Jaden said.

She went over to a wall safe and spun the lock. She brought out a piece set in a bed of velvet and brought it to Vanessa to show it to her.

Vanessa smiled and looked.

It was the mermaid. The mermaid of which she had bought a copy the other day, the pendant that had hung around the neck of Dona Isabella.

This one was, however, far more ornate. Emeralds blazed from the eyes, rubies adorned her scales. The mermaid was large and heavy, and the gold in the workmanship was rich and deep.

"Here," Jaden said.

"Oh, I don't really want to touch it," Vanessa said. "Sticky fingers—body oils, whatever!" she explained quickly. "Funny thing—I purchased a copy from one of the pirate vendors the other day, and I saw the picture of Dona Isabella wearing the pendant."

"It really is a museum piece," Jaden said.

They were all startled by a sudden jerking sound—and a very strange sound, an expulsion of air as soft as a sigh.

Ricky moved back.

A mist of time escaped the trunk, was visible for a split second, and then evaporated into the air.

"Think there might have been a dangerous buildup of gas?" Ted asked. "Wow, sorry, a little late for me to think of that."

"Crank up the air purifiers," Sean suggested. "But I don't think anything lethal just escaped."

"We can lift the lid," David said.

"Go for it," Sean said.

"Vanessa?" David said, looking at her. He smiled. "Your discovery."

She shook her head. "You and Sean are leading the adventure."

Sean stepped forward and shrugged at David.

They each reached for a side of the lid. And lifted.

They were both dead silent, staring downward into the chest.

"Well, well, come on, what is it?" Ted demanded.

Still, neither man moved. Ted went rushing over and looked down, as well. "Holy shit!" he exclaimed—his voice filled with horror, not wonder.

"What?" Katie asked weakly.

Jay walked up next. He clapped his hand over his mouth and turned away.

Vanessa knew from Jay's reaction that it was bad. She steeled herself and walked forward and looked down into a chest.

At first she didn't realize what she was seeing.

And then she did.

The chest contained the oddly mummified and distorted remains of a human body. The clothing remained; the head was at an awkward angle. A hat still sat upon a skeletal head. The skin was dark and stretched over the frame, and the fabric of the clothing was stained, probably by the body fluids that had oozed from the corpse soon after death.

The eye sockets were empty.

And yet they seemed to stare and tear into Vanessa's heart.

All she could remember at that moment were Sean's earlier words.

The trunk, and its contents, are yours.

9

"It's Dona Isabella," Marty said knowingly.

"It can't be Dona Isabella. She wasn't killed until the pirates reached Haunt Island," David said. "According to legend, at any rate. Although, frankly, everything about what happened is legend—after the pirate ship attacked the *Santa Geneva*."

"We'll have to wait, and that's all there is to it—hope that the forensic anthropologist can help us," Sean said.

"It wasn't a treasure," Jay said mournfully.

"If the body sheds light on history, the find is a treasure," Sean said.

They were gathered at O'Hara's. The trunk and body were locked in the workroom at the shop, and they were all lined up at the bar.

Vanessa was next to Sean. He had worried about her at first—neither she nor Katie had seemed thrilled about the discovery from the start. But oddly enough, once she had seen what was in the trunk, she had seemed more relaxed. Maybe she had somehow intuited that they weren't going to bring in a stash of silver and gold, and maybe she felt that, this way, eventually, Dona Isabella would get the funeral she deserved—belatedly—and that there would be some kind of finality for someone, at least.

She had been fine in the showroom, and fine on the walk here. She had applauded and laughed with the rest of them when they had come in to the sounds of a singer doing a version of a Denis Leary number that was tawdry to say the least, but very well done.

Now, at the bar, she was nervously drinking a Scottish single-malt whiskey.

"Maybe the legend has been all wrong—maybe Dona Isabella survived the massacre and was later murdered and tossed over the remains of the *Santa Geneva,*" Jay suggested.

Sean looked at Vanessa. She didn't seem to be listening.

"Maybe it's not Dona Isabella, but Jim Morrison of the Doors," he said, touching Vanessa's hand.

She started, and looked at him. "Well, of course, that's a theory," she said.

He smiled. "A penny for your thoughts. A gold cob, rather," he said.

She arched a brow, opened her mouth and shut it. She tried to speak again. Before she could, Jay exclaimed, "Why, as I live and breathe. Hail, hail, the gang's all here!"

Sean spun around on his stool. Four people had just come into O'Hara's. There was a tiny, pretty woman; a tall, broad-shouldered and all-around big man; and two more men who appeared to be in their early twenties, average in height and size, both with sun-bleached brown hair.

"Your crew?" Sean asked Vanessa.

She nodded. "Zoe Cally, Barry Melkie, Bill Hinton and Jake Magnoli. Jake is taller and tends to slouch, and he's no relation to Bill, though they do look kind of like two peas in a pod, in a way. Barry is the really tall guy, and Zoe is the woman. Obviously."

"I didn't know that they were all here," he said.

"Neither did I. But Zoe and Barry told me earlier that they'd gotten hold of the kids."

He knew the names. He'd looked up what he could find on the film crew and the events that had occurred around the filming. She had mentioned the names as well, telling him what she had seen and experienced the night of the murders.

"I had no idea that Bill and Jake were already here," Vanessa added. "They had heard about your documentary, too. Before you had Liam find them all and call them, they all planned to come and try to get work with you."

Sean was surprised to feel irritated.

This was so…pat.

He'd thought they'd have to hunt the crew down. He looked over at Vanessa, and he wondered if he hadn't fallen into what she wanted as easily as any idiot.

Jay was by David. He looked stunned, and he stared at Vanessa. "Hey, wait, I didn't even know those guys were in Key West," he protested.

"Vanessa did," he said.

There must have been something in his voice that accused her—or else she felt guilty about the situation.

Because she had planned it all this way from the

beginning, and he had walked into it just the way she had intended all along?

It was probably a good thing that he'd never wanted to be an actor.

His face apparently gave away his thoughts. Vanessa was up in an instant, but she didn't turn on him first. She looked at Jay, and then at him.

"Damn you, Jay, don't you understand? They think it was set up that you showed up down here, too." She stood tall and angry, and tossed a length of her hair over her shoulder as she spoke. "What? Are you all suddenly the KGB or the CIA? Why does something have to be a setup? Why isn't it obvious to you all that something absolutely horrible happened? Two people were murdered. Maybe three. Two people we knew well—we'd been working with them for weeks. *We* found them, *we* saw them dead in the sand. Is it so odd that, hearing about your project, this group has all found its way to you?"

David was staring at Vanessa, surprised. He turned to Sean. "I thought you had Liam try to reach the rest of the crew."

"I did," he said.

Vanessa flushed. She winced. "I don't know how everyone managed to be here so quickly. I'm sorry. I... Oh, never mind. It is going to work out best this way."

By then, the group was coming their way, having seen Vanessa and Jay. Zoe Cally came forward with a huge, trusting smile.

As if she hadn't any inkling they might not be wanted.

"There are large tables out back in the patio area.

We'll head out there," Sean said. "We'll go talk where we can hear."

A would-be soprano was belting out a number from *Phantom* that was far out of her range and it seemed to him to be nothing more than a very loud screech at the moment.

He headed out back, waving to the others to follow him.

Clarinda, Jamie's favorite server and Katie's close friend, stopped him as he headed out. "Sean, should I set you all up out there? Do you want dinner and drinks, and should I be steering other people away?"

He paused, feeling a break in his temper at last. "Yeah, thanks, Clarinda, that would be great." Come to think of it, they hadn't eaten.

The contents of the chest had made them all forget the fact that they hadn't had dinner.

She smiled sympathetically and moved on; Clarinda would have known, from Katie, what they had discovered in their "treasure" find.

He walked on out to the patio. It was typical Key West, lots of shrubs and trees surrounding Cuban tile flooring and wooden tables, some round, some square, some oblong. Umbrellas over the tables shaded them from heat during the day and were enough shelter against rain when it was light. He stood by the table, waiting.

The group began to trail out, Vanessa in the lead. Once they could hear, she began the introductions.

There was a large crowd outside by then, so it seemed. Vanessa, Jay and the film crew, himself, David, Jaden and Ted. Jaden and Ted were quiet, watching, as if they were suddenly part of an unexpected reality TV show.

Vanessa was quiet after the introductions, taking a seat at one of the long, oblong tables.

"You all know what we're planning on doing, right?" Sean asked.

"Yes!" Barry said. "It's great. We're so pleased. We were all going to ask you guys for work anyway, and then we talked to your cousin, Liam, and he explained that you wanted those of us who were involved to talk about what happened on camera. But we can help you enormously in other ways," he said.

"Great," Sean said. "I'm sure you all work well together. And that's great. But what we really want is to get each one's perspective of what went on at Haunt Island."

Zoe began speaking quickly. "We're so grateful for this opportunity."

Clarinda came out in the midst of it all.

"Okay, guys, let me get your orders in. The place is getting busy," she said.

Beer seemed to be the main order for the night, and O'Hara's offered a vast variety. There was confusion as people took seats so that she could take food orders.

Sean wound up at the head of the table at one end, David at the other. They did resemble some kind of strange patriarchs in a ragtag family.

"We've already started filming," Jay told the newcomers excitedly. "And guess what? Vanessa found a corpse!"

"A corpse?" Zoe demanded, staring down the table at Vanessa.

"We thought we had a treasure chest. It was a corpse," Vanessa said.

"Well, it was a chest—it just wasn't filled with treasure," Jay said. "It held a corpse. But you know what? We think it might be Dona Isabella."

"We don't know anything yet," Jaden protested softly. She joined the discussion with enthusiasm. "We don't know anything, really, but the preservation is remarkable. Somehow, when the poor woman was murdered and stuffed in the chest, she became mummified. The chest was sealed, as if…as if…oh, I don't know. Maybe someone felt remorse and wanted to see that she was preserved in her tomb in the sea. It's eerie. She's all there…clothes and all, and she's at an strange angle… neck broken, at least that's what it looks like."

"Dona Isabella? I thought she died during the massacre on Haunt Island, or if not, when the pirate ship went down southwest of the Bahamas," Zoe said.

"Everything about Mad Miller, Kitty Cutlass and Dona Isabella is pure speculation, really," Vanessa said. "There were one or two survivors who actually made it to shore when the *Santa Geneva* went down. They were the ones who told of the pirate attack. The *Santa Geneva* was accosted, there was some kind of communication between Mad Miller and her captain, and then the *Santa Geneva* was fired upon. Before she sank, the pirates boarded, cutting down the crew and kidnapping Dona Isabella. We know, too, that there was a massacre on Haunt Island, because the Bahamians found the remains. They knew that the pirate ship had come there, and that it had sailed. We know that it went down in a hurricane, because it was seen by an American ship when that ship barely survived the same storm. In fact, sailors swore that the pirate ship went down when a massive burst of fire flared in the sky. If the Bermuda Triangle had been labeled the Bermuda Triangle back then, it might have taken the blame. They called it an act of God. At least they didn't think that aliens came down and swept up the pirate ship."

Zoe giggled. "Well, if aliens came down, they missed poor Dona Isabella's treasure-chest tomb. Hey, I know debris travels, but not that far. The *Santa Geneva* went down off Key West, and the pirate ship—however it went!—perished off of South Bimini and Haunt Island. So the story is all wrong somewhere along the line."

"If that *is* Dona Isabella," Vanessa said.

Jay laughed, pretended a shiver and let out an "Oooooh! Well, of course, it has to be Dona Isabella. And her evil is rising—that's why you two were afraid of the chest."

"I wasn't afraid of the chest," Vanessa said, her tone aggravated.

"Right," Jay said with a shrug.

Food came. The conversation changed to where everyone was staying on the island—Bill and Jake had taken rooms at the Banyan while Barry and Zoe were in the guesthouses on Duval, a couple blocks down from where Vanessa was staying.

Everyone talked about different projects. Barry admitted that he had looked up information on David and Sean and been impressed with their separate bodies of work. The evening wore on, then Jaden and Ted called it a night, promising to call Sean and David the minute they heard from Tara Aislinn, the woman who was coming down from the University of Florida, the forensic anthropologist they had reached who was fascinated by the find and delighted to come down and examine the body in the chest.

Before the group broke up, Sean said, "David and I are going to do some planning tomorrow. We'll call you when we're set with the decision on when to leave."

Bill and Zoe decided to roam Duval and Barry went back to his room. Jay asked Vanessa if she wanted a walk down the street; he was tired and leaving. To Sean's surprise, she stood and agreed.

David and Sean stood, as well. Vanessa came around the table and gave David a kiss on the cheek. As she neared him, Sean saw that her eyes were sharp.

He stopped her and asked, "What's that look for?"

She shook her head and said softly, "You think that I set this up. You still say that I brought Jay in all the time, and I saw how suspicious you were earlier."

"Admit it, Vanessa. They were all here already."

"Admit it?" she inquired, her voice rising.

"Admit that…it all looks suspicious."

"Whatever it looks like, it isn't. And I guess I want more faith. You stared at me tonight as if you were suddenly certain that I'd planned the entire thing, our old crew taking over your project."

"That's not true," he said. "Yes, it's strange, but—"

"You're a liar."

"We can talk," he said.

She shook her head. "No. Not tonight. I need some time. We can talk tomorrow. Tonight, well, tonight I need to take a look at everything that's gone on."

He was hurt, angry—and baffled, still feeling himself

to be the injured party. He was doing exactly what she wanted.

But he wasn't ready to throw it all over, and he wasn't thinking about the project.

Vanessa...

The ego in him wanted to shrug and tell her that it wouldn't be necessary to talk about anything intimate, if those were her feelings.

But he realized, too, that she must certainly have her own pride.

And he knew, too, that "talking tomorrow" was better than a real break. He'd give her the space she needed.

He was startled as she walked on by him, waiting for Jay. She was truly upset.

Jay gave David a cheery good-night and shook Sean's hand. "What a day, eh?"

"Yeah, what a day."

Jay hesitated. "Honest to God, this wasn't any kind of a setup."

"I never said that it was," Sean told him.

Jay shrugged. "I saw the way that you looked at Vanessa."

Lord. Were his suspicions—his thoughts—really that apparent? Even Jay had read his expression.

"You're mistaken," he lied.

Jay shrugged.

Vanessa was waiting for Jay on the sidewalk. He joined her, and Sean watched as they started north on Duval together.

"Well, that was interesting," David commented.

"I'm sorry—doesn't it feel a bit weird to you? First

Vanessa shows up, pitching her slant to our project, then Jay. Then we think that it might make for a really interesting piece and put out a call to find the rest of the crew, and almost *instantaneously* they all show up?"

"Yes and no," David said. He shrugged. "Maybe they did all hear about it and contacted one another. I don't find it all that odd if they did. Trust me, I know. Events can change your life and haunt you day after day."

David Beckett had once stood accused of murder—if not by law, in the minds of many people who had heard what had happened.

Sean let out a long breath.

Back then, he and David had been friends. Close friends. And he hadn't known what to believe. All he had known was that he had wanted to get away from home, and for years and years he had traveled, staying mainly away from home. Knowing the truth about the past—even though he had not been directly involved, like David—*had* changed everything.

And it was true, too, that he had returned home in all haste when he had heard that David Beckett was here. And then he had been glad as hell, because he had found that David and his sister had become a duo.

"Honestly, I don't care one way or another," David said. "Here's what I care about—Liam doing background checks on them, finding out their work schedules—or with the young ones, their graduation status—whether they've really got the credentials they claim, all that. Parking tickets are okay—I get enough of those myself. But nothing else."

Sean shook his head. "I don't know."

"Yes, you do. You know that you're more intrigued

by this now than ever," David said. "And hell, Vanessa Loren is like a damned dousing rod. One day, a pendant. The next, a chest. With a body. Let's face it, we're in it now."

"Have you talked to Marty? And Jamie? Are they in?"

"They were in from the beginning, too. I say we get Liam on the background checks and plan to head out soon. I'll warn Katie."

"All right," Sean said.

She had just walked away.

Clarinda came out to finish clearing the table. "Hey, this is really getting wild, huh? All these people—and a body!" She shivered, placing empty glasses on her tray.

"It's a very old body, Clarinda," Sean said.

Katie came out the back door and strode toward them. Sean and David had taken their chairs again—at opposite ends of the long oblong table.

"Well. I guess you two scared everyone off," she said. She frowned and looked at Sean. "Where's Vanessa?"

"She went to her room."

Katie's brows shot up. "What did you do to her?"

"Not a thing. She chose to go home," he said, irritated. He didn't feel like explaining himself to his sister. Somewhere in his mind, he recognized the double standard—he had felt like a pit bull when he had first found out about David and Katie.

"You must have done something," Katie persisted.

He stood. "Katie, you and Jamie set me up with her—under false pretenses."

"What?"

"You didn't mention that she was a friend of yours—you had Jamie call me in to talk to her, and you knew all along what she wanted," she said.

"Hey, hey, let's not have a sibling war here," David protested.

"No war," Sean said. "All I know is that Key West is suddenly hosting a whole crew of people—who, incidentally, were all on that island when the murders happened—and it all started with your friend, Miss Loren, and now she's mad at me for what I consider a perfectly reasonable question about how it all came to happen!"

"You probably accused her—basically—of being a liar," Katie said.

"I did not," he said.

"Then you implied that she was a liar."

"Who are you related to here?" Sean demanded. "Never mind. I'm going to go and get some sleep. We'll talk in the morning. Oh—Katie, sign the bill to me, will you, please. And make sure that you—"

"Take care of Clarinda. Of course."

"Good night," he managed, waving to the two of them.

As he walked the back way to his house, he wondered if he had been unreasonable.

But there was something everyone did seem to be forgetting.

Those six people had been on Haunt Island when Georgia and Travis had been murdered, decapitated and chopped into pieces.

Filming a horror movie that had turned very real.

* * *

Jay was cheerful as they walked. "You seem to have some kind of a regular homing beacon for finding things on that wreck. Wonder who the body is. Think it could really be Dona Isabella?"

"I don't know. And I don't care right now. I'm exhausted." They had reached Vanessa's inn. She gave him a hug and a kiss on the cheek. "We'll talk tomorrow, all right?"

"Okay, kid. Sleep well." He started away and turned back. "Hey, Nessa."

"Yeah?"

"Love you, kid. As a friend, you know."

She laughed. "Love you, too. Good night."

Upstairs, Vanessa was glad that her room was on Duval, and that she could hear the faint sounds of music, laughter and conversation. She turned on the lights, wondering if she had done the right thing or not. She cared about Sean, she was attracted to him in a way she might never have been to anyone before, but he had looked at her with suspicion when all four of the others had walked in.

And he had been the one to say that he wanted them all!

Even if they hadn't known each other long, they had known each other *well,* and it was disturbing to her to know someone that well and not be trusted by him.

They might have gotten together too heavily and too fast. They needed the night apart.

And she was right; she was not apologizing for what she didn't do.

That didn't change the fact that her room seemed

impersonal and cold. Nor that she felt incredibly alone, which didn't usually happen to her. Normally, she liked her own company.

She couldn't change things, and she was exhausted. She changed into a giant T-shirt, scrubbed her face and teeth and headed to bed.

She turned off the lights and tried to listen to the revelry from Duval Street.

It wasn't enough.

She turned on MTV—music and videos. The two just might lull her to sleep.

She did fall asleep. And for a while, it was wonderful.

And then the dreams came again.

There was Georgia Dare's head and sand.

Georgia's lips were moving. She was talking.

"Oh, please! Listen. If you'll just pay attention! You know now that I wasn't being silly and hysterical and there were no jokes being played!"

One of Georgia's disarticulated arms moved in the sand; she waved her well-manicured fingers in the air.

"Listen…pay attention, oh, please, Vanessa, you can do it!"

"Please!" Travis begged, his mouth moving. He moaned as his head rolled in the sand.

"There's nothing I can do!" Vanessa protested.

She felt as if she were in a wind tunnel then, being sucked away from them. She was out on the sea, and then she was in the water, and she had a camera in her hand.

The figurehead appeared before her. It seemed that it,

too, had arms, and that the head was real and the entire thing was an animate object—a person.

She saw the face on it that she had always seen.

That of Dona Isabella.

The figurehead was smiling and beckoning to her.

She protested, speaking, or telling the figurehead how she felt in her mind, she wasn't even sure.

"No. I don't want to find more bodies."

"But you want the truth," the figurehead said to her.

"There should be justice."

Suddenly, the image of the face began to change. It morphed, and it seemed that its cheeks struggled to stay cheeks.

Brows became higher and more arched and changed again.

The nose and mouth went through transformations.

The figurehead had changed. It held a different face. But she knew that face, too.

She had seen it that afternoon. She had seen it on the woman who had tried to talk to her. The pirate woman who had been sitting at the table on the patio.

The woman who had disappeared.

"Stop, please, stop, you're being led, you must take care, you don't understand the innocent!" the figurehead told her.

Then she thought she heard a terrible laughter.

"I'm trying to help you! I have helped you. Listen… listen…listen…your friends have pleaded with you, you must listen. Once you didn't pay heed."

The face on the figurehead began to morph again.

Then she saw…

The horrible, mummified, darkened, distorted and decaying face of the woman they had found in the sunken chest.

10

"Here's another one," David said. He tapped on his computer screen. "Another incident that might prove that what happened to the film crew wasn't so bizarre. Bring up the *Herald,* December twentieth, last year."

Sean typed in the key words and waited for Google to bring up the paper and the date, and glanced over at David. They were working together at the Beckett mansion, computers at opposite ends of the table, maps and charts spread out between them.

"Any particular page?"

"Front page. You can't miss it."

David's eyes quickly scanned the bold-type headline. "Modern-Day Pirates at Work? Islanders Claim Devil's Play."

"Ah, I see," Sean said. He read the article aloud.

> "On December tenth, a charter boat, the *Delphi,* captained by Tom Essling, an experienced seaman, USN, disappeared while on route to the Bahamas. Captain Essling left Fort Lauderdale, Florida, on December tenth with his first mate and wife of thirty years, Sharon Biddle Essling, and

four passengers for a cruise down the Keys due south and southwest, with stops at Islamorada and Key West. As per plan, Captain Essling docked in Key West for a two-day stay, and began his journey east and across the Straits of Florida, an area that's also known as the New Bahama Channel, the body of water that connects the Gulf of Mexico to the Atlantic and continues eastward, beginning the Gulf Stream and separating Florida and the Keys from the Bahamas, the Great Bahama and Little Bahama banks. The length of the straits extends for more than three hundred miles and enters through the region known as the Bermuda Triangle. The width is 60 miles in areas and approximately 100 in others. The greatest depth of the channel has been sounded at 6,000 feet.

"On December 18, all contact with the charter boat was lost soon after the *Delphi* sailed due east of Miami, approaching the southern Bahamas. Relatives were concerned because the captain excused himself in the middle of a phone call and never came back on. None aboard answered cell phones, and radio contact could not be made. American Coast Guard and Bahamian officials began a search that continued with daybreak. Many speculate that the Bermuda Triangle has taken more victims, while others rationalize that traffic has been heavy through the straits since the beginning of the passage of Spanish treasure fleets, has always been heavy, naturally accounting for more misfortune. Until early in the nineteenth century, the region was constantly plagued by pirates, a rising concern among seamen and carriers as piracy resurges in contemporary times, even within such heavily traveled waters."

Sean glanced at the sea chart spread out on the table between them. He stood, glancing at his computer, checking latitude and longitude on the charter ship's last known location.

"This disappearance—last contact with the boat was right about where the Mad Miller's pirate ship went down, right where the pirates met their demise," Sean told David.

"Interesting. I thought I had another, but they caught the culprits. Idiots pirated another charter boat and threw the crew overboard. They wanted to hijack it to Cuba. They didn't realize it needed gas," David said, shaking his head.

"Maybe," Bartholomew mused, twirling a lock of ghostly hair—great hair at that—as he leaned against the table, "there is something to be said for the Bermuda Triangle. Maybe it emits…evil," he suggested. "Evil creates a vortex, and men become mad in that vortex, and begin to rip one another asunder."

"Bartholomew, Mad Miller's ship went down in a storm," Sean reminded him.

"I believe that something happens in that area," David said. "But I don't think it's evil oozing out of the earth. There is a scientific explanation."

Bartholomew studied his fingers and said dryly, "Yes, of course. And I'm here—through the effects of man's science. You see me, some people don't. Ah! There's a genetic trait that allows certain eyes to pick out roving ectoplasm in the air!"

Sean sat back in chair, nearly grinning. "Bartholomew, you may have something there. It is possible that some people are born with something within their genes that we haven't discovered as yet."

Bartholomew threw his hands into the air. "Something that can be developed? Such as a talent? My friend, ye of little faith, who could not see or hear me for the longest time? Ah, trust is something that cannot be touched, either, and you needed proof rather than trust your own sister for a very long time. Everything is not science, indeed, it is not, my ever wary and doubting friend. Take faith—faith is belief in the unseen. If you have any kind of faith, you already believe in the unseen. We all believe in good—and trust me, I believe in the evil that lies in the hearts of mankind! Anyway, here's what throws me. I knew Kitty Cutlass, and I knew Mad Miller, and yes, Mad Miller turned to piracy, but the legend that has come down about him is pure bunk—which I've told you. If he slaughtered men in the water and murdered Dona Isabella in a rage, it would be a surprise to me. And Kitty! The most naive harlot I ever did come across!"

"Naive harlots can be jealous and vengeful," Sean commented.

"True, maybe," Bartholomew said.

"You saw the chest—tell me something, Bartholomew. Was that Dona Isabella? You may not have known her as an acquaintance or even a friend, but you saw her around town," Sean said.

"We did not socialize," Bartholomew said. "I spent

my time with the English and Americans, while Dona Isabella was the elite of the remaining Spanish society. But yes, I saw her."

"So?"

"So?" Bartholomew shuddered. "I didn't stare into the chest, my good fellow! That was a horrendous sight, what was once life…so heinously destroyed and mangled and…ghastly! And if I had stared and stared, the way that the decay had set in and the bones had mummified and the fabric of the clothing had clotted with blood and ooze…I'd not have recognized my own dear mother!"

"Have you heard any more from Jaden and Ted?" David asked Sean. "When is the forensic anthropologist due?"

"Later today, I believe," Sean said. "I talked to Ted earlier—a Dr. Tara Aislinn is due in with her colleague, Dr. Latham. I believe they're planning on bringing the body back to a lab in Gainesville. They have the facilities for all the testing they want to do. They're extremely excited, they can find out about dental hygiene, diet, health, parasites—all manner of information."

"You saw today's paper?" he asked Sean.

Sean nodded.

Neither of them had accepted an interview, and to Sean's knowledge, neither had Katie, Jay or Vanessa. But it had been apparent yesterday that they had made a discovery, and there was an article stating that local divers had found a historical artifact and the object was under investigation now.

That afternoon, one of them would take an interview

so that the concept that they were "treasure hunting" would not be taken out of context.

David's cell phone rang and he picked it up. He listened for a moment and looked at Sean, nodding.

He hung up.

"That was Liam. They checked out—the film crew, that is. The two grad students, Bill and Jake. And Barry Melkie has worked for several major motion-picture companies, and Zoe, though not as well-known, has certainly had an excellent employment record. There's not so much as a night in jail, a dismissed charge or a single mark."

"They're just seeking truth," Bartholomew said.

Sean started to speak, but he could have sworn that he heard Bartholomew mutter, "Dumb ass!" just beneath his breath.

"What was that?" he demanded.

"Pardon?" Bartholomew said innocently.

"You just called me a dumb ass!"

"Did I? I didn't mean to speak aloud, which, sadly, in most cases, with most people, I actually don't," Bartholomew said.

Sean rose and approached Bartholomew. "Is it possible you could go haunt someone else for a while?"

"Of course. There seems nothing I can do about the fact that you—behave like a dumb ass."

Sean let out a groan of aggravation. "Because?"

"That young woman did nothing to you."

"Wow, excuse me. Are you missing the fact that two people were heinously killed?"

Bartholomew looked away. "Yes, there is that. But you know that she had nothing to do with that."

"And how do I know that? Maybe she was the

murderer, maybe Jay is a maniacal killer—maybe one of the others," Sean said.

"They were there," David agreed.

"But do you really believe that bringing them all in was some kind of a setup?" Bartholomew said. "If so, you are certainly thinking and behaving as—a dumb ass."

"Bartholomew—" Sean began.

"Yes, yes, fine! Remember, my friends, you may need me. But for now, I'll go haunt someone else!" Bartholomew responded, aggravated. Shoulders high, posture proud, he strode through the room—and through the front door.

"They check out," David said to Sean, when Bartholomew was gone. "So what do you want to do?"

"Two boats," Sean said. "Which is what we've always planned, *Conch Fritter* and Jamie's *Claddagh*. Jamie can captain his own boat, and he's a hell of a dive master. Katie and you with Jamie, and I'll take Ted and Jaden, and we'll bring Marty along, as long as he's still interested, and, of course, Liam. Four of us on each boat. We'll split up the six from the original trip."

"You think that they were involved in a conspiracy—all of them—to kill their leading couple and leave them outrageously staged in the sand?"

"No. But two people died. Somebody killed them."

David shook his head. "There have been a lot of disappearances and bad things happening out in that area—we've just dug up reports of several that occurred in the last couple of years. And it's not like there's one bad guy out there. There are probably a lot of less than honest people plying a pirating trade in the straits. Drug runners, people who smuggle cargo, taking them for whatever they might have, to get them into the United States. Whoever committed the crimes may be long gone, killing people in the streets of Venezuela for all we know."

"Those two weren't just murdered," Sean argued. "They were displayed. They were displayed in a way that played into the movie being made." He hesitated. "As if someone didn't want the movie made? God knows—but whatever did or didn't happen, I think we need to keep the original six split up."

"Agreed," David said. "So when do you want to head out?"

"Day after tomorrow. I want to revise the original shooting schedule and make sure that we have both boats stocked. And—" he hesitated and shrugged "—I want to spend some time at the shooting range with Liam—it's been a long time since I shot at something with anything other than a camera."

"You really think we'll come across trouble?" David asked.

"I really want to be prepared—hell, in the last few years, from what we've seen, too many charters and pleasure boats have been lost. Even without what happened with the film crew, I think it might have been a nice wake-up call to be ready—for anything," Sean said.

His cell started ringing. He picked it up. Liam was on the line.

"Is David with you?" Liam asked.

"Yes."

"Anyone else?"

"No," Sean said.

"Put the phone on speaker, will you, please?"

He did so.

"I don't know if this means anything or not," Liam said. "But I have a report on my desk about another boat that has disappeared—with all four aboard. She's called the *Happy-Me.* She's a thirty-footer that can sleep six, top-of-the-line radio, sonar, all that. She was owned by a retired couple, Jenny and Mark Houghton, who were traveling with another couple, Dale and Gabby Johnson. They were headed out for a couple of weeks, stopping different places. They had notified the Bahamian authorities that they'd be visiting a few different ports in the Bahamas."

"How long have they been missing?" Sean asked.

"A couple of days," Liam told him.

"There's still the possibility that they're fine, that they had trouble, that they're on an island, waiting for a search party," David said.

"There's the possibility. But the couples' children have been calling every law-enforcement agency in the area. One of the daughters says she knows that her parents are dead. They *never* failed to check in," Liam told them.

"Are there search parties out there?" Sean asked.

"Of course," Liam said. "Coast Guard, Bahamians, volunteer rescue societies. But there's been no sight of the boat or any survivors. Of course, it might have no connection with Haunt Island as well, *but* Haunt Island was on their agenda."

"Thanks, Liam," Sean said. "We were just reading

about another disappearance in the area. A boat called the *Delphi*."

"The *Delphi* went missing a year ago," Liam said. "So, two years ago, the film crew is attacked. Last year around the same time, a boat goes missing. And now another."

"There have been other boats that have vanished," David pointed out.

"Right. But these two went down somewhere near Haunt Island," Sean said.

"If this one is down—we don't actually know that yet," Liam said.

Sean was thoughtful.

"So?" Liam asked.

Sean looked at David. "So I say that we really have to be prepared for anything and keep our eyes open at all times."

"Did you hear anything about the body in the chest yet?" Zoe asked Vanessa.

Vanessa shook her head. She and Zoe were down by Fort Zachary Taylor, cruising through the many booths the vendors had set up near the "pirate" campgrounds.

"Not yet. I believe that the person Jaden contacted is on the way down but is planning on bringing the body back to a lab at the university," she said. They were at a booth that displayed books—some old rare, and very expensive, and some copies—sea charts and maps. One large map that included the Gulf of Mexico, Caribbean ports, Florida and the Bahamas was hung on a supporting beam of the booth. It was large and glass-encased, and Zoe paused, looking at it and shivering. "I think I'm crazy myself!" she said. She followed a path from Key West, up around the islands to Miami, and then across to Bimini. "That's it—that's our route. Look at all the little red crosses on it! Those are all ships that have gone down or disappeared over the last decades—and centuries! I think I'm crazy, wanting to do this. No, I have to do this. I can't wait to actually sleep again."

Vanessa was silent. *Yes, she still had to do this, too. But now…she felt a strange numbness. She didn't date easily; she didn't fall for people…she wasn't good at accepting a casual drink. She had never gone out and slept with a man on a first, second, or even third date. But she had felt something about Sean, as if there were something real and deep that made intimacy heady and natural, and something that should have…*

Should have been allowed to mature into more. She felt ridiculously empty and alone, and something inside her ached, and she still felt that she had to hold the distance, because it was wrong not to be trusted, and worse to want someone so badly that she might not care….

She realized she was staring blankly at the chart, lost in her thoughts, which had nothing to do with shipwrecks, when she heard her name called.

"Vanessa!"

She turned around to see that Katie was hurrying toward her through the crowd.

Katie—dressed up in pirate attire that appeared authentic and still attractive. She wasn't dressed as a wench—no heaving bosom above a low-cut shirt and corset—but more like a man, in breeches, buckled boots, a poet's shirt and frock coat, and an over-the-shoulder holster that carried several pistols and ammunition, while the broad leather belt wrapped around her hips held a sailor's cutlass.

Vanessa laughed, seeing her. "Wow! You look great. What's up?"

"I need you. Hey, Zoe, how are you?" she asked, acknowledging Zoe.

"Fine, thanks. And you do look great. I costume people, and I couldn't have done better," Zoe said.

Katie rolled her eyes. "This is Pirates in Paradise. You have avid historians around here. Vanessa, Marty sent me out to ask you to come and be a part of the program."

"What?" Vanessa said. "Katie, I don't know anything about what they're doing, I'd be a bump on the log, and it would just be..."

"Oh, don't be silly, Vanessa!" Zoe said, enthused. "Come on, you've played a monster, a corpse and...and a body a zillion times. Why not find out about it?"

"Come on!" Katie drew her along. Vanessa did her best to lag. She liked being behind a camera. She loved being the eye that found the visions.

But Katie was determined. They came to Marty's booth, and he greeted her with a huge kiss and was pleased to meet Zoe. "It's the trial—just respond as you would if you'd been arrested," Marty said. "Ah, come now, I did tell you girls that I might need some help."

"Whose trial? If it's Anne Bonny and Mary Reid, I don't know enough of the history—"

Marty shook his head. "Look, everyone knows that a body was found, and everyone knows that Sean and David and crew are about to set off to explore the Mad Miller legend. It's a mock trial, and you're going to be

Kitty Cutlass—and you just respond however you feel you should. It's based on the premise that Kitty Cutlass was saved."

"But Katie is a performer—she'd make a far better Kitty Cutlass," Vanessa argued.

"I'm the narrator," Katie said. "Oh, come on, Vanessa. It will be fun. It will take the…well, it will occupy your mind while we all…wait."

"But—" Vanessa began.

"Oh, come on, please!" Zoe said. "I'll help get you all set. Marty, are there costumes somewhere?"

"Great—just go down the path there to my friend Sally, the one dressed up as Queen Isabella. She'll give you everything that you need."

Despite her protests, Vanessa soon found herself dressed up as Kitty Cutlass. She was not given a chaste costume like Katie's. She was in a low-cut blouse with flaring white sleeves, a workaday corset and a billowing skirt and petticoat. Zoe arranged her hair so it was halfway tied high on her head, but with curling blond tendrils around her face.

She did not get any kind of holster—she had been stripped of her weapons.

She got handcuffs.

A large area of park had been set up for readings and theatrics; there was a modular stage, simple, with a judge's bench and just a few stark wooden pews, and a box for the defendant. Vanessa was surprised to see Jamie O'Hara dressed up as the judge, sitting behind the bench. Marty himself was the prosecutor, Katie the narrator and, apparently, she didn't have a defense attorney.

She was led through the crowd by a couple of Marty's cronies. She was stunned to see that a full audience had gathered around and that, while they awaited the beginning of the mock might-have-been trial, they were chatting, arguing amiably amongst themselves and giving their opinions. There were avid-eyed children lined up and seated Indian-style before the stage.

Katie introduced the situation in her little speech, and then explained what might have happened had Kitty Cutlass, a woman who was a known accomplice of Mad Miller and accused of the murder of Dona Isabella, been saved from the sinking of the pirate ship and brought in to face the music—the law!

Vanessa, rudely cast into the little box on the stage, almost jumped when Marty began his prosecutorial tirade of her horrible crimes.

Listening to him, she suddenly found herself ready to enter into the game. She didn't interrupt him; she waited until he was done and denied everything, assuring him that every shred of evidence he had against her was hearsay, circumstantial and in no way proof of any evil deed she might have performed. She had been guilty of loving Mad Miller, and nothing more. And they were wrong about Mad Miller, too. He had never been a murderer. Rather, he had been a man drawn to the life, eager for the rewards of the trade, but a man without a shred of bloodlust in his body.

As she spoke, she looked out at the audience at various times, demanding that they give an opinion. It had all been made up, conjured out of thin air, because every single *fact* that they were bringing forward was nothing more than speculation.

Jamie O'Hara raged from behind the bench that he would give the prisoner a chance—he would listen to thoughts and recommendations of her peers since the prosecution had failed woefully in bringing forth the burden of proof.

As she looked out then, Vanessa froze.

Many men were dressed as pirates. Many women were wenches, ladies and female pirates, and even the children in the crowd were in various stages of fun costume dress.

But there was one man standing behind the proceedings. He had a rich, full black beard and a headful of curly, almost ink-black hair. He was a tall man, and sturdy and strong. He had been watching from behind a group to the far rear, close to a row of merchants, which ended at a large growth of pines that grew raggedly before giving way to the white sands of the beach.

Her jaw dropped.

She'd never seen him with long hair or a beard.

But she knew him.

It was Carlos Roca.

His eyes, she was certain, met hers across the distance.

She cried out, ready to run after him.

But, of course, everyone thought it was part of the theatrics. She nearly shouted his name, but refrained, and when she tried to burst out of the box, Jamie O'Hara thundered his gavel on the bench, and Marty's friends came rushing up to secure the prisoner in the docket.

She flushed, angry, feeling ridiculously desperate, and yet…

She didn't want to shout his name.

And…

He was gone. Where he had stood, there was another man. Another pirate, quite a dandy of a pirate, really. This one had really rich long hair, queued at his nape, and he wore a cocked and sweeping plumed hat. His frock coat was brocade, his stockings and breeches were amazingly authentic. His face was aristocratic and handsome, and he was frowning at her as if she had truly lost her mind.

"What say you?" Jamie O'Hara roared.

"Guilty! I believed her until she tried to run!" a boy cried from the front row.

"Guilty! And sentencing for pirates, be they men or women, is that they be hanged from the neck until dead!" Jamie O'Hara roared with glee.

She felt blank, numb and disturbed. Had she been mistaken? Had she seen Carlos because…

Had she seen him because of this charade, because she wanted to see him, she had admired and cared about Carlos, and…

Her jaw fell open. The man who had taken his place seemed to be staring straight into her eyes, as well. He stiffened.

And seemed to disappear, as if he were fog.

Her knees felt like rubber. The world around her seemed to be a fog. She was going to pass out!

Good God! She didn't pass out. She wasn't the kind to be afraid of her own shadow, she had faced nightmares and the tricks the mind could play again and again. She wasn't weak, and she wasn't going to fall apart.

"Wait!" she suddenly shouted, remembering all that she could of pirate history.

To her surprise, everyone went still. The audience was dead silent.

"I cannot be hanged at this time. I plead my belly!" she announced.

"Brilliant!" someone in the crowd said. And there was laughter, and then applause.

"Well, then, we shall see! Sentence to be carried out when the condemned is delivered of her child, and so be it!" Jamie announced. His gavel slammed down again, and the charade was over. Marty hugged her and told her she was great, and Katie and Jamie were grinning proudly at her. Audience members greeted them all, asking pirate questions, and she stood and listened and spoke, and wasn't sure what she said, or what she heard.

She was searching the audience.

She didn't see Carlos Roca.

Nor did she see the "pirate" who had seemed to disappear into thin air.

Eventually, she made it back to Queen Isabella's costume booth and the little makeshift tent where she had changed. Back in her clothing, she came out to find that Katie and Zoe were deep in conversation with Marty.

"I just talked to my brother. He and David spent a lot of the day working, looking up all kinds of things and planning what they want to do. It's a go with a schedule—the crews are all set. We'll be heading out on two boats, Sean's and my uncle Jamie's. Jamie is coming, of course, captaining his boat. Marty is coming, Liam and I, and Sean and David and Ted and Jaden. And your six, Vanessa. You and Jay, Barry, Jake, Zoe and Bill. We'll set out the day after tomorrow."

"Oh, Vanessa!" Zoe said, throwing her arms around her. "This is wonderful. Maybe…maybe we'll figure things out!"

"Most likely we won't," Vanessa said. She didn't know why she was now being disparaging. This might well be their only hope, considering the fact that no one else was still actively investigating and they all knew that there were still dozens of unanswered mysteries. "I mean, we can only go through the motions, and try to remember every little thing, and see if there isn't something, some clue somewhere, that everyone has missed. And still, we may not find what we're looking for…or even the kind of peace and closure it seems that we're all hoping to find somehow."

"But we may!" Zoe argued. "I'm so excited. I'm going—I'm going to go and find Barry and let him know when we're leaving right away."

"Okay, great," Vanessa said. "And I guess you're in touch with Bill and Jake somehow? Better let them know, too."

"I'm on it!" Zoe said happily.

"Ah, for me?" Marty said, his eyes sparkling. "A chance of a lifetime! On the trail of one of the most infamous pirate tales ever!"

Vanessa tried to smile for him.

She had come here for this. And now…now she wasn't sure about anything.

Katie turned to Vanessa. "Sean wanted to speak to you. I told him you were changing and that I'd have you call him."

Vanessa nodded. Her heart seemed to take a little

leap, and she wanted to kick herself. He probably wanted to give her a list of rules.

"Sure. But, Katie, I'm going to head back to my room for a bit first—too much costume and makeup for me. I need a shower. Oh—thank you," she said.

"Thank me?" Katie said, laughing. "See, you are a ham, and you didn't even know it. You were great."

Vanessa shook her head. "No. Thank you. For influencing David, for introducing me to Jamie—I'm not sure I broached it all right with your brother, but this… well, if anything can be discovered, I think that this is the crew to do it."

Katie grinned happily. "Sure. And hey, I'm on this adventure, too!"

Adventure…

Vanessa wasn't at all sure she saw it that way.

With a wave, she headed out of the park, leaving all the pirate booths behind her. As she watched, she searched the crowds.

Had she imagined them both?

Many a big tall man with dark hair *might* look like Carlos Roca.

And in the midst of would-be pirates, imagining another pirate…

Face it: she wasn't getting enough sleep.

It was a long walk back to her room, but Vanessa was almost glad of it. She needed to walk, to stride, to burn more energy.

She needed to call Sean.

She wasn't ready to do so.

Reaching Duval and starting toward the north end, she realized that she was looking in shops and bars.

She couldn't shake the belief that she had seen Carlos Roca.

But if Carlos was alive, then…

Did that mean he had murdered the others?

As she neared her inn, she glanced across the street at a group of "pirates" gathered in front of the Irish bar across the street.

One relaxed against the door frame, watching the band, listening to the music. He had dark hair. He was the man she had thought had to be Carlos Roca.

He looked at her. He looked straight at her.

It was Carlos Roca. It had to be Carlos Roca. It was his face.

He turned and disappeared into the bar.

11

"Carlos, no! Wait, stay! It's me, Vanessa!" she cried. She raced across the street. It seemed that pirates had spread across the place, and she tried to excuse herself and wend her way through big frock coats, big hair and bigger hats. She made her way through the bar, searching faces to see Carlos's once again.

But she walked all way through to the emergency exit, and he wasn't there. She burst into the kitchen, only to be shown out. The place was ridiculously crowded, and she realized he might have walked out through the gift shop, slipped through another wall of pirates when she wasn't looking.

At last she gave up and walked her way through the pirates once again to the street.

She walked across, and straight into Sean.

He was standing in front of her inn, leaning against the wall, as if he had been there for some time. He seemed curious that she had come from the Irish bar, and was probably impatient, as well.

"I've been calling you," he said.

"I'm sorry."

"I'd have thought that you might have been more

interested in everything going on. Especially as far as getting ready to head out—with your friends all involved now."

"Look, Sean, they're my friends, but not my *friends.* Jay, yes, I've known forever. And I like the others, but I didn't bring them here."

"I'm not holding any of it against you," he said.

"How magnanimous," she murmured, looking away. She wanted to shout that she thought she had seen Carlos Roca. She might have been wrong. And if she'd seen Carlos, everyone would decide that, since he was alive, he was guilty. Until she saw him, really saw him, she couldn't say anything.

What if he was guilty? What if he had seen her, and knew that she had seen him? What if? He had seen her, he had looked straight at her before disappearing.

"Is that all?" she asked him. "It's been a long day, and I'd really like to take a shower, if you'll excuse me. I'll be ready to work whenever you need anything, but for now..."

She started to walk by him. He blocked her path. She looked up and was surprised to see that his golden eyes were opened wide and that everything about him was just slightly awkward. "Vanessa...I'm not good at this. And I'd like you to understand how things looked.... I'm sorry."

She was startled by the apology. It was amazing, coming from him under the circumstances.

Maybe he just missed the sex. But then again, so did she.

And still...

"I don't lie, Sean," she said stiffly.

"I didn't accuse you of lying."

"Well, yes, actually you did."

"I…I'm sorry. Okay, I'm not good at this…I don't know what else to say," he told her. "I'll ask you again, see it from my side."

She nodded and smiled slowly. "Just say that you know that I don't lie, and that you'll believe in me in the future. That will work."

"I know that you don't lie. I'll believe you in the future," he said, his smile broad.

"Thank you," she said softly. They stood there for a moment, looking at one another, not quite touching, and yet…

"I played a pirate about to be hanged today," she told him. "I really need a shower."

"Okay."

"You're not moving."

"You haven't invited me up."

"Come on up."

Maybe showers were destined to be something special between them. And maybe there was something that was just right, amazing, or the intangible bit of animal magnetism, chemistry, or whatever it was that made one person choose another over others. There was nothing awkward in her room, and there was no pretense between either of them. When she walked into the shower, she knew he was behind her. She turned into his arms, euphoric with the feeling that he was there, hard-bodied, rock-solid, vibrant, hot and real. Thoughts and fears left her mind for excruciating moments as she simply lost herself in the beauty and urgency of touch, running her hands down the wet sleekness of his flesh, his sex, along his spine and buttocks, and feeling the deep thrust and hot persistence of his kiss, his tongue and his hands upon her.

They made love with the rush of the water and then, still enwrapped and absorbed in one another, they found towels and made their way to the bed. Once there, he started with a kiss again, hovering over her, golden eyes burning into hers, and then that kiss, his mouth on hers, and then moving to her throat, where he paused, feeling the thunder of her pulse, and moved on, sending a streak of lightning through her as he teased a breast and trailed his kisses onward again. His caresses were slow, a touch of agony in the midst of exhilaration and wonder. He touched and teased, drawing to a point of complete intimacy, and she twisted and writhed until her frantic energy and demand brought him back to her, and they locked together in a storm of frenetic energy that brought her to a point of climax after climax, shuddering in his arms.

He held her close then, murmuring, his kisses tender.

Eventually, their bodies cooled. Their hearts beat at normal rates, and the ragged sound of their breath was no longer a cacophony in the room.

He held her against him and then groaned softly. "Strange. I don't want to get up. I'm starving, and there are things to do, and I don't ever want to leave this bed."

She laughed. "Of course you do. Eventually, you'd get bored here."

"When the sun froze over," he told her.

She stroked his face. "That was good. That makes up for your rather stilted apology."

"Excuse me, that was real and heartfelt."

"We could order food to be brought here," she said.

He nodded and turned from her for a moment, staring at the ceiling. "We're supposed to go over to Ted and Jaden's workshop—the doctor of forensic anthropology arrived, and she's been studying the trunk as we found it. She'll give us what she can before she does all the tests on the body. Anything in the sea that long—even mummified, as the body appears—is very fragile."

"Of course," Vanessa said. She hesitated, wondering why she was so uneasy about the trunk.

Pandora's box? If so, it was already open.

And yet, it hadn't been something actually *evil* that she felt, just as if the chest was going to be a catalyst, and she wasn't sure if she liked what it might cause to come about.

"Do you not want to come over there with me?" Sean asked.

"No, no, of course I want to come," she said.

"Then I guess we have to get moving." He stood, his back to her. "You know, I think you should get the tail end of your things out of here for good."

She rose as well, coming around to look at him. "You want me to come over because I'll be safer? Or because you want me there?"

"I'd say both, and that's pretty obvious," he said. She smiled.

She was glad to be invited.

Ecstatic, actually!

And it was true that she didn't want to be here alone.

She had horrendous nightmares, she saw figureheads in the water, and on top of that, she kept thinking that she saw Carlos Roca and an unknown pirate who looked at her—and then faded into the air.

Really. They were going to have to lock her up soon.

"It's late," he said huskily. "Let's grab pizza downstairs and then get over to Ted and Jaden's."

Dr. Tara Aislinn was in her midfifties, an energetic and enthusiastic woman who greeted Sean and Vanessa with real warmth. Her colleague, Ned Latham, was more subdued but apparently just as eager to be there. They had studied the chest and the victim within but hadn't taken the body from the chest. They had come down in their van and, with permission, of course, would be moving the chest and the body to the lab in Gainesville.

Liam and David had come and gone, Sean discovered. They were late, of course, really late, but in his mind, that was fine. He hadn't been in a serious relationship in a long time; he didn't think he'd ever been in a relationship where he'd felt so lost and empty when it seemed that it had ended. David and Liam were capable, as were Jaden and Ted, and he knew that he'd never understand half of what the scientists could learn from the body, so everything had gone in the right direction without him.

"David is calling the media and letting them know what it was you brought out of the water," Jaden told him.

"What exactly is he telling them?" Sean asked.

Dr. Aislinn laughed softy. "Just that we have arrived and are taking the chest and the body, and that we believe that the chest is early eighteen hundreds, and that a unique set of circumstances have preserved the body of a woman who died in the early eighteen hundreds, as well. More details will follow after we have conducted out tests."

"And what can you really tell us?" Sean asked.

"That she's *not* Dona Isabella!" Jaden burst out.

"What?" Vanessa said.

"Come, come, I'll show you," Dr. Aislinn said. "Dr. Latham, if you'll assist me?"

They walked over to the chest and Latham carefully opened it and offered Dr. Aislinn a set of latex gloves from his pocket. After pulling them on, she reached in and touched the woman's bodice. "This is cotton, and if you'll notice—it's difficult to see with the staining. If you'll hold the flashlight up, Dr. Latham?—that's home sewing. Dr. Latham, the hands if you will? I can't draw them out—we'd break up the mummy—but you'll note the nails. They're chipped and broken, and not the nails of a lady. Whoever this woman was, she didn't grow up in the lap of luxury. From what I've learned about this story, your Dona Isabella was supposedly killed on Haunt Island—or she went down with the ship in the storm. I don't know who this is, but it's not a lady of the time."

"Can you date the corpse to a certain age?" Sean asked.

"Not without a more comprehensive examination," Dr. Aislinn said. "But..." She shrugged. "My guess? Between twenty and thirty. I'm going to need X-rays of the teeth and skull, the hips—all those things help establish age. However, I think you've found a pirate's wench, perhaps a poor girl traveling as a maid or a servant."

"We hope to be able to give you a great deal more," Dr. Latham said.

"I'm sure you're disappointed that it wasn't a chest of gold doubloons, but this is just an amazing scientific find!" Dr. Aislinn said. She looked at Vanessa. "It's extraordinary. I heard you also discovered the pendant—the exquisite mermaid pendant—that Ted showed me earlier. You're quite an amazing woman, Miss Loren. You might have missed your calling as a salvage diver or treasure seeker!"

To Sean's surprise, Vanessa's smile seemed forced and her face seemed pale.

"Oh, I rather like what I do," she said.

"How did you find these relics?" Dr. Latham asked.

"Beginner's luck," she said with a shrug. "And I wasn't looking? I don't know."

"Well," Dr. Aislinn said. "You have made an absolutely amazing discovery here. The mermaid pendant, of course, is beautiful. But the body! We can't thank you enough. We're delighted to be doing the research!"

"Wait!" Ted said. "You didn't tell them the most gruesome part yet." He looked at Sean and Vanessa and shook his head. "I mean, we know that the pirates could be violent. And what with the story of Haunt Island, it shouldn't be surprising."

Jaden said, "Horrible, just horrible. But—of course, long over now."

"What?" Sean demanded.

"At first," Dr. Aislinn said, "I thought that someone must have cared for this young woman deeply. Most of the time, those who died at sea were wrapped in shrouds—if that!—and sent overboard. This young woman was sealed in a chest. I thought that we'd discover that the cause of death had been consumption or the ravages of some other disease. But look at the neck—that's not just decayed fabric there, or a shawl or scarf or any other such object. She was strangled. That's the fabric with which she was strangled. I'm not sure what it is yet. We'll know when we take a sample."

"She was murdered," Vanessa murmured.

"As you said," Sean noted, "violence was common, I'm afraid."

"Yes, but it's curious," Dr. Latham commented. "Pirates blew one another to bits with cannons. They slashed with swords and cutlasses, and they shot one another with their pistols. It's unusual that they would have strangled a woman."

"She must have made someone very angry," Jaden said.

"It's going to be just fascinating to try to discover just who she was!" Dr. Aislinn said. "Of course, I understand all of you are heading out soon to start filming—a most fascinating documentary, I must say! But I'll be in touch constantly by cell phone, and you can reach me anytime you like."

"Thank you," Sean told her.

"So," Ted said, "we're packing her up—the chest and the mummy—in the university van tomorrow morning. Tara and Dr. Latham are leaving then. But Jaden and I are about to take them out for a night on the town, Key West–style. Can you join us?"

Sean didn't have a chance to reply.

Vanessa spoke quickly. "Oh, thank you, and I hope you'll forgive me. It's been a long day, and I didn't get a lot of sleep last night, I'm afraid. But hey, you guys—take them to O'Hara's. They'll have a great time there."

"O'Hara's?" Dr. Aislinn said, grinning and looking at Sean.

"It's my uncle's place, and you will have a great time," Sean said.

"Sean, I'm sorry, I'm really exhausted, but you, of course, are more than welcome to join them," Vanessa said quickly.

She seldom looked vulnerable; for some reason that night she did. Sean felt a surge of tenderness, wanting to make sure that she was safe and warm and protected at all times.

"Sorry, all, and forgive me, too. These have been really long days. My uncle's place has good food, reasonable drinks, and my sister is doing karaoke tonight. It's a bit of a walk down Duval," he said.

"Well, I do love walking, and I don't get down here nearly enough!" Dr. Aislinn said.

Sean and Vanessa left, thanking them again. As they walked down the street, he took her hand—it was crowded that night. Girls were out in skimpy outfits and wench attire; some men were still in pirate costume while others were in jeans and T-shirts. It was Key West. A little cool that night for anything so simple as body paint, but anything might have been worn along Duval.

Vanessa was quiet, and she still seemed disturbed. "What's wrong?" he asked her.

She made a face. "The body is creepy. I'm glad they're taking it to Gainesville."

"It's not really creepy. It's another mystery. We—*you*—found a pendant, which did belong to Dona Isabella, at least according to historical sketches. Then, we—*you*—find a body in a chest, and it proves *not* to be Dona Isabella. That's interesting. I don't remember anything about a maid traveling with her, though, of course, a woman of her stature probably did travel with a servant. Ah, maybe Mad Miller threatened her by killing the maid, and then gave her something of a decent burial. Or, God knows, maybe Kitty Cutlass did the deed."

Vanessa shrugged. "I don't know. We'll have to see what they discover. Both of those doctors seemed fascinated and thrilled, so it was an incredible discovery."

She was silent.

"Hey, you all right?"

"Of course."

"You're the only person who makes incredible finds who seems depressed by their talent. The pendant... well, I can see that as a fluke. But none of that chest was showing above the sand. How in hell *did* you become so certain there was something there?"

She paused and stopped walking and stared at him. "You really want to know? If you make fun of me now, I'll never forgive you."

"I will not make fun of you."

She took a deep breath, her eyes sharp on his. "I keep thinking that I see a figurehead in the water. I dream about it, actually. It's scary and creepy. It has Dona Isabella's face."

He felt his lips start to twitch and remembered he had promised not to make fun of her.

"I see," he managed to say.

"You don't believe a word," she said.

"I'm not saying that!" he protested quickly. He started walking again, eager to get to his home on Elizabeth Street before he somehow managed to lose her once again. "Here's what I think," he said, still holding her hand, and swinging their arms easily between them as they walked. "The story goes that poor Dona Isabella was kidnapped from her transport to Spain by Mad Miller and his pirates. She was forced to Haunt Island and either murdered by Mad Miller or Kitty Cutlass, or still a prisoner—probably one who was raped and abused—when the pirate ship went down in the storm. So you see the face of Dona Isabella because you feel such sympathy for her. And it would be natural that you see the face in the water—as a figurehead—when you are instinctively honing in on something. How's that?"

"Psychology 101?" she asked dryly.

"The mind can do amazing things," he told her. "Then, face it, you've had horrible nightmares since your friends were murdered on Haunt Island—and you found them. There are all kinds of wonderful defense mechanisms in the mind."

"What if the spirit of Dona Isabella is lurking in the water?" Vanessa asked. "Or...worse! What if Mad

Miller is a decayed old pirate like Geoffrey Rush in *Pirates of the Caribbean?*"

He laughed.

Then he realized that she was serious.

"I remember one time, when Katie and I were small, and we were at the old cemetery, bringing flowers to the grave of one of my mom's friends. Katie was acting nervous. My dad told her that the dead were the safest people in the world—that they couldn't hurt anyone. He told her that she had to learn to be very smart and wary and savvy—it was the living who hurt one another."

She nodded. "Of course. I didn't think that Mad Miller or Kitty Cutlass rose out of the sea to kill and dismember Georgia and Travis."

"Of course not. It's sad to say, because I know you liked him, that most probably Carlos Roca was responsible."

She seemed to start, and to shudder.

He set his arm around her and pulled her close.

"Hey, sorry!"

"It's all right," she murmured. "I just— I doubt it. All right, I know that there have been horrible serial killers who had neighbors who had sincerely believed they were just nice, quiet people. But I knew Carlos. And I don't think so—no matter how it looked."

They had reached the house and he opened the door, drawing her in. He locked the door and asked, "Do you want something to drink? A shot of...something. Kahlúa and cream, cup of tea, water, cola, soda...?"

She laughed. "Hmm. Tea and whiskey."

"The old Irish remedy for anything that ails you," he said. He walked into the kitchen and put the kettle on.

As the water boiled, he tried to casually look around the house for Bartholomew. The ghost was nowhere to be seen.

Probably out with his lady in white, Lucinda, the new love of his life.

Probably still angry with him.

That was all right; he didn't want to be haunted that night.

The water boiled. Vanessa got out two cups and he procured the tea cups and the whiskey. When both were prepared, he suggested, "Let's take them up to bed."

She nodded. "Works for me."

He meant to have a little finesse. Give her a few minutes, watch a bit of a late-night comedy. But they were still too new to one another. Once they had shed their clothing, they made love. He couldn't bemoan his lack of subtle courtesy, because she was so passionate, so urgent, and completely and erotically seductive. She seemed to come beneath his very skin. It was one thing to feel the ultimate in climax and satiation. Sex was instinct, it was breathing, it happened all the time. But it was something else to feel the wonder when he lay with her after, something else to feel that nothing in the world could ever be so complete, so fulfilling… even so necessary.

They drank their tea then, cold, and though she kept drifting to sleep at his side, she would awake again and again with a start.

He found the remote and at long last turned on a late-night talk show. The noise seemed to soothe her.

She slept next to him as if he were a bastion against the edge of eternal darkness.

* * *

Waking with Sean was amazing; she had felt his body and warmth throughout the night, and she had slept deeply. She opened her eyes and felt wonderful. He had been on his stomach at an angle, and she had been sleeping against his back. Great back, broad shoulders, long clean lines, bronze flesh. She drew her finger down the length of his spine delicately, waking him immediately.

He woke well, too. It was all so new and amazing, of course. He turned and took her into his arms, a wicked look in his eyes, and they made love to start the day.

Afterward, Vanessa headed to Katie's room to shower and leave Sean in his own space, and once she was dressed, she came downstairs and to the back of the house where he'd set up his office. He was there already, telling her that coffee was poured and that when she was ready, they'd go over the shooting schedule and she could tell him anything that she thought he might have missed.

Walking into the kitchen while reading the schedule that Sean had printed for her, she stopped, stunned—as if she'd been hit by a brick.

For a moment—just for a moment—she thought that she saw the pirate again. Tall, lean, dashing, rich black hair, plumed hat, standing thoughtfully by the dining-room window, staring out at the day.

She saw him in such detail!

And then he was gone.

She blinked. There was nothing there. Sun streaming in played on the dust motes in the air.

She hurried over to the coffeepot and poured a large

cup. She nearly scalded her throat in her hurry to drink it down.

Now she was seeing things nearly on an hourly basis. And after such a miraculous night of deep and undisturbed sleep.

Sean walked into the kitchen to pour himself more coffee. He frowned, looking at her. "What's the matter?"

"Nothing."

"Really? You look—scared."

She smiled. "With you in the room? Never," she said with a laugh. She walked over and hugged him and drew away quickly. "I had another thought that we might add in on your schedule."

"Right," Sean said, smiling. "What scene would you add?"

"Jay and me at night, walking down to where we saw nothing. Where I found the bodies the next morning. Very descriptive without being gruesome."

"I like it. Write it in. Obviously, we'll film hours that we'll wind up editing out, but any scene that you think might enhance the project, just tell me."

Vanessa lowered her head and smiled. It was amazing that he might have hurt her so much and made her so angry—and that, as far as a working relationship went, he was completely confident and comfortable. He knew what he wanted; he knew where he was going. It occurred to her then that they both wanted the same thing. She hoped they made an excellent documentary that was engrossing and made others think, as well.

Until that moment, she realized, she'd been thinking of her own agenda.

The phone rang, causing her to nearly jump out of her skin.

Sean arched a brow to her. "Hey, telephone. It's a landline—remember those? Granted, we don't use them much anymore." He walked over to answer it.

She couldn't be so jumpy. They would lock her up—before they could even get to the project.

Sean answered the phone. He frowned and reached into his pocket. "Sorry, forgot to plug it in last night." He glanced at Vanessa and smiled. "I got distracted," he said.

Then his smile faded. "You're kidding!" he said.

He listened again.

"I'll be right there," he said.

He hung up and stared thoughtfully at Vanessa.

"What?" she demanded.

"The body was stolen."

"What?" she repeated.

"I'm heading out to meet Liam. I won't be long. The body was stolen out of the university van. The problem is, no one knows when. They'd packed it up this morning, and Doctors Aislinn and Latham were at a Cracker Barrel in the middle of the state when they decided to check to make sure that the chest wasn't moving around too much. Well, it wasn't moving. It was gone."

"Someone stole the body out of the van?" she repeated incredulously.

He nodded.

"Who in the hell would want to steal a mummified body?" she demanded.

"Here's my question," he said. "Who in hell would even know that it was there to be stolen?"

* * *

Liam was in his office, filling out paperwork. He looked up the minute Sean came in and glumly waved toward a chair on the other side of his desk.

"Anything?" Sean asked him.

"Nothing—this may be worse than the damned Bermuda Triangle. Most of the time, we can't even find a stolen car, and then we find them half the time because they have LoJack, but they're stripped. But this isn't a car we're looking for, it's a chest with a body in it! This is going to be impossible. They don't know when it happened. They had just left a Cracker Barrel in the center of the state when Dr. Latham decided to check on their cargo. So—they'd stopped for breakfast in Florida City. The van might have been broken into then. It could have happened when they pulled off a few times along the way. So, it might have been stolen anywhere from Key West to Orlando. They believed that their cargo was safe—who tries to steal a corpse?"

"Is there anything we can do?" Sean asked.

"We have reports filled out and sent around the state," Liam said. "They've dusted for fingerprints. The lock was sprung with a pick, but that doesn't really help any. The door could still be secured, so it doesn't mean that the chest was stolen later than earlier." He shook his head. "Someone must have thought it was a treasure chest."

"There was an article that ran in the paper this morning—David talked to a reporter last night, and I believe it went around on the wire and on the Internet. The article announced that it was a body that had been found."

"Maybe the thieves weren't on the Internet, and God knows, they probably didn't read the newspaper, either," Liam said. "The officers here are livid, of course. Keys police tend to be very territorial—they take the theft personally. She was *our* creepy old body, the way they look at it. They'll be doing everything they can, searching for anything suspicious. Obviously, you need a reason to stop people and search their trucks or vans, but we're good and subtle around here—learned a lot from the drug traffic. Someone may just find the chest somewhere—I mean, once they've discovered they haven't any gold, silver or precious gems, they may just abandon the chest."

Sean shook his head. "I don't think so," he said.

"Why?"

"I don't know. I think that the body was stolen on purpose."

"What? By gang members? Like some kind of initiation? If we have a large clan of devil worshipers down here, I don't know anything about it," Liam said.

"I don't think it was gang members or devil worshipers. I think it was someone…I don't know. Someone involved, somehow," Sean said.

"And recently, two unexplained disappearances," Liam said.

"We may be getting into something very bad."

"Well, I am a cop. It's the kind of thing I'm supposed to be doing," Liam said dryly.

"Are you set for tomorrow?" Sean asked.

"I am—shifts covered for two weeks," Liam told him. "Why?"

"I'd like to go for some target practice sometime before tomorrow."

"Target practice?"

"It's been a while for me," Sean said.

"You are really expecting trouble," Liam said.

"Hey—now a nearly two-hundred-year-old body has been stolen. Yes, I guess I am expecting trouble."

"And you still want to proceed?"

Sean hesitated. "I think I feel now more than ever that we have to," he said. "Maybe stealing the body was someone's idea of a prank. And maybe there is something here that we're not seeing—but maybe we're close, and there was something we weren't meant to discover. I don't know. Not much makes sense yet. But yes. With what and who we have—hell, yes, we have to move forward now."

While Sean was gone, Vanessa continued to study the schedule, adding in notes and suggestions. She liked reviewing his work, and going over all the notes he had made about supplies, lighting and editing in the scenes that would go with the narrative.

She rose at one point, realizing that they'd had coffee but not breakfast. Now it was nearly lunchtime, and she was hungry.

She heard the sound of the air-conditioner kicking on as she walked to the kitchen. It might be late fall, but the day was growing warm. The sun was bright outside, casting the dancing rays of rebounding sunlight into the room to play with dust motes in the air again.

She froze again.

He was there again.

Someone by the window. Someone in pirate attire.

She nearly screamed. She felt again the weakness of her legs buckling.

At first, her mind raced in a somewhat rational direction.

Carlos. It was Carlos Roca. She had seen him, and he was real, and she was wrong, and Sean was right, and he was guilty of murder, and now he had come for her.

But it wasn't Carlos.

It was the pirate—the dandy pirate.

The tall, striking fellow with the sweeping hat and brocade coat. The one she had seen yesterday, and then briefly again just this morning.

She would blink, and he would go away. He wasn't real. He was her mind playing tricks.

Really no. She was seeing things.

But she blinked, and this time he remained. She realized that he was staring at her with equal consternation. He jumped up, his eyes locked with hers, and gasped.

"Oh my God!" he cried.

She was hearing things, as well as seeing them. Not just a figurehead through a camera lens. Oh, no, this was much worse. This was a walking, talking pirate ghost.

In her room.

She let out a weak scream.

He let out a weak scream.

Her mouth worked hard.

"Mad Miller!" she gasped.

"Good God, no!" the apparition replied in horror.

Replied. It was talking to her, the images talked to her now, even when she was awake.

She fell back against the door, her hand flying to her throat.

"You're not there," she gasped out.

"My God! You can see me!" he cried. "You can really see me!"

Her knees were really buckling now. And he seemed to be fading in and out, and she wasn't sure what she saw, or what she heard.

"Who are you?" she demanded.

"A friend, I swear. All right, I'm dead, I'm a ghost—but I'm a friend, honest to God, please don't scream again!"

She didn't.

So much for being strong. So much for being the kind of woman who just didn't *pass out.*

She slumped against the wall and sank to the floor, entering a sweet world of darkness and silence.

12

As he headed back to his house, Sean tried not to dwell on the stolen corpse. He called different suppliers, making sure that everything was set for them to leave in the morning. He had a few calls to make, since they needed everything from diving supplies to film, memory cards, backup equipment and groceries.

David called to let him know that he and Jamie were at the dock and that things were coming as promised.

He tried calling Vanessa, but she didn't pick up.

She was at his house—locked in.

But he found himself hurrying. He didn't know why the theft of the body disturbed him so much. Liam had been right—it had probably been some kind of a prank. Or, God knew, maybe an eccentric collector had decided that he just had to have a mummified murder victim from the early eighteen hundreds.

Still, as he neared his house, he was almost running. It occurred to him that he'd been gone a long time. Liam had not been able to leave the station then—he'd been tying up his paperwork and transferring his workload to other detectives throughout the day in preparation for taking his vacation time with Sean and David and the crew.

An hour at the range had been good. He'd always had a clear eye and a steady aim, but since guns weren't in his workaday world, he hadn't carried one in a long time.

The day's events at the fort and beach would be drawing to a close, but there would be parties, lectures and "pirate" entertainment as the night arrived. Once again, pirates and their consorts would be roaming the streets. At the moment, it was one of the most beautiful times of the day; there was nothing like a Key West sunset. The bright sunlight gave way to a gentle, pale yellow, and the brilliant blue of the sky overhead became a silver-gray. Then the sun started down, and it seemed that the horizon and everything around was shot full with a palette of unbelievable colors, from deep magenta to the most delicate pink, shimmering gold to gentle rose. It was most amazing to watch the sun set over the water, but to Sean, the colors were still visible, and the colors were what created the beauty.

The brighter shades were just giving way to violet, silver and gray when he reached his house. Once there, he bounded up the walk and fitted his key into the lock, calling Vanessa's name.

In the foyer, he paused, calling her name again.

Vanessa was there. She walked to the foyer from the center of the house and the kitchen and dining-room area.

She stared at him with immense eyes that seemed to accuse him of the foulest of heinous deeds.

"Sean," she said.

He noticed that she had shampooed her hair and that she was wearing a white halter dress that showed off the tan of her skin.

"Are we going somewhere?" he asked.

"Oh, yes. Bon voyage party at O'Hara's. All of our friends will be joining us," she told him. "It will be Katie's last night for now, so she's going to be there in case Clarinda needs her. David said as long as we're all ready and aboard by ten we'll be fine...oh, and Marty has turned his booth over to his friend for pirate fest—you have been gone awhile. Did you learn anything?"

"No. The police barely know where to start searching for the chest. I went—I went to target practice with Liam."

"We're having guns aboard?" she asked, frowning.

"Think about it. Yes," he said.

"Well, we don't have to leave right away. Come in and sit down and let's talk for a minute, shall we? Sit, please. Can I get you something? It is your house, of course. Thank goodness, the choices here are much broader than what I have up in my room. Beer? Wine? Soda, soda and whiskey, or whiskey. Rum! That's right. It's a pirate drink. Strange, I've had this growing affection for a good stiff drink from just about the time I arrived here."

She was definitely behaving strangely, and yet she certainly seemed stone-cold sober.

He followed her to the dining room. He noticed that Bartholomew was there. He was seated at the dining-room table. He looked at Sean with a guilty expression.

Sean frowned, feeling a sensation of dread.

"I'll take a beer," Sean said. "But I can get it myself."

"No, no, let me. Sit," she said.

He took a chair at the end of the table. Bartholomew—for once—was silent.

Vanessa set a beer in front of him. She had taken one for herself, and walked around to take a seat at the other end of the dining-room table.

"Sean, I mentioned to you that I see a figurehead—with Dona Isabella's face on it—in the water, and it leads me to things beneath."

"Yes," he said slowly. Carefully.

She learned toward him, eyes snapping with light and anger.

"You hypocrite!"

"What?"

"You tell me everything is a trick of the mind—when you live with a ghost!"

He was certain that his jaw fell. Then, of course, he gave himself away by staring at Bartholomew. She saw him! She saw Bartholomew.

"What a jerk!" she told him. "You might have mentioned your pirate friend to me!"

"Privateer," Bartholomew said, but weakly.

"You see him," he said, his voice just as pale.

"Yes, and he nearly gave me a heart attack. You should have told me. When I saw him, I thought that he might have been Mad Miller—"

"That was terribly insulting," Bartholomew interjected.

"How was I supposed to know?" Vanessa snapped

to him. She wagged a finger at Sean. "You should have told me!"

He opened his mouth but no sound came. He cleared his throat and tried again. "You would have thought that I was crazy."

"Really? That's great. Instead, I've been thinking that I'm crazy."

"You can see him—clearly?" Sean asked.

"She's far more perceptive than you'll ever be," Bartholomew said.

"Thank you so much," Sean said dryly.

"You want everything to be black and white," Bartholomew said. "You want science and explanations."

"There is probably a science to everything," Sean said. He looked at Bartholomew. "We just haven't figured it all out yet."

"I hope not—I hope something is left to a—a dimension of faith, or the next world, be it Heaven or Hell," Bartholomew said earnestly. "God forbid someone discovers how to force a soul to stay on this earthly plain."

Sean looked from Bartholomew to Vanessa. "You hear him clearly, too?"

"Perfectly. Actually, we had a lovely discussion this afternoon. He's been around watching out for me a great deal of the time. I kept feeling as if there were…something. Of course, I didn't believe in *ghosts*," she said. "But now…"

"Oh, please," Bartholomew said. "You are not all sharing a mental experience, or conjuring the same imaginary friend."

Vanessa smiled and laughed easily. "No. Now I know," she told him. She spoke to him fondly.

Well.

"You…should have told me that you…that you knew there might be some things that were—unexplainable," Vanessa said. "It would have helped me a lot."

He got up and walked around the table to her, taking her hands. "Vanessa…trust me, if I hadn't thought that…well, seriously, you know…*most* people can't see Bartholomew."

"Frankly, I was stunned," Bartholomew said.

"I—think we're at a point where we need to trust one another," Vanessa said.

He kissed her gently on the lips. "Yes, but you must understand—"

"Oh, yes. I do. Just as you really need to understand that I came here not knowing that Jay and the others would show up—and that when you think about it, it's not odd at all," she said solemnly.

He pulled her to her feet. He smoothed her hair back. "I'll never doubt you again," he said softly.

"Oh, good God," Bartholomew said. "I thought we were going out."

They both turned to look at him.

"Never mind. I'm going out." He looked at them, shook his head and made a tsking sound. "I shall see you when you get there."

Vanessa wound her arms around Sean's neck and kissed him. A few minutes later, he told her huskily that if they were going to leave, they needed to go. And they did.

* * *

O'Hara's was insane that night, inside. People had heard about the excitement of finding a pendant from the ill-fated *Santa Geneva* that had once graced the neck of Dona Isabella, and then the discovery of a body in a chest—and the theft of the body in the trunk. For a while, as everyone arrived, they stayed inside, but when they had all gathered at last, Jamie suggested the patio, a private area in the back, and they all agreed.

Everyone in their group who would be heading out the following day was there.

Clarinda was doing her first night as a karaoke hostess, and despite her innate shyness, she was doing very well.

They could hear the singers and the music faintly, and the night was typically beautiful, not really cool but not hot.

Vanessa sipped a Guinness, enjoying the taste and leaned back against Sean, oddly relaxed. She'd seen a ghost.

And the ghost had proved to be real, or a real mass hallucination. Apparently, Bartholomew had actually been Katie's ghost and helped out in David's time of trouble; though Liam wasn't really in on actually seeing and conversing with the ghost, he knew there was *something.*

And as crazy as it sounded, she wasn't frightened anymore—she was in awe. It was actually something of a dream come true, actually conversing with someone who had lived almost two centuries ago. He had told her his own sad story, which had connected bizarrely with David's, and then he had told her that somehow, he knew it just wasn't right for him to leave yet—follow the light to wherever it might bring him—because he felt he was still needed on Earth. Which was really fine now, because after years and years and years, he had finally met the lady in white, his Lucinda, who had been a lonely figure walking up and down Duval and haunting the cemetery for years—afraid to reach out to others. Bartholomew had no explanation as to why some people had a sense of something, and some actually saw ghosts. Some saw particular ghosts and not others and, of course, there were plenty of ghosts to be seen! The streets of Key West were often riddled with ghosts; after all, people had been dying there forever.

Bartholomew hadn't come to O'Hara's with them; he was determined to join the film project, and so he would spend the night with his beautiful Lucinda.

Vanessa was leaning against Sean. They sat at one of the benches horse-style and it was easy and comfortable to lean against his back.

Sean and David had spent some time delineating duties for each member of the crew and assigning boats. Then Sean lifted his beer. "To success—and safety!" he said.

They all toasted.

The conversation turned to the chest Vanessa had discovered—and the stolen mummified body.

"What if," Jay said, thinking as he went, "what if… what if it was Dona Isabella? The anthropologist might have been wrong. Maybe they dressed her up in peasant garb. Maybe she broke free herself, and was going to come after everyone in…revenge for what happened to her?" he asked, wide-eyed.

"Jay!" Vanessa snapped. "That's...ridiculous. Mummies don't come to life, and why would Dona Isabella want revenge on anyone living? You're talking as if you're plotting out another horror movie, and we're doing a documentary."

"It would be a great and creepy premise," Barry said.

"A sequel!" Zoe said.

Vanessa glared at her. "There isn't going to be a sequel—there was never really a movie. Therefore, you can't have a sequel."

"Well, actually..." Jay said.

Vanessa felt her muscles tighten up with tension. It had been a nice night—thus far. Sipping Guinness, munching on O'Hara's specials such as Shillelagh Sticks—rolled and baked corned beef in pastry—and Tam O Shanters—something like sliders. Such a nice night. She'd been so amazed—and pleased—about Bartholomew. She'd been so happy to be with Sean.

And now...

"Jay, what are you talking about?" she demanded.

He flushed, and lifted his hands uneasily. "I've had a call from a rep with a national distributor. He thinks we have a surefire hit—especially with everything else that went on."

Vanessa sat up, staring at Jay. "Jay—our lead actors were murdered."

"Bad things have happened before and movies have still come out and been very successful—and it was really a wonderful chance for fans to say goodbye," Jay said, defending himself.

"When the leads were murdered?" Vanessa asked icily.

"I'm sure somewhere along the line, yes…but think of the real things out there! Poor Heather O'Rourke of *Poltergeist* died very young—and they've used her scenes in tacky advertisements! When they filmed the *Twilight Movie* years ago, a star and two children were killed, and it aired. People said goodbye to Bruce Lee, Brandon Lee, Heath Ledger and many more actors when their movies aired after their deaths."

Vanessa felt Sean holding her back, but she stood anyway, walking over to Jay. "That would be the height of bad taste, and I put my money into that film, too, and I won't allow it."

"That's great for you—you've hit jobs that pay well. I need to make some money, Nessa," Jay pleaded.

"Jay, it's wrong."

Sean stepped into it then. "Well, the surviving members of your crew are here, Jay. Why don't you find out how they all feel?"

Bill spoke up first. "All right, I was more or less a lowly production assistant on the shoot. But…I liked Georgia and Travis. And they have family living now. Family—who might be hurt."

Barry cleared his throat. "I don't know what I feel. Georgia wanted to be a star. And she survived in the movie. She might be happy."

"Yeah, Georgia was sweet. Dumb, but sweet," Zoe said. "But Travis…Travis was a jerk."

"Zoe!" Bill gasped, horrified.

"Hey, I'm sorry—it's horrible that he died the way he did, yes. But was he a nice guy? No!"

"My money was in it, Jay," Vanessa said. "And I say no."

Jay inhaled and stared at her. He exhaled and took a long sip of his beer, and looked at her again. "What if we find out what happened?" he asked.

"What?" she said.

"We all came here. We heard about Sean and David and their project, and we all came here. Doesn't that mean something? We all care, we were all horrified. Vanessa, I own the majority share—fifty-one percent."

"You slimy basta—" she began.

"Wait, please!" Jay said. "Let's see what we can discover on this documentary project. And then, if there's really a story to be told about what happened to us, it would only be right to release the movie that we filmed."

Sean leaned forward. "Jay, if you want to throw threats around, you'll note that David and I own this particular project."

Jay's jaw fell. He hadn't thought that he might get kicked off the new project.

Sean smiled pleasantly. "We didn't draw up any contracts."

"I'm not threatening anyone. I'm just...I'm just mentioning facts," Jay said.

"And so am I," Sean told him politely.

Jay looked at Vanessa pleadingly. "Will you think about it when this project is done?"

The conversation had been bouncing between them with everyone there staring at them. She didn't want to get into a huge fight with Jay that would naturally begin to involve all the others. The whole project could become an antagonistic disaster by the morning. She didn't want any hostility on the trip or involved with the filming.

For a moment, Vanessa felt the silence that fell among the group.

"You're right," she said. "Let's see what happens on this trip. If we find out something new about what happened, if there is a prayer of solving the murders, then I'll think about it. But if we find nothing at all and their deaths remain mysteries, Jay—please. Let's shelve it."

Jay looked at her, then looked away. "All right."

"Promise," Vanessa insisted.

"I promise," he said dourly.

There was a silence again. Then Katie stood, raising her glass. "Here's to great camaraderie and a wonderful work experience. Here's to tomorrow!"

Again, glasses clinked, and they all toasted one another. The joy of the evening had faded, though, and soon, one by one, they were taking leave.

As they walked home, Sean told Vanessa, "You know, I can fire his ass now, if you want."

She looked at him and flashed a smile. "No, Jay is good. And he promised, and he is my friend."

"He's your broke friend, it sounds like. And in a way, he has a point. I agree with you, but he has a point. Here's the thing that I'll say in his defense—he didn't try to cash in on a tragedy. He had invested his life's savings into that movie. He didn't rush out and try to give it to anyone right after it happened."

"You think he's right?" Vanessa protested.

Sean shook his head. "Me? I don't think I could do

it—not when both of the victims were so young, not when they had family still living." He slipped his arm around her. "*Titanic* the musical played on Broadway. I thought that a musical based on such a horrific event was in terrible taste. Katie wanted to see it, so the family went. And it was actually something that I wound up enjoying, that gave a certain honorable memorial to many of the people involved. Much better than the movie!" he told her, smiling gently.

"Sean—this was a slasher flick."

"I know. Anyway, let's get home and get some sleep, shall we?"

They didn't get to sleep right away. They made love again, and it still seemed so amazing and new, and there was still so much they had to learn about one another. When she drifted to sleep, she was warm, secure and comfortable, and being with him seemed like a bastion against the world. It was ridiculous to think that she could actually fall in love with anyone so quickly, and yet, in the time they had known one another, she had come to realize that now she couldn't imagine a time without him. She had let her pride stand in the way once—he had been a jerk—but he had proven himself, coming to her, and she thought that finding the right relationship had been as hard in the past for him as it had been for her, none of which mattered, because when she was with him, feeling his warmth and the vibrant pulse of his heart so near to hers, she didn't envision the future beyond tomorrow.

She should have slept as sweetly and deeply as she had the night before.

But the dreams came again, though they took a different twist.

She was back at O'Hara's, sitting on the bench at the patio, and Jay was speaking again.

"What if the mummy came to, and broke out..."

Then she was walking down Duval, and it was odd, because no one was there.

She was alone.

And then she wasn't.

The streets were filled with pirates. She told herself that naturally the pirates were there. Pirates in Paradise was happening, and there were events to the last minute, and even then, some people stayed and dressed up, loath to get back to reality.

But they weren't real pirates.

They were ghosts.

Ghosts existed.

They walked along, some in a hurry, some strolling together. Some talked and teased with wenches, some joked with one another. They strode, they swaggered, and one limped on a peg leg. They paid her no heed.

Then she heard carriage wheels. They seemed to come slowly, ominously. The sky blackened and a chill fog sprang out from the sea. The mist whirled in shades of gray, and the clip-clop of the horse's hooves came ever more slowly.

She turned, aware that the carriage was coming to a halt, and that it was coming to a halt near her.

Or perhaps it was coming for her.

A woman, an elegant woman in silk and high fashion, stepped from the carriage, her every movement in slow motion. She looked straight at Vanessa, and Vanessa knew her. She knew the mermaid pendant the woman wore around her neck, and she knew the face—she had seen it on a figurehead that had led her to strange discoveries beneath the sea.

"You must help. You must listen. You must find the truth," the woman said. She smiled at Vanessa, and produced a hatbox. She opened the hatbox, and lifted something.

It was Georgia Dare's head.

"Vanessa!" Georgia cried to her pathetically.

Dona Isabella let the head fall back into the hatbox. She looked around her. Vanessa did the same. The pirates on the street were changing. They seemed to turn into black ooze. They cried out and screamed, and seemed as if they were moving in a black, malevolent mass toward the woman and the carriage.

The wind began to whip up. Vanessa knew that she had to wake up; the evil pirates were coming for Dona Isabella, but she was in their way.

"Here, here!" came a cry.

She turned.

And it was the mummy. The mummy from the pirate's chest.

The face was leathered and dark and decayed. The hands were bony, with dead skin stretched out over them far too tightly. The clothing was stained and ripped, and the eye sockets were empty, nothing but black stygian pits.

"Come, come!" the mummy cried.

Her jaw fell open in horror. The bony fingers were coming closer and closer to her.

"No!" she whispered.

"Yes!" Someone was behind her. She felt the presence and spun around in terror.

The street was still dark; the carriage bearing Dona Isabella away was beginning to move. It was still in slow motion, yet it was trying so hard to pick up speed. Dona Isabella was running now from the wrath of the pirates. She sought escape, as she hadn't found in the past.

Vanessa thought that she should have leaped into the carriage.

Because now she was caught between the mummy…

And the living, breathing man behind her.

Carlos Roca. She stared at him.

"Am I seeing you? Are you dead? Did you kill them, Carlos, did you have us all fooled?" she demanded.

He stood there, frozen in silence.

"I am alive," he told her. "And I am innocent."

He looked at the black shadows. "Come with me!"

"Come, come quickly!" the mummy begged.

She spun around. The mummy was there. So pathetic. So sad.

"Vanessa, you know me!" Carlos said.

Yes, she knew him, and he was there. Was he really alive, and was he running, too, or was he part of a black swirling mass of ooze and evil that was winding slowly down the street, ready to devour her…?

"You don't understand," the mummy said.

And the dead, leathered fingers, bones sticking out, nearly touched her.…

She screamed.

And awoke.

And Sean was with her, holding her in his arms,

smoothing back her damp hair, whispering words of assurance.

She felt the terror of the dream slip away from her, and she felt the strength of his arms. She ceased to shake and she turned him. "I'm so sorry…I didn't think…when I was with you…"

He touched her face. "I'm not the monster in the dream, right?"

She laughed shakily. "No."

"Then it's much better to have nightmares with me than without me, right? Although," he admitted, "these nightmares seem to plague you so cruelly, a therapist might be in order."

"I had a therapist once," she said. "It didn't help."

He rocked with her in silence for a minute, then said, "Then somehow, we have to find the truth. Catch a killer. And put the past to rest."

The morning was a whirlwind of activity. There were dozens of air tanks that needed to be stowed, and though David had overseen the loading of the boats with grocery supplies, ice, film, memory cards, cords, computer needs, batteries, flashlights, flares and every conceivable necessity, they all had their personal gear to stow, as well.

Jamie had David and Katie, Liam, Barry and Bill and Jake aboard the *Claddagh.* Sean had Vanessa, Jay, Ted and Jaden, Marty and Zoe aboard the *Conch Fritter.*

And Bartholomew, of course.

The boats would follow one another through the day, hugging the Intracoastal up to Jewfish Creek, and heading out to the Atlantic at Key Largo. David and Barry would take turns with the camera during the day on the *Claddagh* while Sean, Jay, and Vanessa would trade off on the *Conch Fritter.* They would drop anchor that night southwest of Miami, and in the morning start filming at the first reef where the previous crew had begun their offshore work. Sean felt that he had had enough of Pirate's Cut and that they should start filming in other areas. He had the Marty footage and the footage that Vanessa and Jay had already shot at Pirate Cut.

The first day was easy; it was getting to know the boat, the equipment and one another.

The boats met up at about 4:30 p.m., and tied on together—Sean wanted footage taken on board that night. He and David took turns in front of the camera, describing the voyage and their plans, and the film taken would be edited in with the shots they'd taken of leaving port that morning.

Jamie O'Hara had a portable barbecue grill that extended from the boat's hull, and that night, the *Claddagh*'s crew was responsible for dinner. While Jamie and David barbecued, Katie and Bill prepared salads and green beans. Barry kept the camera going as they cooked and the group settled around to eat.

He took beautiful shots as the sun fell.

Vanessa enjoyed dinner; they all piled aboard the hull and deck of the *Claddagh* for their first major meal together, and she sat back with Katie, enjoying the light sway of the boat in the still night. That morning, the nightmare had all but faded away, and yet she was left to wonder if she had really seen Carlos Roca, if her dreams weren't some kind of a warning.

And if she should tell Sean that she had seen him.

But everyone seemed to think that he had to be guilty. If she told anyone else at all—even Sean—and he appeared again somewhere, someone might shoot to kill.

She had to have imagined Carlos.

Except that she hadn't imagined a dead pirate.

Odd, but true.

And Bartholomew was there. He hadn't come across to the *Claddagh*. He stood at the bow of the *Conch Fritter,* just looking out over the sea. She wondered what he was thinking or feeling, or if—without flesh and substance—he couldn't feel, and yet she thought that he could. She decided then that the soul had to consist of both intelligence and the heart, and it was rather sad, because pain could then remain long after death.

Marty played his guitar and sang on deck, and Katie joined him. Bill and Zoe engaged in a game of chess. Jamie, Liam, David and Sean closed themselves away in the cabin of the *Claddagh* for about an hour, planning and charting, and when they were through, Vanessa was ready to return to the *Conch Fritter* and head into bed.

It was nice to sleep with the captain, she decided. The master cabin very comfortable. Marty was given the convertible couch in the main cabin, while Ted and Jaden were portside and Jay and Zoe were in the slim bunks on the starboard side.

Vanessa went to bed by herself because Sean took first watch on the *Conch Fritter* while Liam took first watch on the *Claddagh.*

Watches were in four-hour shifts. As she curled comfortably into the master cabin's bed, Vanessa realized that the schedule for watch duty included everyone—but someone in Sean's group would be on one of the decks at all times.

Did he distrust someone he had hired on? she wondered. Or was he always that careful and wary?

She thought about Jay wanting to sell their film; a major distributor could mean really decent money, and she knew that he needed the money—and that he still had dreams of producing and directing his own films.

It just disturbed her.

She stared at the small table by the bed that held a reading lamp. She noticed that there was a newspaper there, beneath one of Sean's books. She glanced at the book and noticed that it was on the numerous wrecks in the area. She pulled out the newspaper beneath it.

The headline on the page read, "Missing!"

Beneath it was a picture of two couples standing on a dock. They wore white casual boating clothes and hats, and they were all older, attractive people with happy smiles.

Sean had told her about more disappearances. Disappearances in the area. She scanned the article. Both Mark Houghton and Dale Johnson were experienced captains. They loved traveling together, and though they had made more distant trips, they were sun and warm-water people and set off every couple of months together to tour a part of the Caribbean.

They enjoyed camping on Haunt Island.

She winced and set the article down. She'd been so busy lately that she hadn't seen anything on the disappearance. Of course Sean had known about it.

There had always been disappearances. But now this. A year after the *Delphi.*

Two years after the murders of Travis and Georgia.

She closed her eyes and tried to sleep.

A while later, she felt Sean crawling in beside her, and she sidled up against the warmth of his naked length and lay awake for a very long time.

The sun was rising in the east.

It was almost morning, almost time for their first dive as a complete crew.

She wondered if she was afraid.

No, Vanessa thought. She wasn't afraid of diving. She wasn't afraid of figureheads in the water, or even the absurdity of her dreams.

She was afraid of reaching Haunt Island.

13

The dive that morning was beautiful and uneventful. They went down to several of the wrecks on the Shipwreck Trail in Biscayne National Park. Reefs were beautiful, and though modern technology helped, ships and boats still had to be wary. The *Alicia,* built in Scotland, had slammed into the Ajax reef and the outline of the ship hosted a massive ecosystem of brilliantly colored fish, rays, nurse sharks, groupers and more. It was a beautiful wreck to film, and it was one that Vanessa had filmed before. They had shot scenes of their characters off enjoying themselves before they had stumbled upon the legend and the horror of the ghosts who had come back to tear them to shreds.

That afternoon, they docked at Dinner Key in Miami, since they would begin the voyage across the straits—in the Bermuda Triangle—to reach Haunt Island in the morning. They had a late lunch at Monty's on the water, and after, Sean announced that they were all welcome to do what they wished as long as they were aboard and ready to leave again first thing in the morning.

Vanessa was surprised when Sean suggested that she

and Katie and whoever else wanted to should explore the area, go to a club, do something enjoyable.

He didn't tell her what he had planned. She decided to ask him point-blank—they were supposed to be trusting one another.

"So? Where are you going, what are you up to?" she asked him.

Sean hesitated. "I'm off to see a Coast Guard friend of Liam's," he told her.

"I should come," she said.

He shook his head. "He's told us that they didn't get anything."

"Then why are you seeing him?"

"Because I'm hoping to trigger something. Spend the afternoon and evening with Zoe and Katie—and whoever you wish. Jamie won't leave his boat, and Marty has determined that he's going to keep watch over the *Conch Fritter.* Ted and Jaden have some friends to see. So…Katie will stick with you like glue," he said.

She frowned. "I don't need to be careful here, do I?"

"You need to be careful everywhere," he assured her. "Just stay in public places, and call me if anything disturbs you at all. At all—okay?"

As the others left one by one, Jay told Vanessa, "I have an idea."

She groaned. "I don't think I want to hear any more of your ideas."

He grimaced. "There's a beautiful little park just north of here, and it has great views of the bay and bridges and downtown Miami. I'd like to take some footage of you there, talking about the time we spent in Miami, and how this had been Georgia's destination the night she—died."

She started to protest. Katie was at her side. "Actually, it doesn't sound like a terrible idea," she said. "We can grab a cab and get there while it's still daylight. And it's not the Keys, but it's a beautiful day, and it should be fine footage. I'll go with you," Katie assured her.

"And I'll come," Zoe said.

"Hey, Barry, Ted—Bill. What are you doing tonight?"

"There's a theater up the street," Bill said. "I thought I'd take in a movie—okay, and do some barhopping in Coconut Grove."

"Barry?" Vanessa asked.

He smiled. "The barhopping sounded good to me, too."

Jake told them, "I'll come with you. I guess we need two cabs, though."

"No big deal, it's right down the street," Jay told them.

They left the restaurant and easily hailed cabs.

The park was beautiful. There were wide-open spaces, and areas for volleyball, little pavilions for picnics and separations that were composed of overgrown trees and rich foliage. Beautiful bougainvillea crawled over the pavilions, and majestic oaks vied with palms. They were on a deepwater channel, but the view of the water was spectacular, and as they arrived, the colorful lights of downtown Miami were just beginning to grace the skyscrapers in the distance.

Jay found the perfect place for her to stand. She was on a small mound with bougainvillea and the richness of the foliage to her left as she faced him while a view of the water, the bridge and downtown were just over her shoulder.

Jay set her up where he wanted her and gave her directions. She told him that they hadn't come up with any kind of a script and he told her just to talk. She'd seen Sean do it, easily and naturally, and she tried to emulate what he did. Actually, it was easy. She just talked.

"One more time," Jay told her. "And…action."

She started to talk.

She looked at Zoe, who smiled at her with a thumbs-up gesture. Katie nodded, as well.

The sun was setting in the west, away from the water. The sky was beautiful and the night was balmy. She looked toward the foliage near the entry of the park, and she fell silent.

There he was.

He was in jeans, a T-shirt and a windbreaker. His hair was long, but he had shaved the beard.

Carlos Roca.

He stood on the path, watching her.

He beckoned to her.

But then he saw the others start to stare at Vanessa in her sudden, still silence, and twist to see what had caused her reaction.

He turned his back and moved quickly down the path to the right, into the concealment of the rich foliage.

"Vanessa, I just wanted one more take!" Jay said. "What's the matter with you?"

Vanessa ignored him.

And ran after Carlos Roca.

They met Andy Jimena at the yacht club where the Coast Guardsman kept a membership. It was beautiful, on the bay, and afforded a view of a host of sailboats and pleasure craft. Jimena was an experienced officer who had been with the patrol boat asked in by the Bahamian government. He was fifty, graying and still as sturdy as a rock.

He and his crew had arrived on the island late in the afternoon after the heads and arms of the murder victims had been found onshore.

"I don't know how much I need to tell you all about the way the sea and the sand can hide evidence, or how deep the channel can be in places and how wind and weather can wreck anything on the sand. I'm telling you, here were the problems—the sand on the beach by the victims was dead dry. There were no prints. No footprints whatsoever. Obviously, someone put those bodies there. We found some smashed bracken nearby and further inland, so I'm assuming that Travis was murdered earlier, and that the killer was either Carlos Roca and he came back with Georgia, killed her, too, cut up the bodies and escaped in the night, or—there had been someone else on the island, that person had a boat, maybe something really small, got in, killed Travis, pirated Carlos Roca, killed him and the actress, and went back to pose the bodies."

"What about the people on the island?" Sean asked him.

Jimena shrugged. "They all looked as if they were shell-shocked. Lewis Sanderson, a Bahamian national and guide, was with them, and he was in control but equally horrified. The tents the film crew slept in were all near one another. Apparently, they'd been working all day, work was over, they were about to split open some champagne, and Georgia came down the beach screaming. Sanderson said that he walked down the beach with Jay Allen and Vanessa Loren and that they found nothing—except that someone had been digging in the sand, right where the heads and arms were found later. We searched the shoreline and the surrounding water. We sent out divers. We never found the rest of the bodies, Carlos Roca or the boat. Bahamian officials questioned everyone on that island, and although it's a sovereign country, the Bahamians invited the FBI in and their men questioned everyone involved, as well."

"So what did you believe in the end?" Liam asked him.

"Let's see…one woman told me that alien monsters lived in the Bermuda Triangle and that they rose from the depths to kill. But that's not what I believe. I believe that the most logical answer is that Carlos Roca killed the actor—Travis—and came back to camp and behaved normally. Then he left with the girl, killed her, came back and staged the scene—and disappeared himself. It might have been hard for him at first. But there are a lot of places where you can go by boat, and I don't care how any government or law-enforcement group tries—there are just miles and miles and miles of coast around here, along Florida and in the Caribbean. It's possible to disappear. And after a few years, he could establish a new name, and eventually, people would forget to look for him."

"What about the others on the island?" Sean persisted. Jimena frowned, having answered the question once.

"We're working with what was left of that crew now.

I'd like to know what you thought of all of them—and if you think it was possible that whoever carried out those murders had an accomplice," Sean explained.

Jimena arched his brows. "Well...I suppose it's possible. It seemed to me that they were all in reach of one another, but...I suppose you'd have to ask them all if they're really certain they were all together at the times when it occurred. I know that when the investigations took place, no one suspected the survivors of being guilty."

"That doesn't mean that they weren't," David said quietly.

"Well, no, of course not. All I can tell you is that it was...clean, if that makes sense. There were no mounds of drying blood. There were no footprints, no fingerprints, and there wasn't a murder weapon to be found, and they had to have been chopped to pieces. We searched for the boat and never found it. If you're out with that crew and you're the least bit suspicious, well—I'd keep one hell of a good eye on them." Solid, experienced man that Jimena was, he shuddered. "That was one hell of a scene on Haunt Island. One hell of a scene."

Soon after, they left Jimena, thanking him for his help.

"I think there's something we should start doing," Sean said as he, David and Liam headed back.

Liam looked at him sharply.

"I've charted a number of recent disappearances. I think we might want to make another chart and do some comparisons. You're the only one with the contacts to do it, Liam," Sean told him.

"All right. What am I doing?" Liam asked.

Sean explained.

"Vanessa! Vanessa!"

It was natural, of course, that the others ran after her.

She ignored them at first, running as fast as she could to the path, and then frantically searching the smaller trails among the foliage, hoping against hope that she would find Carlos, that he would be alive and real, and ready to tell her the truth about what had happened—including the fact that he was innocent.

But Carlos was nowhere to be found, and she was left on a path, frustrated and breathless.

A twig snapped behind her and she jumped, suddenly aware that the sun had fallen, she was in the midst of bushes—and she was supposed to be careful and wary.

She spun around.

It was Jay.

He was angry.

He held the camera at his side. It slapped against his leg.

"What the hell are you doing?" he demanded.

He took a step toward her. In her life, she had never been afraid of Jay. She reminded herself that she had known him forever. He was the little kid her own age who lived down the street.

But she stepped back.

Jay started to lift the camera. She had the bizarre fear that he was about to crash it down on her head.

But Zoe came running down the path, crashing into Jay's back. And Jake was right behind Zoe.

"Hey!" Jake said, trying to defuse the situation. Apparently, Jake realized that Jay was really angry.

"Vanessa!" Zoe gasped.

Katie came running from the other direction. She was armed.

She held a giant stick in her hand.

"Vanessa, oh, thank God!" Katie breathed.

"What in hell were you doing?" Jay demanded, still angry.

She opened her mouth. She didn't want to tell anyone about Carlos. Especially not Jay. Not at that moment.

"I was imagining things," she said. "Silly. Ridiculous. I—I thought I saw Dona Isabella standing here."

"What?" Jay exclaimed.

Zoe gasped. "What?"

"It's ridiculous. I'm a little unnerved, I guess. Finding a corpse, finding out the corpse was stolen. I'm sorry, guys, really, I saw a lady standing here and thought it was Dona Isabella. Actually, I scared the poor woman half to death. She was a young Cuban woman, strikingly beautiful, just like Dona Isabella," Vanessa said. The lying was coming too easily, but then, she had thought once that she'd seen Dona Isabella, or she did see her often, her face carved as a figurehead, in her dreams... Maybe reality and imagination were blending so that the line was barely there anymore, this lie was coming so easily.

"Oh, Lord, oh, Lord!" Zoe exclaimed, horrified.

Maybe she should have said that she'd seen Carlos

Roca. Jay was staring at her as if she was crazy, and Zoe looked terrified.

"Look, I'm sorry, I ruined your brilliant idea. It's getting really dark, they must be about to send the rangers in to close this place, and I want to get back to the boats," she said.

Jay looked at her and then sighed. "Well, the first take was good. And when you took off, I wound up with some fantastic shots of the sky. But get a grip, girl!"

"Dammit, Jay, just give me a break, okay?" Vanessa asked. She cursed herself. Surely she could have thought of a different lie! One that wasn't—supernatural.

"Oh, God, oh, God!" Zoe said.

"Hey, there's a cute little restaurant bar just down from Dinner Key marina—we'll go and indulge in big stiff drinks and feel better all the way around!" Jake suggested.

Vanessa didn't want a drink. She wanted to be away from all of them. Except for Katie.

But Katie wanted peace and happiness all the way round. "One big stiff drink apiece," she said. "We'll have a long day tomorrow. One big friendly drink."

"And Vanessa will start seeing little green people, aliens in the Bermuda Triangle," Jay said.

Jake punched Jay in the arm—not hard, but soundly. "Jay, stop!"

Jay stared at Jake. He had a superior, angry look in his eyes for a moment. The look seemed to say *Hey, I'm a director/producer, I'm the boss.*

But Jay wasn't a producer/director on this shoot.

He let out a breath suddenly. "Jake, thanks—I needed that," he said with a laugh. "Vanessa, I'm sorry. I was just— You looked so beautiful there, your hair kind of floating in the breeze, with the lights and the bridge and the foliage. And it was forlorn, it had…oh, well. I'm a great editor. I'll make it work, and Sean and David will love it."

He was Jay again. The Jay she had known forever. She felt silly, being afraid of him.

"Let's get that drink," she said.

They had fun. Vanessa was pleased that she hadn't insisted she was going back.

The bar was composed of a small number of tables with palm-frond shelters over them, their waitress was nice, and a single guitarist played and sang.

When they returned to the boat, Marty was on deck, taking his guard duty very seriously.

"Ahoy, who goes there?" he demanded.

"It's us—we're back," Vanessa told him. She was capable of jumping down to the deck, as were Zoe and Jay, but Marty rose, ever the gentleman, to help them on board.

"Are the guys back yet, Marty?" Vanessa asked.

"Jaden and Ted came back half an hour ago, and they're both in bed. Sean, Liam and David are still out, but they'll be along soon, I warrant," he said cheerfully. "I'll be right here, right here on deck, if you need me, though."

"Thanks, Marty," she told him. "I guess I am calling it a night. Good night, Jay."

"Good night, Vanessa," Jay said. "I'll hang out here with Marty a bit, I guess." He was silent, looking at her. "Good night," he said again, and then, his back to Marty, he mouthed, "I'm sorry. I'm really sorry."

She smiled and nodded. "See you in the morning."

In the master's cabin, she started. Bartholomew was next to the bed, one ghostly buckle-shoe foot upon it as he stood in a Captain Morgan stance. He gave her a start, and she thought again that she was having trouble with reality and fiction or imagination.

He was a ghost, he was real. As real as a ghost could be. Others saw him.

He was glaring at her.

"What?" she murmured.

He shook his head, and then wagged a finger at her.

"I followed you today," he said.

"You did? Well, that was…nice of you? Or nosy of you?" she asked.

He sighed, set his foot on the floor and walked to her. It was odd. She could feel him. At first, she had thought that he was cold. A cold breeze.

But now she thought that he offered a strange warmth. She saw his eyes, and he was concerned. Bartholomew liked her. She was glad.

She would have liked him.

"Vanessa, I don't know what you're thinking, but you have to tell Sean the truth," Bartholomew said.

"What truth?"

"That Carlos Roca was in the park, following you. At least, I think that's who it is. And he was in Key West, too, at the pirate festivities. He's been watching you—and following you," Bartholomew said.

Vanessa gasped. She sank down on the bed in the cabin, and Bartholomew sank down beside her.

"He's real," she whispered.

"Yes," Bartholomew said.

"Real—and alive?" Vanessa asked.

"The man was no ghost. Trust me, sadly, I know," Bartholomew said. He sighed. "Obviously, I can tell Sean and David, because they have a right to know. But I really don't like telling tales when it's someone else's business. But people were killed. They might have been killed by Carlos Roca. The man might be stalking you. You might be his next intended victim. Vanessa, this is scary. Terrifying. And I think you've suspected that he's out there. Why haven't you told Sean?"

She was about to answer when she heard Jay's voice, whispering to her from just beyond the door. "Vanessa? Is something wrong? Are you all right?"

"Fine, Jay!" she replied in a loud whisper. "Fine—I was singing, that's all. Sorry!"

He laughed. "Now you're singing! Night, sweetie."

"Night!"

Vanessa waited until she heard him move away and then she whispered to Bartholomew. "I just can't believe it. I really can't. What if Carlos is trying to reach me because he is innocent, because he needs my help, because he suspects or knows what really happened?" she asked.

"You still need to tell Sean. Look, there are other lives at stake here," he reminded her.

He touched her cheek with a ghostly hand. She thought that she could feel the warmth and tenderness. "I'm going topside, help old Marty keep watch," he said.

She nodded. He stood and looked at her.

"I'll tell him," she said.

He nodded, and disappeared through the door.

Sean was surprised and glad when he arrived back on the boat to find that Vanessa was awake. She stirred when he quietly entered the cabin and stripped down to join her in bed.

"Hey," he said softly.

She smiled in the dim light that filtered through from the dock.

"You aren't on guard duty," she said.

"Ted is taking a turn," he told her. "Had to get Marty to get some sleep," he added dryly. "Did you have a nice night? What did you do?"

She studied him carefully. "We went to a park. Jay took some footage. Let's see, Bill and Barry went bar-hopping, but Zoe, Jay, Jake, Katie and I went to a park. Jay had an idea for a scene, and he's all excited. He thinks you're going to like it."

"I probably will. He's good."

She was still searching out his eyes. He smiled and kissed her lips. She drew the covers more tightly around her and she frowned, trying to understand her sudden reticence with him.

She let out a deep, pent-up breath. "Sean, I saw Carlos Roca."

"What?" He sat up, staring at her, trying to fathom her eyes in the shadows.

"Actually, I had just *thought* that I'd seen Carlos,

but…Bartholomew was with us, following us, and he said that it was Carlos Roca."

"So the man has been hiding in Miami," Sean said, "hiding in plain sight." He started to rise.

"Sean, wait. Where are you going?" she asked.

"To notify the authorities," he said.

"But what if he's in hiding—because he's innocent?" Vanessa asked.

"Vanessa, if he's innocent, he'll be able to prove it."

"How? We both know that he looks guilty as hell, and that innocent men do go to prison," she argued.

He stared down at her and shook his head sadly. "Vanessa, I have to notify the authorities. If he's been living here—"

"He hasn't been living here," she said.

"What? How do you know? Did he accost you?" he asked, coming down beside her again, drawing her to him. "Did he hurt you, did he threaten you, did—"

"No, no, no. I never got close to him. But he was in Key West."

He eased away, trying to study her face again. "You saw him in Key West, and you didn't tell me?" he asked her.

"I didn't know that I had seen him. I *thought* that I might have seen him," she said. "But then, God knows what I see anymore!"

"So he is following you," Sean said.

"I don't know that. And if he is, I swear, I think it's because he needs help."

"Vanessa, what happened to the trust thing that was

supposed to be going on between us?" he asked her softly.

"I do trust you. I just know how you feel."

He nodded slowly. "You wouldn't have told me now—except that Bartholomew saw him, too."

"Your *ghost,*" she reminded him dryly.

He stood. He reached for his jeans again. "Sean—"

"Vanessa, I'm really sorry. The authorities have to know," he told her. He walked to the deck. Ted was leaning back on the aft cushions, watching the stars—and the dock.

"What's up?" he asked.

"A Carlos Roca sighting," he said. "I'm going up to radio the Coast Guard and let the police know that the man was seen in Miami."

"Roca?" Ted sat up straight. "Do you think… Wow. Do you think he'll come after the rest of that crew?"

"Ted, we're traveling the way we are just to make sure we don't have trouble and that no one can take us by surprise. But if you're worried about you and Jaden, I can leave you here and you can get a rental car to take home."

"No. No," Ted told him. "We're on this. We've discussed it. We're with you all the way. And I'm ready. Trust me. I'm ready." He showed Sean that he had a speargun down by his side. "I know how to use this faster than a winking eye, and you know it."

Sean nodded. "Yeah, I know."

He radioed the Coast Guard first, and then called the police, and then David. Bartholomew was seated in the companion seat, aware of Ted just below.

"She told you," Bartholomew said.

Sean nodded.

Bartholomew looked out at the water, at the various boats docked at the public marina. "You had to know," he said.

"Yep."

"I'll be on deck," Bartholomew said.

Sean smiled. "Thanks."

He went back down, telling Ted that he'd spell him in three hours.

He went back to his cabin.

Vanessa's eyes were closed. He didn't think that she was sleeping, but he lay down beside her without touching her.

A moment later she spoke in the darkness. "You called the police?"

"Yes."

She was silent, staying on her own side of the bed. He didn't press the matter. He had done what he had to do, even if he understood that the man had been her friend and she believed in him.

But everyone on that island had been her friend. She trusted them all.

And the more he thought about it all, the more he learned, Sean didn't believe that there had been someone in a boat who had slipped onto the island, killed Travis, gone after Carlos Roca and Georgia, killed Georgia, dismembered two bodies, and escaped with the boat and Carlos Roca, who was now miraculously alive and well.

That was too suspect.

Someone in that film crew had been guilty. Someone knew more than they were saying. And with the violence and brutality of the murders, he doubted that it was someone who had killed only once, for a purpose. That someone had killed before, had probably killed again, and would keep killing. It seemed likely that maybe that person was involved in a murder conspiracy with Carlos Roca.

"I'm sorry," Sean said.

"So am I," she said.

He smiled. "Are you sorry that I called the police—or sorry that you didn't tell me earlier?"

"Both," she said after a moment.

He rolled toward her and reached for her, pulling her into his arms. "Please understand. It's a dangerous world out there," he said softly.

"I know," she told him gravely.

He nodded. He wasn't sure what else to say. He kissed her. And then he knew that he'd have to leave soon enough, take his turn on guard duty.

He made love to her, slowly, tenderly, and she responded, making love in turn, her kisses gentle, her whispers soft…her movement fluid. They winced together at one point—it was a boat, and they were trying to be quiet, and they were, but…

They lay together afterward, and the boat rocked gently, and he heard a distant bell.

"I don't think that it will matter that I called the Miami police," he told her.

"Why not?"

"Because I think he's already out there. Carlos Roca knows where we're going, he knows our route, and he knows we're headed for Haunt Island.

"And he's already on his way."

14

"Let's head straight on over, set up camp on the island and work backward from there," Sean suggested. He and David had met at the breakfast bar near the marina. He opened the book he kept on their schedule with relevant sea charts and maps. "We're clear with the Bahamian authorities, and I started doing calculations on what I could find regarding the current at the time, the time of year and the storm—and I think that once the pirate ship started to take on water and break up during the storm, it would have been forced out of the deep water where it was always assumed to have sunk, and that the debris field would stretch out not far from the first drop-off to the southwest of Haunt Island."

"I like the logic of getting there, setting up a base and moving on from Haunt Island," David said. "You like the split that we have of people? Yesterday was the first time it seemed you didn't trust everyone with us."

"I don't. I don't trust anyone right now."

"Especially Carlos Roca? And you really think that Vanessa saw him—and that it was him?"

Sean shrugged, looking toward the marina. "There are just so many factors in this situation that make no sense. I'm going to try to get Vanessa to take me through it all again, step by step, from earlier in the afternoon *before* Georgia Dare came running down the beach. The thing is, I don't think that one person could have done all this. I think that if Carlos was guilty, he had to have had an accomplice. If he wasn't guilty, two people had to be involved. Yes, it's possible that there was a boat at anchor near the island that was hidden from view behind palms or foliage or even the curve of the shoreline. But the thing is—*why?* Don't you think that someone must have had a reason—no matter how psychotic—to butcher bodies and leave them on display?"

"There's the outside chance that an islander, dismayed with what they were doing on Haunt Island, lay in wait, and that the murders were because of outrage over making a film based on the massacre," David said.

"Yes, there's an outside chance," Sean agreed. "I know that Liam ran everything he could on Lew Sanderson, the Bahamian guide who was with them."

"The man is squeaky-clean. He's worked with dignitaries from around the world. He's a family man, married twenty years, two children, and known for helping out in times of distress, such as doing volunteer road work and clearance after storms. His neighbors love him—he's an open book, so it seems," David said. He drummed his fingers on the breakfast table. "I think your idea of matching up people and places over the last two years is a good one, and I know that Liam is on the computer now. It doesn't seem possible to me that someone could commit such a horrible crime, then go back to a normal life as if nothing ever happened."

"That's my point. And I still say…I don't know, we're

missing something, and I think it has to do with the *why*, and if we could just figure that out, we'd discover the *who*."

David leaned back, shaking his head. "Well, there are plenty of theories. First, chalk it up to the Bermuda Triangle. Second, it *is* called Haunt Island."

"We both know that a ghost—or even ghosts—didn't commit those murders."

"Agreed—I'm just throwing out the theories," David said.

"Right," Sean agreed. "Third theory—modern-day pirates, cleverly plotting. They committed gruesome murders and stole a boat and dumped Carlos Roca's body overboard. But now Carlos Roca has been seen, so that theory is out. Okay, fourth theory. It was Carlos Roca, and he had friends—modern-day pirates—in on it. Fifth theory, Carlos was innocent, and he was hit on the head and is walking around suffering from amnesia. But that's unlikely, considering the fact that there was an intensive manhunt going on for him after it first happened. Sixth theory—someone on the film crew was in on it with Carlos Roca. That's why he's alive and well, it's how he managed to stay 'missing' all this time, and it's why he seems to be following us now."

"We're still back to why," David said. "All those people had good careers. What would make a professional with no record whatsoever suddenly commit murder?"

"That's something we have to find out," Sean said. "It's going to be interesting, though. All of us so close together. And that's how we're going to stay. The film crew—or at least the majority of it—wasn't expecting anything bad to happen. They were working. They were in a place that was a pristine hangout for boaters. There was no reason to expect anything. And we know damned well that bad things happen. So..." Sean hesitated. "Maybe Katie should stay here, in Miami," he said. "I asked Ted last night...but he wants in."

"Katie won't go back—you know your sister," David said. "Look, I really think that we're dealing with cowards here. The whole company wasn't killed. Travis was probably taken by surprise. And as far as Carlos and Georgia and the boat...well, any way you look at it, it was one man who was the surprise, or was taken from the back in the dark. We'll be all right. Marty and Jamie are fierce old pirates, we've got Liam, you and me. Once we're on the island, we'll have perimeter, with one us on guard at all times, maybe two of us. So here's the thing. We do it or we don't. And at this point, I say we do it."

Sean nodded and called for the check.

It was a beautiful day for the trip across the straits from Miami to Haunt Island. The boats moved parallel across fairly calm seas, the sky was a pristine blue with only a few puffs of white clouds, and the sun shone down brilliantly throughout the day.

Seated in the companion seat, Vanessa was glad enough to laze the time away. Marty took the helm several times, and Jay and Sean spent the hours filming the voyage. Sean did a few minutes on the straits, the proximity of the Bahamas to Florida, and how the voyage would have been different in the eighteen hundreds when the wind played such an important role in travel. They pointed out the area where Mad Miller's pirate ship had supposedly gone down, and Sean gave his calculations on the currents of the time, estimating that the debris field had to extend farther than it had often been presumed.

Vanessa was roused for a few moments to do a two-minute take on her research regarding Dona Isabella, Mad Miller and Kitty Cutlass, and how they had followed the same path when they had been making the film.

She was surprised when Sean filmed Jay, asking him about his feelings on the distribution of the film. Jay sounded sincere when he said that he believed that Georgia and Travis would have wanted it shown—they had been actors, after all—and that he hoped they could find the truth, see that the murderer was punished and be able to distribute the film feeling that they had justice and closure at last.

Jay's speech seemed heartfelt.

From her comfortable perch, a warm poncho around her shoulders against the chill of the wind, Vanessa observed Sean's questions as he interviewed Zoe and Jake, wanting to know everything that had happened on the island the day that Georgia and Travis had been murdered. Jake had been in charge of props, and he explained that it was easy to understand why they had all dismissed Georgia's fears—any one of them might have played a prank.

When she had come screaming down the sand, he had been in his little tent, getting ready to come on out and share the champagne.

Zoe talked about her love of the period costumes

and relayed the story about the afternoon when they'd dressed Vanessa up as a deceased Dona Isabella and gotten a bit carried away, forgetting that she was floating in the ocean in heavy materials. She had last seen Travis that afternoon, when they had filmed the scene in which help had come to the island at last. She, too, had been in her tent, pleased with the film and hoping for great distribution and big notches on their résumés for future work.

Vanessa noted that Bartholomew was silent, watching their destination before them and listening intently to the interviews. He seemed thoughtful.

They arrived at the island at just about three that afternoon.

She rose and went aft, watching as they came upon Haunt Island and trying to remember when she had been there last. Now it all seemed such a blur. The island appeared lovely and tropical, totally benign in the bright sunlit day. She had thought she would feel something. She had thought that she'd be afraid. She wasn't. It was just an island.

Lew Sanderson was standing at the end of the dock, waiting to greet them. He waved a welcome and caught the ties as the *Conch Fritter* drew in first. Vanessa hopped to the dock and was enveloped in a huge hug by the big man.

It felt good.

The *Claddagh* pulled into the dockage behind the *Conch Fritter.* Vanessa and Lew caught her ties, and soon everyone was standing on the dock. Lew greeted those he knew and met those he didn't, and the next two hours were spent setting up camp on the island.

There was nothing terribly rustic about camping on the island; the tents were large, the camp bunks were not uncomfortable, they had an impressive barbecue area and a battery-operated coffeemaker, not to mention that showers could be had back at the boats—they were well supplied.

By the time all the work was done, they were exhausted, and Vanessa thought that they might have forgotten that terrible things had happened here. They had all seemed to work very well together, hauling boxes and bags to the beach, setting up the tents and then, when all was done, digging a pit and starting a fire on the beach. Sean had brought a good supply of torches as well, and as darkness settled, their area of the beach was still aglow. The sea remained calm and easy and the sound of the waves was lulling. She was amazed to enjoy the glow and the company as they worked together and finally sat down to a meal.

She, Jay, Sean and Barry had taken turns with cameras during the day, documenting their setup. She forgot that Barry was still filming as dinnertime rolled around—Zoe in charge that night, supervising Bill fondly as she barbecued hot dogs and hamburgers and warmed baked beans in a huge pot, and announcing—with a smile for the camera—that she also had spinach so that they could make certain the meal was healthful. They had to keep up their strength, of course.

Then they sat by the fire, eating. It seemed relaxed. But Vanessa was aware that five people had subtly been changing an important position throughout the day. Guard duty. As Sean took a seat beside her, she saw that his uncle Jamie was standing at the perimeter of the group, watching the dock, the sea and the foliage. He was wearing a windbreaker, and she thought there was a bulge beneath his arm. Jamie was carrying a gun.

If there was tension within their group, Lew Sanderson didn't seem to know it. He entertained them with a Bahamian tale about a talking raccoon, and they all laughed, and then he told them another story, his face dark and mysterious as it was caught in the glow of the fire. "They say we are in the Bermuda Triangle, but long before it had such a name, the people here knew that there was something special about the air. The earth herself is mysterious, and as man has come to learn all about technology and science, he has often forgotten that no matter how far we go, we are dots in the universe, and the universe itself is a mystery. Now, you know, my ancestors who came to these islands came as slaves, and they brought with them a certain magic that belonged to their ancestors. They were open to the world, open to life and death, and aware that all things were not to be seen. Nowadays, we claim that there are underwater forces here. There are the currents, there are the wicked wonders and destruction of the storms and hurricanes that ravage the area. Ah, yes! There are magnetic forces in the earth as well, and they cause confusion, the horizon itself can trick a pilot or a captain. But my people believed that there were gods and devils that dwelled on earth, between the realms of life and death. Forces, for good and for evil. Kiandra, the sea god, once appeared as an ugly thing in need before two sisters. The first spurned him and married a handsome man. The second felt pity, fed him and married him, and went to live with him in his fine kingdom in the sea, bearing many children. The handsome man the sister married proved to be a *kishi,* an evil devil or demon. She had a child with a human head and a hyena head, and in the end, her husband devoured her. Her spirit remained, evil and bitter, and when Africans came here, many believed that what we call the Bermuda Triangle now was where the first sister's bitter soul came to dwell and that now, while the sea god Kiandra and his wife seek to save those who travel the sea, the evil sister's influence can make men crazy, can make the evil dead within the ocean rise and cause all kinds of havoc. There are those who believe that the magnetic forces that cause compasses to spin and ships and planes to go astray are merely the toys of the spirit of the evil sister, and that she teases her prey before she kills, just like a great cat of the sea."

Zoe laughed softy, but the sound seemed a little nervous. "Lew! You don't believe that story, do you?"

Lew smiled. "It is a tale, it is a legend. All people have tales and legends, and perhaps they come from a grain of truth." He shrugged. "I do believe in good and evil, and they dwell within all of us."

"On that, I'll have more coffee!" Bill said. He stood, and having been sitting next to Zoe, he asked her, "Zoe, more coffee? You're shivering."

"I admit to being a little nervous," she said.

He smiled at her. "Don't be. I'll protect you," he said.

Watching them, Vanessa smiled. She hadn't realized—though perhaps she should have—that Bill seemed to have a crush on Zoe. Ah, the slightly older woman. She smiled back at Bill. Maybe Zoe had a crush on the younger man, as well. "Thanks," Zoe said. "I'll hold you to that!"

Well, that was good. Zoe would have Bill with her, and she wouldn't be as nervous, and there was always safety in numbers.

"I think I'm just calling it a night," Katie said, yawning. "I imagine we want to start out on a dive pretty early?" she asked.

"Actually, I was thinking just after twelve tomorrow," Sean said. "I want to take some footage with the original film crew, each person talking a bit more about what they did. And we'll take a walk down the beach, see what we see. Maybe discern if another boat might have come in during the night."

"Well, a boat had to have come in—I think," Barry said. He was frowning. "I mean, if a boat didn't come in, it means…Carlos…or…" He fell silent.

The group was silent.

The fire snapped and crackled.

"One of us will be on guard all night, every night," Sean said.

"One of us?" Jake asked.

"One of us who *wasn't* with the original crew," Sean said.

There was silence again. "Well, good night, all," Katie said, and she left the group.

Sean rose and talked to Marty for a moment. The others began to rise and murmur good-nights and head for their tents.

Vanessa realized that Marty was going to bed; that Sean was taking the first watch.

He looked at her and she smiled, nodded and turned

to head for their tent. She slipped inside and almost started—she still wasn't accustomed to Bartholomew showing up all the time.

"Sean is on first watch," he said softly.

She sat at the foot of her canvas bunk, smiling. "And you're watching over me?"

He winced. "Hey, I can *watch* over you at least. And I can make a few things happen. I can push buttons…I can trip people. I'm not bad at manifestations, but…"

"What?" Vanessa asked.

"I was listening to that fellow tonight, the Bahamian, Lew Sanderson," Bartholomew said.

"He was telling a story," Vanessa said. "An African legend."

"Yes, of course. But often…well, gods and goddesses, angels and demons…it's strange how the world can be so different, and yet so much the same. The Norse had Odin, the Romans, Jupiter, and the Greeks had Zeus, and he was nearly one and the same. The Christian, Jewish and Muslim faiths recognize one God, but he lives in Heaven with the angels, and the angels often have characteristics that line up with the lesser gods in other religions."

She was startled at first that he seemed so philosophical, but then she realized that he was seriously troubled by Lew's story.

"You're talking about the fact that people here thought the bitter sister's soul haunted the ocean, while many people now believe there's something eerie about the Bermuda Triangle?" Vanessa asked.

He nodded. He stared at her. "Well, I told you—the legend that has come down about Mad Miller and Kitty

Cutlass…well, there's just something wrong with it. Mad Miller got his name because another fellow was making fun of him one day and called him *mad* because he was…well, he was a bit of a fop. He hated blood. And Kitty…Kitty was in love with Mad Miller because he was the best thing that ever came along in her sad and pathetic life. You were making a film about them and Dona Isabella. I was thinking that…well, obviously, *I'm* still around, and maybe they are, too."

"Bartholomew, we've all agreed that ghosts couldn't have committed the murders," Vanessa said. "I mean, thank God…thank God we do have you, because we know what ghosts can and can't do. And I always believed that ghosts stayed behind because…they were lost, or they needed help, or justice, or they stayed behind to help others."

"Maybe," Bartholomew said.

"What do you mean *maybe?* You are a ghost!" Vanessa reminded him.

He nodded. "It doesn't mean I have all the answers. Hey, I was a decent fellow in life. I'm a damned decent fellow in death. But perhaps, if you were a bastard in life, you stay a bastard in death."

"You keep telling me that Mad Miller was basically a prissy-ass pansy," Vanessa said with a sigh.

"Yes, I know, though your language is quite colorful," Bartholomew said.

"Sorry."

"That's why I'm perplexed," Bartholomew said. "Ah, well, you had best get some sleep. I think you'll need it in the days to come." He stood. "I'll be near," he promised her.

She smiled, thanked him and bid him good-night.

It wasn't until he was gone and she lay back and watched the fire dancing on the canvas of the tent that she felt alone and uneasy—and suddenly fully aware of the last time she had lain in a tent on the beach at Haunt Island.

She remembered dreaming first that Georgia had come to her. She had almost heard the young woman's voice in the shadows of the night as tears streamed down her cheeks.

I told you there were monsters.

Then Georgia's image had faded, and she must have seen the shadows against the canvas of the tent even in her sleep, because they had seemed like giant monsters rising from the sea, made of seaweed, forming arms, reaching into the sky.

She sighed and lay awake, and thought that she would do so until Sean's watch was over.

But somewhere along the line, she fell asleep, and she didn't dream. She was vaguely aware of Sean coming into the tent, and she was comfortably aware that she tried to get close to him.

Then she let out a startled little cry—completely unaware that she had fallen.

"Vanessa!" It was Sean's voice, and a light suddenly flared in their little tent. She was on the ground between the two cots. They'd been pushed together, but in trying to get too close, she had wedged them apart.

Sean was stretched out on his own, flashlight in one hand as he smiled and reached for her hand with the other.

She grimaced ruefully. "I suppose I forgot where we were."

"Hey!"

"Vanessa!"

"What's going on?"

There was a chorus of voices just outside the tent. She scrambled up, glad that she had chosen to sleep in an encompassing flannel gown. She pushed open the flap to the tent just as Katie was nervously opening it.

"Vanessa!" Katie said.

David was behind her, Liam was behind him, and it seemed that everyone was gathered outside their little tent.

"You screamed!" Zoe said.

Barry cleared his throat. "Um, it didn't sound like a scream of…um, er, happiness."

Sean was behind her then. "Sorry, all."

"I fell off the cot," Vanessa said, aware of the flush that was rising to her cheeks like fire.

"What?" Bill said, and then started to laugh.

"Oh, Lord! You scared us silly," Zoe said, laughing, as well.

"No more even slightly scary stories around the campfire," Lew Sanderson said, shaking his head. "May I suggest you pull the cot mattresses down and leave them on the sand?"

"Great idea, Lew, thanks," Sean said. "Forgive us, folks, and get some sleep."

The good thing was that everyone seemed to be amused. The negative, of course, was seeing just how on edge they had all been.

And probably would remain.

Sean looked down at her, his grin broad. He pulled her into his arms. "Let's get those mattresses down, huh? We'll fold up the bunks—I think we'll wind up with more room."

She agreed. It was really late; they were both exhausted, and aware of the thinness of the canvas that separated them from the others.

And still...

It was good to be close. Seaweed monsters were just shadows on canvas, and Georgia Dare did not return that night with tears streaming down her face to plague Vanessa's dreams.

She thought the morning might be bad as well, with the interviews on the beach. But the sun was shining, the day was bright, and it was hard to imagine that anything horrible had happened in such a beautiful place on such a pristine beach.

They were surrounded by people.

That was good.

Marty and Jamie O'Hara seemed large, wise and imposing, and as she watched the men, naturally taking positions that seemed to guard the group from opposite angles, she realized that they had been asked along from the very beginning because Sean had felt that he needed a security force of those he knew and trusted. They were able seaman, divers and outdoorsmen, but they took no part in any of the filming. They simply watched, interested.

The only one missing during the morning was Liam. Sean told her he was doing some work on his computer on the boat. He didn't mention what. But Liam was a police officer, and he had taken leave at a time when the force was short, and she assumed he was keeping in contact with his colleagues, keeping up on events in Key West.

She was interviewed with Jay, who was matter-of-fact. She spoke about seeing the heads when she had come down the beach. Jay walked to the sand and winced as he told about his disbelief at what they had come upon.

They were all quiet and somewhat mournful when they finished the segment. They walked back to the encampment in comparative silence. Once there, however, everyone set about the business of a light lunch, since they'd head out to the reefs and an afternoon dive soon after. Zoe and Katie went about setting out the sandwich meats, cheeses, lettuce, tomatoes and condiments, but everyone helped themselves, and everyone picked up after themselves.

It was decided that Lew, Marty, Ted, Jaden and Zoe would stay behind to keep an eye on the encampment. They would take out Jamie's boat, the *Claddagh,* because he had recently purchased new sonar equipment, and Sean and David were eager to see if his calculations might be right, if they might find some of the debris from the pirate ship in shallower water.

There was an hour of busywork, coming and going from the *Conch Fritter* and the *Claddagh* as they transferred dive equipment and supplies from one boat to the other, but in the end, once again, it seemed that they all moved smoothly.

As the divers and crew climbed aboard, Vanessa

noted that Bill looked forlornly back at Zoe, and that Zoe smiled and waved.

The romance was blooming.

Bartholomew seemed torn. At the last minute, however, he came aboard the boat.

They set out, running slowly due southwest of the island. Sean grew excited at a blip on the screen, but a study of the sea charts showed that it was a World War II ship that had gone down in 1943; at war's end, it was already becoming part of a growing reef.

"Wait," Sean said. "Uncle Jamie, let's bring her around. If there is something here, that could be a reason that it has never been found!"

"Sean, good call—worth an exploration, at least," David said. "That happened with the old British ship *Renegade* in the Bay of Bengal. She had twisted beneath a trawler that went down several hundred years later."

Barry was filming the discussion. "Wow, yeah, we might have found something!"

His excitement was such that he forgot that he was filming.

"Ahem, camera, my friend!" Jay reminded him.

"Let's break out the diving gear and the casements for the cameras," Sean said. "David, obviously, you and Katie. Jamie—"

"I'll be aboard, keeping watch on the line and my boat!" Jamie said firmly.

"You want me on board or in the water?" Jay asked.

Sean seemed to hesitate for just a second.

He doesn't trust Jay! Vanessa thought.

"What about me?" Barry asked.

"Barry, you're up here, camera ready, with Jamie," Sean said.

Barry frowned. "I—"

"You're the soundman, Barry, and you're good with a camera, too. Be ready when we come up," Sean said.

"Where do you want me?" Bill asked.

"Make it a threesome with Vanessa and me," Sean said. "And, Jake—you tag on with Katie and David."

He had done it again, Vanessa realized—divided the old group. Jamie would watch Barry. Marty was onshore, along with Ted and Jaden, keeping an eye on Lew and Zoe. Liam—David's cousin and Sean's close friend—would be watching Jay. David would have his eye on Jake.

Barry seemed unhappy but resigned. He brightened while the others got into their gear and asked Jamie if he had any fishing equipment.

Jamie scowled. "You'll be catching the divers!"

"No!" Barry protested. "I'll be catching fresh fish for dinner!"

Jamie shook his head but assured Barry he had fishing equipment, but that Barry needed to remember that he was in charge of filming when the divers surfaced.

As Vanessa slipped her mask and regulator on and held the mask in place in order to slip over the hull backward, she noticed Bartholomew. He was standing aft, looking back at the island.

As they descended, the water was clear and beautiful until they reached thirty-three feet and paused to pressurize. Another twenty feet down, and while visibility was still good, the sunlight didn't penetrate as well.

Vanessa saw the hull of the old World War II vessel

and followed Sean around the portside, aware that Bill was keeping pace with her. Sean had the camera, and Vanessa was glad.

It was the camera lens that seemed to play tricks on her.

Sean motioned Bill, instructing him down to the sand where something peculiar seemed to be stuck just beneath the vessel.

It was while they were occupied that Vanessa saw the figurehead.

It was just feet in front of the men. She wouldn't be leaving her partners to follow it, to see if it was real.

To see if it led her to an old treasure again, a pendant.

Or a dead body.

She moved toward it in the water and realized that it was actually within a torn segment of the World War II ship's hull. No. She wasn't going to follow—not without her fellow divers knowing that she was entering the wreck.

She turned, giving a massive kick with her flippers, only to realize that she was already inside the ship. She moved toward the hole through which she had entered, only to discover that the ship seemed to have shifted; the entryway—the exit!—was no more.

And there was no figurehead to be seen.

For a split second, she nearly panicked.

It had all scrambled her mind; she was going ever-so-slightly crazy—and now it was going to trap her and kill her.

She braced herself, checked her air gauge and her compass, and knew that her partners weren't far away.

She moved in the opposite direction from the false lure of the figurehead with the face of Dona Isabella *that didn't really exist.*

The tear in the giant craft was just ahead of her. As she reached it, she saw that the ship had probably been sunk by a torpedo—there was a giant hole extending beneath its watery graveyard in the sand. And beneath it…

There was something.

It looked like a broken shaft of wood. There were clumps and lumps all over it, encrusted in barnacles and sea growth. She reached for it with gloved hands and struggled to pull it free. It gave, but it was heavy.

She banged against the hull of the ship with her dive knife. A second later, Sean came through water toward her, his eyes showing concern through his mask.

She'd never let him know that she had nearly panicked, and thought herself trapped!

She smiled around her regulator and gave him an okay signal. He saw what she had.

He lifted the camera as Bill moved himself through the water to help her grasp the heavy object. He signed to her, and they carried it between them with Sean following. They made their way to the anchor line and moved up to thirty-three feet, waited and moved up again, following the line.

The others had seen them. They begin to ascend, as well.

Jamie was at the dive platform, ready to help them. Vanessa heard Barry say a quick "Oh, shit!" And then he had a camera rolling. Bill climbed out first and shed his tank and BCV in order to help Jamie shift the piece from the dive platform to the boat. Katie followed, throwing her flippers on board and hauling herself up. Sean was quickly behind her, and she reached for the camera. Soon, they were aboard, and the piece she had found was lying on the stern section of the deck with the group gathered around to stare at it.

"It's a piece of a mast," Jamie said.

"And the clumps?" Barry asked.

Jamie stared at Barry, grinning, and then looked at Sean. "Ted and Jaden will have some work to do tonight. Look at the circular patterns. You've found a stash of coins, my friends. Gold and silver, I'd wager. And if I'm right, and if our experts can clean them and give us some dates, I think we'll find that you're right, Sean. We've come upon a debris field of the pirate ship, if not the pirate ship itself."

Sean turned to Vanessa and pulled her close, planting a huge kiss on her lips.

"You're amazing!" he told her.

She smiled uneasily.

She had followed the figurehead again.

But the figurehead had nearly trapped her that day. Had it been leading her to treasure?

Or trying to lure her to her death?

15

"Oh my God!" Jaden cried, delighted with the discovery. "Ted, look…it's definitely a cache of coins. I'd say it is a piece of the mast. Maybe the new wreck crushed the old wreck. I think that Sean was right, and that it was a long debris field…and still, what's left of the pirate hull might be there…it's possible. It's certainly not *impossible!*"

"This is really fabulous," Ted said. "The last time I saw something like this it was…wow, it was a display from the *Atocha.*" He turned to Jaden. "We can get started. We brought supplies. I can't wait to see the dates on the coins and find out what was on that ship. I can't wait to see the coins. I think there are definitely some cobs attached there—those are bits taken off the gold bars. They could have been stolen from anyone, French, English, Spanish or Americans!" he said excitedly.

They were back on the beach and the heavy piece of mast with its encrusted treasure lay in the center of a tarp while they gathered around it and stared.

"It's amazing," Zoe breathed, looking at Vanessa. "And you found this, too?"

"More or less. I was diving with Sean and Bill," Vanessa said.

"You really missed your calling," Zoe said.

"Hey, Bahamian or International waters?" Jay asked, looking at Lew.

Lew smiled broadly. "Bahamian! Yeah!"

"Ah, there goes the treasure," Jay said sadly.

Vanessa stepped back, not really thrilled with the fact that she had once again discovered a find in the water. She couldn't help but think about Lew's story—and the things Bartholomew had said.

But…

Say there was a ghost that somehow haunted her in the water. First off, why would Dona Isabella, so cruelly taken and murdered, want to cause evil to anyone?

And second, ghosts didn't have the power to do what had been done.

She realized that she had backed out of the group, and she was sorry that Sean was so concerned with safety that they couldn't possibly have a minute alone. Not alone, maybe. But…with just Katie and David.

She started as she stood in the back of the group—something had hit her on the back. She spun around and looked down. A tiny pinecone lay there in the sand. She frowned, and then looked up.

Carlos Roca.

She stared at him. He was real. Alive—and on the island. She couldn't begin to fathom how he had followed them so easily.

Unless, of course, he was good at that kind of thing.

She looked at him, at the misery in his eyes, at the

pleading within them. She saw that his face had grown gaunt; he looked like a man haunted by a million demons.

He was beckoning to her. He drew a finger to his lips.

She'd be crazy to walk to him in the brush. Alone.

She winced. She wondered if there was such a thing as instinct, and if her belief in the man was actually crazy. After all, he was there.

He hadn't been killed.

She turned, thinking she could grab Katie or someone.

They were all still discussing the coins. Jaden was explaining how many people used something like an electrode to clean such pieces, but they had always had good luck with certain chemical washes and delicate handwork.

Everyone was staring at the treasure thoughtfully or looking at Jaden.

She hesitated and then took another step back, and another. And when no one noticed her moving at that point, she turned and headed into the brush and the pines.

She had unbuckled her dive knife earlier and shoved it into the pocket of her jeans, and she had her jeans on now....

Right. Like a dive knife could save her against the maniac who had decapitated and dismembered two people!

She entered a tree-shaded trail, and felt as if a mist and darkness gathered around her. It did not; it was just that the sun wasn't penetrating through the pines.

"Carlos?" she said softly.

He stepped out in front of her.

"Jesus Cristo!" he said, and crossed himself. "I have been waiting for you. I have tried so hard to reach you. I need for you to understand."

There had been so much commotion over Vanessa's discovery that they had finally broken to go about different tasks when Sean realized that he didn't see Vanessa anywhere in the group. He saw Katie laying towels over one of the support ropes for her tent to dry, and he hurried over to her. "Katie! Where's Vanessa?"

"What? Well, she was there with the rest of us, listening to Jaden, and then..."

Her voice trailed away and she stared at him with fear in her eyes.

Sean was afraid that she was going to scream or alert the others. He was terrified that she had been dragged into the pine woods and brush, and he quickly looked around the encampment, searching for members of the original film team.

Zoe was with Bill, preparing the barbecue. Barry was showing Jay the fish he had caught that afternoon while they'd been diving—two snappers and a medium-size grouper.

David came over as he searched the group.

"What's wrong?" David asked.

"Vanessa," Sean said.

"I'll help you search."

"No—I'll find her. Make sure that everyone else stays around here, David."

"Right. If you're not back in ten minutes, though, I'll send Liam and Jamie after you."

Sean nodded and hurried back toward the pines. There was a trail—small and overgrown, but it had been traveled recently.

He ran down the trail, afraid to call her name and afraid not to, his heart thundering. He reminded himself that he was certain that the murders had not been committed by one person alone, that whoever had done it had to have had some assistance.

And they were all back at the beach. All of them except for Vanessa. Lew Sanderson had been there as well, rinsing dive gear with Jamie on the *Claddagh*.

Carlos Roca.

He was alive. He had been in Key West. He had followed them to Miami.

And now he was here. On the island.

And he had Vanessa.

He drew out the .38 Special he had stuffed under his jacket and kept moving as quietly as he could along the trail. Visions of what might have happened plagued the back of his mind.

Vanessa. Down on the sand, beautiful blond hair trailing out over it.

Eyes open with horror...

He was about to scream out her name, scream with a desperation that would be heard throughout the island.

He bit back the cry and hurried onward, then paused, listening.

He heard conversation. Hushed. Two people. Whispering. To his right.

He broke through the trees and brush then and burst upon the two of them—Vanessa, perfectly fine, standing in the clearing with her arm on Carlos Roca's shoulder, as if she had been urging him to do something.

He aimed the .38 Special at Carlos Roca's head and said flatly, "I spent time at target practice before the trip. At this distance, I can guarantee a clean shot between your eyes. Step away from Vanessa. Now."

Roca instantly moved to do so.

And Vanessa stepped in front of him, lifting a pleading hand to Sean.

"No, no, please, Sean! Carlos is innocent. He's been desperate all this time. He's been following us—at great risk to himself—determined to keep anything horrible from happening again."

Sean grated down on his teeth, tension bracing his muscles. "Vanessa, get away from him."

"Sean! You have to listen."

"Fine. Carlos, we'll walk back to the encampment. And you can talk to everyone there."

Carlos looked at Vanessa.

"No, Sean, please, no!" Vanessa begged.

He eased the gun down, still ready to lift it again if need be. He didn't want to keep it aimed at Vanessa.

"Please! Sean!" Vanessa pleaded again, wincing. "Sean—we can't let anyone know that Carlos is here. He's watching…watching after us. Sean, listen to him."

"It's one of them," Carlos said quietly and with dignity. "It's one of them. We were barely out at sea when I was attacked at the helm. I never saw who was there. I was struck so hard I went down. I was tossed overboard, and somehow, by the grace of God, the cold woke me up. I was dazed, my head was bleeding. I don't remember much else. I swam. I found a piece of driftwood and clung to it. I came to on one of the small islands, tended by a fisherman's wife. Then, I found out that *I* was wanted for murder. I have a Bahamian friend who got me a false ID claiming that I'm a fisherman from the Dominican Republic. I have been trying to find out what did happen ever since, lying low...and studying disappearances in the air and acts of piracy."

"Why should we believe you?" Sean asked, not moving, his voice cold and steely. "Why should I believe that this isn't a game you're playing, that you don't have an accomplice among the crew, and that if I keep the secret that you're here, you won't be waiting for the right time to kill again?"

"You can ask Lew," Carlos said quietly. "I told you, I came to on a Bahamian island. The people who found me were decent people. They contacted him and got him to come to me. He was there to see the fifty stitches in my head. He knows that I'm telling the truth. The night I left with Georgia, one of them either hid on the boat or found a way onto the boat. I was attacked from behind. God help me, the person just wanted Georgia. I sleep at night, still hearing her screaming!"

Sean still stared at Carlos. He saw that Vanessa believed in the man, believed with every fiber of her being.

She had from the start.

If he was innocent, he was a valuable ally on the island. He was the unknown that they could have in their favor.

And if he wasn't…

He was aware that Bartholomew was at his side.

"I believe he's telling the truth. I followed Vanessa into the woods. There were tears in his eyes. He pleaded. No man is that good an actor," Bartholomew said.

"Someone was on the boat. When you left, who did you see on the dock?" Sean asked.

"Vanessa and Jay. I saw them both," Carlos said.

"That wouldn't mean that either of them was innocent—they might have been an accomplice to whomever slipped aboard. Or are you certain that they slipped aboard before you left? Could someone have come broadside and slipped on?"

Carlos took a deep breath. "It was night. I was moving slowly."

"You have to make a decision," Bartholomew said. "Someone will be coming after you within a few minutes now."

Vanessa came hurrying toward him. She caught his hand and stared into his eyes. "He's telling the truth. I know that he's telling the truth."

"How?" he grated.

"I know. I know!" she said, slamming a fist against her chest. "Sometimes…you *know*."

Sean stared at Carlos over Vanessa's head. "If you're not telling the truth, you're a dead man."

"I am telling the truth. And I am watching. And I am waiting, unknown now, to find out who did this. Because they are here, and they will strike again," Carlos said.

Sean winced and turned, sliding the safety on and the gun beneath his jacket and waistband, and taking Vanessa's hand. When they neared the beach, he slowed his pace and came out of the trees calmly, hoping no one but Katie and David had noticed their absence.

Miraculously, it seemed that no one had. Zoe, Barry, Bill and Jake were standing around the barbecue, chatting excitedly. Jay was staring out at the water. Jamie, Marty, Ted and Jaden were still inspecting the mast and the cache of coins.

Only Liam stood tensely with Katie and David, trying to pretend casual conversation.

"We'll need somewhere alone—guaranteed alone," Sean said quietly. "Liam, how have you been doing on that task I asked you about yesterday?"

"Hopefully, I'll have some information back by the morning," Liam said.

"We're going to need it," Sean told him.

Liam looked at Vanessa, frowning. "What the hell is going on?" he demanded.

"Let's take a walk to the *Conch Fritter,*" he suggested. He turned and stared at Vanessa. "All of us!"

She nodded, and the group walked toward the boat.

"Hey!" Barry called after them.

"Yeah?" Sean yelled back.

"Bring another bag of charcoal, will you please?" Barry asked.

Sean nodded.

Aboard the boat, he looked back to shore, assuring himself that the others had remained behind. Then he looked at Vanessa. "Why don't you tell them? You're the one with complete faith."

She stared at him, and then at David, Liam and Katie. "Carlos Roca is on the island."

Liam stiffened. "All right. We'll figure out a way to

keep you safe while we flush him out. No one is more fierce at protection than Jamie O'Hara, and between Sean, David and me—"

"No, Liam, no!" Vanessa said. "He's hiding. He's watching out—for us."

"He said he was attacked on the ship, and he knows it had to be by one of the crew. He was struck on the head. He says Lew Sanderson will vouch for all this. He's been keeping his secret all this time. He was tossed overboard, assumed dead or left to drown."

"This is crazy," David said.

"Vanessa, can *Lew* actually be an alibi? You don't know that Lew wasn't guilty," Liam pointed out.

"Oh, please, I can't believe that Carlos is lying." She stared at them all. "Ask Bartholomew! *Your friendly neighborhood ghost* believes in him. We all know that faith can't be held or seen, and I have faith in Carlos."

"I hope you're right, Vanessa," Liam said softly. "I really hope you're right. If not, you've just fed into the psychosis of a savage murderer."

"Vanessa?" Katie asked.

"I know I'm right."

"I'll tell Uncle Jamie what's going on, and he'll let Marty know," Sean said.

David nodded. "What do you think he's waiting for?" he asked.

"The murderers to show themselves," Sean said.

"And how will they do that?" Liam asked dryly.

"They'll try to find a way to separate someone from the rest—and murder them, as well," Sean said.

Liam nodded. "Somehow, we'll have to find a way to bait them."

* * *

That night, Vanessa knew that Sean was still angry with her.

He played his part well in front of others, but she knew. She knew the tension that knotted his body, and she knew the tone of his voice.

It wasn't until they had gone to bed for the night that she realized just how angry.

"First you lied to me about him," he told her, keeping his distance, arms locked behind his head as he stared up at their canvas roof. "You lied about seeing him. Then you did the most horrendously stupid thing in the world. You walked off into the woods." He stared at her then. "Don't! Don't even try to get mad at me for saying it was horrendously stupid because you know it was."

"Yes."

"That's all you have to say?"

"I know it was stupid," she said softly. "Sean, I'm sorry."

He shook his head. "Sorry? Vanessa…that can't always cut it, you know," he told her.

She fell silent for a moment, aware of his distance. "Want me to sleep somewhere else?" she asked, praying that he would say no.

"I'm angry, Vanessa. Furious. You risked your life, you risked other lives. I'm disturbed about this trust thing we've got going—or not going. But your plan is to walk away anytime it gets rough between us. No. I don't want you to go away—and I don't want you running away from me when I'm right to be angry."

She stared at him, not knowing what to say. She could

have told him that she was pretty sure that she never wanted to leave.

But she didn't know if that would be right at the moment.

She eased down by his side and laid her head on his chest.

After a moment, she felt his hand on her hair. And in time, he drew her to him.

That night, she dreamed. In the dream, she was still in his arms. She woke because there was a woman in the tent, standing before her.

She wasn't afraid, and she didn't know why she wasn't afraid.

She had seen the woman before, on a crowded afternoon in Key West, when pirates and wenches were everywhere.

She should be afraid. She was certain that the woman was Kitty Cutlass. Pretty, not quite beautiful. Not dressed elegantly. Worn, tired.

"Please, if you would just understand," she said.

"I think I do," Vanessa told her. "You didn't kill Dona Isabella. Dona Isabella planned the attack. The ship had riches on it that were supposed to go with her to her husband in Spain. She didn't want to go to Spain, and she didn't want her husband. She arranged with Mad Miller that he should attack the ship, but…she wanted to control the pirates, and she didn't want you. You were the body in the chest, Kitty. It was you."

The woman, the ghost in front of her, smiled sadly. "She is evil."

"She is dead now, too, Kitty," Vanessa said. "She died in the storm."

"Evil doesn't die," Kitty said. "You must be careful. Evil doesn't die."

Kitty faded away.

A few moments later, Vanessa awoke. She looked around the tent and realized quickly that there was no place for anyone to hide in the small tent.

She lay back and listened to Sean's breathing, felt his warmth and the pulse of his heart.

She wondered if she had been guessing at the truth all along, and if the figurehead image of Dona Isabella leading her into a trap that day hadn't finally made it clear in her mind.

Then she had straightened it all out in a dream.

Either that, or…

The ghost of Kitty Cutlass had been in her tent.

Either way, she felt that it was important that she knew what had happened. Somehow, letting everyone know the truth was going to help them solve the mystery.

In the morning, Sean announced that he wanted to make another trip out to the site where Vanessa had found the broken shaft of old mast with the encrusted coins, but that they'd start out again just after noon—first, they would set up to film Ted and Jaden working with the heavy cache of broken mast and encrusted coins. Ted said he'd be the display hands—Jaden would do the talking.

He and Jaden had freed and cleaned a few of the coins, and Jaden was happy to display them and happy to talk about what they had found and what they had done. "This was someone's personal treasure, I believe, *before* it became the property of the pirate crew," Jaden said, speaking to the camera. "We have a mixture here of gold and silver, and coins that show different mint marks, beneath different rulers. This coin bears a mark showing that it was minted in Peru, and here we have one that is very old, and I'm still working very delicately to see if we still have a mint mark. I would judge it was one of the first coins to come out of the mines of South America. This is why I think that the pirates didn't actually amass the treasure, but that in sinking the *Santa Geneva,* they happened upon a collection of personal riches belonging to Dona Isabella's husband and traveling back to Spain with her."

Jaden displayed her work and spoke of the patience that was needed. Different people worked in different ways when working with centuries-old salvage, but she had Ted had both grown up in Key West and had worked with Jaden's father, a salvage expert from the time he was a child, to learn their craft.

When they finished with the segment, Vanessa asked Sean if she could put forth a theory. He was surprised, but shrugged and told her that she was certainly welcome to do so.

"Walking along the beach?" Jay suggested.

"Sure," Vanessa agreed.

"We'll use two handhelds?" Jay asked Sean.

"I'll observe on this," Sean said.

Vanessa was aware that the group was mostly together, and that was what she wanted. Marty and Liam were at the boats, and Jamie had remained at the encampment while Ted and Jaden continued to work with the treasure.

But Jay was filming and Barry had the second camera while Bill and Jake held the light shield. Zoe was hovering, just in case she was needed. David walked with Sean, discussing shots and angles, and Katie followed, curious to hear Vanessa's theory. Lew walked behind as well, arms crossed over his chest. He was watching out for everyone, and watching the terrain around them. Sean hadn't said so, but she was pretty sure that he had found a few moments during the activity of the first filming to casually corner Lew—and demand to know what he knew about Carlos Roca.

It seemed that whatever Lew had told Sean, it had satisfied him.

There had been no call for a manhunt to drag Carlos out of the pine and shrub forest, nor had there been any suggestion that they weren't alone on the island.

She wondered if what she was about to do was crazy, or necessary.

She walked slowly along the beach, almost unaware of the cameras or the reflector shield being wielded by Bill and Jake. "Yesterday," she began, "we made an amazing find. People often wonder why, when a wreck has rested in the ocean so long and we have so much advanced equipment to put to work in the oceans these days, it hasn't been previously discovered. As Sean O'Hara noted, we have to remember that conditions in the past might have been different, and that the ocean is always shifting and hiding her treasures. What we refer to as the Bermuda Triangle is a busy area where currents and weather are particularly active and where, perhaps, there are major magnetic fields at work. Basically, it's natural phenomena that dictate what happens beneath the waves. Mad Miller's pirate ship was taken down by a force of nature. And the force of nature, over the years, shifted the wreckage, and created a long debris field. Despite sonar, seagoing robots and other technical devices, treasures and wrecks can hide in plain sight. As in this case, the great metal hull of a World War II ship has hidden a great deal of the wreckage. What we have discovered this time is treasure. It's my belief that we have imagined the real story of Mad Miller, Kitty Cutlass and Dona Isabella wrong. We saw what happened as Dona Isabella would have *wanted* the world to see it. She was a beautiful woman, a proud and haughty woman. She lived life as she chose in Key West in luxury. She traveled the Caribbean, and she took on lovers as she chose, all with her husband's riches. I believe that she made a deal with Mad Miller. Somewhere, she met the pirate. She told him the course of the *Santa Geneva* and what riches the ship would carry. In return, they would split the bounty. It would be assumed that she'd died in captivity—but not until a ransom had been paid. Dona Isabella would then take on a new identity and live richly—without the yoke of her husband's financial power over her—wherever she chose. I can't imagine just what seductive power or force the woman wielded, because earlier, at the site of the *Santa Geneva* wreck, we pulled up a chest that held the body of a murdered woman. The 'treasure chest' of her body was stolen somewhere en route to a lab in Gainesville, but the experts noted immediately that she was not decked out in great finery. It's my belief that Dona Isabella was entranced with the pirate way of life and perhaps with Mad Miller himself. Either on her own—or with his blessing—Dona Isabella murdered the one person who stood in her way in the act of completely subduing the pirate Mad Miller to her total control. In remorse, Mad Miller saw to it that Kitty Cutlass went to the bottom of the sea in a sealed tomb. With Dona Isabella now calling the shots like a true pirate queen, she and the remaining crews of the ships sailed on to Haunt Island, where the massacre of all those who would not bow down before her took place. She was truly in her power when she and Mad Miller then set sail again, only to sail into the embrace of a massive storm, and a watery graveyard for all aboard. How furious she must have been—furious with God and the heavens. She had at last obtained freedom, power and control—only to fall victim to the revenge of the sea herself. Once, Africans brought to these islands believed that the tempest within this area—now known as the Bermuda Triangle—was caused by the bitter fury of a woman who had not been kind, while her sister had taken pity on a poor and broken man who proved to be a god. The haughty sister married a rich and handsome man who turned out to be a demon who killed her and devoured her. Her fury caused the thunder and waves and strange phenomena that brought down ships and planes. Perhaps, in later years, sailors—pirates, patriots, merchants and pleasure seekers—might well find that same evil spirit rests in the bitter and furious soul of the heartless woman who murdered for power and riches."

She stopped walking, and smiled.

Jay lowered the camera and looked into her eyes. The reflector shields fell, and Sean came walking toward her, taking her by the shoulders, his grin deep, his eyes admiring.

"Fantastic!" he said.

"Oh!" Katie gasped. "That's brilliant, Vanessa, and you probably got it all right after all these years of us believing that Kitty Cutlass was a murderess!"

"It makes perfect sense," David agreed.

"But wait—I'm confused," Zoe said. "You found Dona Isabella's pendant. That was the first find that you made."

"Yes—I'm sure she purposely lost that pendant, and someone was supposed to have found it years and years before I did. When salvage divers came out to the wreck, they would believe that the pendant was wrenched from her neck in the struggle. Maybe they wouldn't find it, but the seeds were planted for her story—the story she wanted people to believe—to come to light. Of course, this is my theory. I'm not sure that I can prove it in any way, and the body is gone now, but from what Dr. Aislinn said when we did have the body, it seems likely that it was Kitty Cutlass," Vanessa said.

"Oh, Lord, and what a cool bit!" Barry said to her, grinning. "Dona Isabella can be seen as the evil that lurks in the Bermuda Triangle. I love it!"

"After all these years of man being man, war and devastation, I'm sure a lot of evil energy went down in the ocean," Sean said dryly.

"Evil is in the mind, really, isn't it?" Jay asked.

"And in idle hands, right?" Zoe asked, grimacing.

"Well, in the mind—and in the hands of those it inhabits, I guess," Barry noted, grinning. He frowned and stared at Vanessa. "You're not suggesting that the evil spirit of Dona Isabella came up from the sea to somehow decapitate and dismember Georgia and Travis."

Vanessa shook her head. "Hey—I just put forth a new theory, that's all. A theory. We've always worked on theories and suppositions."

"Fascinating," Bill Hinton said, nodding in thought.

"Creepy," Barry said.

"Ah, but it's all in the mind, really, isn't it?" Jay asked. He looked at Vanessa, frowning. "In an odd way, maybe Dona Isabella was getting her evil revenge. *You* wrote our script, relying on supposed history and legend. Maybe Dona Isabella wanted it all remembered that way."

"Why kill Georgia and Travis—if evil ghosts of the past had anything to do with it?" Vanessa asked.

"Hey, I don't know," Jay said, shrugging. He rolled his eyes. "Maybe evil spirits demand sacrifices!"

"Human hands committed murder," Sean said. "Anyway, let's get back to working on what we've begun to find. Light lunch again, and an afternoon dive. That was great footage, Vanessa, great. I loved it. Let's see what else we can find."

While lunch was being prepared, Sean went aboard the *Conch Fritter,* where Liam had been on the computer using his various contacts to try to track the movement of the original film crew in more detail over the last two years when the other two boats disappeared.

"Some of this we knew. Vanessa has been doing commercial shoots. Three of the others, Barry Melkie, Bill Hinton and Zoe Cally, were part of a crew that filmed in the Bahamas. Jay hasn't done as well as the others. He's had a few dry spells in there. So really, anyone could have easily been around when the other disappearances occurred."

"Good to know. I guess it's still not proof of anything. And I'm still trying to figure out *why.* Vanessa's theory on Dona Isabella being in collusion with Mad Miller was fascinating, and rings true, and it had all kinds of motive—for Dona Isabella. I don't see the motive in the killings now—if, indeed, some of these disappearances were caused by the same murderer or murderers who killed Georgia and Travis," Sean said, perplexed. "There was no financial gain, not that I can see. The deaths of Georgia and Travis put Jay into financial difficulty. It's true that the water can be rough around here and that ships have disappeared in the area forever, but other disappearances now might be related. David and I read about the *Delphi.* It seemed it disappeared into thin air, and the boat was captained by an experienced man. There should have been a distress call, something."

"You can't make a distress call if you're taken by surprise," Liam pointed out.

"We could still be way off course," Sean said. "But you're right. And Carlos thought someone was aboard the boat because he was knocked out—taken by surprise."

"If we're not being taken in by Carlos," Liam said.

"I don't think we are." He hesitated. "I think that the man is telling the truth, and that someone with us is guilty. Carlos Roca is convinced someone on the island at the time was involved."

"We're taking a leap of faith to believe in Carlos Roca," Liam noted.

Sean nodded. "Yes and no," he said softly. "Vanessa has…something. Like Katie. The thing I always wanted to deny. Until Bartholomew. Now I know that things do exist that we can't see. She has instincts and…something. I trust that something."

"Let's hope you're right," Liam said.

Everyone wanted to dive that day. Sean, however, didn't want to leave the encampment alone, nor did he want to leave Ted and Jaden alone to keep guard. In the end, it was agreed both boats would go out that day with Jamie O'Hara remaining topside on his *Claddagh* and David and Katie remaining topside on the *Conch Fritter.*

They followed one another going down, but the World War II vessel was a huge hulk, and they split to follow it around in different directions. Vanessa led, bringing her partners around to the gash in the giant hull that had probably caused its sinking. They began to explore the area, Sean turning the camera on the wreck and then the different divers.

Vanessa realized that they were in an equipment room, and she began to study the dials and levers on one side of the wall. She followed them to the sandy bottom, where in some places they were on the ocean floor and in others she heard the metallic clink of the vessel's flooring. She kept searching the flooring, aware that her fellow divers were near.

She found an uneven patch in the sand and started carefully moving the sand around it. She grew excited as she realized that she had come across something. There was a piece of something that glittered. She moved more sand and realized that one object was laid atop another. She picked up the first and was surprised to see that it was a knife. It wasn't old; the hilt was wearing and the blade was dull and crusted, but it was a modern diving knife. She slipped it into her belt and looked at the object beneath it. It was long and wedged tightly between the rip in the hull's floor and the sand.

She looked for the others and saw that Zoe was at a hatch, struggling with the door. She swam toward her just as the door gave.

Vanessa ducked the massive sheet of steel that seemed to have some kind of spring; Barry, shooting ahead of her, did not.

She heard the thud as he crashed, headfirst, into the steel.

He shot back, his regulator falling from his mouth. She realized that he was unconscious and hurried toward him, catching his drifting weight and gripping her backup regulator to force it immediately into his mouth. Zoe shot for her, trying to help, but she was panicking and in the way. Sean let the camera fall, suspended, to his side, shooting toward them. He signaled that they needed to surface, which, of course, they knew.

Decompression time had to be taken, but between them, they kept the air going into Barry's lungs and bubbles coming out into the water. When they surfaced, Zoe began to shout, drawing David's attention. He was quickly at the dive platform with Katie, and between them they got Barry's body on deck, stripped of dive gear and wrapped in a towel.

Sean stood over him and looked the ten feet over to the *Claddagh*. The other divers were up, and Liam shouted over to Sean. "What happened?"

"Barry took a beating from a spring-loaded hatch," Sean cried.

"It was my fault. I should have known," Zoe moaned. She was flustered, fluttering over Barry, trying to touch him, whispering that she was sorry.

"He's got to get to medical care," Sean said. "He might have had some oxygen deprivation, though Vanessa got to him quickly."

"I'll tie up and take Barry on board the *Claddagh.* She's got a bit of speed on your Sunray, Sean. I'll radio ahead and they'll be ready for him in Bimini," Jamie called to him.

"All right," Sean conceded.

"I can't believe I did this," Zoe said.

"Zoe, you didn't do it—the door sprang right when Barry was heading for it," Vanessa said. She glanced at Sean and realized that he thought that Zoe's ministrations might prove to be too much for the poor man. "Barry will be fine. Jamie's boat is fast. We've got him breathing, and he has a weak but steady pulse going."

"Grab the bumpers," Jamie called to his crew aboard the *Claddagh.*

Vanessa and Jay ran to do the same for the *Conch Fritter.* A few minutes later, Barry was aboard the *Claddagh,* and it was agreed that David and Katie would go with him while the rest of the crew came aboard the *Conch Fritter* to head back to the island.

Vanessa watched the *Claddagh* sail away, and she waved to Katie and David.

She felt a chill.

They would be all right. They had to be all right. They were close to Bimini, it was still daylight and there were three of them aboard with Barry.

She still felt an ominous sense of dread that something horrible would happen before she saw them again. The sea wind suddenly seemed chill, and when she turned away, she felt the strange sting of tears in her eyes.

16

"Barry could die," Zoe said, watching as the *Claddagh* disappeared into the horizon.

"He's not going to die," Vanessa assured her, giving her shoulders a hug. "It's going to be fine."

Zoe looked at her and tried to smile. "And I didn't find a thing," Zoe said.

Vanessa tried to brighten. "I did."

They all looked at her.

"Well, of course you did," Jay said. "What?"

She looked around at the faces. Sean was just waiting, Liam at his side. Bill, Jake, Jay and Zoe were wide-eyed.

"I don't know," she said.

That wasn't true. She knew that she had found a modern dive knife. Maybe it wasn't indicative of anything—perhaps a diver had lost it. But for some reason, she decided not to tell them all about the knife—just what was beneath it.

"The floor was uneven, and it was all crusted…I think it might have been what remained of a sword or a cutlass. I didn't have time to try to figure it out—Barry was hit. But we can find out tomorrow. I know exactly where it is," Vanessa said. She smiled. She was proud of this find. She hadn't seen a ghostly figurehead in the water. She had found it on her own.

She saw that Bartholomew was standing just behind Liam and Sean; he watched her solemnly.

"It might have been German, or fairly modern," she said. "It was impossible to tell."

"We should go back down right now," Jay said.

"No. Not today," Sean said. "Today, we had a member of our crew injured. We'll head back and let the others know what happened, and wait to hear about Barry's condition."

"Oh my God, you are worried he could die!" Zoe said.

"No. He just needs care. But this is it for the day," Sean said. He headed to the helm. Vanessa came and curled up on the companion seat, hugging a throw around her shoulders—she hadn't been able to shake the chill that had seized her as she had waved goodbye to Katie.

She was anxious to hear that the *Claddagh* had arrived safely in Bimini.

Liam was seated aft.

Watching, she thought.

Watching Zoe, Bill and Jake.

They didn't have far to come in to the island, but she decided that the demand for a freshwater shower on the one boat might be high that night, and she slipped off the seat, telling Sean that she was going to take a quick shower. It was good, though quick. Zoe followed her lead while the guys washed off on the deck, using the equipment hose.

She felt better once she was dressed in jeans and a sweater. And in another few minutes, she heard Sean calling for the ties and the bumpers. They had returned to Haunt Island.

A fire had been built and the barbecue had been set to blaze and dinner put on in their absence. Jaden, busy flipping thin flank steaks, was horrified when she heard about Barry, and Ted had to take the barbecue fork from her hand to save a piece of meat.

"It was an accident," Jay said, "nothing but an accident." He set a hand gently on Zoe's shoulders.

"And he's going to be all right," Vanessa added.

"They'll call soon," Sean said.

Vanessa felt she had to escape for a few moments at least. She murmured something about needing to put a few things away in her tent. She glanced at Sean, hoping that he would follow her.

She started entering the tent. Bartholomew had preceded her entry and was seated on the ground, Indian-style, hands folded prayer-fashion and tapping his lower jaw. He started to rise when he saw her, but she shook her head and sank down beside him.

"I've been thinking all day," he said.

"And?"

"And your theory is right. It has to be. I told you—I knew them, Mad Miller and Kitty…and they weren't evil or cruel. Mad Miller must have made a financial agreement with Dona Isabella. She traveled a lot—they could have met at several ports. He was…he was soft. Once he had stopped her ship, she took control. She insisted it be sunk, and she murdered Kitty. It all makes sense now."

Vanessa shook her head. "It still doesn't make sense. I kept seeing Dona Isabella's face on a figurehead—she was the one leading me around."

The tent flap opened and they started, but it was Sean, and evidently he had heard them.

Sean shook his head. "Whatever type of spirit she is, she's been playing with you. She's been leading you. She wanted you to find the pendant, because that lent credence to the tale. That would bring everyone aboard to follow this whole route again. And—just in case it didn't—she then had you find the body. She probably didn't realize that a forensic anthropologist would immediately realize that it was the wrong body."

"But the body disappeared," Vanessa said.

"She led you—and she's leading someone else," Sean said.

Bartholomew nodded.

"Oh!" Vanessa said, and dug into her bag. "I did pick up something today, but no one led me to it. It was in the gap in the ship, on top of the object I was describing." She produced the knife and showed it to Sean. He studied it, rolling it over in his hand and chipping at the crust on it.

"T-B-E," Sean read. "Tom Essling," he said.

"I'm sorry?" Vanessa asked.

"Tom Essling—he was captain of a boat that disappeared in that area just last year. If we further our search, I have a feeling we'll find his boat, the *Delphi,* too," he said grimly.

"So…someone has been pirating other vessels near here. Someone maybe using Haunt Island as their base, as if it's their…their home fort," Vanessa said.

"I don't know. It's all supposition," Sean said.

"She's right. I know she's right," Bartholomew said. "But I'm watching…I'm always watching, and I can't figure it out yet."

"Well, it has been figured out to this," Sean said. "Someone here knows much more than he or she is saying. Someone is—" He broke off, looking at Vanessa. "A killer, I believe," he said softly.

From outside the tent, they heard Jaden call out loudly. "Dinner, folks, dinner! Come and get it now!"

"Let's go on out," Sean told Vanessa. "We'll keep up all appearances."

As they walked over to the barbecue area, Vanessa asked Sean, "David hasn't called yet. Why hasn't David called?"

"He will," he assured her.

Unless what Barry had done had been an act. Barry was a big man, muscular, powerful. The kind who could wield a knife and a bone saw, if needed. What if he had been pretending the entire event, and he had known that they would save him, bring him to the surface.

And rush him to a hospital.

She began to fear that Barry would suddenly rise, taking David and Jamie by surprise. He would attack from the rear, when they weren't expecting it. He would toss them overboard as he had done with Carlos, and then he would come for Katie.…

She clenched her fists, knowing that she was letting her imagination run away from her.

But she was scared.

And she wanted David to call, or Katie, or anyone.

Jaden and Ted tried to be cheerful and upbeat as they

doled out dinner. Marty, however, appeared wary and watchful.

Lew Sanderson sat on the beach alone, watching the others as they ate.

Liam stayed on one side of the group and Sean on the other.

When Sean's cell phone started ringing, they all jumped. He answered it quickly, and then breathed a sigh of relief as he looked at the others.

"They are in Bimini, and the doctors believe that Barry will pull through," he told them.

It seemed that everyone let out a sigh. And then they began to chat with relief, and in a few minutes, they were even joking with one another.

David, Jamie and Katie wouldn't return until the next morning, which meant that Sean had lost three of the people he trusted most for the night.

Lew—he thought he trusted, but he didn't know.

Ted and Jaden he trusted, but they were really scholars, not fighters, though Ted did know how to use a speargun.

Carlos was an unknown element in the whole game.

Still, he had himself and Liam and Marty. And they were guarding a tiny blonde woman and two twenty-somethings who didn't appear to be musclemen.

Maybe there was something he still wasn't seeing. One of the group had been involved, but they'd had outside help.

Everyone seemed tired that night. He told Liam about the knife they had found, and they both knew that they'd be searching for the *Delphi* the next day.

"Tonight?" Liam asked.

"We all stay on guard. Marty, Ted, you and I. And Lew. But I'm uneasy now, and we'll actually be watching Lew, as well. I'm thinking that when David and Katie and my uncle Jamie return, it may be time to put an end to this. I think a killer is in reach, but I don't want to risk anyone else's life. We need a larger crew—a totally trustworthy crew. Anyway, we'll each take a few hours, and stand guard in threes through the night," Sean said.

"You want some time first?" Liam asked.

"Sure. Thanks. I'd like that," Sean admitted.

Vanessa was already in their little tent. She had seemed chilled during the day, and was wearing her flannel nightdress again. He smiled at her, coming in to zip the flap on the tent.

He came to her, taking her by the shoulders, and she looked up at him expectantly.

"These are really tight quarters," he whispered. "And we are really, really close to other tents, but..."

He loved her smile, loved her eyes. "We're very good at whispered conversations," she said.

"There are many ways to communicate, you know."

Her arms wrapped around him. She drew him down with her to the thin mattresses on the canvas floor of the tent and he reflected that it was really one of the finest beds he'd ever seen. Any bed was fine, if Vanessa was there. He cupped her face in his hands and kissed her slowly, and she slid her fingers beneath his shirt, teasing the flesh of his abdomen, then drawing the shirt up and over his head. They came together again, and she felt his blood begin to burn as her fingers dipped into the waistband of his jeans. She went still as she felt his gun.

"I'm sorry," he whispered.

"I'm not. I'm damned glad you have it. And I'm definitely glad it was a gun. It seemed a very strange place to have such a body part," she teased.

"I'll show you body parts," he whispered.

"Promises, promises…"

They quickly grew breathless and winced here and there, pressing their fingers to each other's lips, smiling, laughing, making love just a bit awkwardly and with just a bit of difficulty and yet finding that the smiles, the whispered warnings and the laughter itself made the moment sweeter and more frantic, and even in hushed gasps the moment of climax incredible and shattering. Then they lay together, damp and breathing deeply, hearts thundering, interlocked, and strangely silent.

"You're going out, aren't you?" Vanessa whispered.

He nodded. "I just…I…I needed this time," he said. He'd never realized that he didn't know how to speak to a woman. Not true, speech had been easy. But he had never intended to become involved, never realized that he could feel that he needed to wake up with someone every morning. He let out a breath and turned to her and just let the words come. "I think I love you," he said.

She smiled. "I think I love you, too."

"I think…I think that when this is over you shouldn't leave," he said. "I think that we should both see where this thinking is going. I think the thinking could become certainty."

She brushed her lips against his, and her eyes, so dark

and beautiful a blue in the shadows, met his. "I think that I'll be here," she said softly.

He didn't want to leave her; he had to. He knew that he was right, that even if the three of them guarding the place appeared to be overkill, it was necessary.

He rose, reaching for his clothes and dressing quickly in the cramped quarters. Vanessa slipped back into the flannel gown. "I'll come with you."

"No."

"But—"

"Get some sleep. Tomorrow will be a long day, and… well, you are distracting," he told her.

"All right," she said softly.

He unzipped the flap on the tent and slipped away.

Despite everything that had happened during the day—or perhaps because of it—Vanessa found herself falling into a deep sleep almost immediately after Sean left her.

For a while, even in sleep, she knew the comfort of the sweet rest.

Then she felt as if she was being touched.

She opened her eyes. It was dark in the tent, though the many torches set into the sand kept the area light enough. Strange patterns and shadows were dispersed between faint lights.

She must have still been sleeping. She could see a face. It wasn't the face that had been on the figurehead, not that of Dona Isabella.

It was the face of the blonde woman, not as pretty, just a little worn. Kitty. Kitty Cutlass.

And her eyes were tinged with worry now.

She was dreaming again, of course.

"Come, come…come on. You must leave, please, hurry!" the woman warned her.

She had been sleeping so, so deeply.…

She was still struggling to rise when she saw another face.

Zoe's. Zoe was shaking her and half sobbing, very softly. "Vanessa, you have to come. Quickly."

Vanessa sat up instantly. "What's wrong?"

"It's Bill…he's… Please, you can't wake the others. You can't let…you can't let Lew see us. You have to come quickly. He knows something, and if you let out the alarm, Lew will come and kill him. Please, Vanessa, hurry! Be silent."

Tears streamed down Zoe's delicate cheeks. "All right, all right, Zoe. We have to get to Sean—"

"Yes, but after you see Bill. You'll have to make Sean understand!"

She slipped quietly out of the tent with Zoe, her heart racing. *Lew? She had trusted him! He had a family, little children…*

She crept low, but they had barely gone a few steps before she heard Sean's voice.

"Hey. What's going on?" he asked.

Zoe stared at him without speaking.

"Sean," she said softly. "You need to be quiet and not raise an alarm."

"What's going on?" Sean repeated.

"Zoe—"

"Zoe's tired of waiting and being pushed around," Zoe said flatly. Her voice was deep and coarse and dry, and not her at all.

Sean drew his gun but not quickly enough. Vanessa felt the steel prod of Zoe's weapon at her back. "Set it down, Sean. Shooting Vanessa will be a piece of cake."

"Zoe, what do you think you'll accomplish?" Sean asked her.

"Satisfaction—and her rewards," Zoe said.

"But you can't get off this island alive," Sean argued.

"Put your gun down, Sean. I'm good with weapons. This is a Magnum .45—Vanessa's entire chest will burst out in your face, and it will be all your fault," Zoe said.

"Shoot her, too, Sean," Vanessa said. "She intends to kill me in the end anyway!"

They could both sense Zoe's delicate finger on the trigger. Sean set his gun on the ground.

"Now step out of my way," Zoe said. "Vanessa and I have a little business together."

By then, the others had come running.

Ted with his speargun, Liam with his police revolver. But Zoe was calm and resolved. "Put the weapons down. I cannot tell you what it will look like if I fire into Vanessa's flesh and blood and bone!" She said the last with relish.

Liam held on to his gun for a moment.

Suddenly, he stiffened.

"Down, my friendly neighborhood cop," Bill Hinton said. "Set it down, come on now, good cop! Zoe, go on, take her. I've got the situation here."

"Hell, no!" Liam said. He spun quickly, but not quickly enough. Bill Hinton brought the butt of his gun down on Liam's head with a savage vengeance and turned to shoot at Marty's foot. Marty, stunned, let out a roar of pain and fell to the sand.

"I said to drop all the weapons!" Bill thundered. He turned his gun on Jaden. "She'll look great with a shattered kneecap!"

The entire group was still. "Take her, and I'll be right behind," Bill said, his voice bizarrely gentle as he spoke to Zoe.

"Hey, I'll be all right," Vanessa said. "We're just going for a little walk in the woods."

Her heart was racing. She saw the trapped fury in Sean's eyes, and she was afraid that he'd wind up dead in the sand himself if she didn't defuse the immediate situation. "Please, stand back," she begged Sean. "I'll be all right."

She wasn't going to be all right. She couldn't believe that Zoe—who had cried in fear of what she had done to Barry that day—could be this person. But she had been fooled—Zoe was petite, delicate. Zoe was a murderess, apparently. And she had probably managed to spring the door on purpose, knowing it would bring a weakening of the ranks.

Zoe dragged her into the trail where she had first traveled to find Carlos.

Zoe meant to kill her, just as she had killed Georgia Dare. It wasn't for money. It was because she had become strangely...*possessed.*

Sean made a dive into the sand, rolling to retrieve his weapon.

In all honesty, he wasn't sure if he would make it or not.

But it didn't matter.

Just as Bill started to rage at him, his attention distracted as he tried to take aim at Sean, something came leaping from the tent behind Liam's prone body—something! A whir of motion and of fury.

Sean got his hands on his gun just as Carlos Roca brought Bill down to the ground. Bill twisted, trying to aim his gun at Carlos Roca's face.

Sean fired, as carefully as he could, praying that his aim would be true.

It was. Bill Hinton screamed in agony as his hand exploded and his gun went flying. Carlos Roca did not find mercy at that cry of pain. He slammed a bone-crunching fist into Hinton's face, and the cry was cut off cleanly. Hinton was out.

"Jesus!" Jaden cried, almost sinking to her knees, then rising, going one way, and then the other, not certain whether to see to Liam or Marty first.

"Liam!" Ted suggested, and they crossed one another as Ted raced to Marty and Jaden hurried on to Liam.

Jake Magnoli stood in the middle of the group, his jaw wide with astonishment and horror.

"Zoe? Bill?" he breathed.

Jay had been frozen in place. He moved, pacing, looking at Sean. "She's crazy. She's got to be crazy. She's got Vanessa. Why Vanessa?"

"We've got to hurry, track them, run…!" Lew Sanderson cried.

"No! No, we have to track them, but she can't see us," Sean said. "She'll kill. I know she'll kill. We have to take her by surprise." He looked up. Bartholomew was at the start of the trail. He looked at Sean, and he began to run into the darkness of the pines.

"She can't hear us, she can't see us!" Sean said. "Carlos…come. Lew and the rest of you, stay here. Help Liam and Marty. Call for the authorities!"

He ran toward the trail, his heart thundering.

Zoe? Zoe Cally? The little bitty blonde…

The little bitty bloodthirsty blonde.

"All right, I admit to being incredibly confused," Vanessa said, trying to keep her voice calm and her words conversational. "I did figure out the truth behind Dona Isabella, right? What I'm trying to understand is how on earth you came to be so…"

"Crazy?" Zoe asked. "I'm not crazy. She's here. She *is* the power of the sea. Eventually, she'll reward us, and we'll live like royalty within her realm!"

"What are you talking about? She made you kill people. You ruined your own work with the movie—"

"Oh, right! The only people who would have made money on that movie were you and Jay," Zoe said. "While Dona Isabella…you must understand. She thrives on blood, she needs so much blood in the sea. Souls are good, too, but she really likes a good machete massacre."

"She thrives on blood?" Vanessa said. "Zoe, when did you start this? How? Why?"

"How? I was chosen, don't you see? I knew the legend, good God, we all knew the legend. I used to love to come here and wonder what it was like in my own mind. And I sat here once and she came to me, and I knew. I knew what she wanted. She needed to be fed lots of blood. Then there was a bit filmed here for one of the history channels…let me see, that was four or five years ago. Bill was playing a bit part, and

I saw that he would have loved to have been a pirate. It was so easy then...." She broke off, laughing softly. "We had to learn, of course. We started with a girl who was diving here...a Bahamian. We didn't really know what we were doing and it was a very messy murder, but luckily, no one was around. And I'm so good with costumes and makeup, when the film that you and Jay were doing came up, well...it was just brilliant. Wonderful! We became pirates. Travis was easy. We terrified him before we killed him. And then we got on board the boat when Carlos tried to take Georgia away. Oh, it was so much fun. And the more blood Dona Isabella got, the more power she had, the more power she gave to us! But you! You went and found the trunk. That was very tricky, because we had to pretend to be just hanging around Key West while we caught up with that doctor and her assistant and stole it back, then got a boat and dumped it back out at sea...but we're wonderful at getting rid of things in the sea. The sea is merciless, don't you agree?"

"A year ago, you killed the people on the *Delphi.* And you just killed more people, those retired people, on the *Happy-Me.*"

Zoe appeared indignant. "Dona Isabella needed her strength for this." She smiled. "Sometimes you have to seize your chances when they appear. Picking off retirees on boats that are just anchored here? Now and then you can have fun. You can do the whole pirate thing. Ghosts rising from the sea in flesh and blood with machetes!" She smiled, so proud of herself. "All you need is a place to run, excellent diving abilities and sheer talent. Oh, Vanessa! Murder is really ridiculously easy.

The tricky part, always, was pulling off the crimes and then being back to appear to be innocent as hell. Actually, the hardest night was when we both had to slip out of our tents to catch up with Georgia and Carlos when they left that night. Catch up with them and get back into our own tents so we could wake up in horror and come see what had happened, what was lying on the sand. But it was wonderful!"

Zoe might have been describing an incredible trip abroad, or a loving sexual encounter. She appeared ecstatic.

Vanessa tried to keep her talking.

"Zoe, you need to stop now. I'll help you. If not, you'll wind up arrested. You may get the needle instead of life in prison," Vanessa warned. She could still feel the prod of the gun so sharply against her back.

"No. Dona Isabella will protect me," Zoe said. "Won't you?" Zoe smiled slyly at Vanessa, then looked to her side.

Vanessa looked, too.

And there she was. The ghost of Dona Isabella, haughty, proud and cruel, and highly amused as they walked through the pines.

"You," Vanessa said, "will surely rot in all the fires of hell, and soon."

Zoe looked shocked. "You see her?" she demanded.

Dona Isabella looked furious. She spoke with a sultry voice, pleasantly, despite her words. "Zoe will kill you slowly, Vanessa. Slowly. You will bleed into the sand and into the sea."

Zoe looked distracted for a minute. "Where's Bill?"

"I'm sure he's dead," Vanessa said. "You think those men just let a boy playing with a gun stop them?"

The nose of the gun pressed harder.

Vanessa realized that they were coming through the trees to the other side of the island. When they reached the sand, she thought, she would be in trouble.

The moon was out, and they neared the water. She could hear the waves, the sound lulling. They were about to break through the trees.

They did.

To Vanessa's surprise, they came to a sudden halt. "Ah, well, if it isn't the Spanish whore of all time!" came a voice.

Bartholomew. The ghost was awaiting them.

"Pirate scum!" Dona Isabella said. "Go—out of my way. Push through him. Just push through him. He is nothing but a mass in the air."

"As you are," Vanessa said.

She was stunned when the ghost swung about, when she saw hands of mist come toward her and encircle her throat. She felt the pinch…

And then she refused to do so.

"You bitch! You let her go!" Bartholomew said.

Zoe let out a little cry, thrusting Vanessa forward so that she fell onto the sand. She lifted the gun, but her hand was shaking as Bartholomew pitched himself at Dona Isabella and the spirits went flying downward in the night in a mist of white and sand.

And just as they did, Vanessa heard something like

a whir, a motion so fast it seemed more ethereal than the ghostly specters in the sand.

Sean.

He flew into Zoe so fast, pitching himself from the trees, that she didn't even have a split second to pull the trigger. She fell to the earth, and Jay, behind Sean, swept up her gun. Zoe began to toss and writhe and scream incoherently.

Sean kept her down.

Lew Sanderson walked out of the trail and approached the ghosts locked in combat on the sand. And he began to speak, too, some kind of an ancient dialect, his booming voice rising over Zoe's desperate tirade and screams.

Then Lew's words changed to Latin, and he lifted a cross, speaking the same words over and over. He reached into his pocket. From the sand, Vanessa stared at him, afraid that he had a gun, that he would begin to shoot needlessly at the mist…

But it wasn't a gun. It was a vial of water, and he sprinkled it again and again.…

Suddenly, a piercing scream of agony and terror erupted from the sand. Vanessa looked toward the sea. It seemed that her monsters had risen, but they were seaweed monsters of darkness and fire.…

Black mist rose like fierce, roiling thunderclouds, seeming both unreal and with substance, a viscous mass that steadily came forward.

Dona Isabella stared at it, screaming in a rage. Words of protest tumbled from her mouth.

It seemed that thunder roared, silencing her.

She backed away.

But it did no good.

The darkness had come for her.

The black, roiling mass washed its way over the shoreline, an unstoppable army of oily shadows, somehow alive and furious, bearing red eyes that spoke of all the demons of hell.

Coming for Dona Isabella.

The mass enveloped her. She screamed and writhed, but to no avail. She became part of the mass, and it ripped her from shore, bearing her back to the water again.

Vanessa blinked. It was over; she was gone. Her heart flew to her throat because she didn't see Bartholomew, either. All there was to be seen was Zoe, now suddenly silent, almost catatonic.

Lew turned to them. "She is gone," he said simply.

Jay blinked. "Who is gone?" he whispered.

He didn't know what he had seen. Now, as the waves lapped gently again, as the moon rode over the water, Vanessa wasn't sure, either.

Lew Sanderson stooped down by Zoe. "I will take her. She will go to the Bahamian authorities," he said. "And perhaps face charges elsewhere."

Sean left Zoe to Lew.

He walked to Vanessa, caught her hand and drew her up into his arms. He was shaking.

"You know what I think?" he whispered.

"What?"

"I don't need to think anymore. I know that I love you," he said, and he drew her hard against him, still shaking as he held her there.

* * *

The remains of the *Happy-Me* were found the following week, and the *Delphi* was found two weeks later. Once in custody, Bill and Zoe seemed to have no problem talking, even though most of the law-enforcement officials they spilled their souls to thought they were crazy.

It was Dona Isabella. She taught them how to be pirates. She helped them slip aboard boats, kill the crew one by one and make them disappear into the ocean.

The film shoot had been so easy. They had made a point of switching places constantly, so that neither could really be accused. For instance, Zoe had made certain that Bill was working when she took down the *Delphi*, just as Bill had made sure that Zoe was seen at the time he lured Travis out to the sand during the making of the horror movie. Travis! Conceited oaf. He had died quickly and easily. And it was bizarre that the authorities had never found the machete that they had used to cut up the bodies—they had left it hidden in the pine forest on the island. They had sunk Jay's boat—as they sank all the boats, stealing off them little by little. They weren't bad people—they were chosen. They were chosen by Dona Isabella to help her rule the sea.

There were a dozen times when Vanessa wanted to turn to Sean and say, "Did that really happen? Did we see what we saw? Did an evil ghost walk the world just as easily as the pained spirits of those who had been wronged, or who sought to help others?"

She never spoke. Maybe they both knew that the world was composed of good and evil. As Bartholomew had suggested, good men were good men.

And evil men—and women—were evil.

Just how crazy had Zoe become?

And did it make them all a little mad?

They were questions that haunted Vanessa at first. But they weren't about to stop her from living her life, from being with Sean. Barry healed quickly, and Marty was thrilled to walk around with a cane for a while. Liam came to before the authorities even arrived, furious with himself for having fallen prey to a pathetic little bastard like Bill Hinton.

But they had survived, and they had found a certain truth—if not the total truth. No one would really know what had happened on the pirate ship—and man might never really know what had caused hundreds of years of wild weather and strange occurrences in the Bermuda Triangle.

They didn't expect to solve that riddle.

They weren't salvage divers, either. They were filmmakers.

And so they became the filmmakers who worked with the salvage divers who brought up the pirate ship.

Vanessa still had a strange knack for finding treasure. She'd be led sometimes by a gentle presence in the water—a blonde woman who had worked too hard in life, fallen in love with a pirate and been murdered for that love. Kitty Cutlass.

She had feared for Bartholomew that night. But he had joined her later in the confusion on the shore, and he had assured her that he was not going to the place that was now hosting Dona Isabella. He wouldn't say more, just that he was destined for a better end, and that he was actually quite anxious to get back to Key West.

It wasn't long before they had a break and spent time in the city. And it was at dinner at O'Hara's where she saw that Bartholomew was really all right. He had been sitting with them idly at the bar, and then…

His Lucinda, his lady in white, came by, and he was gone, hurrying out to the street to meet her, where he held her tenderly in his arms, where their eyes met, and he kissed her.

"Very romantic!" she said, pleased.

Sean pulled her into his arms. "Let's go home," he said softly. "And I'll show you romantic."

She smiled, and slipped from the bar stool.

She turned into his arms. "I don't need to think much at all anymore, Sean O'Hara. I know. I know that I love you."

"I know…that I love you," he said.

And they left the bar, and went home, and made good on their words to each other.

* * * * *

Author's Note

Key West is known as the Conch Republic; those born there are known as Conchs and those who have been there for more than seven years are known as Freshwater Conchs.

Naturally, in Key West, you're going to come upon many conch offerings. The Bahamians and the Keys' people tend to believe they've both created the same recipes, but you'll find subtle flavor variations wherever you go.

But when in Rome—or the Conch Republic—it's great to try the local dishes. And conch chowder and conch fritters—two very popular uses for the shellfish—can be absolutely delicious.

One thing to remember—conch meat can be tough and rubbery. In any recipe, it's best to bring a heavy-duty meat mallet, and be ready for dicing and grinding!

These recipes may not be low-cal—but if you've been imbibing a few of the local drink choices, you won't care too much!

Key West Conch Chowder

(8 servings)

Ingredients:

2 cups fresh or frozen conch meat, well ground or chopped
4 cups potatoes, peeled and diced
2 quarts water
4 cups diced lean pork meat (bacon may be substituted)
1 cup fresh or canned tomatoes, diced
2 small onions, chopped fine
2 cloves garlic, chopped fine
1 green pepper, chopped fine
Salt and pepper to taste
2 tablespoons olive oil
2 tablespoons butter

Directions:

Place conch in half olive oil, half butter, and heat on low heat; do not brown, just allow to heat. Add potatoes and water and bring to a boil; reduce heat. In a separate pan, sauté lean pork (bacon) and tomatoes, peppers, onions and garlic until tender. Add to the conch mixture and allow to cook thirty to forty-five minutes, covered, until a creamy texture is reached and conch is tender. Add salt and pepper to taste—and enjoy!

Key West Conch Fritters

Ingredients:

3 cups flour
1 tablespoon baking powder
1 ½ cups pounded and diced conch
1 clove garlic
⅛ cup minced onion
⅛ cup finely diced red bell pepper
⅛ cup finely diced green bell pepper
2 tablespoons finely chopped parsley
4 eggs (or substitute such as Eggbeaters)
Salt and pepper to taste
(For a spicy Bahamian version, add 1 tablespoon finely chopped jalapeño pepper and a dash of cayenne pepper or a touch of hot sauce.)

Directions:

Sift the flour and baking powder together, mix other ingredients with eggs, then blend together. Season as desired. (Mild, or with a kick!) Form fritters, and deep-fry in vegetable oil until crispy and golden-brown. Great when served with a Key lime mayonnaise. Add some cayenne to the mayonnaise for those who love more spice.

Look for the next book in the exciting
BONE ISLAND TRILOGY,
GHOST MOON, coming in September 2010.

There were so many things in the room that Liam didn't even see the dead man at first. Like one of his relics, Cutter Merlin was covered in a thin patina of dust. Old and frail, his hair long and white, his cheeks covered in a stubble of white beard, he looked as if he might speak. But of course, he would never speak again.

Liam felt his heart sink. He found himself suddenly wishing that he—or someone—had kept up with the old recluse. Then there had been the strange rumors about the old hermit and his collections. He practiced black magic. He made deals with the devil.

Liam softly walked toward the old man. The corpse's mouth was slightly open, his eyes wide behind steel-framed reading glasses. It was as if he stared toward the front entry, terrified of whatever he saw there. The expression on his face was so filled with horror that Liam found himself turning to look. But there was nothing there.

"So old Merlin finally bit the dust, eh?" said Valaski, the medical examiner, shaking his head sadly. "I had all but forgotten the old bastard was out here...."

His voice trailed off, as if he were deep in thought.

"Valaski?"

Valaski looked up. He seemed to give himself a shake, physically and mentally.

"Nothing. Nothing, really. It's just that...well, he seems to be wearing the same expression as his daughter. You remember her. She was such a beautiful woman. She fell down the stairs—down that beautiful curving stairway right there. She died of a broken neck, and yet...well, she had the

MIRAEXP328155

exact same expression on her face. She seemed to be staring at the most terrifying thing in the universe. Just like Cutter here. Good God, I wonder what it was that they saw?"

MIRAEXP328155